Acclaim for Ellen Gilchrist's

Collected Stories

"Ellen Gilchrist chose the thirty-four stories herself from seven of her books, spanning nearly twenty years, and chose them not for posterity, but for now. Each is still as charged and crackling with its own centrifugal emotion as the day it was written. . . . By placing these stories in close proximity within the same book, the effect is almost unearthly. . . . Once you have read these stories you won't be able to pass a stranger on the street without wondering what his story is, and knowing if Gilchrist were there, she wouldn't hesitate to tell it."
— Tommy Hays, *Atlanta Journal-Constitution*

"Gilchrist's voice has become an integral part of American literature. . . . She grants readers the boon of her humor, wisdom, and beautifully crafted prose." — Donna Seaman, *Booklist*

"A new collection of short stories from a master of the form. . . . Readers who know Ms. Gilchrist only through *Sarah Conley* or who haven't yet entered her world at all will find *Collected Stories* the perfect place to begin. . . . Gilchrist is a master at layering a remarkably funny surface over a foundation of immense sadness and anxiety."
— Ron Carter, *Richmond Times-Dispatch*

"Being a newcomer to Gilchrist's writing, I was immediately struck by two aspects of her work. The first is the way Gilchrist excels in describing the human condition, warts and all. . . . The other outstanding feature about her writing is that she creates entire lives. . . . Gilchrist's world is full of people who survive self-inflicted misfortunes. And, when they do, we aren't sorry. What we really want to know is, what will they be doing next?" — Amrita Shlachter, *Fort Worth Star-Telegram*

"Gilchrist is very good. . . . She surprises with something so striking and new that it seems necessary to reread what has gone before."
—

"Gilchrist is an important voice in contemporary Southern fiction. . . . Highly recommended." —Christine DeZelar-Tiedman, *Library Journal*

"Like a good magician, Ellen Gilchrist keeps her talents impressive and invisible at the same time. Her stories effortlessly convey the complexity of human relationships without abandoning simplicity. . . . Gilchrist compiled many of her favorite creations into *Collected Stories*, spreading their honest, eccentric, and endearing narratives throughout the collection in chronological order. It's a pleasure every time the author offers an update on naïve would-be anarchist Nora Jane Whittington or headstrong Rhoda Manning. . . . Gilchrist's greatest trick could be the way she avoids the trappings of much contemporary Southern fiction." —Joshua Klein, *The Onion*

"*Collected Stories* is cause for celebration. . . . Gilchrist is such a persuasive writer that we feel a kinship with her characters' messy, interesting lives, are fascinated by their quirky sensibilities." —Nancy Pate, *Orlando Sentinel*

"In this golden age of feel-good fiction, Gilchrist must be credited for grappling with the truth in all its ugliness. . . . The roughness of her composition works in her favor, conveying the immediacy of deeply felt moments in the lives of her characters." —Jason K. Friedman, *San Francisco Chronicle*

"I was struck by the power of Gilchrist's last lines, the way she builds on readers' expectations and then shatters them. . . . She is also one of the finest writers of a rarest species: the happy story." —Susan Salter Reynolds, *Los Angeles Times Book Review*

"There is such wisdom and strength and optimism in Gilchrist's writing. At her best, the prose is so clear it all but forces the reader toward clarity. . . . She has an uncanny ability to impart both the joy and the considerable brutality of romantic love and family relationships. . . . In the end, almost all of Gilchrist's stories are about hope, our ability to triumph in ways large and, mostly, small." —Julia Reed, *Vogue*

ELLEN GILCHRIST

COLLECTED STORIES

ELLEN GILCHRIST

COLLECTED STORIES

BACK
BAY
BOOKS
LITTLE, BROWN

LITTLE, BROWN AND COMPANY

BOSTON   NEW YORK   LONDON

ORIGINALLY PUBLISHED IN HARDCOVER BY LITTLE, BROWN, DECEMBER 2000
FIRST BACK BAY PAPERBACK EDITION,
DECEMBER 2001

THE CHARACTERS AND EVENTS IN THIS BOOK ARE FICTITIOUS.
ANY SIMILARITY TO REAL PERSONS, LIVING OR DEAD,
IS COINCIDENTAL AND NOT INTENDED BY THE AUTHOR.

Library of Congress Cataloging-in-Publication Data

Gilchrist, Ellen.
  [Short stories. Selections]
  Collected stories / Ellen Gilchrist — 1st ed.
    p. cm.
  ISBN 0-316-29948-0 (hc) / 0-316-19365-8 (pb)
  1. Southern States — Social life and customs — Fiction.   I. Title.
PS3557.I34258 A6 2000
813'.54 — dc21   00-035667

10 9 8 7 6 5 4 3

BOOK DESIGN BY ROBERT G. LOWE

Q-MART

PRINTED IN THE UNITED STATES OF AMERICA

For Don Congdon and Roger Donald

CONTENTS

ELLEN GILCHRIST

COLLECTED STORIES

THE FAMOUS POLL
AT JODY'S BAR

IT WAS NINETY-EIGHT DEGREES in the shade in New Orleans, a record-breaking day in August.

Nora Jane Whittington sat in a small apartment several blocks from Jody's Bar and went over her alternatives.

"No two ways about it," she said to herself, shaking out her black curls, "if Sandy wants my ass in San Jose, I'm taking it to San Jose. But I've got to get some cash."

Nora Jane was nineteen years old, a self-taught anarchist and a quick-change artist. She owned six Dynel wigs in different hair colors, a makeup kit she stole from Le Petit Theatre du Vieux Carre while working as a volunteer stagehand, and a small but versatile wardrobe. She could turn her graceful body into any character she saw in a movie or on TV. Her specialties were boyish young lesbians, boyish young nuns, and a variety of lady tourists.

Nora Jane could also do wonderful tricks with her voice, which had a range of almost two octaves. She was the despair of the sisters at the Academy of the Most Holy Name of Jesus when she quit the choir saying her chores at home didn't allow her to stay after school to practice.

The sisters made special novenas for the bright, lonely child whose father died at the beginning of the Vietnam War and whose pretty alcoholic mother wept and prayed when they called upon her begging her to either put away the bottle and make a decent home for Nora Jane or allow them to put her in a Catholic boarding school.

Nora Jane didn't want a decent home. What she wanted was a steady boyfriend, and the summer she graduated from high school she met Sandy. Nora Jane had a job selling records at The Mushroom Cloud, a record shop near the Tulane campus where rich kids came to spend their parents' money on phonograph records and jewelry made in the shape of coke spoons and marijuana leaves. "The Cloud" was a nice place, up a flight of narrow stairs from Freret Street. Nora Jane felt important, helping customers decide what records to buy.

The day Sandy came into her life she was wearing a yellow cotton dress and her hair was curling around her face from the humidity.

Sandy walked into the shop and stood for a long time reading the backs of jazz albums. He was fresh out of a Texas reform school with $500.00 in the bank and a new lease on life. He was a handsome boy with green eyes as opaque and unfathomable as a salt lake. When he smiled down at Nora Jane over a picture of Rahshaan Roland Kirk as The Five Thousand Pound Man, she dreamed of Robert Redford as The Sundance Kid.

"I'm going to dedicate a book of poems to this man's memory," Sandy said. "I'm going to call the book *Dark Mondays*. Did you know that Rahshaan Kirk died last year?"

"I don't know much about him. I haven't been working here long," Nora Jane said. "Are you really a writer?"

"I'm really a land surveyor, but I write poems and stories at night. In the school I went to in Texas a poet used to come and teach my English class once a month. He said the most important writing gets done in your head while you think you're doing something else. Sometimes I write in the fields while I'm working. I sing the poems I'm writing to myself like work songs. Then at night I write them down. You really ought to listen to this album. Rahshaan Kirk is almost as good as Coltrane. A boy I went to school with is his cousin."

"I guess I have a lot to learn about different kinds of music," Nora Jane answered, embarrassed.

"I'm new in town," Sandy said, after they had talked for a while, "and I don't know many people here yet. How about going with me to a political rally this afternoon. I read in the paper that The Alliance for Good Government is having a free picnic in Audubon Park. I like to find out what's going on in politics when I get to a new town."

"I don't know if I should," Nora Jane said, trying not to smile.

"It's all right," Sandy told her. "I'm really a nice guy. You'll be safe with me. It isn't far from here and we have to walk anyway because I don't have a car, so if you don't like it you can just walk away. If you'll go I'll wait for you after work."

"I guess I should go," Nora Jane said. "I need to know what's going on in politics myself."

When Nora Jane was through for the day they walked to Audubon Park and ate free fried chicken and listened to the Democratic candidate for the House of Representatives debate the Republican candidate over the ERA and the canal treaties.

It was still light when they walked back through the park in the direction of Sandy's apartment. Nora Jane was telling Sandy the story of her life. She had just gotten to the sad part where her father died when he stopped her and put his hands around her waist.

"Wait just a minute," he said, and he walked over to the roots of an enormous old live-oak tree and began to dig a hole with the heel of his boot. When he had dug down about six inches in the hard-packed brown soil he took out all the change he had in his pockets, wrapped it in a dollar bill and buried it in the hole. He packed the dirt back down with his hands and looked up at her.

"Remember this spot," he said, "you might need this some day."

Many hours later Nora Jane reached out and touched his arm where he stood leaning into the window frame watching the moon in the cloudy sky.

"Do you want to stay here for a while?" he asked, without looking at her.

"I want to stay here for a long time," she answered, taking a chance.

So she stayed for fourteen months.

Sandy taught her how to listen to jazz, how to bring a kite down without tearing it, how to watch the sun go down on the Mississippi River, how to make macrame plant holders out of kite string, and how to steal things.

Stealing small things from elegant uptown gift shops was as easy as walking down a tree-lined street. After all, Sandy assured her, their insurance was covering it. Pulling off robberies was another thing. Nora Jane drove the borrowed getaway car three times while Sandy cleaned out a drugstore and two beauty parlors in remote parts of Jefferson Parish. The last of these jobs supplied her with the wigs. Sandy picked them up for her on his way out.

"I'm heading for the west coast," he told her, when the beauty parlor job turned out to be successful beyond his wildest dreams, netting them $723.00. He had lucked into a payroll.

"I'll send for you as soon as I get settled," he said, and he lifted her over his head like a flower and carried her to the small iron bed and made love to her while the afternoon sun and then the moonlight poured in the low windows of the attic apartment.

Robbing a neighborhood bar in uptown New Orleans in broad daylight all by herself was another thing entirely. Nora Jane thought that up for herself. It was the plan she settled upon as the quickest way to get to California. She planned it for weeks, casing the bar at different times of the day and night in several disguises, and even dropping by one Saturday afternoon pretending to be collecting money to help the Crippled Children's Hospital. She collected almost ten dollars.

Nora Jane had never been out of the state of Louisiana, but once she settled on a plan of action she was certain all she needed was a little luck and she was as good as wading in the Pacific Ocean. One evening's work and her hands were back in Sandy's hair.

She crossed herself and prayed for divine intervention. After all, she told herself, robbing an old guy who sold whiskey and laid bets on athletic events was part of an anarchist's work. Nora Jane didn't like old guys much anyway. They were all wrinkled where the muscles ought to be and they were so sad.

She took the heavy stage pistol out of its hiding place under the sink and inspected it. She practiced looking tough for a few minutes and then replaced the gun in its wrapper and sat down at the card table to go over her plans.

Nora Jane had a methodical streak and liked to take care of details.

II

"The first nigger that comes in here attempting a robbery is going to be in the wrong place," Jody laughed, smiling at Judge Crozier and handing him a fresh bourbon and Coke across the bar.

"Yes, sir, that nigger is gonna be in the wrong place." Jody fingered the blackjack that lay in its purple velvet sack on a small shelf below the antiquated cash register and warmed into his favorite subject, his interest in local crime fueled by a report in the *Times-Picayune* of a holdup in a neighborhood Tote-Sum store.

The black bandits had made the customers lie on the floor, cleaned out the cash register, and helped themselves to a cherry Icee on the way out. The newspaper carried a photograph of the Icee machine.

The judge popped open his third sack of Bar-B-Que potato chips and looked thoughtful. The other customers waited politely to see what he had to say for himself this morning concerning law and order.

"Now, Jody, you don't know how a man will act in an emergency until that emergency transpires," the judge began, wiping his hands on his worn seersucker pants. "That's a fact and worthy of all good men to be accepted. Your wife could be in here helping tend bar. Your tables could be full of innocent customers watching a ball game. You might be busy talking to someone like that sweet little girl who came in last Saturday collecting for the Crippled Children's Hospital. First thing you know, gun in your back, knife at your throat. It has nothing at all to do with being brave." The judge polished off his drink and turned to look out the door to where the poll was going on.

Jody's Bar didn't cater to just anyone that happened to drop by to get a drink or lay a bet. It was the oldest neighborhood bar in the Irish Channel section of New Orleans, and its regular customers included second- and third-generation drinkers from many walks of life. Descendants of Creole blue bloods mingled easily with house painters and deliverymen stopping by for a quick one on their route.

Jody ran a notoriously tight ship. No one but Jody himself had ever answered the telephone that sat beneath a framed copy of The Auburn Creed, and no woman, no matter what her tale of woe, had ever managed to get him to call a man to the phone.

"Not here," he would answer curtly, "haven't seen him." And

Jody would hang up without offering to take a message. If a woman wanted a man at Jody's she had to come look for him in person.

There was an air of anticipation around Jody's this Saturday morning. All eight of the stools were filled. The excitement was due to the poll.

Outside of Jody's, seated at a small card table underneath a green-and-white-striped awning, Wesley Labouisse was proceeding with the poll in a businesslike manner. Every male passerby was interviewed in turn and his ballot folded into quarters and deposited in the Mason jar with a pink ribbon from an old Valentine's box wrapped loosely around it.

"Just mark it yes or no. Whatever advice you would give your closest friend if he came to you and told you he was thinking of getting married." Wesley was talking to a fourteen-year-old boy straddling a ten-speed bike.

"Take all the time you need to make up your mind. Think about your mother and father. Think about what it's like to have a woman tell you when to come home every night and when to get up in the morning and when to take a bath and when to talk and when to shut up. Think about what it's like to give your money to a woman from now till the day you die. Then just write down your honest feelings about whether a perfectly happy man ought to go out and get himself married."

Wesley was in a good mood. He had thought up the poll himself and had side bets laid all the way from The New Orleans Country Club to the Plaquemines Parish sheriff's office.

There was a big sign tacked up over the card table declaring THIS POLL IS BEING CONDUCTED WITHOUT RE-GARD TO SEX OR PREVIOUS CONDITION OF SERVI-TUDE. Wesley had made the sign himself and thought it was hilarious. He was well known in New Orleans society as the author of Boston Club Mardi Gras skits.

The leading man in the drama of the poll, Prescott Hamilton IV, was leaning into Jody's pinball machine with the dedication of a ballet dancer winding up *The Firebird*. He was twelve games ahead and his brand-new, navy blue wedding suit hung in its plastic see-through wrapper on the edge of the machine swaying in rhythm as Prescott nudged the laws of pinball machines gently in his favor. He was a lucky gambler and an ace pinball-machine player. He was a general favorite at Jody's, where the less aristocratic customers loved him for his gentle ways and his notoriously hollow leg.

Prescott wasn't pretending to be more interested in the outcome of the pinball-machine game than in the outcome of the poll that was deciding his matrimonial future. He was genuinely more interested in the pinball machine. Prescott had great powers of concentration and was a man who lived in the present.

Prescott didn't really care whether he married Emily Anne Hughes or not. He and Emily Anne had been getting along fine for years without getting married, and he didn't see what difference his moving into Emily Anne's house at this late date was going to make in the history of the world.

Besides he wasn't certain how his Labradors would adjust to her backyard. Emily Anne's house was nice, but the yard was full of little fences and lacked a shade tree.

Nonetheless, Prescott was a man of his word, and if the poll came out in favor of marriage they would be married as soon as he could change into his suit and find an Episcopal minister, unless Emily Anne would be reasonable and settle for the judge.

Prescott was forty-eight years old. The wild blood of his pioneer ancestors had slowed down in Prescott. Even his smile took a long time to develop, feeling out the terrain, then opening up like a child's.

"Crime wave, crime wave, that's all I hear around this place anymore," the judge muttered, tapping his cigar on the edge of the bar and staring straight at the rack of potato chips. "Let's talk about something else for a change."

"Judge, you ought to get Jody to take you back to the ladies' room and show you the job Claiborne did of patching the window so kids on the street can't see into the ladies'," one of the regulars said. Two or three guys laughed, holding their stomachs.

"Claiborne owed Jody sixty bucks on his tab and the window was broken out in the ladies' room so Jody's old lady talked him into letting Claiborne fix the window to pay back part of the money he owes. After all, Claiborne is supposed to be a carpenter." Everyone started laughing again.

"Well, Claiborne showed up about six sheets in the wind last Wednesday while Jody was out jogging in the park and he went to work. You wouldn't believe what he did. He boarded up the window. He didn't feel like going out for a windowpane, so he just boarded up the window with scrap lumber."

"I'll have to see that as soon as it calms down around here," the judge said, and he turned to watch Prescott, who was staring passionately into the lighted TILT sign on the pinball machine.

"What's wrong, Prescott," he said, "you losing your touch?"

"Could be, Judge," Prescott answered, slipping another quarter into the slot.

The late afternoon sun shone in the windows of the bare apartment. Nora Jane had dumped most of her possessions into a container for The Volunteers of America. She had even burned Sandy's letters. If she was caught there was no sense in involving him.

If she was caught what could they do to her, a young girl, a first offender, the daughter of a hero? The sisters would come to her rescue. Nora Jane had carefully been attending early morning mass for several weeks.

She trembled with excitement and glanced at her watch. She shook her head and walked over to the mirror on the dresser.

Nora Jane couldn't decide if she was frightened or not. She looked deep into her eyes in the mirror trying to read the secrets of her mind, but Nora Jane was too much in love to even know her own secrets. She was inside a mystery deeper than the mass.

She inspected the reddish-blond wig with its cascades of silky Dynel falling around her shoulders and blinked her black eyelashes. To the wig and eyelashes she added blue eye shadow, peach rouge, and beige lipstick. Nora Jane looked awful.

"You look like a piece of shit," she said to her reflection, adding another layer of lipstick. "Anyway, it's time to go."

On weekends six o'clock was the slow hour at Jody's, when most of the customers went home to change for the evening.

Nora Jane walked down the two flights of stairs and out onto the sidewalk carrying the brown leather bag. Inside was her costume change and a bus ticket to San Francisco zippered into a side compartment. The gun was stuffed into one of the Red Cross shoes she had bought to wear with the short brown nun's habit she had stolen from Dominican College. She hoped the short veil wasn't getting wrinkled. Nora Jane was prissy about her appearance.

As she walked along in the August evening she dreamed of Sandy sitting on her bed playing his harmonica while she pretended to sleep. In the dream he was playing an old Bob Dylan love song, the sort of thing she liked to listen to before he upgraded her taste in music.

Earlier that afternoon Nora Jane had rolled a pair of shorts, an old shirt, and some sandals into a neat bundle and hidden it in the low-hanging branches of the oak tree where Sandy had planted her money.

A scrawny-looking black kid was dozing in the roots of the tree. He promised to keep an eye on her things.

"If I don't come back by tomorrow afternoon you can have

this stuff," she told him. "The sandals were handmade in Brazil."

"Thanks," the black kid said. "I'll watch it for you till then. You running away from home or what?"

"I'm going to rob a bank," she confided.

The black kid giggled and shot her the old peace sign.

Wesley walked into the bar where Prescott, Jody, and the judge were all alone watching the evening news on television.

"Aren't you getting tired of that goddamn poll," Prescott said to him. "Emily Anne won't even answer her phone. A joke's a joke, Wesley. I better put on my suit and get on over there."

"Not yet," Wesley said. "The sun isn't all the way down yet. Wait till we open the jar. You promised." Prescott was drunk, but Wesley was drunker. Not that either of them ever showed their whiskey.

"I promised I wouldn't get married unless you found one boy or man all day who thought it was an unqualified good idea to get married. I didn't ever say I was interested in waiting around for the outcome of a vote. Come on and open up that jar before Emily Anne gets any madder."

"What makes you think there is a single ballot in favor of you getting married?" Wesley asked.

"I don't know if there is or there isn't," Prescott answered. "So go on and let the judge open that goddamn jar."

"Look at him, Wesley," Jody said delightedly. "He ain't even signed the papers yet and he's already acting like a married man. Already worried about getting home in time for dinner. If Miss Emily Anne Hughes wakes up in the morning wearing a ring from Prescott, I say she takes the cake. I say she's gone and caught a whale on a ten-pound test line."

"Open the jar," Prescott demanded, while the others howled with laughter.

✳   ✳   ✳

Nora Jane stepped into the bar, closed the door behind her, and turned the lock. She kept the pistol pointed at the four men who were clustered around the cash register.

"Please be quiet and put your hands over your heads before I kill one of you," she said politely, waving the gun with one hand and reaching behind herself with the other to draw the window shade that said CLOSED in red letters.

Prescott and the judge raised their hands first, then Wesley.

"Do as you are told," the judge said to Jody in his deep voice. "Jody, do what that woman tells you to do and do it this instant." Jody added his hands to the six already pointing at the ceiling fan.

"Get in there," Nora Jane directed, indicating the ladies' room at the end of the bar. "Please hurry before you make me angry. I ran away from DePaul's Hospital yesterday afternoon and I haven't had my medication and I become angry very easily."

The judge held the door open, and the four men crowded into the small bathroom.

"Face the window," Nora Jane ordered, indicating Claiborne's famous repair job. The astonished men obeyed silently as she closed the bathroom door and turned the skeleton key in its lock and dropped it on the floor under the bar.

"Please be very quiet so I won't get worried and need to shoot through the door," she said. "Be awfully quiet. I am an alcoholic and I need some of this whiskey. I need some whiskey in the worst way."

Nora Jane changed into the nun's habit, wiping the makeup off her face with a bar rag and stuffing the old clothes into the bag. Next she opened the cash register, removed all the bills without counting them, and dropped them into the bag. On second thought she added the pile of IOUs and walked back to the door of the ladies' room.

"Please be a little quieter," she said in a husky voice. "I'm getting very nervous."

"Don't worry, Miss. We are cooperating to the fullest extent," the judge's bench voice answered.

"That's nice," Nora Jane said. "That's very nice."

She pinned the little veil to her hair, picked up the bag, and walked out the door. She looked all around, but there was no one on the street but a couple of kids riding tricycles.

As she passed the card table she stopped, marked a ballot, folded it neatly, and dropped it into the Mason jar.

Then, like a woman in a dream, she walked on down the street, the rays of the setting sun making her a path all the way to the bus stop at the corner of Annunciation and Nashville Avenue.

Making her a path all the way to mountains and valleys and fields, to rivers and streams and oceans. To a boy who was like no other. To the source of all water.

REVENGE

⤳ ⤶

IT WAS THE SUMMER of the Broad Jump Pit.

The Broad Jump Pit, how shall I describe it! It was a bright orange rectangle in the middle of a green pasture. It was three feet deep, filled with river sand and sawdust. A real cinder track led up to it, ending where tall poles for pole-vaulting rose forever in the still Delta air.

I am looking through the old binoculars. I am watching Bunky coming at a run down the cinder path, pausing expertly at the jump-off line, then rising into the air, heels stretched far out in front of him, landing in the sawdust. Before the dust has settled Saint John comes running with the tape, calling out measurements in his high, excitable voice.

Next comes my thirteen-year-old brother, Dudley, coming at a brisk jog down the track, the pole-vaulting pole held lightly in his delicate hands, then vaulting, high into the sky. His skinny tanned legs make a last, desperate surge, and he is clear and over.

Think how it looked from my lonely exile atop the chicken house. I was ten years old, the only girl in a house full of cousins.

There were six of us, shipped to the Delta for the summer, dumped on my grandmother right in the middle of a world war.

They built this wonder in answer to a V-Mail letter from my father in Europe. The war was going well, my father wrote, within a year the Allies would triumph over the forces of evil, the world would be at peace, and the Olympic torch would again be brought down from its mountain and carried to Zurich or Amsterdam or London or Mexico City, wherever free men lived and worshiped sports. My father had been a participant in an Olympic event when he was young.

Therefore, the letter continued, Dudley and Bunky and Philip and Saint John and Oliver were to begin training. The United States would need athletes now, not soldiers.

They were to train for broad jumping and pole-vaulting and discus throwing, for fifty-, one-hundred-, and four-hundred-yard dashes, for high and low hurdles. The letter included instructions for building the pit, for making pole-vaulting poles out of cane, and for converting ordinary sawhorses into hurdles. It ended with a page of tips for proper eating and admonished Dudley to take good care of me as I was my father's own dear sweet little girl.

The letter came one afternoon. Early the next morning they began construction. Around noon I wandered out to the pasture to see how they were coming along. I picked up a shovel.

"Put that down, Rhoda," Dudley said. "Don't bother us now. We're working."

"I know it," I said. "I'm going to help."

"No, you're not," Bunky said. "This is the Broad Jump Pit. We're starting our training."

"I'm going to do it too," I said. "I'm going to be in training."

"Get out of here now," Dudley said. "This is only for boys, Rhoda. This isn't a game."

"I'm going to dig it if I want to," I said, picking up a shovelful of dirt and throwing it on Philip. On second thought I picked up another shovelful and threw it on Bunky.

"Get out of here, Ratface," Philip yelled at me. "You German spy." He was referring to the initials on my Girl Scout uniform.

"You goddamn niggers," I yelled. "You niggers. I'm digging this if I want to and you can't stop me, you nasty niggers, you Japs, you Jews." I was throwing dirt on everyone now. Dudley grabbed the shovel and wrestled me to the ground. He held my arms down in the coarse grass and peered into my face.

"Rhoda, you're not having anything to do with this Broad Jump Pit. And if you set foot inside this pasture or come around here and touch anything we will break your legs and drown you in the bayou with a crowbar around your neck." He was twisting my leg until it creaked at the joints. "Do you get it, Rhoda? Do you understand me?"

"Let me up," I was screaming, my rage threatening to split open my skull. "Let me up, you goddamn nigger, you Jap, you spy. I'm telling Grannie and you're going to get the worst whipping of your life. And you better quit digging this hole for the horses to fall in. Let me up, let me up. Let me go."

"You've been ruining everything we've thought up all summer," Dudley said, "and you're not setting foot inside this pasture."

In the end they dragged me back to the house, and I ran screaming into the kitchen where Grannie and Calvin, the black man who did the cooking, tried to comfort me, feeding me pound cake and offering to let me help with the mayonnaise.

"You be a sweet girl, Rhoda," my grandmother said, "and this afternoon we'll go over to Eisenglas Plantation to play with Miss Ann Wentzel."

"I don't want to play with Miss Ann Wentzel," I screamed. "I hate Miss Ann Wentzel. She's fat and she calls me a Yankee. She said my socks were ugly."

"Why, Rhoda," my grandmother said. "I'm surprised at you. Miss Ann Wentzel is your own sweet friend. Her momma was your momma's roommate at All Saint's. How can you talk like that?"

"She's a nigger," I screamed. "She's a goddamned nigger German spy."

"Now it's coming. Here comes the temper," Calvin said, rolling his eyes back in their sockets to make me madder. I threw my second fit of the morning, beating my fists into a door frame. My grandmother seized me in soft arms. She led me to a bedroom where I sobbed myself to sleep in a sea of down pillows.

The construction went on for several weeks. As soon as they finished breakfast every morning they started out for the pasture. Wood had to be burned to make cinders, sawdust brought from the sawmill, sand hauled up from the riverbank by wheelbarrow.

When the pit was finished the savage training began. From my several vantage points I watched them. Up and down, up and down they ran, dove, flew, sprinted. Drenched with sweat they wrestled each other to the ground in bitter feuds over distances and times and fractions of inches.

Dudley was their self-appointed leader. He drove them like a demon. They began each morning by running around the edge of the pasture several times, then practicing their hurdles and dashes, then on to discus throwing and calisthenics. Then on to the Broad Jump Pit with its endless challenges.

They even pressed the old mare into service. Saint John was from New Orleans and knew the British ambassador and was thinking of being a polo player. Up and down the pasture he drove the poor old creature, leaning far out of the saddle, swatting a basketball with my grandaddy's cane.

I spied on them from the swing that went out over the bayou, and from the roof of the chicken house, and sometimes from the pasture fence itself, calling out insults or attempts to make them jealous.

"Guess what," I would yell, "I'm going to town to the

Chinaman's store." "Guess what, I'm getting to go to the beauty parlor." "Doctor Biggs says you're adopted."

They ignored me. At meals they sat together at one end of the table, making jokes about my temper and my red hair, opening their mouths so I could see their half-chewed food, burping loudly in my direction.

At night they pulled their cots together on the sleeping porch, plotting against me while I slept beneath my grandmother's window, listening to the soft assurance of her snoring.

I began to pray the Japs would win the war, would come marching into Issaquena County and take them prisoners, starving and torturing them, sticking bamboo splinters under their fingernails. I saw myself in the Japanese colonel's office, turning them in, writing their names down, myself being treated like an honored guest, drinking tea from tiny blue cups like the ones the Chinaman had in his store.

They would be outside, tied up with wire. There would be Dudley, begging for mercy. What good to him now his loyal gang, his photographic memory, his trick magnet dogs, his perfect pitch, his camp shorts, his Baby Brownie camera.

I prayed they would get polio, would be consigned forever to iron lungs. I put myself to sleep at night imagining their labored breathing, their five little wheelchairs lined up by the store as I drove by in my father's Packard, my arm around the jacket of his blue uniform, on my way to Hollywood for my screen test.

Meanwhile, I practiced dancing. My grandmother had a black housekeeper named Baby Doll who was a wonderful dancer. In the mornings I followed her around while she dusted, begging for dancing lessons. She was a big woman, as tall as a man, and gave off a dark rich smell, an unforgettable incense, a combination of Evening in Paris and the sweet perfume of the cabins.

Baby Doll wore bright skirts and on her blouses a pin that

said REMEMBER, then a real pearl, then HARBOR. She was engaged to a sailor and was going to California to be rich as soon as the war was over.

I would put a stack of heavy, scratched records on the record player, and Baby Doll and I would dance through the parlors to the music of Glenn Miller or Guy Lombardo or Tommy Dorsey.

Sometimes I stood on a stool in front of the fireplace and made up lyrics while Baby Doll acted them out, moving lightly across the old dark rugs, turning and swooping and shaking and gliding.

Outside the summer sun beat down on the Delta, beating down a million volts a minute, feeding the soybeans and cotton and clover, sucking Steele's Bayou up into the clouds, beating down on the road and the store, on the pecans and elms and magnolias, on the men at work in the fields, on the athletes at work in the pasture.

Inside Baby Doll and I would be dancing. Or Guy Lombardo would be playing "Begin the Beguine" and I would be belting out lyrics.

> *"Oh, let them begin . . . we don't care,*
> *America all . . . ways does its share,*
> *We'll be there with plenty of ammo,*
> *Allies . . . don't ever despair . . ."*

Baby Doll thought I was a genius. If I was having an especially creative morning she would go running out to the kitchen and bring anyone she could find to hear me.

"Oh, let them begin any warrr . . ." I would be singing, tapping one foot against the fireplace tiles, waving my arms around like a conductor.

> *"Uncle Sam will fight*
> *for the underrr . . . doggg.*
> *Never fear, Allies, never fear."*

A new record would drop. Baby Doll would swoop me into her fragrant arms, and we would break into an improvisation on Tommy Dorsey's "Boogie-Woogie."

But the Broad Jump Pit would not go away. It loomed in my dreams. If I walked to the store I had to pass the pasture. If I stood on the porch or looked out my grandmother's window, there it was, shimmering in the sunlight, constantly guarded by one of the Olympians.

Things went from bad to worse between me and Dudley. If we so much as passed each other in the hall a fight began. He would hold up his fists and dance around, trying to look like a fighter. When I came flailing at him he would reach underneath my arms and punch me in the stomach.

I considered poisoning him. There was a box of white powder in the toolshed with a skull and crossbones above the label. Several times I took it down and held it in my hands, shuddering at the power it gave me. Only the thought of the electric chair kept me from using it.

Every day Dudley gathered his troops and headed out for the pasture. Every day my hatred grew and festered. Then, just about the time I could stand it no longer, a diversion occurred.

One afternoon about four o'clock an official-looking sedan clattered across the bridge and came roaring down the road to the house.

It was my cousin, Lauralee Manning, wearing her WAVE uniform and smoking Camels in an ivory holder. Lauralee had been widowed at the beginning of the war when her young husband crashed his Navy training plane into the Pacific.

Lauralee dried her tears, joined the WAVES, and went off to avenge his death. I had not seen this paragon since I was a small child, but I had memorized the photograph Miss Onnie Maud, who was Lauralee's mother, kept on her dresser. It was a photograph of Lauralee leaning against the rail of a destroyer.

Not that Lauralee ever went to sea on a destroyer. She was spending the war in Pensacola, Florida, being secretary to an admiral.

Now, out of a clear blue sky, here was Lauralee, home on leave with a two-carat diamond ring and the news that she was getting married.

"You might have called and given some warning," Miss Onnie Maud said, turning Lauralee into a mass of wrinkles with her embraces. "You could have softened the blow with a letter."

"Who's the groom," my grandmother said. "I only hope he's not a pilot."

"Is he an admiral?" I said, "or a colonel or a major or a commander?"

"My fiancé's not in uniform, Honey," Lauralee said. "He's in real estate. He runs the war-bond effort for the whole state of Florida. Last year he collected half a million dollars."

"In real estate!" Miss Onnie Maud said, gasping. "What religion is he?"

"He's Unitarian," she said. "His name is Donald Marcus. He's best friends with Admiral Semmes, that's how I met him. And he's coming a week from Saturday, and that's all the time we have to get ready for the wedding."

"Unitarian!" Miss Onnie Maud said. "I don't think I've ever met a Unitarian."

"Why isn't he in uniform?" I insisted.

"He has flat feet," Lauralee said gaily. "But you'll love him when you see him."

Later that afternoon Lauralee took me off by myself for a ride in the sedan.

"Your mother is my favorite cousin," she said, touching my face with gentle fingers. "You'll look just like her when you grow up and get your figure."

I moved closer, admiring the brass buttons on her starched uniform and the brisk way she shifted and braked and put in the clutch and accelerated.

We drove down the river road and out to the bootlegger's shack where Lauralee bought a pint of Jack Daniel's and two Cokes. She poured out half of her Coke, filled it with whiskey, and we roared off down the road with the radio playing.

We drove along in the lengthening day. Lauralee was chain-smoking, lighting one Camel after another, tossing the butts out the window, taking sips from her bourbon and Coke. I sat beside her, pretending to smoke a piece of rolled-up paper, making little noises into the mouth of my Coke bottle.

We drove up to a picnic spot on the levee and sat under a tree to look out at the river.

"I miss this old river," she said. "When I'm sad I dream about it licking the tops of the levees."

I didn't know what to say to that. To tell the truth I was afraid to say much of anything to Lauralee. She seemed so splendid. It was enough to be allowed to sit by her on the levee.

"Now, Rhoda," she said, "your mother was matron of honor in my wedding to Buddy, and I want you, her own little daughter, to be maid of honor in my second wedding."

I could hardly believe my ears! While I was trying to think of something to say to this wonderful news I saw that Lauralee was crying, great tears were forming in her blue eyes.

"Under this very tree is where Buddy and I got engaged," she said. Now the tears were really starting to roll, falling all over the front of her uniform. "He gave me my ring right where we're sitting."

"The maid of honor?" I said, patting her on the shoulder, trying to be of some comfort. "You really mean the maid of honor?"

"Now he's gone from the world," she continued, "and I'm marrying a wonderful man, but that doesn't make it any easier. Oh,

Rhoda, they never even found his body, never even found his body."

I was patting her on the head now, afraid she would forget her offer in the midst of her sorrow.

"You mean I get to be the real maid of honor?"

"Oh, yes, Rhoda, Honey," she said. "The maid of honor, my only attendant." She blew her nose on a lace-trimmed handkerchief and sat up straighter, taking a drink from the Coke bottle.

"Not only that, but I have decided to let you pick out your own dress. We'll go to Greenville and you can try on every dress at Nell's and Blum's and you can have the one you like the most."

I threw my arms around her, burning with happiness, smelling her whiskey and Camels and the dark Tabu perfume that was her signature. Over her shoulder and through the low branches of the trees the afternoon sun was going down in an orgy of reds and blues and purples and violets, falling from sight, going all the way to China.

Let them keep their nasty Broad Jump Pit I thought. Wait till they hear about this. Wait till they find out I'm maid of honor in a military wedding.

Finding the dress was another matter. Early the next morning Miss Onnie Maud and my grandmother and Lauralee and I set out for Greenville.

As we passed the pasture I hung out the back window making faces at the athletes. This time they only pretended to ignore me. They couldn't ignore this wedding. It was going to be in the parlor instead of the church so they wouldn't even get to be altar boys. They wouldn't get to light a candle.

"I don't know why you care what's going on in that pasture," my grandmother said. "Even if they let you play with them all it would do is make you a lot of ugly muscles."

"Then you'd have big old ugly arms like Weegie Toler," Miss

Onnie Maud said. "Lauralee, you remember Weegie Toler, that was a swimmer. Her arms got so big no one would take her to a dance, much less marry her."

"Well, I don't want to get married anyway," I said. "I'm never getting married. I'm going to New York City and be a lawyer."

"Where does she get those ideas?" Miss Onnie Maud said.

"When you get older you'll want to get married," Lauralee said. "Look at how much fun you're having being in my wedding."

"Well, I'm never getting married," I said. "And I'm never having any children. I'm going to New York and be a lawyer and save people from the electric chair."

"It's the movies," Miss Onnie Maud said. "They let her watch anything she likes in Indiana."

We walked into Nell's and Blum's Department Store and took up the largest dressing room. My grandmother and Miss Onnie Maud were seated on brocade chairs and every saleslady in the store came crowding around trying to get in on the wedding.

I refused to even consider the dresses they brought from the "girls'" department.

"I told her she could wear whatever she wanted," Lauralee said, "and I'm keeping my promise."

"Well, she's not wearing green satin or I'm not coming," my grandmother said, indicating the dress I had found on a rack and was clutching against me.

"At least let her try it on," Lauralee said. "Let her see for herself." She zipped me into the green satin. It came down to my ankles and fit around my midsection like a girdle, making my waist seem smaller than my stomach. I admired myself in the mirror. It was almost perfect. I looked exactly like a nightclub singer.

"This one's fine," I said. "This is the one I want."

"It looks marvelous, Rhoda," Lauralee said, "but it's the wrong color for the wedding. Remember I'm wearing blue."

"I believe the child's color-blind," Miss Onnie Maud said. "It runs in her father's family."

"I am not color-blind," I said, reaching behind me and unzipping the dress. "I have twenty-twenty vision."

"Let her try on some more," Lauralee said. "Let her try on everything in the store."

I proceeded to do just that, with the salesladies getting grumpier and grumpier. I tried on a gold gabardine dress with a rhinestone-studded cummerbund. I tried on a pink ballerina-length formal and a lavender voile tea dress and several silk suits. Somehow nothing looked right.

"Maybe we'll have to make her something," my grandmother said.

"But there's no time," Miss Onnie Maud said. "Besides first we'd have to find out what she wants. Rhoda, please tell us what you're looking for."

Their faces all turned to mine, waiting for an answer. But I didn't know the answer.

The dress I wanted was a secret. The dress I wanted was dark and tall and thin as a reed. There was a word for what I wanted, a word I had seen in magazines. But what was that word? I could not remember.

"I want something dark," I said at last. "Something dark and silky."

"Wait right there," the saleslady said. "Wait just a minute." Then, from out of a prewar storage closet she brought a black-watch plaid recital dress with spaghetti straps and a white piqué jacket. It was made of taffeta and rustled when I touched it. There was a label sewn into the collar of the jacket. *Little Miss Sophisticate*, it said. *Sophisticate*, that was the word I was seeking.

I put on the dress and stood triumphant in a sea of ladies and dresses and hangers.

"This is the dress," I said. "This is the dress I'm wearing."

"It's perfect," Lauralee said. "Start hemming it up. She'll be the prettiest maid of honor in the whole world."

All the way home I held the box on my lap thinking about how I would look in the dress. Wait till they see me like this, I was thinking. Wait till they see what I really look like.

I fell in love with the groom. The moment I laid eyes on him I forgot he was flat-footed. He arrived bearing gifts of music and perfume and candy, a warm dark-skinned man with eyes the color of walnuts.

He laughed out loud when he saw me, standing on the porch with my hands on my hips.

"This must be Rhoda," he exclaimed, "the famous red-haired maid of honor." He came running up the steps, gave me a slow, exciting hug, and presented me with a whole album of Xavier Cugat records. I had never owned a record of my own, much less an album.

Before the evening was over I put on a red formal I found in a trunk and did a South American dance for him to Xavier Cugat's "Poinciana." He said he had never seen anything like it in his whole life.

The wedding itself was a disappointment. No one came but the immediate family and there was no aisle to march down and the only music was Onnie Maud playing "Liebestraum."

Dudley and Philip and Saint John and Oliver and Bunky were dressed in long pants and white shirts and ties. They had fresh military crew cuts and looked like a nest of new birds, huddled together on the blue velvet sofa, trying to keep their hands to themselves, trying to figure out how to act at a wedding.

The elderly Episcopal priest read out the ceremony in a gravelly smoker's voice, ruining all the good parts by coughing. He was in a bad mood because Lauralee and Mr. Marcus hadn't found time to come to him for marriage instruction.

Still, I got to hold the bride's flowers while he gave her the ring and stood so close to her during the ceremony I could hear her breathing.

The reception was better. People came from all over the Delta. There were tables with candles set up around the porches and sprays of greenery in every corner. There were gentlemen sweating in linen suits and the record player playing every minute. In the back hall Calvin had set up a real professional bar with tall, permanently frosted glasses and ice and mint and lemons and every kind of whiskey and liqueur in the world.

I stood in the receiving line getting compliments on my dress, then wandered around the rooms eating cake and letting people hug me. After a while I got bored with that and went out to the back hall and began to fix myself a drink at the bar.

I took one of the frosted glasses and began filling it from different bottles, tasting as I went along. I used plenty of crème de menthe and soon had something that tasted heavenly. I filled the glass with crushed ice, added three straws, and went out to sit on the back steps and cool off.

I was feeling wonderful. A full moon was caught like a kite in the pecan trees across the river. I sipped along on my drink. Then, without planning it, I did something I had never dreamed of doing. I left the porch alone at night. Usually I was in terror of the dark. My grandmother had told me that alligators come out of the bayou to eat children who wander alone at night.

I walked out across the yard, the huge moon giving so much light I almost cast a shadow. When I was nearly to the water's edge I turned and looked back toward the house. It shimmered in the moonlight like a jukebox alive in a meadow, seemed to pulsate with music and laughter and people, beautiful and foreign, not a part of me.

I looked out at the water, then down the road to the pasture. The Broad Jump Pit! There it was, perfect and unguarded. Why had I never thought of doing this before?

I began to run toward the road. I ran as fast as my Mary Jane pumps would allow me. I pulled my dress up around my waist and climbed the fence in one motion, dropping lightly down on the other side. I was sweating heavily, alone with the moon and my wonderful courage.

I knew exactly what to do first. I picked up the pole and hoisted it over my head. It felt solid and balanced and alive. I hoisted it up and down a few times as I had seen Dudley do, getting the feel of it.

Then I laid it ceremoniously down on the ground, reached behind me, and unhooked the plaid formal. I left it lying in a heap on the ground. There I stood, in my cotton underpants, ready to take up pole-vaulting.

I lifted the pole and carried it back to the end of the cinder path. I ran slowly down the path, stuck the pole in the wooden cup, and attempted throwing my body into the air, using it as a lever.

Something was wrong. It was more difficult than it appeared from a distance. I tried again. Nothing happened. I sat down with the pole across my legs to think things over.

Then I remembered something I had watched Dudley doing through the binoculars. He measured down from the end of the pole with his fingers spread wide. That was it, I had to hold it closer to the end.

I tried it again. This time the pole lifted me several feet off the ground. My body sailed across the grass in a neat arc and I landed on my toes. I was a natural!

I do not know how long I was out there, running up and down the cinder path, thrusting my body further and further through space, tossing myself into the pit like a mussel shell thrown across the bayou.

At last I decided I was ready for the real test. I had to vault over a cane barrier. I examined the pegs on the wooden poles and chose one that came up to my shoulder.

I put the barrier pole in place, spit over my left shoulder, and marched back to the end of the path. Suck up your guts, I told myself. It's only a pole. It won't get stuck in your stomach and tear out your insides. It won't kill you.

I stood at the end of the path eyeballing the barrier. Then, above the incessant racket of the crickets, I heard my name being called. Rhoda . . . the voices were calling. Rhoda . . . Rhoda . . . Rhoda . . . Rhoda.

I turned toward the house and saw them coming. Mr. Marcus and Dudley and Bunky and Calvin and Lauralee and what looked like half the wedding. They were climbing the fence, calling my name, and coming to get me. Rhoda . . . they called out. Where on earth have you been? What on earth are you doing?

I hoisted the pole up to my shoulders and began to run down the path, running into the light from the moon. I picked up speed, thrust the pole into the cup, and threw myself into the sky, into the still Delta night. I sailed up and was clear and over the barrier.

I let go of the pole and began my fall, which seemed to last a long, long time. It was like falling through clear water. I dropped into the sawdust and lay very still, waiting for them to reach me.

Sometimes I think whatever has happened since has been of no real interest to me.

THERE'S
A GARDEN OF EDEN

SCORES OF MEN, including an ex-governor and the owner of a football team, consider Alisha Terrebone to be the most beautiful woman in the state of Louisiana. If she is unhappy what hope is there for ordinary mortals? Yet here is Alisha, cold and bored and lonely, smoking in bed.

Not an ordinary bed either. This bed is eight feet wide and covered with a spread made from Alisha's old fur coats. There are dozens of little pillows piled against the headboard, and the sheets are the color of shells and wild plums and ivory.

Everything else in the room is brown, brown velvet, brown satin, brown leather, brown silk, deep polished woods.

Alisha sleeps alone in the wonderful bed. She has a husband, but he isn't any fun anymore. He went morose on Alisha. Now he has a bed of his own in another part of town.

Alisha has had three husbands. First she married a poor engineer and that didn't work out. Then she married a judge and that didn't work out. Then she married a rich lawyer and that didn't work out.

Now she stays in bed most of the day, reading and drinking

coffee, listening to music, cutting pictures out of old magazines, dreaming, arguing with herself.

This morning it is raining, the third straight day of the steady dramatic rains that come in the spring to New Orleans.

"It's on the TV a flood is coming," the maid says, bringing in Alisha's breakfast tray. Alisha and the maid adore each other. No matter how many husbands Alisha has she always keeps the same old maid.

"They always say a flood is coming," Alisha says. "It gives them something to talk about on television all day."

"I hope you're right," the maid says. "Anyway, your mother's been calling and calling. And the carpenter's here. He wants to start on the kitchen cabinets."

"Oh," Alisha says, "which carpenter?"

"The new one," the maid says, looking down at her shoes. "The young one." Blue-collar workers, she says to herself. Now it's going to be blue-collar workers.

"All right," Alisha says. "Tell him I'll talk to him as soon as I get dressed. Fix him some coffee."

Alisha gets out of bed, runs a comb through her hair, pulls on a pair of brown velvet pants, and ties a loose white shirt around her waist. I've got to get a haircut, she says, tying back her thick black curls with a pink ribbon. I've really got to do something about this hair.

The carpenter's name is Michael. He used to be a Presbyterian. Now he is a Zen Buddhist carpenter. When he uses wood he remembers the tree. Every day he says to himself, *I am part of the universe. I have a right to be here.*

This is something he learned when he was younger, when he was tripping with his wild friends. Michael is through with tripping now. He wants to go straight and have a car that runs. He wants his parents to call him up and write him letters and lend him money. His parents are busy pediatricians. They kicked him out for tripping. They don't have time for silly shit about the universe.

Alisha found Michael in a classified ad. "Household repairs done by an honest, dedicated craftsman. Call after four."

Alisha called the number and he came right over. As soon as she opened the door she knew something funny was going on. What kind of a carpenter shows up in a handmade white peasant shirt carrying a recorder.

"Can I put this somewhere while you show me what needs fixing?" he said, looking at her out of dark blue eyes.

"What is it?" she said, taking it from him, laying it on a sofa.

"It's a musical instrument," he said. "I play with a group on Thursday nights. I was on my way there."

She led him around the house showing him things that were broken, watching his hands as he touched her possessions, watching his shoulders and his long legs and his soft hair and his dark blue eyes.

"This is a nice house," he said, when he had finished his inspection. "It has nice vibrations. I feel good here."

"It's very quiet," she said.

"I know," he said. "It's like a cave."

"You're right," she said. "It is like a cave. I never would have thought of that."

"Do you live here alone?" he said, holding his recorder in his arms. The last rays of the afternoon sun were filtering in through the leaded glass doors in the hallway, casting rainbows all over the side of his face. Alisha was watching the blue part of the rainbow slide along the hollows of his cheeks.

"Most of the time," she said. "I have a husband, but he's almost never here anymore."

"It feels like only one person lives here," he said. "Everything seems to belong to you."

"It's very astute of you to see that," she began in a serious voice, then broke into a giggle. "To tell the truth, that's why my husband left. He said only Kierkegaard would believe I loved him. He said the longer he stayed in this house the smaller he became. He said he had gotten to be about the size of an old golf ball in the corner."

"Why did he let you do that to him?" Michael said.

"He did it to himself," she said. "I don't take responsibility for other people's lives. I don't believe in being a scapegoat. That's a thing Jews are historically pretty good at, you know, so I'm always watching out for it in myself. Women are pretty good at it too, for that matter."

"You're a pretty smart lady."

"No, I'm not," she said. "I'm just trying to make it through the days like everybody else."

"I should be leaving," he said. "I'm having a hard time leaving this house."

"Come back, then," she said. "As soon as you have time. I'm looking forward to getting things fixed up around the place."

Now he was back, leaning on a counter in her spotless kitchen, cradling a cup of coffee, listening intently to something the maid was telling him.

"Have you been sick?" Michael asked, looking up from his coffee.

"Not really," she said. "I just stay in bed a lot."

"Do you want me to start on these cabinets?" he said. "I could come back another day."

"Oh, no," she said. "Today is fine. It was nice of you to come out in this weather."

"It says on the television two pumping stations are out," the maid said. "It says it's going to flood and your mother's been calling and calling."

"Maybe you should go home then," Alisha said. "Just in case."

"I think I will," the maid said. "They might let the schools out early and I'm taking care of my grandchild this week."

"Go on then," Alisha said. "I can manage here."

"What about the cabinets?" the maid said. "I was going to put in shelf paper when he finished."

"It doesn't matter," Alisha said. "I'll do it. Look out there. The sky is black as it can be. You better call a cab."

Michael finished his coffee, rinsed out the cup in the sink, set it nearly upside down to dry and began to work on the hardware of the cabinet doors, aligning them so they stayed closed when they were shut.

"They go out of tune," he said, "like a piano. I wonder who installed these to begin with. He must have been an impatient man. See how he drove these screws in. I should take the hardware off and start all over."

"Will that take a long time?" she said.

"Well," he laughed, "you'd probably have to refinish the cabinets if I did that."

"Then do it," she said. "Go on. Fix them right while you're here."

"I'll see," he said. "Perhaps I will change the worst ones, like the ones over the stove."

He went back to work. Outside torrents of rain beat against the windows and the sky was black as evening. Alisha moved around the kitchen straightening things inside the cabinets. She had not looked inside these cabinets in ages. She had forgotten all the interesting and beautiful things she owned. There were shelves of fine Limoges china and silver serving pieces wrapped carelessly in cellophane bags from the dry cleaners. There were copper pans and casserole dishes. There were stainless-steel mixing bowls and porcelain soufflé dishes and shelves and shelves of every sort of wineglass from the time when she gave dinner parties. There was one cabinet full of cookbooks and recipe folders and flower vases and candles and candleholders.

She took down a cookbook called *The Joy of Cooking.* Her first mother-in-law had given it to her. On the flyleaf was an inscription, "Much love for good cooking and a few fancy dishes." Underneath the inscription the maid had written TAKE FROM THE LEFT, SERVE FROM THE RIGHT, in large letters.

Alisha laughed out loud.

"What's so funny," the carpenter said.

"I found a book I used to use when I gave dinner parties," she said. "I wasn't very good at dinner parties. I was too ambitious. I used to make things with *curry.* And the maid and I used to get drunk while we were waiting for the guests to arrive. We never could remember which side to serve the vegetables from. No matter how many dinner parties we had we never could remember."

"Why did you get drunk?" Michael said. "Were you unhappy?"

"No," she said. "I don't think so. To tell the truth I think I was hungry. I used to take diet pills so I wouldn't eat any of the good things I was always cooking. I would be so hungry by nighttime I would get drunk if I only had a glass of wine."

"Why did you do all that?" he said, wondering if she always said anything that came into her head.

"I did it so I would look like Audrey Hepburn," she said. "At that time most of the women in the United States wanted to look like Audrey Hepburn."

"Really?" he said.

"Well, all of my friends did at least. I spent most of my waking hours trying not to eat anything. It was a lot of trouble, being hungry all the time."

"It sounds terrible," Michael said. "Do you still do it?"

"No," she said. "I quit giving a damn about Audrey Hepburn. Then I quit taking diet pills, and then I quit drinking, and then I quit giving dinner parties. Then I quit doing anything I didn't like to do."

"What do you like to do?" he asked.

"I don't know," she said. "I haven't found out yet."

"Your phone is ringing," he said. "Aren't you going to answer it?"

"No," she said. "I don't like to talk on the telephone."

"The maid said your mother had been trying to call you."

"I know. That's probably her on the phone now."

"You aren't going to answer it?"

"No. Because I already know what she's going to say. She's going to tell me a flood is coming. Don't pay any attention to the phone. It'll stop in a minute."

He put down his tools and turned around to face her. "There's a whole lot going on in this room right now," he said. "Are you aware of that?" He looked very serious, wiping his hands across his sleeves.

"How old are you?" Alisha said.

"What difference does that make?" he said and crossed the room and put his arms around her. She felt very nice in his arms, soft and brave and sad, like an old actress.

"Oh, my," she said. "I was afraid this was going to happen." Then they laid down their weapons and walked awkwardly down the hall to the bedroom, walking slowly as though they were going to do something embarrassing and awkward and absurd.

At the door to the bedroom he picked her up and carried her to the bed, hoping that was the romantic thing to do. Then he saw it. "What in the name of God is this?" he said, meaning the fur bedspread.

"Something my mother gave me," she said. "Isn't it the tackiest thing you've ever seen in your life."

"Your body is very beautiful," she said when he had taken off his clothes and was standing before her, shy and human. "You *look* like a grown man. That's a relief."

"Do you always say whatever comes into your head?" he said.

"Oh, yes," she said. "I think everyone knows what everyone

else is thinking all the time anyway. Do you mind? Do you think I talk too much?"

"Oh, no," he said. "I like it. It keeps surprising me."

"Do you like my body?" she said, for now she had taken off her clothes and had struck a pose, sitting cross-legged on the bed.

"Of course I do," he said. "I've been wanting to touch your tits ever since the first moment I saw you. The whole time we were walking around your house I was wanting to touch your tits."

"Oh, my," she said. "Not my tits again. For years I believed men liked me for my mind. Imagine that! I read hundreds of books so they would like me better. All the time they were only wanting to touch my tits. Think of that!"

"Now you're talking too much," he said.

Then Alisha closed her eyes and pretended she was an Indian princess lying in a tent deep in a forest, dressed in a long white deerskin robe, waiting for Jeff Chandler to come and claim her for his bride. Outside the wind and rain beat down upon the forest.

Then Michael closed his eyes and pretended he was a millionaire going to bed with a beautiful, sad old actress.

The phone woke them with its ringing. Alisha was startled for a moment. Then she settled back down, remembering where she was. Michael's legs were smooth and warm beside her. She was safe.

"You really ought to answer that," he said. "This is quite a storm we're having."

She picked his shirt up off the floor, put it on for a bathrobe, and went into the other room to talk.

"That was my mother," she reported. "She's crying. She's almost got her companion crying. I think they're both crying. He's this real sensitive young man we found in the drama department at Tulane. They watch TV together. He's learning to be an actor watching TV."

"Why is she crying?" Michael said, sitting up in bed, pulling the plum-colored sheets around his waist.

"She's crying because the basement of her house is flooding. It always does that in heavy rains. She lives on Jefferson Avenue, around the corner. Anyway, she can't find one of her cats and she thinks he's getting wet."

"Her cats?"

"She has six or seven cats. At least six cats. Anyway, she thinks the water is going to keep on rising and drown her cats."

"You'd better go and see about her then. We'd better go and help her."

"Help her? How can we help her? It's a flash flood on Jefferson Avenue. It'll go away as soon as the pumping stations start working. I told her to sell that goddamn house the last time this happened."

"It's flooding your mother's house and you don't want to go and help her?"

"It's only flooding the basement."

"How old is she?"

"My mother? She's seventy-eight. She has a companion. Besides, she does anything she wants to do. Last year she went to *China*. She's perfectly all right."

"Then why is she crying?"

"Because she thinks her silly goddamn cats are getting wet."

"Then we'll have to go and help her."

"How can we. It's *flooded* all the way down Jefferson Avenue."

"Does that canoe in the garage work?"

"I think so. No one's ever used it. Stanley ordered it last year when he got interested in the Sierra Club. But no one's ever *used* it."

"Then we'll go in that. Every time I see a flood on television and people going to get other people in boats I want to be one of them. This is my chance. We can take the canoe in my truck to where the water starts. Go on. Call your mother back and tell her we're coming to save her. Tell her we'll be right there. And, Alisha."

"Yes."

"Tell her to stop crying. After all, she is your mother."

"This is a great canoe," he said, maneuvering it down from the floored platform of the garage. "Your husband never uses it?"

"He never uses anything," she said. "He just likes to have things. To tell the truth he's almost never here."

"Then why are you married?" he asked.

"That's a good question," Alisha said. "But I don't know the answer to it."

"Well, look, let's go on over there. I can't wait to put this in the water. I'm afraid the water will go down before we get there."

"It's really nice of you to do this," Alisha said, standing close to him, smelling the warm smell of his clothes, taking everything that she could get while she could get it.

"Everybody loves to be a hero," Michael said, putting his arms around her again, running his hands up and down her strange soft body.

"Say I'm not your mother," she said.

"You're not my mother," he said. "Besides, it doesn't matter. We're probably only dreaming."

They drove down Freret Street with the city spread out before them, clean and shining after the rain. The sun was lighting up the red tile roofs of the houses, and Tulane students were on the porches with glasses in their hands, starting their flood parties.

The inside of Michael's truck was very cozy. He used it for a business office. File folders stuffed with bills and invoices were piled in one corner, and an accounting book was on the dashboard.

"Will I make love to you again?" Alisha said, for she was too old to play hard to get.

"Whenever you want to," he said. "As soon as we finish saving your mother."

They could see the flood now. They took the canoe out of the back of the truck and carried it to where the water began at the foot of Skippy Nevelson's front yard. Alisha sat in the bow and Michael waded out pushing her until it was deep enough for him to climb in.

"I don't believe I'm doing this," she said. "You're the craziest man I ever met in my life."

"Which way is the house," he said.

"It's the second house off Willow," Alisha said. "I guess we'll just go down Jefferson and take a right at Willow."

They floated along with Michael paddling. The water was three feet deep, thick and brown and slow-moving. An envelope floated by, then an orange barrette, then a purple Frisbee.

Alisha was feeling wonderful. If Skippy Nevelson was leaning out of her front window with her eyes the size of plates, if the WDSU Minicam crew was filming her for the evening news, if the levee broke and carried them all out to sea, what was that to Alisha, who had been delivered of an angel.

"What will happen next?" she asked, pushing her luck.

"Whatever we want to happen," he said, lifting the paddle and throwing the muddy water up into the air.

"Oh, my," she said to no one in particular. "This was the year I was going to stop dyeing my hair."

Now they were only a block away from their destination. Alisha kept her face to the front wishing she had a hat so Michael couldn't see her wrinkles. I have to remember this a long time, she told herself. I have to watch everything and hear everything and smell everything and remember everything. This may have to last me a long, long time.

Then Alisha did a stupid thing. She wrote a little script for herself. This is the very last time I will ever love anyone she told herself. I will love this boy until he leaves me. And then I will never love another human being.

And he will leave me, because no man has ever left me in my whole life and sooner or later it has to be my turn. After a while he will stop loving me and nothing will bring him back, not all the money or love or passion in the world will hold him. So he will leave me and go into the future and I will stay here and remember love. *And that is what I get for devoting my life to love instead of wisdom.*

So Alisha sat in the bow and wrote a script for herself and then she went to work to make it all come true.

"There it is," she said, spotting the house. "The one with the green awnings. See the balconies on the top. When I was a child I always dreamed of walking out there and waving to people, but the windows were always locked so I wouldn't fall to my death on Willow Street."

"That's terrible," he said. "You had a fancy place like that and you couldn't even walk out on the balconies."

"I couldn't do anything," she said. "They were too afraid I'd get hurt. That's how wealthy Jews used to raise their children. They didn't let me ride a bicycle or roller skate or swim or anything."

"You don't know how to *swim!*" he said.

"No," she said. "Isn't that dreadful?"

"Then what are you doing in this boat?"

"Hoping it won't turn over," she said, smiling a wonderful mysterious French smile, holding on lightly to the gunwales while he rowed her to her mother's doorstep.

IN THE LAND
OF DREAMY DREAMS

ON THE THIRD OF MAY, 1977, LaGrande McGruder drove out onto the Huey P. Long Bridge, dropped two Davis Classics and a gut-strung PDP tournament racket into the Mississippi River, and quit playing tennis forever.

"That was it," she said. "That was the last goddamn straw." She heaved a sigh, thinking this must be what it feels like to die, to be through with something that was more trouble than it was worth.

As long as she could remember LaGrande had been playing tennis four or five hours a day whenever it wasn't raining or she didn't have a funeral to attend. In her father's law office was a whole cabinet full of her trophies.

After the rackets sank LaGrande dumped a can of brand-new Slazenger tennis balls into the river and stood for a long time watching the cheerful, little, yellow constellation form and re-form in the muddy current.

"Jesus Fucking A Christ," she said to herself. "Oh, well," she added, "maybe now I can get my arms to be the same size for the first time in my life."

LaGrande leaned into the bridge railing, staring past the white circles on her wrists, souvenirs of twenty years of wearing sweatbands in the fierce New Orleans sunlight, and on down to the river where the little yellow constellation was overtaking a barge.

"That goddamn little new-rich Yankee bitch," she said, kicking the bridge with her leather Tretorns.

There was no denying it. There was no undoing it. At ten o'clock that morning LaGrande McGruder, whose grandfather had been president of the United States Lawn Tennis Association, had cheated a crippled girl out of a tennis match, had deliberately and without hesitation made a bad call in the last point of a crucial game, had defended the call against loud protests, taken a big drink of her Gatorade, and proceeded to win the next twelve games while her opponent reeled with disbelief at being done out of her victory.

At exactly three minutes after ten that morning she had looked across the net at the impassive face of the interloper who was about to humiliate her at her own tennis club and she had changed her mind about honor quicker than the speed of light. "Out," she had said, not giving a damn whether the serve was in or out. "Nice try."

"It couldn't be out," the crippled girl said. "Are you sure?"

"Of course I'm sure," LaGrande said. "I wouldn't have called it unless I was sure."

"Are you positive?" the crippled girl said.

"For God's sake," LaGrande said, "look, if you don't mind, let's hurry up and get this over with. I have to be at the country club for lunch." That ought to get her, LaGrande thought. At least they don't let Jews into the country club yet. At least that's still sacred.

"Serving," the crippled girl said, trying to control her rage.

LaGrande took her position at the back of the court, reached up to adjust her visor, and caught the eye of old Claiborne Redding, who was sitting on the second-floor balcony watching the match. He smiled and waved. How long has he been standing there, LaGrande wondered. How long has that old fart been watching me? But she was too busy to worry about Claiborne now. She had a tennis match to save, and she was going to save it if it was the last thing she ever did in her life.

The crippled girl set her mouth into a tight line and prepared to serve into the forehand court. Her name was Roxanne Miller, and she had traveled a long way to this morning's fury. She had spent thousands of dollars on private tennis lessons, hundreds of dollars on equipment, and untold time and energy giving cocktail parties and dinner parties for the entrenched players who one by one she had courted and blackmailed and finagled into giving her matches and return matches until finally one day she would catch them at a weak moment and defeat them. She kept a mental list of such victories. Sometimes when she went to bed at night she would pull the pillows over her head and lie there imagining herself as a sort of Greek figure of justice, sitting on a marble chair in the clouds, holding a scroll, a little parable of conquest and revenge.

It had taken Roxanne five years to fight and claw and worm her way into the ranks of respected Lawn Tennis Club Ladies. For five years she had dragged her bad foot around the carefully manicured courts of the oldest and snottiest tennis club in the United States of America.

For months now her ambitions had centered around LaGrande. A victory over LaGrande would mean she had arrived in the top echelons of the Lawn Tennis Club Ladies.

A victory over LaGrande would surely be followed by invitations to play in the top doubles games, perhaps even in the famous Thursday foursome that played on Rena Clark's private tennis court. Who knows, Roxanne dreamed, LaGrande might even ask her to be her doubles partner. LaGrande's old doubles partners were always retiring to have babies. At any moment she

might need a new one. Roxanne would be there waiting, the in-
defatigable handicapped wonder of the New Orleans tennis world.

She had envisioned this morning's victory a thousand times,
had seen herself walking up to the net to shake LaGrande's hand,
had planned her little speech of condolence, after which the two
of them would go into the snack bar for lunch and have a heart-
to-heart talk about rackets and balls and backhands and forehands
and volleys and lobs.

Roxanne basked in her dreams. It did not bother her that
LaGrande never returned her phone calls, avoided her at the club,
made vacant replies to her requests for matches. Roxanne had
plenty of time. She could wait. Sooner or later she would catch
LaGrande in a weak moment.

That moment came at the club's 100th Anniversary Celebration.
Everyone was drunk and full of camaraderie. The old members
were all on their best behavior, trying to be extra nice to the new
members and pretend like the new members were just as good as
they were even if they didn't belong to the Boston Club or the
Southern Yacht Club or Comus or Momus or Proteus.

Roxanne cornered LaGrande while she was talking to a famous psychiatrist-player from Washington, a bachelor who was
much adored in tennis circles for his wit and political connections.

LaGrande was trying to impress him with how sane she was
and hated to let him see her irritation when Roxanne moved in
on them.

"When are you going to give me that match you promised
me?" Roxanne asked, looking wistful, as if this were something
the two of them had been discussing for years.

"I don't know," LaGrande said. "I guess I just stay so busy.
This is Semmes Talbot, from Washington. This is Roxanne,
Semmes. I'm sorry. I can't remember your last name. You'll have
to help me."

"Miller," Roxanne said. "My name is Miller. Really now, when will you play with me?"

"Well, how about Monday?" LaGrande heard herself saying. "I guess I could do it Monday. My doubles game was canceled." She looked up at the doctor to see if he appreciated how charming she was to everyone, no matter who they were.

"Fine," Roxanne said. "Monday's fine. I'll be here at nine. I'll be counting on it so don't let me down." She laughed. "I thought you'd never say yes. I was beginning to think you were afraid I'd beat you."

"Oh, my goodness," LaGrande said, "anyone can beat me, I don't take tennis very seriously anymore, you know. I just play enough to keep my hand in."

"Who was that?" Semmes asked when Roxanne left them. "She certainly has her nerve!"

"She's one of the new members," LaGrande said. "I really try so hard not to be snotty about them. I really do believe that every human being is just as valuable as everyone else, don't you? And it doesn't matter a bit to me what anyone's background is, but some of the new people are sort of hard to take. They're so, oh, well, so *eager*."

Semmes looked down the front of her silk blouse and laughed happily into her aristocratic eyes. "Well, watch out for that one," he said. "There's no reason for anyone as pretty as you to let people make you uncomfortable."

Across the room Roxanne collected Willie and got ready to leave the party. She was on her way home to begin training for the match.

Willie was glad to leave. He didn't like hanging around places where he wasn't wanted. He couldn't imagine why Roxanne wanted to spend all her time playing tennis with a bunch of snotty people.

Roxanne and Willie were new members. Willie's brand-new 15 million dollars and the New Orleans Lawn Tennis Club's brand-new $700,000-dollar mortgage had met at a point in history, and Willie's application for membership had been approved by the board and railroaded past the watchful noses of old Claiborne Redding and his buddies. Until then the only Jewish member of the club had been a globe-trotting Jewish bachelor who knew his wines, entertained lavishly at Antoine's, and had the courtesy to stay in Europe most of the time.

Willie and Roxanne were something else again. "What in the hell are we going to do with a guy who sells ties and a crippled woman who runs around Audubon Park all day in a pair of tennis shorts," Claiborne said, pulling on a pair of the thick white Australian wool socks he wore to play in. The committee had cornered him in the locker room.

"The membership's not for him," they said. "He doesn't even play. You'll never see him. And she really isn't a cripple. One leg is a little bit shorter than the other one, that's all."

"I don't know," Claiborne said. "Not just Jews, for God's sake, but Yankee Jews to boot."

"The company's listed on the American Stock Exchange, Claiborne. It is selling at 16½ this morning, up from 5. And he buys his insurance from me. Come on, you'll never see them. All she's going to do is play a little tennis with the ladies."

Old Claiborne rued the day he had let himself be talked into Roxanne and Willie. The club had been forced to take in thirty new families to pay for its new building and some of them were Jews, but, as Claiborne was fond of saying, at least the rest of them tried to act like white people.

Roxanne was something else. It seemed to him that she lived at the club. The only person who hung around the club more than Roxanne was old Claiborne himself. Pretty soon she was running the place. She wrote *The Lawn Tennis Newsletter*. She circulated petitions to change the all-white dress rule. She campaigned for more court privileges for women. She dashed in and out of the bar and the dining room making plans with the waiters and chefs for Mixed Doubles Nights, Round Robin Galas, Benefit Children's Jamborees, Saturday Night Luaus.

Claiborne felt like his club was being turned into a cruise ship.

On top of everything else Roxanne was always trying to get in good with Claiborne. Every time he settled down on the balcony to watch a match she came around trying to talk to him, talking while the match was going on, remembering the names of his grandchildren, complimenting him on their serves and backhands and footwork, taking every conceivable liberty, as if at any moment she might start showing up at their weddings and debuts.

Claiborne thought about Roxanne a lot. He was thinking about her this morning when he arrived at the club and saw her cream-colored Rolls-Royce blocking his view of the Garth Humphries Memorial Plaque. He was thinking about her as he got a cup of coffee from a stand the ladies had taken to setting up by the sign-in board. This was some more of her meddling, he thought, percolated coffee in Styrofoam cups with plastic spoons and some kind of powder instead of cream.

At the old clubhouse waiters had brought steaming cups of thick chicory-flavored café au lait out onto the balcony with cream and sugar in silver servers.

Claiborne heaved a sigh, pulled his pants out of his crotch, and went up to the balcony to see what the morning would bring.

He had hardly reached the top of the stairs when he saw Roxanne leading LaGrande to a deserted court at the end of the property. My God in Heaven, he thought, how did she pull that off? How in the name of God did she get hold of Leland's daughter.

Leland McGruder had been Claiborne's doubles partner in their youth. Together they had known victory and defeat in New Orleans and Jackson and Monroe and Shreveport and Mobile and Atlanta and as far away as Forest Hills during one never to be forgotten year when they had thrown their rackets into a red Ford and gone off together on the tour.

Down on the court LaGrande was so aggravated she could barely be civil. How did I end up here, she thought, playing second-class tennis against anyone who corners me at a party.

LaGrande was in a bad mood all around. The psychiatrist had squired her around all weekend, fucked her dispassionately in someone's *garçonnière*, and gone back to Washington without making further plans to see her.

She bounced a ball up and down a few times with her racket, thinking about a line of poetry that kept occurring to her lately whenever she played tennis. "Their only monument the asphalt road, and a thousand lost golf balls."

"Are you coming to Ladies Day on Wednesday?" Roxanne was saying. "We're going to have a great time. You really ought to come. We've got a real clown coming to give out helium balloons, and we're going to photograph the winners sitting on his lap for the newsletter. Isn't that a cute idea?"

"I'm afraid I'm busy Wednesday," LaGrande said, imagining balloons flying all over the courts when the serious players arrived for their noon games. "Look," she said, "let's go on and get started. I can't stay too long."

They set down their pitchers of Gatorade, put on their visors and sweatbands, sprayed a little powdered resin on their hands, and walked out to their respective sides of the court.

Before they hit the ball four times LaGrande knew something was wrong. The woman wasn't going to warm her up! LaGrande had hit her three nice long smooth balls and each time Roxanne moved up to the net and put the ball away on the sidelines.

"How about hitting me some forehands," LaGrande said. "I haven't played in a week. I need to warm up."

"I'll try," Roxanne said. "I have to play most of my game at the net, you know, because of my leg."

"Well, stay back there and hit me some to warm up with," LaGrande said, but Roxanne went right on putting her shots away with an assortment of tricks that looked more like a circus act than a tennis game.

"Are you ready to play yet?" she asked. "I'd like to get started before I get too tired."

"Sure," LaGrande said. "Go ahead, you serve first. There's no reason to spin a racket over a fun match." Oh, well, she thought, I'll just go ahead and slaughter her. Of course, I won't lob over her head, I don't suppose anyone does that to her.

Roxanne pulled the first ball out of her pants. She had a disconcerting habit of sticking the extra ball up the leg of her tights instead of keeping it in a pocket. She pulled the ball out of her pants, tossed it expertly up into the air, and served an ace to LaGrande's extreme backhand service corner.

"Nice serve," LaGrande said. Oh, well, she thought, everyone gets one off occasionally. Let her go on and get overconfident. Then I can get this over in a hurry.

They changed courts for the second serve. Roxanne hit short into the backhand court. LaGrande raced up and hit a forehand right into Roxanne's waiting racket. The ball dropped neatly into a corner and the score was 30-love.

How in the shit did she get to the net so fast, LaGrande thought. Well, I'll have to watch out for that. I thought she was supposed to be crippled.

Roxanne served again, winning the point with a short spinning forehand. Before LaGrande could gather her wits about her she had lost the first game.

Things went badly with her serve and she lost the second game. While she was still recovering from that she lost the third game. Calm down, she told herself. Get hold of yourself. Keep your eye on the ball. Anticipate her moves. It's only because I didn't have a chance to warm up. I'll get going in a minute.

*　　*　　*

Old Claiborne stood watching the match from a secluded spot near the door to the dining room, watching it with his heart in his throat, not daring to move any farther out onto the balcony for fear he might distract LaGrande and make things worse.

Why doesn't she lob, Claiborne thought. Why in the name of God doesn't she lob? Maybe she thinks she shouldn't do it just because one of that woman's legs is a little bit shorter than the other.

He stood squeezing the Styrofoam cup in his hand. A small hole had developed in the side, and drops of coffee were making a little track down the side of his Fred Perry flannels, but he was oblivious to everything but the action on the court.

He didn't even notice when Nailor came up behind him. Nailor was a haughty old black man who had been with the club since he was a young boy and now was the chief groundskeeper and arbiter of manners among the hired help.

Nailor had spent his life tending Rubico tennis courts without once having the desire to pick up a racket. But he had watched thousands of tennis matches and he knew more about tennis than most players did.

He knew how the little fields of energy that surround men and women move and coalesce and strike and fend off and retreat and attack and conquer. That was what he looked for when he watched tennis. He wasn't interested in the details.

If it was up to Nailor no one but a few select players would ever be allowed to set foot on his Rubico courts. The only time of day when he was really at peace was the half hour from when he finished the courts around 7:15 each morning until they opened the iron gates at 7:45 and the members started arriving.

Nailor had known LaGrande since she came to her father's matches in a perambulator. He had lusted after her ass ever since she got her first white tennis skirt and her first Wilson autograph racket. He had been the first black man to wax her first baby-blue convertible, and he had been taking care of her cars ever since.

Nailor moonlighted at the club polishing cars with a special wax he had invented.

Nailor hated the new members worse than Claiborne did. Ever since the club had moved to its new quarters and they had come crowding in bringing their children and leaving their paper cups all over the courts he had been thinking of retiring.

Now he was watching one of them taking his favorite little missy to the cleaners. She's getting her little booty whipped for sure this morning, he thought. She can't find a place to turn and make a stand. She don't know where to start to stop it. She's got hind teat today whether she likes it or not and I'm glad her daddy's not here to watch it.

Claiborne was oblivious to Nailor. He was trying to decide who would benefit most if he made a show of walking out to the balcony and taking a seat.

He took a chance. He waited until LaGrande's back was to him, then walked out just as Roxanne was receiving serve.

LaGrande made a small rally and won her service, but Roxanne took the next three games for the set. "I don't need to rest between sets unless you do," she said, walking up to the net. "We really haven't been playing that long. I really don't know why I'm playing so well. I guess I'm just lucky today."

"I just guess you are," LaGrande said. "Sure, let's go right on. I've got a date for lunch." Now I'll take her, she thought. Now I'm tired of being polite. Now I'm going to beat the shit out of her.

Roxanne picked up a ball, tossed it into the air, and served another ace into the backhand corner of the forehand court.

Jesus Fucking A Christ, LaGrande thought. She did it again. Where in the name of God did that little Jewish housewife learn that shot.

LaGrande returned the next serve with a lob. Roxanne ran

back, caught it on the edge of her racket and dribbled it over the net.

Now LaGrande lost all powers of reason. She began trying to kill the ball on every shot. Before she could get hold of herself she had lost three games, then four, then five, then she was only one game away from losing the match, then only one point.

This is it, LaGrande thought. Armageddon.

Roxanne picked up the balls and served the first one out. She slowed herself down, took a deep breath, tossed up the second ball and shot a clean forehand into the service box.

"Out," LaGrande said. "Nice try."

"It couldn't be out," Roxanne said. "Are you sure?"

"Of course I'm sure," LaGrande said. *"I wouldn't have called it unless I was sure."*

Up on the balcony Old Claiborne's heart was opening and closing like a geisha's fan. He caught LaGrande's eye, smiled and waved, and, turning around, realized that Nailor was standing behind him.

"Morning, Mr. Claiborne," Nailor said, leaning politely across him to pick up the cup. "Looks like Mr. Leland's baby's having herself a hard time this morning. Let me bring you something nice to drink while you watch."

Claiborne sent him for coffee and settled back in the chair to watch LaGrande finish her off, thinking, as he often did lately, that he had outlived his time and his place. "I'm not suited for a holding action," he told himself, imagining the entire culture of the white Christian world to be stretched out on some sort of endless Maginot Line besieged by the children of the poor carrying portable radios and boxes of fried chicken.

Here Claiborne sat, on a beautiful spring morning, in good spirits, still breathing normally, his blood coursing through his veins on its admirable and accustomed journeys, and only a few minutes before he had been party to a violation of a code he had lived by all his life.

He sat there, sipping his tasteless coffee, listening to the Saturday lawn mowers starting up on the lawn of the Poydras Retirement Home, which took up the other half of the square block of prime New Orleans real estate on which the new clubhouse was built. It was a very exclusive old folks' home, with real antiques and Persian rugs and a board of directors made up of members of the New Orleans Junior League. Some of the nicest old people in New Orleans went there to die.

Claiborne had suffered through a series of terrible luncheons at the Poydras Home in an effort to get them to allow the tennis club to unlock one of the gates that separated the two properties. But no matter how the board of directors of the Lawn Tennis Club pleaded and bargained and implored, the board of directors of the Poydras Home stoutly refused to allow the tennis-club members to set foot on their lawn to retrieve the balls that flew over the fence. A ball lost to the Poydras Home was a ball gone forever.

The old-fashioned steel girders of the Huey P. Long Bridge hung languidly in the moist air. The sun beat down on the river. The low-hanging clouds pushed against each other in fat cosmic orgasms.

LaGrande stood on the bridge until the constellation of yellow balls was out of sight around a bend in the river. Then she drove to her house on Philip Street, changed clothes, got in the car, and began to drive aimlessly up and down Saint Charles Avenue, thinking of things to do with the rest of her life.

She decided to cheer herself up. She turned onto Carrollton Avenue and drove down to Gus Mayer.

She went in, found a saleslady, took up a large dressing room, and bought some cocktail dresses and some sun dresses and some summer skirts and blouses and some pink linen pants and a beige silk Calvin Klein evening jacket.

Then she went downstairs and bought some hose and some

makeup and some perfume and some brassieres and some panties and a blue satin Christian Dior gown and robe.

She went into the shoe department and bought some Capezio sandals and some Bass loafers and some handmade espadrilles. She bought a red umbrella and a navy blue canvas handbag.

When she had bought one each of every single thing she could possibly imagine needing she felt better and went on out to the Country Club to see if anyone she liked to fuck was hanging around the pool.

1944

⤙ ❧

WHEN I WAS EIGHT YEARS OLD I had a piano made of nine martini glasses.

I could have had a real piano if I had been able to pay the terrible price, been able to put up with piano lessons, but the old German spy who taught piano in the small town of Seymour, Indiana, was jealous of my talent.

"Stop it! Stop it! Stop it!" she would scream in her guttural accent, hitting me on the knuckles with the stick she kept for that purpose. "Stopping this crazy business. Can't you ever listen? Can't you sit still a minute? Can't you settle down?"

God knows I tried to settle down. But the mere sight of the magnificent black upright, the feel of the piano stool against my plump bottom, the cold ivory touch of the keys would send me into paroxysms of musical bliss, and I would throw back my head and begin to pound out melodies in two octaves.

"Stop it," she would be screaming. "This is no music, this crazy banging business. Stop on my piano. Stop before I call your momma!"

I remember the day I quit for good. I got up from the piano

stool, slammed the cover down on the keys, told her my father would have her arrested, and stalked out of the house without my hat and gloves. It was a cold November day, and I walked home with gray skies all around me, shivering and brokenhearted, certain the secret lives of musical instruments were closed to me forever.

So music might have disappeared from my life. With my formal training at this sorry end I might have had to content myself with tap and ballet and public speaking, but a muse looked down from heaven and took pity on me.

She arrived in the form of a glamorous war widow, was waiting for me at the bar when I walked into the officers' club with my parents that Saturday night.

There she sat, wearing black taffeta, smoking long white cigarettes, sipping her third very dry martini.

"Isn't that Doris Treadway at the bar?" my mother said. "I can't believe she's going out in public."

"What would you like her to do," my father said, "stay home and go crazy?"

"Well, after all," my mother whispered. "It's only been a month."

"Do you *know* that lady?" I asked, wondering if she was a movie star. She looked exactly like a movie star.

"She works for your daddy, Honey," my mother said. "Her husband got killed in the Philippines."

"Go talk to her," my father said. "Go cheer her up. Go tell her who you are."

As soon as we ordered dinner I did just that. I walked across the room and took up the stool beside her at the bar. I breathed deeply of her cool perfume, listening to the rustling of her sleeves as she took a long sophisticated drag on her Camel.

"So you are Dudley's daughter," she said, smiling at me. I squirmed with delight beneath her approving gaze, enchanted by the dark timbre of her voice, the marvelous fuchsia of her lips and fingertips, the brooding glamor of her widowhood.

"I'm Rhoda," I said. "The baby-sitter quit so they brought me with them."

"Would you like a drink?" she asked. "Could I persuade you to join me?"

"Sure," I said. "Sure I'll join you."

She conferred with the bartender and waved to my parents who were watching us from across the room.

"Well, Rhoda," she said. "I've been hearing about you from your father."

"What did you hear?" I asked, getting worried.

"Well," she said, "the best thing I heard was that you locked yourself in a bathroom for six hours to keep from eating fruit cocktail."

"I hate fruit cocktail," I said. "It makes me sick. I wouldn't eat fruit cocktail for all the tea in China."

"I couldn't agree with you more," she said, picking up her stirrer and tapping it on her martini glass. "I think people who hate fruit cocktail should always stick together."

The stirrer made a lovely sound against the glass. The bartender returned, bringing a wineglass full of bright pink liquid.

"Taste it," she said, "go ahead. He made it just for you."

I picked up the glass in two fingers and brought it delicately to my lips as I had seen her do.

"It's wonderful," I said, "what's in it?"

"Something special," she said. "It's called a Shirley Temple. So little girls can pretend they're drinking." She laughed out loud and began to tap the glass stirrer against the line of empty glasses in front of her.

"Why doesn't he move the empty glasses?" I asked.

"Because I'm playing them," she said. "Listen." She tapped out a little tune. "Now, listen to this," she said, adding small amounts of water to the glasses. She tapped them again with the stirrer, calling out the notes in a very high, very clear soprano voice. "Do,

Re, Mi, Fa, So, . . . Bartender," she called, "bring us more glasses."

In a minute she had arranged a keyboard with nine perfect notes.

"Here," she said, moving the glasses in front of me, handing me the stirrer, "you play it."

"What should I play," I said. "I don't know any music."

"Of course you know music," she said. "Everyone knows music. Play anything you like. Play whatever comes into your head."

I began to hit the glasses with the stirrer, gingerly at first, then with more abandon. Soon I had something going that sounded marvelous.

"Is that by any chance the 'Air Corps Hymn' you're playing?" she said.

"Well . . . yes it is," I said. "How could you tell?"

She began to sing along with me, singing the words in her perfect voice as I beat upon the glasses. "Off we go," she sang, "into the wild blue yonder, climbing high into the sky, dum, dum, dum. Down we dive spouting a flame from under, off with one hell-of-a-roar, roar, roar . . ."

People crowded around our end of the bar, listening to us, applauding. We finished with the air corps and started right in on the army. "Over hill, over dale, as we hit the dusty trail, and those caissons go marching along, dum, dum, dum . . . In and out, hear them shout, counter march and right about, and those caissons go rolling along. For it's hie, hie, hee, in the field artill-a-reeeee . . ."

A man near me began playing the bass on a brandy glass. Another man drummed on the bar with a pair of ashtrays.

Doris broke into "Begin the Beguine." "When they begin the beguine," she sang, "it brings back a night of tropical splendor. It brings back the sound of music so te-en-de-rr. It brings back a memorreeeeee ever green."

A woman in a green dress began dancing, swaying to our

rhythm. My martini glasses shone in the light from the bar. As I struck them one by one the notes floated around me like bright translucent boats.

This was music! Not the stale order of the book and the metronome, not the stick and the German. Music was this wildness rising from the dark taffeta of Doris's dress. This praise, this brilliance.

The soft delicious light, the smell of perfume and gin, the perfection of our artistry almost overwhelmed me, but I played bravely on.

Every now and then I would look up and see Doris smiling at me while she sang. Doris and I were one. And that too was the secret of music.

I do not know how long we played. Perhaps we played until my dinner was served. Perhaps we played for hours. Perhaps we are playing still.

"Oh, just let them begin the beguine, let them plaaaaay... Let the fire that was once a flame remain an ember. Let it burn like the long lost desire I only remember. When they begin, when they begin, when they begi-i-i-i-in the begui-i-i-i-ine..."

SUMMER, AN ELEGY

HIS NAME WAS SHELBY after the town where his mother was born, and he was eight years old and all that summer he had to wear a little black sling around the index finger of his right hand. He had to wear the sling because his great-granddaddy had been a famous portrait painter and had paintings hanging in the White House.

Shelby was so high-strung his mother was certain he was destined to be an artist like his famous ancestor. So, when he broke his finger and it grew back crooked, of course they took him to a specialist. They weren't taking any chances on a deformity standing in his way.

All summer long he was supposed to wear the sling to limber up the finger, and in the fall the doctor was going to operate and straighten it. While he waited for his operation Shelby was brought to Bear Garden Plantation to spend the summer with his grandmother, and as soon as he got up every morning he rode over to Esperanza to look for Matille.

He would come riding up in the yard and tie his saddle pony to the fence and start talking before he even got on the porch.

He was a beautiful boy, five months younger than Matille, and he was the biggest liar she had ever met in her life.

Matille was the only child in a house full of widows. She was glad of this noisy companion fate had delivered to Issaquena County right in the middle of a World War.

Shelby would wait for her while she ate breakfast, helping himself to pinch-cake, or toast, or cold cornbread, or muffins, walking around the kitchen touching everything and talking a mile a minute to anyone who would listen, talking and eating at the same time.

"My daddy's a personal friend of General MacArthur's," he would be saying. "They were buddies at Auburn. General MacArthur wants him to come work in Washington, but he can't go because what he does is too important." Shelby was standing in the pantry door making a pyramid out of the Campbell Soup cans. "Every time my daddy talks about going to Washington my momma starts crying her head off and goes to bed with a headache." He topped off the pyramid with a can of tomato paste and returned to the present. "I don't know how anyone can sleep this late," he said, "I'm the first one up at Bear Garden every single morning."

Matille would eat breakfast as fast as she could and they would start out for the bayou that ran in front of the house at the end of a wide lawn.

"Did I tell you I'm engaged to be married," Shelby would begin, sitting next to Matille in the swing that went out over the water, pumping as hard as he could with his thin legs, staring off into the sky.

"Her daddy's a colonel in the air corps. They're real rich." A dark, secret look crossed his face. "I already gave her a diamond ring. That's why I've got to find the pearl. So I can get enough money to get married. But don't tell anyone because my momma and daddy don't know about it yet."

"There aren't any pearls in mussels," Matille said. "Guy said so. He said we were wasting our time chopping open all those mussels."

"They do too have pearls," Shelby said coldly. "Better ones than oysters. My father told me all about it. Everyone in New Orleans knows about it."

"Well," Matille said, "I'm not looking for any pearls today. I'm going to the store and play the slot machine."

"You haven't got any nickels."

"I can get one. Guy'll give me one." Guy was Matille's uncle. He was 4-F. He had lost an eye in a crop-dusting accident and was having to miss the whole war because of it. He couldn't get into the army, navy, marines, or air corps. Even the coast guard had turned him down. He tried to keep up a cheerful face, running around Esperanza doing the work of three men, being extra nice to everyone, even the German war prisoners who were brought over from the Greenville Air Force Base to work in the fields.

He was always good for a nickel, sometimes two or three if Matille waited until after he had his evening toddies.

"If you help me with the mussels I'll give you two nickels," Shelby said.

"Let me see," Matille said, dragging her feet to slow the swing. It was nice in the swing with the sun beating down on the water below and the pecan trees casting a cool shade.

Shelby pulled a handkerchief from his pocket and untied a corner. Sure enough, there they were, three nickels and a quarter and a dime. Shelby always had money. He was the richest boy Matille had ever known. She stared down at the nickels, imagining the cold thrill of the slot machine handle throbbing beneath her touch.

"How long?" she said.

"Until I have to go home," Shelby said.

"All right," Matille said. "Let's get started."

They went out to the shed and found two rakes and a small hoe and picked their way through the weeds to the bayou bank.

The mud along the bank was black and hard-packed and broken all along the waterline by thick tree roots, cypress and willow and catalpa and water oak. They walked past the cleared-off place with its pier and rope swings and on down to where the banks of mussels began.

The mussels lay in the shallow water as far as the rake could reach, an endless supply, as plentiful as oak leaves, as plentiful as the fireflies that covered the lawn at evening, as plentiful as the minnows casting their tiny shadows all along the water's edge, or the gnats that buzzed around Matille's face as she worked, raking and digging and chopping, earning her nickels.

She would throw the rake down into the water and pull it back full of the dark-shelled, inedible, mud-covered creatures. Moments later, reaching into the same place, dozens more would have appeared to take their place.

They would rake in a pile of mussels, then set to work breaking them open with the hoe and screwdriver. When they had opened twenty or thirty, they would sit on the bank searching the soft flesh for the pearl. Behind them and all around them were piles of rotting shells left behind in the past weeks.

"I had my fortune told by a voodoo queen last Mardi Gras," Shelby said. "Did I ever tell you about that? She gave me a charm made out of a dead baby's bone. You want to see it?"

"I been to Ditty's house and had my fortune told," Matille said. "Ditty's real old. She's the oldest person in Issaquena County. She's older than Nannie-Mother. She's probably the oldest person in the whole state of Mississippi." Matille picked up a mussel and examined it, running her finger inside, then tossed it into the water. Where it landed a dragonfly hovered for a moment, then rose in the humid air, its electric-blue tail flashing.

"You want to see the charm or not?" Shelby said, pulling it out of his pocket.

"Sure," she said. "Give it here."

He opened his hand and held it out to her. It looked like the wishbone from a tiny chicken. "It's voodoo," Shelby said. He held it up in the air, turning it to catch the sunlight. "You can touch it but you can't hold it. No one can hold it but the master of it. Here, go on and touch it if you want to."

Matille reached out and stroked the little bone. "What's it good for?" she asked.

"To make whatever you want to happen. It's white magic. Momma Ulaline is real famous. She's got a place on Royal Street right next to an antique store. My Aunt Katherine took me there when she was baby-sitting me last Mardi Gras."

Matille touched it again. She gave a little shudder.

"Well, let's get back to work," Shelby said, putting the charm into his pocket, wiping his hands on his playsuit. His little black sling was covered with mud. "I think we're getting someplace today. I think we're getting warm."

They went back to work. Shelby was quiet, dreaming of treasure, of the pearl that lay in wait for him, of riches beyond his wildest dreams, of mansions and fine automobiles and chauffeurs and butlers and maids and money, stacks and stacks of crisp five-dollar bills and ten-dollar bills and twenty-dollar bills. Somewhere in Steele's Bayou the pearl waited. It loomed in his dreams. It lay in wait for him beneath the roots of a cypress or water oak or willow.

Every morning when he woke he could see it, all morning as he dug and raked and chopped and Matille complained and the hot sun beat down on the sweating mud and the stagnant pools of minnows and the fast-moving, evil-looking gars swimming by like gunboats, all day the pearl shone in his mind, smooth and mysterious, cold to the touch.

They worked in silence for a while, moving downstream until they were almost to the bridge.

"Looks like we could get something for all these shells," Matille said, examining the inside of one. It was all swirls of pink and white, like polished marble. "Looks like they ought to be worth something!"

"We could make dog food out of the insides," Shelby said. "Mr. Green Bagett had a dog that ate mussels. My grandmother told me all about it. He would carry them up to the road in his mouth and when the sun made them open he would suck out the insides." Shelby leaned on his hoe, making a loud sucking noise. "He was a dog named Harry after Mr. Bagett's dentist and he would eat mussels all day long if nobody stopped him."

"Why don't we carry these mussels up to the road and let the sun open them?" Matille said.

"Because it takes too long that way," Shelby said. "This is quicker."

"We could make ashtrays out of the shells," Matille said.

"Yeah," Shelby said. "We could sell them in New Orleans. You can sell anything in the French Quarter."

"We could paint them and decorate them with flowers," Matille said, falling into a dream of her own, picturing herself wearing a long flowered dress, pushing a cart through the crowded streets of a city, selling ashtrays to satisfied customers.

Now they were almost underneath the bridge. Here the trees were thicker and festooned with vines that dropped into the water like swings. It was darker here, and secret.

The bridge was a fine one for such a small bayou. It was a drawbridge with high steel girders that gleamed like silver in the flat Delta countryside. The bridge had been built to connect the two parts of the county, and anyone going from Grace to Baleshed or Esperanza or Panther Brake or Greenfields had to pass that way. Some mornings as many as seven cars and trucks passed over it. All day small black children played on the bridge and fished from it and leaned over its railings looking down into the brown water, chunking rocks at the mud turtles or trying to hit the mean-looking gars and catfish that swam by in twos or threes with their teeth showing.

This morning there were half a dozen little black boys on the bridge and one little black girl wearing a clean apron. Her hair was in neat cornrows with yellow yarn plaited into the braids. Her head looked like the wing of a butterfly, all yellow and black and brown and round as it could be.

"What y'all doing?" the girl called down when they got close enough to hear. "What y'all doing to them mussels?"

"We're doing an experiment," Shelby called back.

"Let's get Teentsy and Kale to help us," Matille said. "Hey, Teentsy," she called out, but Shelby grabbed her arm.

"Don't get them down here," he said. "I don't want everyone in the Delta in on this."

"They all know about it anyway," Matille said. "Guy told Granddaddy everyone at the store was laughing about us the other day. He said Baby Doll was busting a gut laughing at us for chopping all these mussels."

"I don't care," Shelby said, putting his hands on his hips, looking out across the water with the grim resignation of the born artist. "They don't know what we're doing it for."

"Well, I'm about worn out," Matille said. "Let's go up to the store and get Mavis to give us a drink."

"Let's open a few more first. Then we'll get a drink and go over to the other side. I think it's better over there anyway. There's sand over there. You got to have sand to make pearls."

"We can't go over there," Matille said. "That's not our property. That's Mr. Donleavy's place."

"He don't care if we dig some mussels on his bayou bank, does he?"

"I don't know. We got to ask him first. He's got a real bad temper."

"Let's try under this tree," Shelby said. "This looks like a good place. There's sand in this mud." He was bending down, trying the mud between his fingers, rubbing it back and forth to test the consistency. "Yeah, let's try here. This feels good."

"What y'all tearing up all those mussels for," Kale called down from his perch on the bridge. "They ain't good for nothing. You can't even use them for bait."

"We're gonna make ashtrays out of them," Shelby said. "We're starting us an ashtray factory."

"Where about?" Kale said, getting interested, looking like he would come down and take a look for himself.

"Next to the store," Shelby said. "We're gonna decorate them and sell them in New Orleans. Rich folks will pay a lot for real mussel ashtrays."

"That ought to hold them for a while," he said to Matille. "Let them talk about that at the store. Come on, let's open a few more. Then we'll get us a drink."

"All right," Matille said. "Let's try under this tree." She waded out into the water until it was up to her ankles, feeling the cold mud ooze up between her toes. She reached out with the rake. It caught, and she began pulling it up the shore, backing as she pulled, tearing the bark off the edges of the tree roots. The rake caught in the roots, and she reached down to free it.

"Matille!" Shelby yelled. "Matille! Look out!" She heard his voice and saw the snake at the same moment, saw the snake and Shelby lifting the hoe and her hand outlined against the water, frozen and dappled with sunlight and the snake struggling to free itself and the hoe falling toward her hand, and she dropped the rake and turned and was running up the bank, stumbling and running, with Shelby yelling his head off behind her, and Teentsy and Kale and the other children rose up from the bridge like a flock of little blackbirds and came running down the hill to see what the excitement was.

"I got him," Shelby yelled. "I cut him in two. I cut him in two with the hoe. I got him."

Matille sank down on the edge of the road and put her head on her knees.

"She's fainting," Kale called out, running up to her. "Matille's fainting."

"No, she ain't," Teentsy said. "She's all right." Teentsy sat down by Matille and put a hand on her arm, patting her.

"It was a moccasin," Shelby yelled. "He was big around as my arm. After I killed him the top half was still alive. He struck at me four times. I don't know if I'm bit or not."

"Where's he gone to now?" Kale said.

"I don't know," Shelby said, pulling off his shirt. "Come look and see if he bit me." The children gathered around searching Shelby's skin for bite marks. His little chest was heaving with excitement and his face was shining. With his shirt off he looked about as big around as a blue jay. His little black sling was flopping around his wrist and his rib cage rose and fell beneath the straps of his seersucker playsuit.

"Here's one!" Teentsy screamed, touching a spot on Shelby's back, but it turned out to be an old mosquito bite.

"Lay down on the ground," Kale yelled, "where we can look at you better."

"Where do you *think* he bit you?" Teentsy said.

But Shelby was too excited to lay down on the ground. All he wanted to do was jump up and down and tell his story over and over.

Then the grown people heard the commotion and came out from the store. Mavis Findley and Mr. Beaumont and Baby Doll and R. C. and Overflow came hurrying down the road and grabbed hold of Shelby so they could see where the snake bit him.

"Didn't nothing bite him, Mr. Mavis," Kale said. "He kilt it. He kilt it with the hoe."

"He almost chopped my hand off," Matille said, but no one was listening.

Then Mavis and Baby Doll and Overflow escorted Matille and

Shelby back to the big house with the black children skipping along beside and in front of them like a disorderly marching band.

By the time the procession reached the house the porch was full of ladies. Matille's mother and grandmother and great-grandmother and several widowed aunts had materialized from their rooms and were standing in a circle. From a distance they looked like a great flowering shrub. The screen door was open and a wasp buzzed around their heads threatening to be caught in their hairnets.

The ladies all began talking at once, their voices rising above and riding over and falling into each other in a long chorus of mothering.

"Thank goodness you're all in one piece," Miss Babbie said, swooping up Matille and enfolding her in a cool fragrance of dotted Swiss and soft yielding bosom and the smell of sandal-wood and the smell of coffee and the smell of powder.

Miss Nannie-Mother, who was ninety-six, kissed her on the forehead and called her Eloise, after a long-dead cousin. Miss Nannie-Mother had lived so long and grown so wise that every-one in the world had started to look alike to her.

The rest of the ladies swirled around Shelby. Matille strug-gled from her grandmother's embrace and watched disgustedly from the door frame as Shelby told his story for the tenth time.

"I didn't care what happened to me," Shelby was saying. "No rattlesnake was biting a lady while I was in the neighborhood. After I chopped it in two the mouth part came at me like a chicken with its head cut off."

"He almost chopped my hand off," Matille said again, but the only ones listening to her were Teentsy and Kale, who stood by the steps picking petals off Miss Teddy's prize pansies and cov-ering their mouths with their hands when they giggled to show what nice manners they had.

"This is what comes of letting children run loose like wild Indians," Miss Teddy was saying, brandishing a bottle of Windsor nail polish.

"Whatever will Rhoda Hotchkiss think when she hears of this?" Miss Grace said.

"She'll be terrified," Miss Babbie answered. "Then go straight to her knees and thank the Lord for the narrow escape."

"I knew something was going to happen," Miss Hannie Clay said, her hands full of rickrack for the smock she was making for her daughter in Shreveport. "I knew something was coming. It was too quiet around here all morning if you ask my opinion."

Matille leaned into the door frame with her hands on her hips watching her chances of ever going near the bayou again as long as she lived growing slimmer and slimmer.

Sure enough, when Matille's grandfather came in from the fields for the noon meal he made his pronouncement before he even washed his hands or hung up his hat.

"Well, then," he said, looking down from his six feet four inches and furrowing his brow. "I want everyone in this house to stay away from the bayou until I can spare some men to clear the brush. Shelby, I'm counting on you to keep Matille away from there, you hear me?"

"Yes sir," Shelby said. He stood up very straight, stuck out his hand and shook on it.

Now he's done it, Matille thought. Now nothing will be the same.

Now the summer wore on into August, and Shelby and Matille made a laboratory in an old chicken house and collected a lot of butterflies and chloroformed them with fingernail polish remover, and they taught a fox terrier puppy how to dance on his hind legs, and spent some time spying on the German prisoners, and read all the old love letters in the trunks under the house, but it was not the same. Somehow the heart had gone out of the summer.

Then one morning the grown people decided it was time for typhoid shots, and no matter how Matille cried and beat her head against the floor she was bathed and dressed and sent off in the back seat of Miss Rhoda's Buick to Doctor Findley's little brick office overlooking Lake Washington.

As a reward Matille was to be allowed to stay over at Bear Garden until the pain and fever subsided.

In those days vaccinations were much stronger than they are now and well-cared-for children were kept in bed for twenty-four hours nursing their sore arms, taking aspirin dissolved in sugar water, and being treated as though they were victims of the disease itself.

Miss Rhoda made up the twin beds in Shelby's mother's old room, made them up with her finest Belgian linens and decorated the headboards with Hero medals cut from cardboard and hand painted with watercolors.

The bedroom was painted ivory and the chairs were covered with blue and white chintz imported from Paris. It was the finest room Matille had ever slept in. She snuggled down in the pillows admiring the tall bookcases filled with old dolls and mementos of Carrie Hotchkiss's brilliant career as a Rolling Fork cheerleader.

Miss Rhoda bathed their faces with lemon water, drew the Austrian blinds, and went off for her nap.

"Does yours hurt yet?" Shelby asked, rubbing his shot as hard as he could to get the pain going. "Mine's killing me already."

"It hurts some," Matille said, touching the swollen area. "Not too much." She was looking at Shelby's legs, remembering something that had happened a long time ago, something hot and exciting, something that felt like fever, and like fever, made everything seem present, always present, so that she could not remember where or how it had happened or how long a time had passed since she had forgotten it.

"Just wait till tonight," Shelby rattled on. "You'll think your arm's fixing to fall off. I almost died from mine last year. One year a boy in New Orleans did die. They cut off his arm and did everything they could to save him but he died anyway. Think about that, being in a grave with only one arm." Shelby was talking faster than ever, to hide his embarrassment at the way Matille was looking at him.

"I can't stand to think about being buried, can you?" he continued, "all shut up in the ground with the worms eating you. I'm getting buried in a mausoleum if I die. They're these little houses up off the ground made out of concrete. Everyone in New Orleans that can afford it gets buried in mausoleums. That's one good thing about living there."

"You want to get in bed with me?" Matille said, surprised at the sound of her own voice, clear and orderly in the still room.

"Sure," Shelby said, "if you're scared. It scares me to death to think about being buried and stuff like that. Are you scared?"

"I don't know," Matille said. "I just feel funny. I feel like doing something bad."

"Well, scoot over then," Shelby said, crawling in beside her.

"You're burning up," she said, putting a hand on his forehead to see if he had a fever. Then she put her hand on his chest as if to feel his heartbeat, and then, as if she had been doing it every day of her life, she reached down inside his pajamas for the strange hard secret of boys.

"I want to see it, Shelby," she said, and he lay back with his hands stiff by his sides while she touched and looked to her heart's content.

"Now you do it to me," she said, and she guided his fingers up and down, up and down the thick wet opening between her legs.

The afternoon went on for a long time, and the small bed

was surrounded by yellow light and the room filled with the smell of mussels.

Long afterward, as she lay in a cool bed in Acapulco, waiting for her third husband to claim her as his bride, Matille would remember that light and how, later that afternoon, the wind picked up and could be heard for miles away, moving toward Issaquena County with its lines of distant thunder, and how the cottonwood leaves outside the window had beat upon the house all night with their exotic crackling.

"You better not tell anyone about this ever, Shelby," Matille said, when she woke in the morning. "You can't tell anyone about it, not even in New Orleans."

"The moon's still up," Shelby said, as if he hadn't heard her. "I can see it out the window."

"How can the moon be up," Matille said. "It's daylight."

"It stays up when it wants to," Shelby said. "Haven't you ever seen that before."

That was the beginning. They cleared out an old playhouse that had belonged to Matille's mother and made a bed from an old cot mattress.

It was Matille who made up the game now. She would lie down on the mattress with her hand on her head pretending to have a sick headache.

"Come sit by me, Honey," she would say. "Pour me a glass of sherry and come lie down till I feel better."

"God can see in this playhouse," Shelby said, pulling his hand away.

"No, he can't, Shelby," Matille said, sitting up and looking him hard in the eye. "God can't see through tin. This is a tin roof and God can't see through it."

"He can see everywhere," Shelby said. "Father Godchaux said so."

"Well, he can't see through tin," Matille said. "He can't be everywhere at once. He's got enough to do helping out the Allies without watching little boys and girls every minute of the night and day." Matille was unbuttoning Shelby's playsuit.

"Doesn't that feel good, Shelby," she said. "Doesn't that make it feel better."

"God can see everywhere," Shelby insisted. "He can see every single thing in the whole world."

"I don't care," Matille said. "I don't like God anyway. If God's so good why did he let Uncle Robert die. And why did he make alligators and snakes and send my daddy off to fight the Japs. If God's so good why'd he let the Jews kill his own little boy."

"You better not talk like that," Shelby said, buttoning his suit back together. "And we better get back before Baby Doll comes looking for us again."

"Just a little bit more," Matille said. "Just till we get to the part where the baby comes out."

August went by as if it had only lasted a moment. Then one afternoon Miss Rhoda drove Shelby over in the Buick to say goodbye. He was wearing long pants and had a clean sling on the finger and he had brought Matille the voodoo bone wrapped in tissue paper to keep for him.

"You might need this," he said, holding it out to her. He looked very grown-up standing by the stairs in his city clothes, and Matille thought that maybe she would marry Shelby when she grew up and be a fine married lady in New Orleans.

Then it was September and the cotton went to the gin and Matille was in the third grade and rode to school on the bus.

One afternoon she was standing by the driver while the bus clattered across the bridge and came to a halt by the store. It was a cool day. A breeze was blowing from the northeast and the cypress trees were turning a dusty red and the wild persimmons and muscadines were making.

Matille felt the trouble before she even got off the bus. The trouble reached out and touched her before she even saw the ladies standing on the porch in their dark dresses. It fell across her shoulders like a cloak. It was as if she had touched a strand of a web and felt the whole thing tremble and knew herself to be caught forever in its trembling.

They found out, she thought. Shelby told them. Now they'll kill me. Now they'll beat me like they did Guy.

She looked down the gravel road to the house, down the long line of pecan and elm trees and knew that she should turn and go back the other way, should run from this trouble, but something made her keep on moving toward the house. I'll say he lied, she thought. I'll say I didn't do it. I'll say he made it up. Everyone knows what a liar Shelby is.

Then her mother and grandmother and Miss Babbie came down off the porch and took her into the parlor and sat beside her on the sofa. And Miss Hannie and Miss Nell Grace and Overflow and Baby Doll stood around her in a circle and told her the terrible news.

"Shelby is dead, Matille," her grandmother said, and the words slid over her like water falling on stones.

Shelby had gone to the hospital to have his finger fixed and he had lain down on the table and put the gas mask over his face and the man who ran the machine made a mistake and Shelby had gone to sleep and nothing could wake him up, not all the screams or shots or slaps in the face or prayers or remorse in the world could wake him. And that was the Lord's will, blessed be the name of the Lord, Amen.

Later the ladies went into the kitchen to make a cold supper for anyone who felt like eating and Matille walked down to the bayou and stood for a long time staring down into the water, feeling strangely elated, as though this were some wonderful joke Shelby had dreamed up.

She stared down into the tree roots, deep down into the muddy water, down to the place where Shelby's pearl waited, grew and moved inside the soft watery flesh of its mother, luminous and perfect and alive, as cold as the moon in the winter sky.

VICTORY
OVER JAPAN

WHEN I WAS IN THE THIRD GRADE I knew a boy
who had to have fourteen shots in the stomach as the result of
a squirrel bite. Every day at two o'clock they would come to get
him. A hush would fall on the room. We would all look down
at our desks while he left the room between Mr. Harmon and
his mother. Mr. Harmon was the principal. That's how important Billy Monday's tragedy was.

Mr. Harmon came along in case Billy threw a fit. Every day
we waited to see if he would throw a fit but he never did. He
just put his books away and left the room with his head hanging down on his chest and Mr. Harmon and his mother guiding
him along between them like a boat.

"Would you go with them like that?" I asked Letitia at recess.
Letitia was my best friend. Usually we played girls chase the boys
at recess or pushed each other on the swings or hung upside down
on the monkey bars so Joe Franke and Bobby Saxacorn could see
our underpants but Billy's shots had even taken the fun out of
recess. Now we sat around on the fire escape and talked about
rabies instead.

"Why don't they put him to sleep first?" Letitia said. "I'd make them put me to sleep."

"They can't," I said. "They can't put you to sleep unless they operate."

"My father could," she said. "He owns the hospital. He could put me to sleep." She was always saying things like that but I let her be my best friend anyway.

"They couldn't give them to me," I said. "I'd run away to Florida and be a beachcomber."

"Then you'd get rabies," Letitia said. "You'd be foaming at the mouth."

"I'd take a chance. You don't always get it." We moved closer together, caught up in the horror of it. I was thinking about the Livingstons' bulldog. I'd had some close calls with it lately.

"It was a pet," Letitia said. "His brother was keeping it for a pet."

It was noon recess. Billy Monday was sitting on a bench by the swings. Just sitting there. Not talking to anybody. Waiting for two o'clock, a small washed-out-looking boy that nobody paid any attention to until he got bit. He never talked to anybody. He could hardly even read. When Mrs. Jansma asked him to read his head would fall all the way over to the side of his neck. Then he would read a few sentences with her having to tell him half the words. No one would ever have picked him out to be the center of a rabies tragedy. He was more the type to fall in a well or get sucked down the drain at the swimming pool.

Fourteen days. Fourteen shots. It was spring when it happened and the schoolroom windows were open all day long, and every afternoon after Billy left we had milk from little waxy cartons and Mrs. Jansma would read us chapters from a wonderful book about some children in England that had a bed that took them places at night. There we were, eating graham crackers and listening to stories while Billy was strapped to the table in Doctor Finley's office waiting for his shot.

"I can't stand to think about it," Letitia said. "It makes me so sick I could puke."

"I'm going over there and talk to him right now," I said. "I'm going to interview him for the paper." I had been the only one in the third grade to get anything in the Horace Mann paper. I got in with a story about how Mr. Harmon was shell-shocked in the First World War. I was on the lookout for another story that good.

I got up, smoothed down my skirt, walked over to the bench where Billy was sitting and held out a vial of cinnamon toothpicks. "You want one," I said. "Go ahead. She won't care." It was against the rules to bring cinnamon toothpicks to Horace Mann. They were afraid someone would swallow one.

"I don't think so," he said. "I don't need any."

"Go on," I said. "They're really good. They've been soaking all week."

"I don't want any," he said.

"You want me to push you on the swings?"

"I don't know," he said. "I don't think so."

"If it was my brother's squirrel, I'd kill it," I said. "I'd cut its head off."

"It got away," he said. "It's gone."

"What's it like when they give them to you?" I said. "Does it hurt very much?"

"I don't know," he said. "I don't look." His head was starting to slip down onto his chest. He was rolling up like a ball.

"I know how to hypnotize people," I said. "You want me to hypnotize you so you can't feel it?"

"I don't know," he said. He had pulled his legs up on the bench. Now his chin was so far down into his chest I could barely hear him talk. Part of me wanted to give him a shove and see if he would roll. I touched him on the shoulder instead. I could feel his little bones beneath his shirt. I could smell his washed-out rusty smell. His head went all the way down under his knees. Over his shoulder I saw Mrs. Jansma headed our way.

"Rhoda," she called out. "I need you to clean off the blackboards before we go back in. Will you be a sweet girl and do that for me?"

"I wasn't doing anything but talking to him," I said. She was beside us now and had gathered him into her wide sleeves. He was starting to cry, making little strangled noises like a goat.

"Well, my goodness, that was nice of you to try to cheer Billy up. Now go see about those blackboards for me, will you?"

I went on in and cleaned off the blackboards and beat the erasers together out the window, watching the chalk dust settle into the bricks. Down below I could see Mrs. Jansma still holding on to Billy. He was hanging on to her like a spider but it looked like he had quit crying.

That afternoon a lady from the PTA came to talk to us about the paper drive. "One more time," she was saying. "We've licked the Krauts. Now all we have left is the Japs. Who's going to help?" she shouted.

"I am," I shouted back. I was the first one on my feet.

"Who do you want for a partner?" she said.

"Billy Monday," I said, pointing at him. He looked up at me as though I had asked him to swim the English Channel, then his head slid down on the desk.

"All right," Mrs. Jansma said. "Rhoda Manning and Billy Monday. Team number one. To cover Washington and Sycamore from Calvin Boulevard to Conner Street. Who else?"

"Bobby and me," Joe Franke called out. He was wearing his coonskin cap, even though it was as hot as summer. How I loved him! "We want downtown," he shouted. "We want Dirkson Street to the river."

"Done," Mrs. Jansma said. JoEllen Scaggs was writing it all down on the blackboard. By the time Billy's mother and Mr.

Harmon came to get him the paper drive was all arranged.

"See you tomorrow," I called out as Billy left the room. "Don't forget. Don't be late."

When I got home that afternoon I told my mother I had volunteered to let Billy be my partner. She was so proud of me she made me some cookies even though I was supposed to be on a diet. I took the cookies and a pillow and climbed up into my treehouse to read a book. I was getting to be more like my mother every day. My mother was a saint. She fed hoboes and played the organ at early communion even if she was sick and gave away her ration stamps to anyone that needed them. She had only had one pair of new shoes the whole war.

I was getting more like her every day. I was the only one in the third grade that would have picked Billy Monday to help with a paper drive. He probably couldn't even pick up a stack of papers. He probably couldn't even help pull the wagon.

I bet this is the happiest day of her life, I was thinking. I was lying in my treehouse watching her. She was sitting on the back steps putting liquid hose on her legs. She was waiting for the Episcopal minister to come by for a drink. He'd been coming by a lot since my daddy was overseas. That was just like my mother. To be best friends with a minister.

"She picked out a boy that's been sick to help her on the paper drive," I heard her tell him later. "I think it helped a lot to get her to lose weight. It was smart of you to see that was the problem."

"There isn't anything I wouldn't do for you, Ariane," he said. "You say the word and I'll be here to do it."

I got a few more cookies and went back up into the treehouse to finish my book. I could read all kinds of books. I could read Book-of-the-Month Club books. The one I was reading now was called *Cakes and Ale*. It wasn't coming along too well.

I settled down with my back against the tree, turning the pages, looking for the good parts. Inside the house my mother was bragging on me. Above my head a golden sun beat down out of a blue sky. All around the silver maple leaves moved in the breeze. I went back to my book. "She put her arms around my neck and pressed her lips against mine. I forgot my wrath. I only thought of her beauty and her enveloping kindness.

"'You must take me as I am, you know,' she whispered.

"'All right,' I said."

Saturday was not going to be a good day for a paper drive. The sky was gray and overcast. By the time we lined up on the Horace Mann playground with our wagons a light rain was falling.

"Our boys are fighting in rain and snow and whatever the heavens send," Mr. Harmon was saying. He was standing on the bleachers wearing an old baseball shirt and a cap. I had never seen him in anything but his gray suit. He looked more shell-shocked than ever in his cap.

"They're working over there. We're working over here. The Germans are defeated. Only the Japs left to go. There're canvas tarps from Gentilly's Hardware, so take one to cover your papers. All right now. One grade at a time. And remember, Mrs. Winchester's third grade is still ahead by seventy-eight pounds. So you're going to have to go some to beat that. Get to your stations now. Get ready, get set, go. Everybody working together . . ."

Billy and I started off. I was pulling the wagon, he was walking along beside me. I had meant to wait awhile before I started interviewing him but I started right in.

"Are you going to have to leave to go get it?" I said.

"Go get what?"

"You know. Your shot."

"I got it this morning. I already had it."

"Where do they put it in?"

"I don't know," he said. "I don't look."

"Well, you can feel it, can't you?" I said. "Like, do they stick it in your navel or what?"

"It's higher than that."

"How long does it take? To get it."

"I don't know," he said. "Till they get through."

"Well, at least you aren't going to get rabies. At least you won't be foaming at the mouth. I guess you're glad about that." I had stopped in front of a house and was looking up the path to the door. We had come to the end of Sycamore, where our territory began.

"Are you going to be the one to ask them?" he said.

"Sure," I said. "You want to come to the door with me?"

"I'll wait," he said. "I'll just wait."

We filled the wagon by the second block. We took that load back to the school and started out again. On the second trip we hit an attic with bundles of the *Kansas City Star* tied up with string. It took us all afternoon to haul that. Mrs. Jansma said she'd never seen anyone as lucky on a paper drive as Billy and I. Our whole class was having a good day. It looked like we might beat everybody, even the sixth grade.

"Let's go out one more time," Mrs. Jansma said. "One more trip before dark. Be sure and hit all the houses you missed."

Billy and I started back down Sycamore. It was growing dark. I untied my Brownie Scout sweater from around my waist and put it on and pulled the sleeves down over my wrists. "Let's try that brick house on the corner," I said. "They might be home by now." It was an old house set back on a high lawn. It looked like a house where old people lived. I had noticed old people were the ones who saved things. "Come on," I said. "You go to the door with me. I'm tired of doing it by myself."

He came along behind me and we walked up to the door and rang the bell. No one answered for a long time although I could hear footsteps and saw someone pass by a window. I rang the bell again.

A man came to the door. A thin man about my father's age.

"We're collecting papers for Horace Mann School," I said. "For the war effort."

"You got any papers we can have?" Billy said. It was the first time he had spoken to anyone but me all day. "For the war," he added.

"There're some things in the basement if you want to go down there and get them," the man said. He turned a light on in the hall and we followed him into a high-ceilinged foyer with a set of winding stairs going up to another floor. It smelled musty, like my grandmother's house in Clarksville. Billy was right beside me, sticking as close as a burr. We followed the man through the kitchen and down a flight of stairs to the basement.

"You can have whatever you find down here," he said. "There're papers and magazines in that corner. Take whatever you can carry."

There was a large stack of magazines. Magazines were the best thing you could find. They weighed three times as much as newspapers.

"Come on," I said to Billy. "Let's fill the wagon. This will put us over the top for sure." I picked up a bundle and started up the stairs. I went in and out several times carrying as many as I could at a time. On the third trip Billy met me at the foot of the stairs. "Rhoda," he said. "Come here. Come look at this."

He took me to an old table in a corner of the basement. It was a walnut table with grapes carved on the side and feet like lion's feet. He laid one of the magazines down on the table and opened it. It was a photograph of a naked little girl, a girl smaller than I was. He turned the page. Two naked boys were standing together with their legs twined. He kept turning the pages. It was all the same. Naked children on every page. I had never seen a naked boy. Much less a photograph of one. Billy looked up at me. He turned another page. Five naked little girls were grouped together around a fountain.

"Let's get out of here," I said. "Come on. I'm getting out of here." I headed for the stairs with him right behind me. We didn't even close the basement door. We didn't even stop to say thank you.

The magazines we had collected were in bundles. About a block from the house we stopped on a corner, breathless from running. "Let's see if there're any more," I said. We tore open a bundle. The first magazine had pictures of naked grown people on every page.

"What are we going to do?" he said.

"We're going to throw them away," I answered, and started throwing them into the nandina bushes by the Hancock's vacant lot. We threw them into the nandina bushes and into the ditch that runs into Mills Creek. We threw the last ones into a culvert and then we took our wagon and got on out of there. At the corner of Sycamore and Wesley we went our separate ways.

"Well, at least you'll have something to think about tomorrow when you get your shot," I said.

"I guess so," he replied.

"Look here, Billy. I don't want you to tell anyone about those magazines. You understand?"

"I won't." His head was going down again.

"I mean it, Billy."

He raised his head and looked at me as if he had just remembered something he was thinking about. "I won't," he said. "Are you really going to write about me in the paper?"

"Of course I am. I said I was, didn't I? I'm going to do it tonight."

I walked on home. Past the corner where the Scout hikes met. Down the alley where I found the card shuffler and the Japanese fan. Past the yard where the violets grew. I was thinking about the boys with their legs twined. They looked like earthworms, all naked like that. They looked like something might fly down and eat them. It made me sick to think about it and I stopped by Mrs. Alford's and picked a few iris to take home to my mother.

Billy finished getting his shots. And I wrote the article and of course they put it on page one. BE ON THE LOOKOUT FOR MAD SQUIRREL, the headline read. By Rhoda Katherine Manning. Grade 3.

> We didn't even know it was mean, the person it bit said. That person is in the third grade at our school. His name is William Monday. On April 23 he had his last shot. Mrs. Jansma's class had a cake and gave him a pencil set. Billy Monday is all right now and things are back to normal.
>
> I think it should be against the law to keep dangerous pets or dogs where they can get out and get people. If you see a dog or squirrel acting funny go in the house and stay there.

I never did get around to telling my mother about those magazines. I kept meaning to but there never seemed to be anywhere to start. One day in August I tried to tell her. I had been to the swimming pool and I thought I saw the man from the brick house drive by in a car. I was pretty sure it was him. As he turned the corner he looked at me. *He looked right at my face.* I stood very still, my heart pounding inside my chest, my hands as cold and wet as a frog, the smell of swimming pool chlorine rising from my skin. What if he found out where I lived? What if he followed me home and killed me to keep me from telling on him? I was terrified. At any moment the car might return. He might grab me and put me in the car and take me off and kill me. I threw my bathing suit and towel down on the sidewalk and started running. I ran down Linden Street and turned into the alley behind Calvin Boulevard, running as fast as I could. I ran down the alley and into my yard and up my steps and into my house looking for my mother to tell her about it.

She was in the living room, with Father Kenniman and Mr. and Mrs. DuVal. They lived across the street and had a gold star in their window. Warrene, our cook, was there. And Connie Barksdale, our cousin who was visiting from the Delta. Her husband had been killed on Corregidor and she would come up and stay with my mother whenever she couldn't take it anymore. They were all in the living room gathered around the radio.

"Momma," I said. "I saw this man that gave me some magazines . . ."

"Be quiet, Rhoda," she said. "We're listening to the news. Something's happened. We think maybe we've won the war." There were tears in her eyes. She gave me a little hug, then turned back to the radio. It was a wonderful radio with a magic eye that glowed in the dark. At night when we had blackouts Dudley and I would get into bed with my mother and we would listen to it together, the magic eye glowing in the dark like an emerald.

Now the radio was bringing important news to Seymour, Indiana. Strange, confused, hush-hush news that said we had a bomb bigger than any bomb ever made and we had already dropped it on Japan and half of Japan was sinking into the sea. Now the Japs had to surrender. Now they couldn't come to Indiana and stick bamboo up our fingernails. Now it would all be over and my father would come home.

The grown people kept on listening to the radio, getting up every now and then to get drinks or fix each other sandwiches. Dudley was sitting beside my mother in a white shirt acting like he was twenty years old. He always did that when company came. No one was paying any attention to me.

Finally I went upstairs and lay down on the bed to think things over. My father was coming home. I didn't know how to feel about that. He was always yelling at someone when he was home. He was always yelling at my mother to make me mind.

"What do you mean, you can't catch her," I could hear him yelling. "Hit her with a broom. Hit her with a table. Hit her with a chair. But, for God's sake, Ariane, don't let her talk to you that way."

Well, maybe it would take a while for him to get home. First they had to finish off Japan. First they had to sink the other half into the sea. I curled up in my soft old eiderdown comforter. I was feeling great. We had dropped the biggest bomb in the world on Japan and there were plenty more where that one came from.

I fell asleep in the hot sweaty silkiness of the comforter. I was dreaming I was at the wheel of an airplane carrying the bomb to Japan. Hit 'em, I was yelling. Hit 'em with a mountain. Hit 'em with a table. Hit 'em with a chair. Off we go into the wild blue yonder, climbing high into the sky. I dropped one on the brick house where the bad man lived, then took off for Japan. Down we dive, spouting a flame from under. Off with one hell of a roar. We live in flame. Buckle down in flame. For nothing can stop the Army Air Corps. Hit 'em with a table, I was yelling. Hit 'em with a broom. Hit 'em with a bomb. Hit 'em with a chair.

MUSIC

꩜ ꩜

RHODA WAS FOURTEEN YEARS OLD the summer her father dragged her off to Clay County, Kentucky, to make her stop smoking and acting like a movie star. She was fourteen years old, a holy and terrible age, and her desire for beauty and romance drove her all day long and pursued her if she slept.

"Te amo," she whispered to herself in Latin class. "Te amo, Bob Rosen," sending the heat of her passions across the classroom and out through the window and across two states to a hospital room in Saint Louis, where a college boy lay recovering from a series of operations Rhoda had decided would be fatal.

"And you as well must die, beloved dust," she quoted to herself. "Oh, sleep forever in your Latmian cave, Mortal Endymion, darling of the moon," she whispered, and sometimes it was Bob Rosen's lanky body stretched out in the cave beside his saxophone that she envisioned and sometimes it was her own lush, apricot-colored skin growing cold against the rocks in the moonlight.

Rhoda was fourteen years old that spring and her true love had been cruelly taken from her and she had started smoking because there was nothing left to do now but be a writer.

She was fourteen years old and she would sit on the porch at night looking down the hill that led through the small town of Franklin, Kentucky, and think about the stars, wondering where heaven could be in all that vastness, feeling betrayed by her mother's pale Episcopalianism and the fate that had brought her to this small town right in the middle of her sophomore year in high school. She would sit on the porch stuffing chocolate chip cookies into her mouth, drinking endless homemade chocolate milkshakes, smoking endless Lucky Strike cigarettes, watching her mother's transplanted roses move steadily across the trellis, taking Bob Rosen's thin letters in and out of their envelopes, holding them against her face, then going up to the new bedroom, to the soft, blue sheets, stuffed with cookies and ice cream and cigarettes and rage.

"Is that you, Rhoda?" her father would call out as she passed his bedroom. "Is that you, sweetie? Come tell us good night." And she would go into their bedroom and lean over and kiss him.

"You just ought to smell yourself," he would say, sitting up, pushing her away. "You just ought to smell those nasty cigarettes." And as soon as she went into her room he would go downstairs and empty all the ashtrays to make sure the house wouldn't burn down while he was sleeping.

"I've got to make her stop that goddamn smoking," he would say, climbing back into the bed. "I'm goddamned if I'm going to put up with that."

"I'd like to know how you're going to stop it," Rhoda's mother said. "I'd like to see anyone make Rhoda do anything she doesn't want to do. Not to mention that you're hardly ever here."

"Goddammit, Ariane, don't start that this time of night." And he rolled over on his side of the bed and began to plot his campaign against Rhoda's cigarettes.

Dudley Manning wasn't afraid of Rhoda, even if she was as stubborn as a goat. Dudley Manning wasn't afraid of anything. He had gotten up at dawn every day for years and believed in himself and followed his luck wherever it led him, dragging his sweet southern wife and his children behind him, and now, in his fortieth year, he was about to become a millionaire.

He was about to become a millionaire and he was in love with a beautiful woman who was not his wife and it was the strangest spring he had ever known. When he added up the figures in his account books he was filled with awe at his own achievements, amazed at what he had made of himself, and to make up for it he talked a lot about luck and pretended to be humble but deep down inside he believed there was nothing he couldn't do, even love two women at once, even make Rhoda stop smoking.

Both Dudley and Rhoda were early risers. If he was in town he would be waiting in the kitchen when she came down to breakfast, dressed in his khakis, his pens in his pocket, his glasses on his nose, sitting at the table going over his papers, his head full of the clean new ideas of morning.

"How many more days of school do you have?" he said to her one morning, watching her light the first of her cigarettes without saying anything about it.

"Just this week," she said. "Just until Friday. I'm making A's, Daddy. This is the easiest school I've ever been to."

"Well, don't be smart-alecky about it, Rhoda," he said. "If you've got a good mind it's only because God gave it to you."

"God didn't give me anything," she said. "Because there isn't any God."

"Well, let's don't get into an argument about that this morning," Dudley said. "As soon as you finish school I want you to drive up to the mines with me for a few days."

"For how long?" she said.

"We won't be gone long," he said. "I just want to take you to the mines to look things over."

Rhoda french-inhaled, blowing the smoke out into the sunlight coming through the kitchen windows, imagining herself on a tour of her father's mines, the workers with their caps in their hands smiling at her as she walked politely among them. Rhoda liked that idea. She dropped two saccharin tablets into her coffee and sat down at the table, enjoying her fantasy.

"Is that what you're having for breakfast?" he said.

"I'm on a diet," Rhoda said. "I'm on a black coffee diet."

He looked down at his poached eggs, cutting into the yellow with his knife. I can wait, he said to himself. As God is my witness I can wait until Sunday.

Rhoda poured herself another cup of coffee and went upstairs to write Bob Rosen before she left for school.

Dear Bob [the letter began],

School is almost over. I made straight A's, of course, as per your instructions. This school is so easy it's crazy.

They read one of my newspaper columns on the radio in Nashville. Everyone in Franklin goes around saying my mother writes my columns. Can you believe that? Allison Hotchkiss, that's my editor, says she's going to write an editorial about it saying I really write them.

I turned my bedroom into an office and took out the tacky dressing table mother made me and got a desk and put my typewriter on it and made striped drapes, green and black and white. I think you would approve.

Sunday Daddy is taking me to Manchester, Kentucky, to look over the coal mines. He's going to let me drive. He lets me drive *all the time.* I live for your letters.

Te amo,

Rhoda

She put the letter in a pale blue envelope, sealed it, dripped some Toujours Moi lavishly onto it in several places and threw herself down on her bed.

She pressed her face deep down into her comforter pretending it was Bob Rosen's smooth cool skin. "Oh, Bob, Bob," she whispered to the comforter. "Oh, honey, don't die, don't die, please don't die." She could feel the tears coming. She reached out and caressed the seam of the comforter, pretending it was the scar on Bob Rosen's neck.

The last night she had been with him he had just come home from an operation for a mysterious tumor that he didn't want to talk about. It would be better soon, was all he would say about it. Before long he would be as good as new.

They had driven out of town and parked the old Pontiac underneath a tree beside a pasture. It was September and Rhoda had lain in his arms smelling the clean smell of his new sweater, touching the fresh red scars on his neck, looking out the window to memorize every detail of the scene, the black tree, the September pasture, the white horse leaning against the fence, the palms of his hands, the taste of their cigarettes, the night breeze, the exact temperature of the air, saying to herself over and over, I must remember everything. This will have to last me forever and ever and ever.

"I want you to do it to me," she said. "Whatever it is they do."

"I can't," he said. "I couldn't do that now. It's too much trouble to make love to a virgin." He was laughing. "Besides, it's hard to do it in a car."

"But I'm leaving," she said. "I might not ever see you again."

"Not tonight," he said. "I still don't feel very good, Rhoda."

"What if I come back and visit," she said. "Will you do it then? When you feel better."

"If you still want me to I will," he said. "If you come back to visit and we both want to, I will."

"Do you promise?" she said, hugging him fiercely.

"I promise," he said. "On my honor I promise to do it when you come to visit."

But Rhoda was not allowed to go to Saint Louis to visit. Either her mother guessed her intentions or else she seized the opportunity to do what she had been wanting to do all along and stop her daughter from seeing a boy with a Jewish last name.

There were weeks of pleadings and threats. It all ended one Sunday night when Mrs. Manning lost her temper and made the statement that Jews were little peddlers who went through the Delta selling needles and pins.

"You don't know what you're talking about," Rhoda screamed. "He's not a peddler, and I love him and I'm going to love him until I die." Rhoda pulled her arms away from her mother's hands.

"I'm going up there this weekend to see him," she screamed. "Daddy promised me I could and you're not going to stop me and if you try to stop me I'll kill you and I'll run away and I'll never come back."

"You are not going to Saint Louis and that's the end of this conversation and if you don't calm down I'll call a doctor and have you locked up. I think you're crazy, Rhoda. I really do."

"I'm not crazy," Rhoda screamed. "You're the one that's crazy."

"You and your father think you're so smart," her mother said. She was shaking but she held her ground, moving around behind a Queen Anne chair. "Well, I don't care how smart you are, you're not going to get on a train and go off to Saint Louis, Missouri, to see a man when you're only fourteen years old, and that, Miss Rhoda K. Manning, is that."

"I'm going to kill you," Rhoda said. "I really am. I'm going to kill you," and she thought for a moment that she would kill her, but then she noticed her grandmother's Limoges hot chocolate pot sitting on top of the piano holding a spray of yellow jasmine, and she walked over to the piano and picked it up and threw it all the way across the room and smashed it into a wall beside a framed print of "The Blue Boy."

"I hate you," Rhoda said. "I wish you were dead." And while her mother stared in disbelief at the wreck of the sainted hot chocolate pot, Rhoda walked out of the house and got in the car and drove off down the steep driveway. I hate her guts, she said to herself. I hope she cries herself to death.

She shifted into second gear and drove off toward her father's office, quoting to herself from Edna Millay. "Now by this moon, before this moon shall wane, I shall be dead or I shall be with you."

But in the end Rhoda didn't die. Neither did she kill her mother. Neither did she go to Saint Louis to give her virginity to her reluctant lover.

The Sunday of the trip Rhoda woke at dawn feeling very excited and changed clothes four or five times trying to decide how she wanted to look for her inspection of the mines.

Rhoda had never even seen a picture of a strip mine. In her imagination she and her father would be riding an elevator down into the heart of a mountain where obsequious masked miners were lined up to shake her hand. Later that evening the captain of the football team would be coming over to the hotel to meet her and take her somewhere for a drive.

She pulled on a pair of pink pedal pushers and a long navy blue sweatshirt, threw every single thing she could possibly imagine wearing into a large suitcase, and started down the stairs to where her father was calling for her to hurry up.

Her mother followed her out of the house holding a buttered biscuit on a linen napkin. "Please eat something before you leave," she said. "There isn't a decent restaurant after you leave Bowling Green."

"I told you I don't want anything to eat," Rhoda said. "I'm on a diet." She stared at the biscuit as though it were a coral snake.

"One biscuit isn't going to hurt you," her mother said. "I made you a lunch, chicken and carrot sticks and apples."

"I don't want it," Rhoda said "Don't put any food in this car, Mother."

"Just because you never eat doesn't mean your father won't get hungry. You don't have to eat any of it unless you want to." Their eyes met. Then they sighed and looked away.

Her father appeared at the door and climbed in behind the wheel of the secondhand Cadillac.

"Let's go, Sweet Sister," he said, cruising down the driveway, turning onto the road leading to Bowling Green and due east into the hill country. Usually this was his favorite moment of the week, starting the long drive into the rich Kentucky hills where his energy and intelligence had created the long black rows of figures in the account books, figures that meant Rhoda would never know what it was to be really afraid or uncertain or powerless.

"How long will it take?" Rhoda asked.

"Don't worry about that," he said. "Just look out the window and enjoy the ride. This is beautiful country we're driving through."

"I can't right now," Rhoda said. "I want to read the new book Allison gave me. It's a book of poems."

She settled down into the seat and opened the book.

> *Oh, gallant was the first love, and glittering and fine;*
> *The second love was water, in a clear blue cup;*
> *The third love was his, and the fourth was mine.*
> *And after that, I always get them all mixed up.*

Oh, God, this is good, she thought. She sat up straighter, wanting to kiss the book. Oh, God, this is really good. She turned the book over to look at the picture of the author. It was a photograph of a small bright face in full profile staring off into the mysterious brightly lit world of a poet's life.

Dorothy Parker, she read. What a wonderful name. Maybe I'll change my name to Dorothy, Dorothy Louise Manning. Dot Manning. Dottie, Dottie Leigh, Dot.

Rhoda pulled a pack of Lucky Strikes out of her purse, tamped it on the dashboard, opened it, extracted a cigarette and lit it with a gold Ronson lighter. She inhaled deeply and went back to the book.

Her father gripped the wheel, trying to concentrate on the

beauty of the morning, the green fields, the small, neat farm-
houses, the red barns, the cattle and horses. He moved his eyes
from all that order to his fourteen-year-old daughter slumped beside him with her nose buried in a book, her plump fingers lan-
guishing in the air, holding a cigarette. He slowed down, pulled
the car onto the side of the road and killed the motor.

"What's wrong?" Rhoda said. "Why are you stopping?"

"Because you are going to put out that goddamn cigarette this
very minute and you're going to give me the package and you're
not going to smoke another cigarette around me as long as you
live," he said.

"I will not do any such thing," Rhoda said. "It's a free country."

"Give me the cigarette, Rhoda," he said. "Hand it here."

"Give me one good reason why I should," she said. But her
voice let her down. She knew there wasn't any use in arguing. This
was not her soft little mother she was dealing with. This was
Dudley Manning, who had been a famous baseball player until
he quit when she was born. Who before that had gone to the
Olympics on a relay team. There were scrapbooks full of his clippings in Rhoda's house. No matter where the Mannings went
those scrapbooks sat on a table in the den. *Manning Hits One
Over The Fence,* the headlines read. *Manning Saves The Day. Manning
Does It Again.* And he was not the only one. His cousin, Philip
Manning, down in Jackson, Mississippi, was famous too. Who
was the father of the famous Crystal Manning, Rhoda's cousin
who had a fur coat when she was ten. And Leland Manning, who
was her cousin Lele's daddy. Leland had been the captain of the
Tulane football team before he drank himself to death in the
Delta.

Rhoda sighed, thinking of all that, and gave in for the moment. "Give me one good reason and I might," she repeated.

"I don't have to give you a reason for a goddamn thing," he
said. "Give the cigarette here, Rhoda. Right this minute." He
reached out and took it and she didn't resist. "Goddamn, these

things smell awful," he said, crushing it in the ashtray. He reached in her pocketbook and got the package and threw it out the window.

"Only white trash throw things out on the road," Rhoda said. "You'd kill me if I did that."

"Well, let's just be quiet and get to where we're going." He started the motor and drove back out onto the highway. Rhoda crunched down lower in the seat, pretending to read her book. Who cares, she thought. I'll get some as soon as we stop for gas.

Getting cigarettes at filling stations was not as easy as Rhoda thought it was going to be. This was God's country they were driving into now, the hills rising up higher and higher, strange, silent little houses back off the road. Rhoda could feel the eyes looking out at her from behind the silent windows. Poor white trash, Rhoda's mother would have called them. The salt of the earth, her father would have said.

This was God's country and these people took things like children smoking cigarettes seriously. At both places where they stopped there was a sign by the cash register, *No Cigarettes Sold To Minors*.

Rhoda had moved to the back seat of the Cadillac and was stretched out on the seat reading her book. She had found another poem she liked and she was memorizing it.

> *Four be the things I'd be better without,*
> *Love, curiosity, freckles and doubt,*
> *Three be the things I shall never attain,*
> *Envy, content and sufficient champagne.*

Oh, God, I love this book, she thought. *This Dorothy Parker is just like me.* Rhoda was remembering a night when she got drunk in Clarkesville, Mississippi, with her cousin Baby Gwen Barksdale. They got drunk on tequila LaGrande Conroy brought back from Mexico, and Rhoda had slept all night in the bathtub so she would be near the toilet when she vomited.

She put her head down on her arm and giggled, thinking about waking up in the bathtub. Then a plan occurred to her.

"Stop and let me go to the bathroom," she said to her father. "I think I'm going to throw up."

"Oh, Lord," he said. "I knew you shouldn't have gotten in the back seat. Well, hold on. I'll stop the first place I see." He pushed his hat back off his forehead and began looking for a place to stop, glancing back over his shoulder every now and then to see if she was all right. Rhoda had a long history of throwing up on car trips so he was taking this seriously. Finally he saw a combination store and filling station at a bend in the road and pulled up beside the front door.

"I'll be all right." Rhoda said, jumping out of the car. "You stay here. I'll be right back."

She walked dramatically up the wooden steps and pushed open the screen door. It was so quiet and dark inside she thought for a moment the store was closed. She looked around. She was in a rough, high-ceilinged room with saddles and pieces of farm equipment hanging from the rafters and a sparse array of canned goods on wooden shelves behind a counter. On the counter were five or six large glass jars filled with different kinds of Nabisco cookies. Rhoda stared at the cookie jars, wanting to stick her hand down inside and take out great fistfuls of Lorna Doones and Oreos. She fought off her hunger and raised her eyes to the display of chewing tobacco and cigarettes.

The smells of the store rose up to meet her, fecund and rich, moist and cool, as if the store was an extension of the earth outside. Rhoda looked down at the board floors. She felt she could have dropped a sunflower seed on the floor and it would instantly sprout and take bloom, growing quick, moving down into the earth and upwards toward the rafters.

"Is anybody here?" she said softly, then louder. "Is anybody here?"

A woman in a cotton dress appeared in a door, staring at Rhoda out of very intense, very blue eyes.

"Can I buy a pack of cigarettes from you?" Rhoda said. "My dad's in the car. He sent me to get them."

"What kind of cigarettes you looking for?" the woman said, moving to the space between the cash register and the cookie jars.

"Some Luckies if you have them," Rhoda said. "He said to just get anything you had if you didn't have that."

"They're a quarter," the woman said, reaching behind herself to take the package down and lay it on the counter, not smiling, but not being unkind either.

"Thank you," Rhoda said, laying the quarter down on the counter. "Do you have any matches?"

"Sure," the woman said, holding out a box of kitchen matches. Rhoda took a few, letting her eyes leave the woman's face and come to rest on the jars of Oreos. They looked wonderful and light, as though they had been there a long time and grown soft around the edges.

The woman was smiling now. "You want one of those cookies?" she said. "You want one, you go on and have one, It's free."

"Oh, no thank you," Rhoda said. "I'm on a diet. Look, do you have a ladies' room I can use?"

"It's out back," the woman said. "You can have one of them cookies if you want it. Like I said, it won't cost you nothing."

"I guess I'd better get going," Rhoda said. "My dad's in a hurry. But thank you anyway. And thanks for the matches." Rhoda hurried down the aisle, slipped out the back door and leaned up against the back of the store, tearing the paper off the cigarettes. She pulled one out, lit it, and inhaled deeply, blowing the smoke out in front of her, watching it rise up into the air, casting a veil over the hills that rose up behind and to the left of her. She had never been in such a strange country. It looked as though no one ever did anything to their yards or roads or fences. It looked as though there might not be a clock for miles.

She inhaled again, feeling dizzy and full. She had just taken the cigarette out of her mouth when her father came bursting out of the door and grabbed both of her wrists in his hands.

"Let go of me," she said. "Let go of me this minute." She struggled to free herself, ready to kick or claw or bite, ready for a real fight, but he held her off. "Drop the cigarette, Rhoda," he said. "Drop it on the ground."

"I'll kill you," she said. "As soon as I get away I'm running away to Florida. Let go of me, Daddy. Do you hear me?"

"I hear you," he said. The veins were standing out on his forehead. His face was so close Rhoda could see his freckles and the line where his false front tooth was joined to what was left of the real one. He had lost the tooth in a baseball game the day Rhoda was born. That was how he told the story. "I lost that tooth the day Rhoda was born," he would say. "I was playing left field against Memphis in the old Crump Stadium. I slid into second and the second baseman got me with his shoe."

"You can smoke all you want to when you get down to Florida," he was saying now. "But you're not smoking on this trip. So you might as well calm down before I drive off and leave you here."

"I don't care," she said. "Go on and leave. I'll just call up Mother and she'll come and get me." She was struggling to free her wrists but she could not move them inside his hands. "Let go of me, you big bully," she added.

"Will you calm down and give me the cigarettes?"

"All right," she said, but the minute he let go of her hands she turned and began to hit him on the shoulders, pounding her fists up and down on his back, not daring to put any real force behind the blows. He pretended to cower under the assault. She caught his eye and saw that he was laughing at her and she had to fight the desire to laugh with him.

"I'm getting in the car," she said. "I'm sick of this place." She walked grandly around to the front of the store, got into the car, tore open the lunch and began to devour it, tearing the chicken off the bones with her teeth, swallowing great hunks without even bothering to chew them. "I'm never speaking to you again as long as I live," she said, her mouth full of chicken breast. "You are not my father."

"Suits me, Miss Smart-alecky Movie Star," he said, putting his hat back on his head. "Soon as we get home you can head on out for Florida. You just let me know when you're leaving so I can give you some money for the bus."

"I hate you," Rhoda mumbled to herself, starting in on the homemade raisin cookies. I hate your guts. I hope you go to hell forever, she thought, breaking a cookie into pieces so she could pick out the raisins.

It was late afternoon when the Cadillac picked its way up a rocky red clay driveway to a housetrailer nestled in the curve of a hill beside a stand of pine trees.

"Where are we going?" Rhoda said. "Would you just tell me that?"

"We're going to see Maud and Joe Samples," he said. "Joe's an old hand around here. He's my right-hand man in Clay County. Now you just be polite and try to learn something, Sister. These are real folks you're about to meet."

"Why are we going here first?" Rhoda said. "Aren't we going to a hotel?"

"There isn't any hotel," her father said. "Does this look like someplace they'd have hotels? Maud and Joe are going to put you up for me while I'm off working."

"I'm going to stay here?" Rhoda asked. "In this trailer?"

"Just wait until you see the inside," her father said. "It's like the inside of a boat, everything all planned out and just the right amount of space for things. I wish your mother'd let me live in a trailer."

They were almost to the door now. A plump smiling woman came out onto the wooden platform and waited for them with her hands on her hips, smiling wider and wider as they got nearer.

"There's Maud," Dudley said. "She's the sweetest woman in the world and the best cook in Kentucky. Hey there, Miss Maud," he called out.

"Mr. D," she said, opening the car door for them. "Joe Samples' been waiting on you all day and here you show up bringing this beautiful girl just like you promised. I've made you some black-berry pies. Come on inside this trailer." Maud smiled deep into Rhoda's face. Her eyes were as blue as the ones on the woman in the store. Rhoda's mother had blue eyes, but not this brilliant and not this blue. These eyes were from another world, another century.

"Come on in and see Joe," Maud said. "He's been having a fit for you to get here."

They went inside and Dudley showed Rhoda all around the trailer, praising the design of trailers. Maud turned on the tiny oven and they had blackberry pie and bread and butter sandwiches and Rhoda abandoned her diet and ate two pieces of the pie, covering it with thick whipped cream.

The men went off to talk business and Maud took Rhoda to a small room at the back of the trailer decorated to match a handmade quilt of the sunrise.

There were yellow ruffled curtains at the windows and a tiny dressing table with a yellow ruffled skirt around the edges. Rhoda was enchanted by the smallness of everything and the way the windows looked out onto layers of green trees and bushes.

Lying on the dresser was a white leather Bible and a display of small white pamphlets, *Alcohol And You, When Jesus Reaches For A Drink, You Are Not Alone, Sorry Isn't Enough, Taking No For An Answer*.

It embarrassed Rhoda even to read the titles of anything as tacky as the pamphlets, but she didn't let on she thought it was tacky, not with Maud sitting on the bed telling her how pretty she was every other second and asking her questions about herself and saying how wonderful her father was.

"We love Mr. D to death," she said. "It's like he was one of our own."

He appeared in the door. "Rhoda, if you're settled in I'll be leaving now," he said. "I've got to drive to Knoxville to do some business but I'll be back here Tuesday morning to take you to the mines." He handed her three twenty-dollar bills. "Here," he said. "In case you need anything."

He left then and hurried out to the car, trying to figure out how long it would take him to get to Knoxville, to where Valerie sat alone in a hotel room waiting for this night they had planned for so long. He felt the sweet hot guilt rise up in his face and the sweet hot longing in his legs and hands.

I'm sorry, Jesus, he thought, pulling out onto the highway. I know it's wrong and I know we're doing wrong. So go on and punish me if you have to but just let me make it there and back before you start in on me.

He set the cruising speed at exactly fifty-five miles an hour and began to sing to himself as he drove.

> *"Oh, sure as the vine grows around the stump*
> *You're my darling sugar lump,"* he sang, and;
>
> *Froggy went a-courting and he did ride,*
> *Huhhrummp, huhhrummp,*
> *Froggy went a-courting and he did ride, Huhhrummp,*
>
> *What you gonna have for the wedding supper?*
> *Black-eyed peas and bread and butter, Huhhrummp, huhhrummp . . ."*

Rhoda was up and dressed when her father came to get her on Tuesday morning. It was still dark outside but a rooster had begun to crow in the distance. Maud bustled all about the little kitchen making much of them, filling their plates with biscuits and fried eggs and ham and gravy.

Then they got into the Cadillac and began to drive toward the mine. Dudley was driving slowly, pointing out everything to her as they rode along.

"Up on that knoll," he said, "that's where the Traylors live. Rooster Traylor's a man about my age. Last year his mother shot one of the Galtney women for breaking up Rooster's marriage and now the Galtneys have got to shoot someone in the Traylor family."

"That's terrible," Rhoda said.

"No it isn't, Sister," he said, warming into the argument. "These people take care of their own problems."

"They actually shoot each other?" she said. "And you think that's okay? You think that's funny?"

"I think it's just as good as waiting around for some judge and jury to do it for you."

"Then you're just crazy," Rhoda said. "You're as crazy as you can be."

"Well, let's don't argue about it this morning. Come on. I've got something to show you." He pulled the car off the road and they walked into the woods, following a set of bulldozer tracks that made a crude path into the trees. It was quiet in the woods and smelled of pine and sassafras. Rhoda watched her father's strong body moving in front of her, striding along, inspecting everything, noticing everything, commenting on everything.

"Look at this," he said. "Look at all this beauty, honey. Look at how beautiful all this is. This is the real world. Not those goddamn movies and beauty parlors and magazines. This is the world that God made. This is where people are really happy."

"There isn't any God," she said. "Nobody that knows anything believes in God, Daddy. That's just a lot of old stuff..."

"I'm telling you, Rhoda," he said. "It breaks my heart to see the way you're growing up." He stopped underneath a tree, took a seat on a log and turned his face to hers. Tears were forming in his eyes. He was famous in the family for being able to cry on cue. "You've just got to learn to listen to someone. You've got to get some common sense in your head. I swear to God, I worry about you all the time." The tears were falling now. "I just can't stand to see the way you're growing up. I don't know where you get all those crazy ideas you come up with."

Rhoda looked down, caught off guard by the tears. No matter how many times he pulled that with the tears she fell for it for a moment. The summer forest was all around them, soft deep earth beneath their feet, morning light falling through the leaves, and the things that passed between them were too hard to understand. Their brown eyes met and locked and after that they were bound to start an argument for no one can bear to be that happy or that close to another human being.

"Well, I'll tell you one thing," Rhoda said. "It's a free country and I can smoke if I want to and you can't keep me from doing it by locking me up in a trailer with some poor white trash."

"What did you say?" he said, getting a look on his face that would have scared a grown man to death. "What did you just say, Rhoda?"

"I said I'm sick and tired of being locked up in that damned old trailer with those corny people and nothing to read but religious magazines. I want to get some cigarettes and I want you to take me home so I can see my friends and get my column written for next week."

"Oh, God, Sister," he said. "Haven't I taught you anything? Maud Samples is the salt of the earth. That woman raised seven children. She knows things you and I will never know as long as we live."

"Well, no she doesn't," Rhoda said. "She's just an old white trash country woman and if Momma knew where I was she'd have a fit."

"Your momma is a very stupid person," he said. "And I'm sorry I ever let her raise you." He turned his back to her then and stalked on out of the woods to a road that ran like a red scar up the side of the mountain. "Come on," he said. "I'm going to take you up there and show you where coal comes from. Maybe you can learn one thing this week."

"I learn things all the time," she said. "I already know more than half the people I know . . . I know . . ."

"Please don't talk anymore this morning," he said. "I'm burned out talking to you."

He put her into a jeep and began driving up the steep unpaved road. In a minute he was feeling better, cheered up by the sight of the big Caterpillar tractors moving dirt. If there was one thing that always cheered him up it was the sight of a big shovel moving dirt. "This is Blue Gem coal," he said. "The hardest in the area. See the layers. Topsoil, then gravel and dirt or clay, then slate, then thirteen feet of pure coal. Some people think it was made by dinosaurs. Other people think God put it there."

"This is it?" she said. "This is the mine?" It looked like one of his road construction projects. Same yellow tractors, same disorderly activity. The only difference seemed to be the huge piles of coal and a conveyor belt going down the mountain to a train.

"This is it," he said. "This is where they stored the old dinosaurs."

"Well, it is made out of dinosaurs," she said. "There were a lot of leaves and trees and dinosaurs and then they died and the coal and oil is made out of them."

"All right," he said. "Let's say I'll go along with the coal. But tell me this, who made the slate then? Who put the slate right on top of the coal everywhere it's found in the world? Who laid the slate down on top of the dinosaurs?"

"I don't know who put the slate there," she said. "We haven't got that far yet."

"You haven't got that far?" he said. "You mean the scientists haven't got as far as the slate yet? Well, Sister, that's the problem with you folks that evolved out of monkeys. You're still half-baked. You aren't finished like us old dumb ones that God made."

"I didn't say the scientists hadn't got that far," she said. "I just said I hadn't got that far."

"It's a funny thing to me how all those dinosaurs came up here to die in the mountains and none of them died in the farm-land," he said. "It sure would have made it a lot easier on us min-ers if they'd died down there on the flat."

While she was groping around for an answer he went right on. "Tell me this, Sister," he said. "Are any of your monkey an-cestors in there with the dinosaurs, or is it just plain dinosaurs? I'd like to know who all I'm digging up . . . I'd like to give credit . . ."

The jeep had come to a stop and Joe was coming toward them, hurrying out of the small tin-roofed office with a worried look on his face. "Mr. D, you better call up to Jellico. Beb's been look-ing everywhere for you. They had a run-in with a teamster orga-nizer. You got to call him right away."

"What's wrong?" Rhoda said. "What happened?"

"Nothing you need to worry about, Sister," her father said. He turned to Joe. "Go find Preacher and tell him to drive Rhoda back to your house. You go on now, honey. I've got work to do." He gave her a kiss on the cheek and disappeared into the office. A small shriveled-looking man came limping out of a building and climbed into the driver's seat. "I'm Preacher," he said. "Mr. Joe tole me to drive you up to his place."

"All right," Rhoda said. "I guess that's okay with me." Preacher put the jeep in gear and drove it slowly down the winding rut-ted road. By the time they got to the bottom Rhoda had thought of a better plan. "I'll drive now," she said. "I'll drive myself to Maud's. It's all right with my father. He lets me drive all the time. You can walk back, can't you?" Preacher didn't know what to say to that. He was an old drunk that Dudley and Joe kept around to run errands. He was so used to taking orders that finally he climbed down out of the jeep and did as he was told. "Show me the way to town," Rhoda said. "Draw me a map. I have to go by town on my way to Maud's." Preacher scratched his head, then bent over and drew her a little map in the dust on the hood. Rhoda studied the map, put the jeep into the first forward gear she could find and drove off down the road to the little town of Manchester, Kentucky, studying the diagram on the gearshift as she drove.

She parked beside a boardwalk that led through the main street of town and started off looking for a store that sold cigarettes. One of the stores had dresses in the window. In the center was a red strapless sundress with a white jacket. $6.95, the price tag said. I hate the way I look, she decided. I hate these tacky pants. I've got sixty dollars. I don't have to look like this if I don't want to. I can buy anything I want.

She went inside, asked the clerk to take the dress out of the window and in a few minutes she emerged from the store wearing the dress and a pair of leather sandals with two-inch heels. The jacket was thrown carelessly over her shoulder like Gene Tierney in *Leave Her to Heaven*. I look great in red, she was thinking, catching a glimpse of herself in a store window. It isn't true that redheaded people can't wear red. She walked on down the boardwalk, admiring herself in every window.

She walked for two blocks looking for a place to try her luck getting cigarettes. She was almost to the end of the boardwalk when she came to a pool hall. She stood in the door looking in, smelling the dark smell of tobacco and beer. The room was deserted except for a man leaning on a cue stick beside a table and a boy with black hair seated behind a cash register reading a book. The boy's name was Johnny Hazard and he was sixteen years old. The book he was reading was *U.S.A.* by John Dos Passos. A woman who came to Manchester to teach poetry writing had given him the book. She had made a dust jacket for it out of brown paper so he could read it in public. On the spine of the jacket she had written *American History.*

"I'd like a package of Lucky Strikes," Rhoda said, holding out a twenty-dollar bill in his direction.

"We don't sell cigarettes to minors," he said. "It's against the law."

"I'm not a minor," Rhoda said. "I'm eighteen. I'm Rhoda Manning. My daddy owns the mine."

"Which mine?" he said. He was watching her breasts as she talked, getting caught up in the apricot skin against the soft red dress.

"The mine," she said. "The Manning mine. I just got here the other day. I haven't been downtown before."

"So, how do you like our town?"

"Please sell me some cigarettes," she said. "I'm about to have a fit for a Lucky."

"I can't sell you cigarettes," he said. "You're not any more eighteen years old than my dog."

"Yes, I am," she said. "I drove here in a jeep, doesn't that prove anything?" She was looking at his wide shoulders and the tough flat chest beneath his plaid shirt.

"Are you a football player?" she said.

"When I have time," he said. "When I don't have to work on the nights they have games."

"I'm a cheerleader where I live," Rhoda said. "I just got elected again for next year."

"What kind of a jeep?" he said.

"An old one," she said. "It's filthy dirty. They use it at the mine." She had just noticed the package of Camels in his breast pocket.

"If you won't sell me a whole package, how about selling me one," she said. "I'll give you a dollar for a cigarette." She raised the twenty-dollar bill and laid it down on the glass counter.

He ignored the twenty-dollar bill, opened the cash register, re-moved a quarter and walked over to the jukebox. He walked with a precise, balanced sort of cockiness, as if he knew he could walk any way he wanted but had carefully chosen this particular walk as his own. He walked across the room through the rectangle of light coming in the door, walking as though he were the first boy ever to be in the world, the first boy ever to walk across a room and put a quarter into a jukebox. He pushed a button and music filled the room.

> *"Kaw-Liga was a wooden Indian a-standing by the door,*
> *He fell in love with an Indian maid*
> *Over in the antique store."*

"My uncle wrote that song," he said, coming back to her. "But it got ripped off by some promoters in Nashville. I'll make you a deal," he said. "I'll give you a cigarette if you'll give me a ride somewhere I have to go."

"All right," Rhoda said. "Where do you want to go?"

"Out to my cousin's," he said. "It isn't far."

"Fine," Rhoda said. Johnny told the lone pool player to keep an eye on things and the two of them walked out into the sunlight, walking together very formally down the street to where the jeep was parked.

"Why don't you let me drive," he said. "It might be easier." She agreed and he drove on up the mountain to a house that looked deserted. He went in and returned carrying a guitar in a case, a blanket, and a quart bottle with a piece of wax paper tied around the top with a rubber band.

"What's in the bottle?" Rhoda said.

"Lemonade, with a little sweetening in it."

"Like whiskey?"

"Yeah. Like whiskey. Do you ever drink it?"

"Sure," she said. "I drink a lot. In Saint Louis we had this

club called The Four Roses that met every Monday at Donna
Duston's house to get drunk. I thought it up, the club I mean."

"Well, here's your cigarette," he said. He took the package from
his pocket and offered her one, holding it near his chest so she
had to get in close to take it.

"Oh, God," she said. "Oh, thank you so much. I'm about to
die for a ciggie. I haven't had one in days. Because my father
dragged me up here to make me stop smoking. He's always trying to make me do something I don't want to do. But it never
works. I'm very hardheaded, like him." She took the light Johnny
offered her and blew out the smoke in a small controlled stream.
"God, I love to smoke," she said.

"I'm glad I could help you out," he said. "Anytime you want
one when you're here you just come on over. Look," he said. "I'm
going somewhere you might want to see, if you're not in a hurry
to get back. You got time to go and see something with me?"

"What is it?" she asked.

"Something worth seeing," he said. "The best thing in Clay
County there is to see."

"Sure," she said. "I'll go. I never turn down an adventure. Why
not, that's what my cousins in the Delta always say. Whyyyyyyy
not." They drove up the mountain and parked and began to walk
into the woods along a path. The woods were deeper here than
where Rhoda had been that morning, dense and green and cool.
She felt silly walking in the woods in the little high-heeled sandals, but she held on to Johnny's hand and followed him deeper
and deeper into the trees, feeling grown up and brave and romantic. I'll bet he thinks I'm the bravest girl he ever met, she
thought. I'll bet he thinks at last he's met a girl who's not afraid
of anything. Rhoda was walking along imagining tearing off a
piece of her dress for a tourniquet in case Johnny was bit by a
poisonous snake. She was pulling the tourniquet tighter and tighter
when the trees opened onto a small brilliant blue pond. The water

was so blue Rhoda thought for a moment it must be some sort of trick. He stood there watching her while she took it in.

"What do you think?" he said at last.

"My God," she said. "What is it?"

"It's Blue Pond," he said. "People come from all over the world to see it."

"Who made it?" Rhoda said. "Where did it come from?"

"Springs. Rock springs. No one knows how deep down it goes, but more than a hundred feet because divers have been that far."

"I wish I could swim in it," Rhoda said. "I'd like to jump in there and swim all day."

"Come over here, cheerleader," he said. "Come sit over here by me and we'll watch the light on it. I brought this teacher from New York here last year. She said it was the best thing she'd ever seen in her life. She's a writer. Anyway, the thing she likes about Blue Pond is watching the light change on the water. She taught me a lot when she was here. About things like that."

Rhoda moved nearer to him, trying to hold in her stomach.

"My father really likes this part of the country," she said. "He says people up here are the salt of the earth. He says all the people up here are direct descendants from England and Scotland and Wales. I think he wants us to move up here and stay, but my mother won't let us. It's all because the unions keep messing with his mine that he has to be up here all the time. If it wasn't for the unions everything would be going fine. You aren't for the unions, are you?"

"I'm for myself," Johnny said. "And for my kinfolks." He was tired of her talking then and reached for her and pulled her into his arms, paying no attention to her small resistances, until finally she was stretched out under him on the earth and he moved the dress from her breasts and held them in his hands. He could smell the wild smell of her craziness and after a while he took the dress off and the soft white cotton underpants and touched

her over and over again. Then he entered her with the way he had
of doing things, gently and with a good sense of the natural
rhythms of the earth.

I'm doing it, Rhoda thought. I'm doing it. This is doing it.
This is what it feels like to be doing it.

"This doesn't hurt a bit," she said out loud. "I think I love
you, Johnny. I love, love, love you. I've been waiting all my life
for you."

"Don't talk so much," he said. "It's better if you stop talking."

And Rhoda was quiet and he made love to her as the sun was
leaving the earth and the afternoon breeze moved in the trees.
Here was every possible tree, hickory and white oak and redwood
and sumac and maple, all in thick foliage now, and he made love
to her with great tenderness, forgetting he had set out to fuck
the boss's daughter, and he kept on making love to her until she
began to tighten around him, not knowing what she was doing,
or where she was going, or even that there was anyplace to be
going to.

Dudley was waiting outside the trailer when she drove up. There
was a sky full of cold stars behind him, and he was pacing up
and down and talking to himself like a crazy man. Maud was inside the trailer crying her heart out and only Joe had kept his
head and was going back and forth from one to the other telling
them everything would be all right.

Dudley was pacing up and down talking to Jesus. I know I
had it coming, he was saying. I know goddamn well I had it coming. But not her. Where in the hell is she? You get her back in
one piece and I'll call Valerie and break it off. I won't see Valerie
ever again as long as I live. *But you've got to get me back my little girl.
Goddammit, you get me back my girl.*

Then he was crying, his head thrown back and raised up to

the stars as the jeep came banging up the hill in third gear. Rhoda parked it and got out and started walking toward him, all bravado and disdain.

Dudley smelled it on her before he even touched her. Smelled it all over her and began to shake her, screaming at her to tell him who it had been. Then Joe came running out from the trailer and threw his hundred and fifty pounds between them, and Maud was right behind him. She led Rhoda into the trailer and put her into bed and sat beside her, bathing her head with a damp towel until she fell asleep.

"I'll find out who it was," Dudley said, shaking his fist. "I'll find out who it was."

"You don't know it was anybody," Joe said. "You don't even know what happened, Mr. D. Now you got to calm down and in the morning we'll find out what happened. More than likely she's just been holed up somewhere trying to scare you."

"I know what happened," Dudley said. "I already know what happened."

"Well, you can find out who it was and you can kill him if you have to," Joe said. "If it's true and you still want to in the morning, you can kill him."

But there would be no killing. By the time the moon was high, Johnny Hazard was halfway between Lexington, Kentucky, and Cincinnati, Ohio, with a bus ticket he bought with the fifty dollars he'd taken from Rhoda's pocket. He had called the poetry teacher and told her he was coming. Johnny had decided it was time to see the world. After all, that very afternoon a rich cheerleader had cried in his arms and given him her cherry. There was no telling what might happen next.

Much later that night Rhoda woke up in the small room, hearing the wind come up in the trees. The window was open and the moon, now low in the sky and covered with mist, poured a diffused light upon the bed. Rhoda sat up in the bed and shivered. Why did I do that with him? she thought. Why in the world did I do that? But I couldn't help it, she decided. He's so sophisticated and he's so good-looking and he's a wonderful driver and he plays a guitar. She moved her hands along her thighs, trying to remember exactly what it was they had done, trying to remember the details, wondering where she could find him in the morning.

But Dudley had other plans for Rhoda in the morning. By noon she was on her way home in a chartered plane. Rhoda had never been on an airplane of any kind before, but she didn't let on.

"I'm thinking of starting a diary," she was saying to the pilot, arranging her skirt so her knees would show. "A lot of unusual things have been happening to me lately. The boy I love is dying of cancer in Saint Louis. It's very sad, but I have to put up with it. He wants me to write a lot of books and dedicate them to his memory."

The pilot didn't seem to be paying much attention, so Rhoda gave up on him and went back into her own head.

In her head Bob Rosen was alive after all. He was walking along a street in Greenwich Village and passed a bookstore with a window full of her books, many copies stacked in a pyramid with her picture on every cover. He recognized the photograph, ran into the bookstore, grabbed a book, opened it and saw the dedication. *To Bob Rosen, Te Amo Forever, Rhoda.*

Then Bob Rosen, or maybe it was Johnny Hazard, or maybe this unfriendly pilot, stood there on that city street, looking up at the sky, holding the book against his chest, crying and brokenhearted because Rhoda was lost to him forever, this famous author, who could have been his, lost to him forever.

Thirty years later Rhoda woke up in a hotel room in New York City. There was a letter lying on the floor where she had thrown it when she went to bed. She picked it up and read it again. *Take my name off that book*, the letter said. *Imagine a girl with your advantages writing a book like that. Your mother is so ashamed of you.*

Goddamn you, Rhoda thought. Goddamn you to hell. She climbed back into the bed and pulled the pillows over her head. She lay there for a while feeling sorry for herself. Then she got up and walked across the room and pulled a legal pad out of a briefcase and started writing.

Dear Father,

You take *my* name off those checks you send those television preachers and those goddamn right-wing politicians. That name has come to me from a hundred generations of men and women . . . also, in the future let my mother speak for herself about my work.

Love,
Rhoda

P.S. The slate was put there by the second law of thermodynamics. Some folks call it gravity. Other folks call it God.

I guess it was the second law, she thought. It was the second law or the third law or something like that. She leaned back in the chair, looking at the ceiling. Maybe I'd better find out before I mail it.

JADE BUDDHAS,
RED BRIDGES,
FRUITS OF LOVE

꙲ ꙳

SHE HAD WRITTEN TO HIM, since neither of them had a phone.

> I'll be there Sunday morning at four. It's called the Night Owl flight in case you forget the number. The number's 349. If you can't come get me I'll get a taxi and come on over. I saw Johnny Vidocovitch last night. He's got a new bass player. He told Ron he could afford to get married now that he'd found his bass player. Doesn't that sound just like him? I want to go to that chocolate place in San Francisco the minute I get there. And lie down with you in the dark for a million years. Or in the daylight. I love you. Nora Jane

He wasn't there. He wasn't at the gate. Then he wasn't in the terminal. Then he wasn't at the baggage carousel. Nora Jane stood by the carousel taking her hat on and off, watching a boy in cowboy boots kiss his girlfriend in front of everyone at the airport. He would run his hands down her flowered skirt and then kiss her again.

Finally the bags came. Nora Jane got her flat shoes out of her backpack and went on out to find a taxi. It's because I was too cheap to get a phone, she told herself. I knew I should have had a phone.

She found a taxi and was driven off into the hazy early morning light of San Jose. The five hundred and forty dollars she got from the robbery was rolled up in her bag. The hundred and twenty she saved from her job was in her bra. She had been awake all night. And something was wrong. Something had gone wrong.

"You been out here before?" the driver said.

"It's the first time I've been farther west than Alexandria," she said. "I've hardly ever been anywhere."

"How old are you?" he said. He was in a good mood. He had just gotten a $100 tip from a drunk movie star. Besides, the little black-haired girl in the back seat had the kind of face you can't help being nice to.

"I'll be twenty this month," she said. "I'm a Moonchild. They used to call it Cancer but they changed. Do you believe in that stuff?"

"I don't know," the driver said. "Some days I believe in anything. Look over there. Sun's coming up behind the mountains."

"Oh, my," she said. "I forgot there would be mountains."

"On a clear day you can see Mount Diablo. You ought to go while you're out here. You can see eighty percent of California from it. You came out to visit someone?"

"My boyfriend. Well, he's my fiancé. Sometimes he has to work at night. He wasn't sure he could meet me. Is it far? To where I'm going?" They were in a neighborhood now, driving past rows of stucco cottages, built close together like houses in the Irish Channel. The yards looked brown and bare as if they needed rain.

"Couple of blocks. These are nice old neighborhoods. My sister used to live out here. It's called the Lewis tract." He turned a corner and came to a stop before a small pink house with an overgrown yard.

"Four fifty-one. Is that right?"

"That's right."

"You want me to wait till you see if anyone's here?"

"No, I'll just get out."

"You sure?"

"I'm sure." She watched as he backed and turned and went on off down the road, little clouds of dust rising behind the wheels. She stood looking up the path to the door. A red tree peeling like a sunburn shaded the yard. Here and there a few scraggly petunias bloomed in boxes. *Get your ass out here and see where the USA is headed,* Sandy had written her. *I've got lots of plans. No phone as yet. Bring some French bread. Everything out here is sourdough. Yours forever, Sandy.* He's here, she thought. I know he's here.

She walked on up the path. There was a spider's web across the screen door. They can make one overnight, she told herself. It's nothing to make one overnight.

She rang the doorbell and waited. Then she walked around to the back and looked in the window. It was a large room with a modern-looking stove and a tile floor. I'm going in, she decided. I'm worn out. I'm going in.

She picked up a rock and broke a pane of glass in the door, then carefully picked out all the broken pieces and put them in a pile under the steps. She reached her hand in the opening, undid the latch and went on in. It was Sandy's house all right. His old Jazzfest poster of Dr. John and the Mardi Gras Indians was hanging on a wall. A few clothes were in the closets. Not many. Still, Sandy traveled light. He'll be back, she thought. He's just gone somewhere.

She walked around the house looking for clues. She found only a map of San Francisco with some circles drawn on it, and a list, on an envelope, from something called the Paris Hotel. Willets, it said. Berkeley, Sebastopol, Ukiah, Petaluma, Occidental.

She walked back into the kitchen looking for something to

eat. The refrigerator was propped open with a blue tile. Maybe he's in jail, she thought. Maybe I got here just in time.

She reached up a fingernail and flipped open a greeting card that was tacked up over the stove. It was a photograph of a snow-covered mountain with purple fields below and blue skies above. A hawk, or perhaps it was a buzzard, was flying over the mountain. FREEDOM IS THE GREATEST GIFT THAT ONE CAN GIVE ANOTHER, the card said. IT IS A GIFT BORN OF LOVE, TRUST, AND UNDERSTANDING. Nora Jane pulled out the pushpin and read the message inside.

Dear Sandy,

I am glad I am going to be away from you during our two weeks of abstinence. You were so supportive once you realized I was freaking out. I want to thank you for being there for me. We have climbed the mountain together now and also the valley. I hope the valley wasn't too low for you.

I know this has been hard on you. You have had to deal with a lot of new feelings and need time to adjust to them. We will both hopefully grow from this experience. I want us to have many more meaningful experiences together. I love you more than words can say. In deepest friendship.

Pam

I'm hungry, Nora Jane thought. I'm starving. She walked over to a bed in a corner. She guessed it was a bed. It was a mattress on top of a platform made of some kind of green stone. It looked more like a place to sacrifice someone than a place to sleep.

She put her pack up on the bed and began riffling through the pockets for the candy bar she had saved from a snack on the plane. When she found it she tore open the cardboard box and began to eat it, slowly at first, then faster. *I don't know,* she thought. *I just don't know.* She leaned up against the green stone platform eating the chocolate, watching the light coming in the window through the leaves of the red tree making patches on the mattress. That's all we are, she decided. Patches of light and darkness. Things that cast shadows.

She ate the rest of the candy, stopping every now and then to lick her fingers. When she was finished she folded the candy box and put it carefully away in her pack. Nora Jane never littered anything. So far in her life she had not thrown down a single gum wrapper.

During the next week there were four earthquakes in the Bay Area. A five point, then a four point, then a two, then a three. The first one woke her in the middle of the night. She was asleep in a room she had rented near the Berkeley campus. At first she thought a cat had walked across the bed. Then she thought the world had come to an end. Then the lights went on. Everyone in the house gathered in the upstairs hall. When the excitement wore down a Chinese mathematician and his wife fixed tea in their room. "Very lucky to be here for that one," Tam Suyin assured Nora Jane. "Sometimes have to wait long time to experience big one."

"I was in a hurricane once," Nora Jane said. "I had to get evacuated when Camille came."

"Oh," Tam said to her husband. "Did you hear that? Miss Whittington have to be evacuated during hurricane. Which one you find most interesting experience, Miss Whittington, earthquake or hurricane?"

"I don't know," Nora Jane said. She was admiring the room, which was as bare as a nun's cell. "I guess the hurricane. It lasted longer."

The next morning she felt better than she had in a week. She was almost glad to be alive. She bought croissants from a little shop on Tamalpais Street, then spent some time decorating her room to look like a nun's cell. She put everything she owned in the closet. She covered the bed with a white sheet. She took down the drapes. She put the rug away and cleaned the floor. She bought flowers and put them on the dresser.

That afternoon she found a theatrical supply store on Shattuck Avenue and bought a stage pistol. It was time to get to work.

"What are you doing?" the proprietor said.

"Happy Birthday, Nora Jane. Have you ever seen it?"

"The Vonnegut play? The one with the animal heads?"

"No, this is an original script. It's a new group on the campus."

"Bring a poster by when you get them ready. We like to advertise our customers."

"I'll do that," she said. "As soon as we get some printed."

"When's it scheduled for?"

"Oh, right away. As soon as we can whip it together."

Freddy Harwood walked down Telegraph Avenue thinking about everyone who adored him. He had just run into Buiji. She had let him buy her a café mocca at the Met. She had let him hold her hand. She had told him all about the horrible time she was having with Dudley. She told him about the au pair girl and the night he threatened her with a gun and the time he choked her and what he said about her friends. It was Freddy she loved, she said. Freddy she adored. Freddy she worshipped. Freddy's hairy stomach and strong arms and level head she longed for. She was counting the days until she was free.

I ought to run for office, he was thinking. And just to think, I could have thrown it all away. I could have been a wastrel like Augustine. But no, I chose another way. The prince's way. Noblesse oblige. Ah, duty, sweet mistress.

Freddy Harwood was the founder and owner of the biggest and least profitable bookstore in northern California. He had one each of every book worth reading in the English language. He had everything that was still in print and a lot that was out of print. He knew dozens of writers. Writers adored him. He gave them autograph parties and unlimited credit and kept their books in stock. He even read their books. He went that far. He actually read their books.

In return they were making him famous. Already he was the hero of three short stories and a science fiction film. Last month *California Magazine* had named him one of the Bay Area's ten most eligible bachelors. Not that he needed the publicity. He already had more women than he knew what to do with. He had Aline and Rita and Janey and Lila and Barbara Hunnicutt, when she was in between tournaments. Not to mention Buiji. Well, he was thinking about settling down. *There are limits,* he said to himself. *Even to Grandmother's money. There are perimeters and prices to pay.*

He wandered across Blake Street against the light, trying to choose among his women. A man in a baseball cap took him by the arm and led him back to the sidewalk.

"Nieman," he said. "What are you doing in town?"

"Looking for you. I've got to see three films between now and twelve o'clock. Go with me. I'll let you help write the reviews."

"I can't. I'm up to my ass in the IRS. I'll be working all night."

"Tomorrow then. I'm at Gautier's. Call me for breakfast."

"If I get through. If I can."

"Holy shit," Nieman said. "Did you see that?" Nora Jane had just passed them going six miles an hour down the sidewalk. She was wearing black and white striped running shorts and a pair of canvas wedgies with black ankle straps, her hair curling all over her head like a dark cloud.

"This city will kill me," Freddy said. "I'm moving back to Gualala."

"Let's catch her," Nieman said. "Let's take her to the movies."

"I can't," Freddy said. "I have to work."

An hour later his computer broke. He rapped it across the desk several times, then beat it against the chair. Still no light. He laid it down on a pile of papers and decided to take a break. An accountant, he was thinking. They've turned me into an accountant.

Nora Jane was sitting by a window of the Atelier reading *The Bridge of San Luis Rey*. She was deep into a description of Uncle Pio. "He possessed the six attributes of an adventurer — a memory for names and faces; with the aptitude for altering his own; the gift of tongues; inexhaustible invention; secrecy; the talent for falling into conversation with strangers; and that freedom from conscience that springs from a contempt for the dozing rich he preyed upon." That's just like me, Nora Jane was thinking. She felt in her bag for the gun. It was still there.

Freddy sat down at a table near hers. Your legs are proof of the existence of God. No, not that. What if she's an atheist? If I could decipher the Rosetta Stone of your anklestraps. My best friend just died. My grandmother owns Sears Roebuck.

"I haven't seen one of those old Time-Life editions of that book in years," he said. "I own a bookstore. May I look at that a minute?"

"Sure you can," she said. "It's a great book. I bought it in New Orleans. That's where I'm from."

"Ah, the crescent city. I know it well. Where did you live? In what part of town?"

"Near the park. Near Tulane."

"On Exposition?"

"No, on Story Street. Near Calhoun." She handed him the book. He took it from her and sat down at the table.

"Oh, this is very interesting, finding this," he said. "This series was so well designed. Look at this cover. You don't see them like this now."

"I've been looking for a bookstore to go to," she said. "I haven't been here long. I don't know my way around yet."

"Well, the best bookstore in the world is right down the street. Finish your coffee and I'll take you there. Clara, I call it. Clara, for light. You know, the patron saint of light."

"Oh, sure," she said. The stranger, she thought. This is the stranger.

They made their way out of the café through a sea of ice cream chairs and out onto the sidewalk. It was in between semesters at Berkeley, and Telegraph Avenue was quiet, almost deserted. When they got to the store Freddy turned the key in the lock and held the door open for her. "Sorry it's so dark," he said. "It's on an automatic switch."

"Is anyone here?" she asked.

"Only us."

"Good," she said. She took the pistol out of her purse and stepped back and pointed it at him. "Where is the office?" she said. "I am robbing you. I came to get money."

"Oh, come on," he said. "You've got to be kidding. Put that gun down."

"I mean it," she said. "This is not a joke. I have killed. I will kill again." He put his hands over his head as he had seen prisoners do in films and led the way to his office through a field of books, a bright meadow of books, one hundred and nineteen library tables piled high with books.

"Listen, Betty," he began, for Nora Jane had told him her name was Betty.

"I came to get money," she said. "Where is the money? Don't talk to me. Just tell me where you put the money."

"Some of it's in my pocket," he said. "The rest is locked up. We don't keep much here. It's mostly charge accounts."

"Where's the safe? Come on. Don't make me mad."

"It's behind that painting. Listen, I'll have to help you take that down. That's a Helen Watermeir. She's my aunt. She'll kill me if anything happens to that painting."

Nora Jane had moved behind his desk. "Try not to mess up

those papers," he said. "I gave up a chance to canoe the Eel River to work on those papers."

"What's it a painting of?" she said.

"It's A.E."

"A.E.?"

"Abstract Expressionism."

"Oh, I know about that. Sister Celestine said it was from painters riding in airplanes all the time. She said that's what things look like to them from planes. You know, I was thinking about that flying up here. We flew over all these salt ponds. They were these beautiful colors. I was thinking about those painters."

"I'll have to let you tell Aunt Helen that. She's really defensive about A.E. right now. That might cheer her up. Now, listen here, Betty, hasn't this gone far enough? Can't you put that gun down? They put people in Alcatraz for that." She was weakening. She was looking away. He pressed his luck. "Nobody with legs like yours should be in Alcatraz."

"This is what I do," she said. "I'm an anarchist. I don't know what else to do." The gun was pointing to the floor.

"Oh," he said. "There are lots of better things to do in San Francisco than rob a bookstore."

"Name one," she said.

"You could go with me," he said. He decided to pull out all the stops. He decided to go for his old standby. "We could go together 'while the evening is spread out against the sky, like a patient etherized upon a table. Oh, do not ask what is it. Let us go and make our visit.'"

"I know that poem," she said. "We had it in English." She wasn't pointing the gun and she was listening. Of course he had never known the "Love Song" to fail. He had seen hardhearted graduate students pull off their sweaters by the third line.

He kept on going. Hitting the high spots. Watching for signs of boredom. By the time he got to "tea and cakes and ices," she had begun to cry. When he got to the line about Prince Hamlet she laid the gun down on top of the computer and dissolved in tears. "My name isn't Betty," she said. "I hate the name of Betty. My name is Nora Jane Whittington and tomorrow is my birthday. Oh, goddamn it all to hell. Oh, goddamn everything in the whole world to hell."

He came around the desk and put his arms around her. She felt wonderful. She felt as good as she looked. "I'm going home and turn myself in," she was sobbing. "They've got my fingerprints. They've got my handwriting. I'm going to have to go live in Mexico."

"No, you aren't," he said. "Come along. Let's go eat dinner. I've been dreaming all day about the prawns at Narsai's."

"I don't want any prawns," she said. "I don't even know what prawns are. I want to go to that chocolate store. I want to go to that store Sandy told me about."

Many hours later they were sitting in the middle of a eucalyptus grove on the campus, watching the stars through the trees. The fog had lifted. It was a nice night with many stars.

"The woods decay, the woods decay and fall," Freddy was saying, but she interrupted him.

"Do you think birds live up there?" she said. "That far up."

"I don't know," he said. "I never thought about it."

"It doesn't look like they would want to nest that high up. I watch birds a lot. I mean, I'm not a birdwatcher or anything like that. But I used to go out on the seawall and watch them all the time. The seagulls, I mean. Feed them bread and watch them fly. Did you ever think how soft flying seems? How soft they look, like they don't have any edges."

"I took some glider lessons once. But I couldn't get into it. I don't care how safe they say it is."

"I don't mean people flying. I mean birds."

"Well, look, how about coming home with me tonight. I want you to spend the night. You can start off your birthday in my hot tub."

"You've got a hot tub in your house?"

"And a redwood deck and a vegetable garden, corn, okra, squash, beans, skylights, silk kimonos, futon, orange trees. If you come over you won't have to go anyplace else the whole time you're in California. And movies. I just got *Chariots of Fire.* I haven't even had time to see it yet."

"All right," she said. "I guess I'll go."

Much later, sitting in his hot tub, she told him all about it. "Then there was this card tacked up over the stove from this girl. You wouldn't believe that card. I wouldn't send anyone one of those cards for a million dollars. We used to have those cards at The Mushroom Cloud. Anyway, now I don't know what to do. I guess I'll go on home and turn myself in. They've got my fingerprints. I left them all over everything."

"We could have your fingers sanded. Did you ever see that movie? With Bette Davis as twin sisters? And Karl Malden. I *think* it was Karl Malden."

"I can't stay out here," she said. "I don't know how to take care of myself out here."

"I'll take care of you," he said. "Listen, N.J., you want me to tell you the rest of that quote I was telling you or not?"

"The one about the trees dying?"

"No, the one about the lice."

"All right," she said. "Go on. Tell the whole thing. I forgot the first part." She had already figured out there wasn't any stopping him once he decided to quote something.

"It's from Heraclitus. Now, listen, this is really good. 'All men are deceived by the appearances of things, even Homer himself, who was the wisest man in Greece; for he was deceived by boys catching lice; they said to him, 'What we have caught and what we have killed we have left behind, but what has escaped us we bring with us.'"

"Am I supposed to say something?" she said.

"Not unless you want to, come on, let's go to bed. Tomorrow we begin the F. Slazenger Harwood memorial tour of the Bay Area. The last girl who got it was runner-up for Miss America. It was wasted on her, however. She didn't even shiver when she put her finger in the passion fruit."

"What all do we have to do?" Nora Jane said.

"We have to see your chocolate store and the seismograph and the Campanile and the Pacific Ocean and the redwood trees. And a movie. At least one movie. There's this great documentary about Werner Herzog playing. He kills all these people trying to move a boat across a forest in Brazil. At the end he says, I don't know if it was worth it. Sometimes I don't know if movies are worth all this."

The tour moved from the Cyclotron to Chez Panisse, from Muir Woods to Toroya's, from the Chinese cemetery to Bolinas Reef.

It began with the seismograph. "That needle is connected to a drum deep in the earth," Freddy quoted from a high-school science lecture. "You could say that needle has its finger on the earth's heart. When the plates shift, when the mantle buckles, it tells us just how much and where."

"What good does that do," Nora Jane said, "if the building you're in is falling down?"

"Come on," he said. "We're late to the concert at the Campanile."

They drove all over town in Freddy's new DeLorean. "Why does this car have fingerprints all over it?" Nora Jane asked. "If I had a car this nice I'd keep it waxed."

"It's made of stainless steel. It's the only stainless steel DeLorean in town. You can't wax stainless steel."

"If I got a car I'd get a baby blue convertible," she said. "This girl at home, Dany Nasser, that went to Sacred Heart with me, had one. She kept promising to let me drive it but she never did."

"You can drive my car," he said. "You can drive it all day long. You can drive it anyplace you want to drive it to."

"Except over bridges," she said. "I don't drive over bridges."

"Why not?"

"I don't know. It always seems like there's nothing underneath them. Like there's nothing there."

He asked her to move in with him but she turned him down. "I couldn't do that," she said. "I wouldn't want to live with anyone just now."

"Then let's go steady. Or get matching tattoos. Or have a baby. Or buy a dog. Or call up everyone we know and tell them we can't see them anymore."

"There isn't anyone for me to call," she said. "You're the only one I know."

In August Sandy found her. Nora Jane was getting ready to go to work. She was putting in her coral earrings when Tam Suyin called her to the phone.

"I was in Colorado," he said. "I didn't get your letter until a week ago. I've been looking all over the place for you. Finally I got Ron and he told me where you were."

"Who's Pam," she said. "Tell me about Pam."

"So you're the one that broke my window."

"I'll pay for your window. Tell me about Pam."

"Pam was a mistake. She took advantage of me. Look, Nora Jane, I've got big plans for us. I've got something planned that only you and I could do. I mean, this is big money. Where are you? I want to see you right away."

"Well, you can't come now. I'm on my way to work. I've got a job, Sandy."

"A job?"

"In an art gallery. A friend got it for me."

"What time do you get off? I'll come wait for you."

"No, don't do that. Come over here. I'll meet you here at five. It's 1512 Arch Street. In Berkeley. Can you find the way?"

"I'll find the way. I'll be counting the minutes."

She called Freddy and broke a date to go to the movies. "I have to talk to him," she said. "I have to give him a chance to explain."

"Oh, sure," he said. "Do whatever you have to do."

"Don't sound like that."

"What do you want me to do? Pretend like I don't care? Your old boyfriend shows up at eight o'clock in the morning . . . the robber baron shows up, and I'm supposed to act like I think it's great."

"I'll call you tomorrow."

"Don't bother. I won't be here. I'm going out of town."

He worked all morning and half the afternoon without giving in to his desire to call her. By two-thirty his sinus headache was so bad he could hardly breathe. He stood on his head for twenty minutes reciting "The Four Quartets." Nothing helped. At three he stormed out of the store. I'm sitting on her steps till she gets home from work, he told himself. I can't make myself sick just to be a nice guy. Unless that bastard picks her up at work. What if he picks her up at work. He'll drag her into drugs. She'll end up in the state pen. He'll put his mouth on her mouth. He'll put his mouth on her legs. He'll touch her hands. He'll touch her hair.

Freddy trudged up Arch Street with his chin on his chest, ignoring the flowers and the smell of hawthorn and bay, ignoring the pines, ignoring the sun, the clear light, the cool clean air.

At the corner of Arch and Brainard he started having second

thoughts. He stood on the corner with his hands stuck deep in the pockets of his pants. A white Lincoln with Colorado plates pulled up in front of Nora Jane's house. A tall boy in chinos got out and walked up on the porch. He inspected the row of mailboxes. He had an envelope in his hand. He put it into one of the boxes and hurried back down the steps. A woman was waiting in the car. They talked a moment, then drove off down the street.

That's him, Freddy thought. That's the little son-of-a-bitch. The Suyins' Pomeranian met him in the yard. He knocked it out of his way with the side of his foot and opened Nora Jane's mailbox. The envelope was there, in between an advertisement and a letter from a politician. He stuck it into his pocket and walked up the hill toward the campus. He stopped in a playground and read the note.

Angel, I have to go to Petaluma on business. I'll call tonight. After eight. Maybe you can come up and spend the weekend. I'm really sorry about tonight. I'll make it up to you. Yours forever.

Sandy

When he finished reading it he wadded it up and stuck it into a trash container shaped like a pelican. "All right," he said to the pelican. "I'll show him anarchy. I'll show him business. I'll show him war."

He walked back down to Shattuck Avenue and hailed a taxi. "Where's the nearest Ford place?" he asked the driver. "Where's the nearest Ford dealer?"

"There's Moak's over in Oakland. Unless you want to go downtown. You want me to take you to Moak's?"

"That's fine," Freddy said. "Moak's is fine with me."

"I wouldn't have a Ford," the driver said. "You couldn't give me a Ford. I wouldn't have a thing but a Toyota."

*   *   *

Moak Ford had just what he was looking for. A pint-sized baby blue convertible sitting in the display window with the sunlight gleaming off its chrome and glass. The interior was an even lighter blue with leather seats and a soft blue carpet. "I'll need a tape deck," he said to the salesman. "How long does it take to install a tape deck?"

At six-thirty he called her from a pay phone near her house. "I don't want to bother you," he said. "I just want to apologize for this morning. I just wanted to make sure you're okay."

"I'm not okay," she said. "I'm terrible. I'm just terrible."

"Could I come over? I've got a present for you."

"A present?"

"It's blue. I bought you something blue."

She was waiting on the porch when he drove up. She walked down the steps trying not to look at it. It was so blue. So very blue. He got out and handed her the keys.

"People don't give other people cars," she said. "They don't just give someone a car."

"I do whatever I need to do," he said. "It's my charm. My fabled charisma."

"Why are you doing this, Freddy?"

"So you'll like me better than old Louisiana Joe. Where is he, by the way? I thought you had a big date with him."

"I broke the date. I didn't feel like seeing him right now. Did you really buy me that car?"

"Yes, I really did. Get in. See how good it smells. I got a tape deck but they can't put it in until Thursday. You want the top down or not?"

She opened the car door and settled her body into the driver's seat. She turned on the key. "I better not put it down just yet. I'll put it down in a minute. I'll stop somewhere and put it down later."

She drove off down Arch Street wondering if she was going crazy. "You don't have to stop to put it down," he said. He reached across her and pushed a button and the blue accordion top folded down like a wing, then back up, then back down again.

"Stop doing that," she said. "You'll make me have a wreck. Where should I go, Freddy? I don't know where to go."

"We could go by the Komatsu showroom and watch ourselves driving by in their glass walls. When I first got the DeLorean I used to do that all the time. Don't look like that, N.J. It's okay to have a car. Cars are all right. They satisfy our need for strong emotions."

"Just tell me where to go."

"I want to take you to the park and show you the Brundage collection but I'm afraid they're closed this time of day. They have this jade Buddha. It's like nothing you've ever seen in your life. I know, let's give it a try. Go down University. We'll drive across a couple of bridges. You need to learn the bridges."

"I can't drive across a bridge. I told you that."

"Of course you can. We'll do the Oakland first, then the Golden Gate. You can't live here if you can't go across the bridges. You won't be able to go anywhere."

"I can't do it, Freddy. I can't even drive across the Huey P. Long, and it's only over the Mississippi."

"Listen to me a minute," he said. "I want to tell you about these bridges. People like us didn't built these bridges, N.J. People like Teddy Roosevelt and Albert Einstein and Aristotle built those bridges. People like my father. The Golden Gate is so overbuilt you could stack cars two deep on it and it wouldn't fall."

"Go on," she said. "I'm listening." She was making straight for the Oakland Bridge, *with the top down*. In the distance the red girders of the Golden Gate gleamed in the sun. She gripped the wheel and turned onto University Avenue leading to the bay.

"All right," he continued, "about these bridge builders. They get up every morning and put on a clean shirt and fill their pockets with pencils. They go out and add and subtract and read blue-prints and put pilings all the way down to the bedrock. Then they build a bridge so strong their great-grandchildren can ride across it without getting hurt. My father helped raise money for the Golden Gate. That's how strong it is."

Nora Jane had driven right by the sign pointing to the Oakland Bridge. The little car hummed beneath her fingers. She straight-ened her shoulders. She kept on going. "All right," she said. "I'll try it. I'll give it a try."

"I wish to hell the Brundage was open. You've got to see this Buddha. It's unbelievable. It's only ten inches high. You can see every wrinkle. You can see every rib. The jade's the color of celadon. Oh, lighter than that. It's translucent. It just floats there."

"Don't talk so much until I get through the gate," she said. She almost sideswiped a black Mazda station wagon. There was a little boy in the back seat wearing a crown. He put his face to the window and waved.

"Did you see that?" Nora Jane said. "Did you see what he's wearing?" She drove through the toll gate and out onto the bridge. She was into it now. She was doing it.

"Loosen up," Freddy said. "Loosen up on the wheel. This Buddha I was telling you about, N.J. It's more the color of seafoam. You've never seen jade like this. It's indescribable. It's got a light of its own. Well, we'll never make it today. I know what, we'll stop in Chinatown and have dinner. I want you to have some Dim Sum. And tomorrow, tomorrow we're going to Mendocino. The hills there are like yellow velvet this time of year. You'll want to put them on and wear them."

I haven't been to confession in two years, Nora Jane was think-ing. What am I doing in this car?

The Mazda passed them again. The boy with the crown was at the back window now. Looking out the open window of the tailgate, eating a package of Nacho Cheese Flavored Doritos and drinking a Coke. He held up a Dorito to Nora Jane. He waved it out the window in the air. The Mazda moved on. A metallic green Buick took its place. In the front seat was a young Chinese businessman wearing a suit. In the back seat, a Chinese gentleman wearing a pigtail.

A plane flew over, trailing a banner. HAPPY 40TH, ED AND DEB, the banner said. Things were happening too fast. "I just saw an airplane fly by trailing breadcrumbs," she said.

"What did you say?" he said. *"What did you just say?"*

"I said . . . oh, never mind. I was thinking too many things at once. I'm going over there, Freddy, in the lane by the water." She put the turn signal on and moved over into the right-hand lane. "Now don't talk to me anymore," she said, squeezing the steering wheel, leaning into it, trying to concentrate on the girders and forget the water. "Don't say any more until I get this car across this bridge."

MISS CRYSTAL'S MAID
NAME TRACELEEN, SHE'S TALKING,
SHE'S TELLING EVERYTHING
SHE KNOWS

ANOTHER TIME, Miss Crystal did a real bad thing at a wedding. It was her brother-in-law's wedding. He was marrying this girl, her daddy was said to be the richest man in Memphis. The Weisses were real excited about it. As much money as they got I guess they figure they can always use some more. So the whole family was going up to Memphis to the wedding, all dressed up and ready to show off what nice people they were. Then Miss Crystal got to get in all that trouble and have it end with the accident.

What they want to call the accident. I was along to nurse the baby, Crystal Anne, age three. I was right there for everything that happened. So don't tell me she fall down the stairs. Miss Crystal hasn't ever fall down in her life, drunk or sober, or have the smallest kind of an accident.

No, she didn't fall down any stairs. She's sleeping now. I got time to talk. Doctor Wilkins be by in a while. Maybe he'll have better news today. Maybe we can take her home by Monday. If I ever get her out of here I'll get her off those pills they give her. Get her thinking straight.

How it started was. We were going off to Memphis to this wedding, Miss Crystal and Mr. Manny and her brother-in-law, Joey, that was the groom, and Mr. Lenny, that runs the store, and Mr. and Mrs. Weiss, senior, the old folks, and me and Crystal Anne and some of Joey's friends. We took up half the plane. Everybody started drinking Bloody Marys the minute the plane left New Orleans. They even made me have one. "Drink up, Traceleen," Mr. Weiss said. "Joey's marrying the richest girl in Memphis."

Miss Crystal started flirting with Owen as soon as the plane left the ground. This big Spanish-looking boy that was Joey's roommate up at Harvard. She'd already seen him up at Joey's graduation in the spring, set her eye on him up there. Well, first thing she does is fix it so she can sit by him on the plane. Me sitting across from them with the baby. Mr. Manny up front, talking business with his daddy.

Owen's telling Miss Crystal all about how he goes scuba diving down in Mexico. Her hanging on to every word. "I'm going to start a dive school down there as soon as I get the cash," he said. "I'm quitting all that other stuff. It's no good to work your ass off all your life. No, I want a life in the water." He poured himself another Bloody Mary. Miss Crystal had her hand on his leg by then. Like she was this nice older lady that was a friend of his. He pretend like he don't notice it was there. Baby climbing all over me, messing up my uniform.

"To hell with graduate school at my age," Owen was saying. "I'm too big for the desks. I'm going back to Guadalajara the minute this wedding's over. Get me a wicker swing and sit down to enjoy life. You come on down and see me. You and Manny fly on down. I'll teach you to dive. You just say the word." Miss Crystal was lapping it up. I could see her fitting herself into his plans. It had been a bad spring around our place. It was time for something to happen.

"Go to sleep now," I'm saying to Crystal Anne. "Get you a

little sleep. Lots of excitement coming up. You cuddle up by Traceleen."

The minute the plane landed there was this bus to take us to the hotel. I'll say one thing for people in Memphis. They know how to throw a wedding. The bus took us right to the Peabody Hotel. They had two floors reserved. Hospitality rooms set up on each floor, stayed open twenty-four hours. You could get anything you wanted from sunup to sundown. Mixed drinks, Cokes, baby food, Band-Aids, sweet rolls, homemade brownies. I've never seen such a spread.

The young people took over one hospitality room and the old people took up the other. Me and Crystal Anne sort of moving from one to the other, picking up compliments on her hair, getting Cokes, watching TV. I was getting sixty dollars a day for being there. I would have done it free. Every now and then I'd put on Crystal Anne's little suit and take her up to the pool. That's where Miss Crystal was hanging out. With Owen. He was loaded when he got off the plane and he was staying loaded. He was lounging around the pool telling stories about going scuba diving. Finally he sent out for some scuba diving equipment to put on a demonstration. That's the type wedding this was. Any of the guests that wanted anything they just called up and someone brought it to them.

It was getting dark by then. The sun almost down. Someone comes up with the scuba diving equipment and Owen puts it on and starts scuba diving all around the pool. He's trying to get Miss Crystal to go in with him but she won't do it. "Come on, chicken," he saying. "It's not going to hurt your hair. You'll be hooked for life the minute you go down. It's like flying in water."

"I can't, Owee," she says. That's what she's calling him now. "I'm in the wedding party. I can't get wet now." Well, in the end he coaxed her into the pool, everyone hanging around the edge watching and cheering them on. All these bubbles coming up from the bottom where I guess she is. Mr. Manny standing with his back to the wall smoking cigarette after cigarette and not saying anything. Miss Crystal and Owen stayed underwater a long time. Crystal Anne, she's screaming, "Momma, Momma, Momma," because she can't see her in the water so I take her to the lobby to see the ducks to calm her down.

The ducks in the lobby of the Peabody Hotel are famous all over the world. There's even a book about them you can buy. What they do is they keep about thirty or forty ducks up on the roof and they bring them down four or five at a time and let them swim around this pool in the lobby. I was talking to this man who takes care of them and brings them up and down in the morning and the afternoon. We were on the elevator with him. He told Crystal Anne she shouldn't chase them or put her hands on them like some bad children did. "You have to stay back and just look at them," he said. "Just be satisfied to watch them swim around." So we go with him to take the old ducks out and put the new ducks in and that satisfies her and she forgets all about her momma up in the pool drowning herself to show off for Owen.

I kept seeing Mr. Manny standing against that wall with a drink in his hand. Not letting anything show. None of the Weisses let anything show. They like to act like nothing's going on. They been that way forever. My auntee worked for the old folks. She says they were the same way then.

Then it's dark and everyone go to their rooms to get ready for the rehearsal dinner. Miss Crystal's in the bathroom trying to do something with her hair. She can't get it to suit herself. She's wearing this black lace dress with no back in it and no brassiere. And some little three-inch platform shoes with that blond hair curling all over her head like it do when she can't get it to behave. Like I said, it'd been a long spring. All that bad time with Mr. Alan breaking her heart. Now Owen.

So she finishes dressing and then she orders a martini from

room service. She's in such a good mood. I haven't seen her like that in a long time. We're in two rooms hooked together with a living room. I had on my black gabardine uniform with a white lace apron and Crystal Anne's in white with lace hairbows. We should have had our picture taken.

"Don't start in on martinis now," Mr. Manny said. "Let's just remember this is Joey's wedding and try to act right." I feel sorry for him sometimes. He's always having to police everything. Come from being a lawyer, I guess. Always down at the law courts and the jail and the coroner's office and all.

"I'm acting right," she says. "I'm acting just fine."

"Don't start it, Crystal." I move in the other room at that.

"I'm not starting a thing," she said. "You started this conversation. And you really shouldn't smoke so much, Manny. The human lungs will only take so much abuse."

Owen was waiting for us at the door of the dining room. He was really loaded now, laughing and joking at everything that happened. He was wearing this wrinkled-looking white tuxedo, big old shoulders like a football player about to bust out of it. He had half the young people at the wedding following him everywhere he'd go. Like he was a comet or something. That's the kind of man Miss Crystal goes for. I don't know why she ever married Mr. Manny to begin with. They not each other's type. It's a mismatch. Anybody could see that.

Well, this night was bound for disaster. It didn't take a fortune-teller to see that. I found Crystal Anne some crackers to chew on and in a little while everyone found their places and sat down. A roomful of people. I guess half of Memphis must have been there. They were all eating and making speeches about how happy Joey and his bride was going to be. She was a wispy little thing. But it was true about the money. Her daddy owns the Trumble Oil Company that makes mayonnaise. All her old boyfriends read poems they wrote about being married and Joey's friends all got up and talked about what a great guy he was. All except Owen, he got up and recited this poem about getting drunk coming home from a fair and not being able to find his necktie the next day. It got a lot of applause and Miss Crystal was beaming with pride. I'm sitting by Crystal Anne feeding her. The bride had insisted Crystal Anne must come to everything.

Then the band came and the dancing started. Mr. Manny, he's sitting way down the table talking to the bride's father about business, just like he's an old man, making jokes about how much the wedding must have cost. I felt sorry for him again. His jokes couldn't take a patch on that poem Owen recited.

Everybody ended up in the hospitality room about one o'clock in the morning. All except Miss Crystal and Owen. They're in his hotel room talking about scuba diving and listening to the radio. They've got this late night station on playing dixieland and I'm in there to put a better look on it. Crystal Anne's asleep beside me. Still in her dress. "Night diving's the best," Owen is telling us. "That's where you separate the men from the boys." He's lying on the bed with his hands behind his head. Miss Crystal's sprawled all over a chair with her legs hooked over the side.

So Mr. Manny comes in. He's tired of pretending he isn't mad. "Get up, Crystal," he says. "Come on, you're going to our room."

"I'm talking to Owen," she says. "He's going to take us diving in Belize."

"Crystal, you're coming to our room."

"No, I'm not. I'm staying here. Go get me a drink if you haven't got anything to do." She look at him like he's some kind of servant. So he moves into the room and takes hold of her legs and starts dragging her. Owen, he stands up and says, stop dragging her like that, but Mr. Manny, he keeps on doing it. Miss Crystal, she's too surprised to do a thing. All I'm thinking about is the dress. Brussels lace. He's going to ruin the dress.

Then Mr. Manny he drag her all the way out into the hall
and to the top of the stairs and they start yelling at each other.
You're coming with me, he's saying, and she's saying, oh, no, I am
not because I can not stand you. Then I heard this scream and I
come running out into the hall and Miss Crystal is tumbling
down those stairs. I heard her head hit on every one. Mr. Manny,
he's just standing there watching her. You should have seen the
expression on his face.

They don't put lawyers in jail for nothing they do. Otherwise,
why isn't Mr. Manny in jail for that night? It's been two months
since I ran down those stairs after Miss Crystal and hold her head
in my lap while I waited for the ambulance to come. I've still got
my apron, stained with her blood. And she's still in this hospital, crazy as a bat and they're feeding her pills all day and she
don't recognize me sometimes when I go to visit. Other times she
does and seem all right but you can't make any sense talking to
her. All she want to do when she's awake is talk about how her
head is hurting or wait for some more pills or make long-distance
calls to her brother, Phelan, begging him to forgive her for turning his antelopes loose and come and bring her a gun to shoot
herself with. And Mr. Manny. He's got her where he wants her
now, hasn't he? Any day when he gets off work he can just drive
down to Touro and there she is, right where he left her, laying in
bed, waiting for him to get there. And my auntee Mae, that worked
for the old people, the Weisses that are dead now. She says that's
just how it started with LaureLee Weiss that ended up in
Mandeville forever because she wouldn't be a proper wife to old
Stanley Weiss. They ended up putting electricity in her head to
calm her down. My auntee has been around these people a long
time. She knows the past of them.

And there she is, Miss Crystal, that has been as good to me
as my own sister. Lying on that bed. I'll get her out of there.

Someday. Somehow. Meantime, she say, *Traceleen, write it down. You got to write it down. I can't see to read and write. So you got to do it for me.*

How to write it down? Number 1. Start at the beginning. That's what Mark advise me to do. So here goes. I remember when Miss Crystal first came to New Orleans as a bride. It was her second time around. There was this call from Mrs. Weiss, senior, and she say, Traceleen, Mr. Manny has taken himself a bride and I would like you to go around and see if you can be the maid. She has a boy she's bringing with her. She's going to need some help.

It's a day in November and I dress up in my best beige walking dress and go on around to Story Street which is where they have their new house. She's waiting on the porch and takes me inside and we sit down in the living room and have a talk and she tells me all about her love affair with Mr. Manny and how her son has been against the marriage but she decided to go on and do it because where they was living in Mississippi he was going to school with a boy that had a Ku Klux Klan suit hanging in his closet and they had meetings in the yard of the school and no one even told them not to. Rankin County, Mississippi.

Then I tell her all about myself and where I am from and she says are you sure you want to go on being a maid, you seem too smart for this work and I says yes, that's all I know how to do. She says, well, I can be the maid for a while but I'll have to get some education part time and let her pay for it because she doesn't believe in people being maids. I've got a lot of machines, she says. You can run the machines. When would you like to start?

I'll start in the morning, I said. I'll be over around nine.

The next day was Saturday but Miss Crystal hadn't even unpacked all the boxes yet and I wanted to help with that so I'd know where things were in the kitchen. I got off the streetcar about a quarter to nine and come walking up Story Street and the first person I run into is King Mallison, junior, Miss Crystal's son by her first marriage. My auntee Mae had already told me what he done at the wedding so I was prepared. Anyway, there he was, looking like a boy in a magazine, he's so beautiful, look just like an angel. He's out on the sidewalk taking his bicycle apart. He's got it laid out all over the front yard. It's this new bicycle Mr. Manny gave him for a present for coming to live in New Orleans.

"I'm Traceleen," I said. "I'm going to be the maid."

"I'm King," he said. "I'm going to be the stepchild."

So that is how that is and a week later the bicycle is still all over the front yard and there's about ten more taken apart in the garage and King says he's started a bicycle repair shop but it turns out it's a bicycle stealing ring and Mr. Manny's going crazy, he thinks he's got a criminal on his hands and Miss Crystal's second marriage is on the rocks. One catch. By then she is pregnant with Crystal Anne.

Number 2. This is a long time later. There has been so much going on around here I haven't had time to write any of it down. First of all Miss Crystal got home from the hospital. I had her room all fixed up with her Belgian sheets and pillowcases and flowers on the dresser and the television at the foot of the bed so we can watch the stories. She didn't even notice. She was so doped up. What she had from the fall was a brain concussion. So why did they give her all those pills? I looked it up in Mr. Manny's *Harvard Medical Dictionary* and it said don't give pills to people that injure their heads.

Then many days went by. Sometimes she would seem as normal as can be. Other days she's having headaches and swallowing all the pills she can get her hands on. Anytime she wants any more she just call up and yell at a doctor and in a little while here comes the drugstore truck delivering more pills, Valium and stuff like that. Then she'd sleep a little while, then get up and start talking crazy and do so many things I can't write them all down. Walk to the drugstore in her nightgown. Call up the President of the United States. Call up her brother, Phelan, and beg him to come shoot her in the head. Mr. Manny he can't do anything with her because she is blaming him for her fall and telling him he tried to kill her so he has got to let her do anything she likes no matter what it costs. But I can tell he don't like her taking all those pills any more than I do.

Meantime King came home from his vacation and start in school. Mr. Manny's having to help him all the time with his homework. Much as they hate each other they have to sit in there and try to catch King up. All this time he still hasn't caught up from the school he went to in Mississippi.

Then Miss Crystal she start talking on the phone every day to this man that is a behaviorist. He's hooked up with this stuff they got going on at Tulane where they are doing experiments on the brain. They got a way they can hook the brain up with wires and teach you how to make things quit hurting you.

Well, behind all our backs Miss Crystal she sign up to go down to the Tulane Hospital and take a course in getting her brain wired to stop pain. Then one afternoon after I'm gone home she get Mrs. Weiss, senior, to come and get Crystal Anne and she goes in a taxicab and checks herself into this experiment place on Tulane Avenue and first thing I know about it is Mr. Manny calling me to find out where she's at. Then he calls back and says he's coming to get me and we're going to this hospital to see what she's up to. King overhears it and he insists on going along.

Here's what it's like at that place. A Loony Bin. All these sad-looking people going around in pajamas with their heads shaved, looking gray in the face. Everybody just crazy as they can be. This doctor that was in charge of things looked crazier than anybody and they had Miss Crystal in a room with a girl that had tried to kill herself. That's where we found her, sitting on a bed trying to talk this girl out of killing herself again. "Oh, hello," she said when we came in. "Tomorrow they're going to teach me to stop the headaches. I'm going to do it by willpower. Isn't that nice, isn't it going to be wonderful."

"Pack up that bag," Mr. Manny said. "You're not staying here another minute, Crystal. This is the end. You don't know what these people might do to you. Come on, pick up that robe and put it on. We're leaving. We're going away from here."

"Come on, Momma," King said. For once he and Mr. Manny had a common cause. "You can't stay here. The people here are crazy."

"I don't care," she said. She laid back on the bed. "I don't care what happens. I have to stop these headaches. Whatever I have to do."

"Please come home with us," I put in. "You don't know what might happen."

"Momma," King said. He was leaning over her with his hands on her arms. "Please come home with me. I need you. I need you to come home." That did it. He never has to ask her twice for anything. She love him better than anything there is, even Crystal Anne.

"My head hurts so much," she says. "It's driving me crazy."

"I know," he said. "When you get home I'll rub it for you." So then she gets up and goes over to the suicide girl's part of the room and explains why she's leaving and we close up her bag and the four of us go walking down the hall to the front desk. This is one floor of a big tall building that's the Tulane Medical Center. It's all surrounded by heavy glass walls, this part of the place. About the time we get to the desk a guard is locking all the doors for the night. Big cigar-smelling man with hips that wave around like ocean waves. Dark brown pants with a big bunch of keys hanging off the back. Light brown shirt.

"Come on," he says. "Visitors' hours are over. You've got to be leaving now."

"We're taking my wife home," Mr. Manny says. "She's checking out."

"She can't leave without authorization from the physician," the boy at the desk says.

Miss Crystal's just standing there, this little bracelet on her wrist like a newborn baby. Only she's Miss Crystal. Now she's getting mad. It had not occurred to her she couldn't leave.

"She's scheduled for surgery in the morning," the deskman says. "You'll have to have Doctor Layman here before I can release her."

"Release her!" Mr. Manny runs a whole law firm. He's not accustomed to anyone telling him what he can do. "She's not a mental patient. She can leave anytime she damn well pleases." I look over at King. He's got this look on his face that anybody that knows him would recognize. Look out when you see him look that way. He's very quiet and his face is real still. The guard has come over to us now to see what the trouble is. We're standing in a circle, with the crazy patients in their pajamas on chairs in front of a television, half watching it and half watching us. Then King he walks around behind the guard and takes his keys. So light I couldn't believe what I was watching. Then he moves closer and reach down and take his gun and back up over beside the television set. "Take her on out of here, Manny," he says. "You can pick me up on Tulane in a minute. Go on, Traceleen, go with them." Mr. Manny, he opens the door and Miss Crystal and Mr. Manny and I are out in the hall. King, he's standing there like in a movie holding that big old heavy-looking pistol.

Then we're out in the hall and down the elevator and running across Tulane Avenue to the parking lot. And we get into the car and circle the block and here comes King. He's locked the guard in the Loony Bin and thrown the keys away but he's still got the gun in his pocket. After all, he was born and raised in Mississippi. Then he's in the car and we are driving down Tulane Avenue. I will never forget that ride. Miss Crystal's crying her heart out on

Mr. Manny's shirt and Mr. Manny and King are so proud of themselves they have forgotten they are enemies. That isn't the end.

When we got home I put Miss Crystal to bed and Mr. Manny he starts going all over the house like he's a madman and throws out every pill he can find and then he comes and stands at the foot of Miss Crystal's bed and he says, "Crystal, get well. Starting right this minute you are not going to take another pill of any kind or call one more goddamn doctor for another thing as long as you live. I have had it. I have had all I can take. *Do you under-stand me. Do you understand what I mean?*"

"He's right, Momma," King says, coming and standing beside him. "We've had all we can take for now."

TRACELEEN,
SHE'S STILL TALKING

ANOTHER TIME, Miss Crystal's brother Phelan bought this car in Germany and shipped it to New Orleans and we had to get it off the boat. There's more to getting a car off a boat than you'd imagine. In the end Miss Crystal had to call her cousin Harry that's a lawyer, and get him to call the owner of the shipyards and I don't know what all. That was just to get it off the boat. Before we even started driving it to Texas.

Miss Crystal is the lady I work for. I nurse her little girl, Crystal Anne, and I run the house. They're rich people, all the ones I'm talking about. Not that it does them much good that I can see. Miss Crystal's married to this man she can't stand. All the money in the world will not make up for that.

I'll say one thing for her though, she manages to have herself a good time. Her and her cousin Harry are always up to something. And Mr. Phelan, her brother that bought the car. He's always in on it too whenever he's in town. He's this big barrel-chested man that talks real low and looks at you out of the bottom of his eyes. Looks like he's sighting you down the barrel of a gun. He's always in Africa or getting married or something, sending

Miss Crystal these clothes she don't wear. Lace dresses and negligees, satin pants, tennis dresses with little flowers appliquéd on them, like that. That's not her style. She like plain things. She never has flowers or writing on anything she wears.

I never had been to Texas before this trip. I'd heard all about it though. One time Mr. Phelan was in town and he got this screen and showed pictures of Texas, where he's got his ranch, and some of Brazil, where he'd been shooting jaguars. He had just got home from Brazil and he had all this jewelry with him made out of jaguar parts. He give Miss Crystal a necklace with a jaguar claw on it to make her play tennis better. She tried it a number of times but it never worked. She was so busy rubbing the claw for luck she forgot to look at the ball.

Finally she got so mad one day she just tore it off her neck, chain and all, and gave it to me. I put it away with the other stuff she gives me, newspaper clippings from when we get our name in the paper for having parties, silver spoons that get caught in the disposal, her old wedding ring. From her other marriage, to King's daddy. King's her son that smokes dope. She gave me the ring one day when she was drunk. I tried and tried to give it back but she made me keep it.

Anyway, it was Mr. Phelan that sent this car. He's her brother but they're not a thing alike. Miss Crystal don't like him very much. She's always bad-mouthing him to Mr. Harry behind his back. Saying her daddy give him all her money. So now it's nine o'clock in the morning and they're calling her to come down to the docks and get this car he shipped over here. Then Mr. Phelan he calls from Texas and begs her to do it. "I can't," she says into the phone. "I've got a match at ten. I can't leave people standing on the court to be your errand boy, Phelan. It's your car, you come and get it."

Well, he finally talked her into it and she puts me in the car with the baby, Crystal Anne, and off we go to the docks. First we have to go in this little smelly office and this Cajun wants her to fill out some forms about who owns the car. Act like he think we're trying to steal it or something.

Well, she raises Cain about the forms and then she calls her cousin Harry and he comes over and gets it straightened out. Mr. Harry's a lawyer, but he only works part time. He doesn't keep regular hours or go in an office or anything. He just does enough to get by. So he dresses and comes on down, all the time we're sitting in that office and I'm trying to keep Crystal Anne from touching anything, everything's so dirty. So finally Mr. Harry comes in wearing this good-looking white suit, all shaved and looking like he owns the world. Miss Crystal's crazy about Mr. Harry. She's always in a good mood when he's around. So he comes and makes all these calls, then everything is okay. Crystal Anne, she's rubbed her hands all over the back of his pants but he doesn't notice it. Miss Crystal's in a better mood now that Mr. Harry has put the Cajun in his place.

What really cheers her up though is the car. "Look at that goddamn car," she says. "Isn't that car just like Phelan. Isn't that the tackiest thing you've ever seen in your life?" We're in a warehouse. Right down on the docks. It's noisy as it can be and this Cajun is driving down a gangplank in the biggest, shiniest dark green car you have ever seen in your life. A Mercedes-Benz number six hundred. It's as big as a hearse and heavy looking. "Just look at it," Miss Crystal says. She's laughing her head off. The driver had got out and was letting her look inside. "Where in the name of God did he get this car?"

"It's the biggest one they make," the Cajun said. "I've never seen one bigger and I unload them all the time." Mr. Harry had the explanation. "He got it from the head of the Mercedes company. It was being custom made for the president of the company. Phelan bought it right off the line and he needs someone to drive it down to Texas. Come on, leave the other cars here. Let's take it for a spin." He gave the Cajun a check and a twenty-dollar tip for putting up with Miss Crystal and the four of us got in the car. Crystal Anne needed changing in the worst way. As soon as we got inside I whipped off the old diaper and put on a new one. She'd been happy as she could be all morning, just good as gold, watching everything the way she do and chewing on her pacifier.

"How much do you think Phelan paid for this thing?" Miss Crystal said. "I bet it cost a fortune. He's gone too far this time, Harry. Even Phelan can't justify this car." She was playing with the radio dials, running the automatic antenna up and down outside the window.

"He needs it for his hunts," Mr. Harry said. "To meet planes when people come down for the hunts. And he needs someone to get it down to Texas right away."

"Well, it won't be me," she said. "I'm not his errand boy. Let him fly up here and get it himself if he needs it so bad."

"He can't. Some men from Jackson are going down this weekend. They're paying two thousand dollars apiece to shoot a wild Russian boar. Phelan's got everything he owns in this operation, Crystal. You ought to want to see him make a go of it. Those animals he imported cost a lot of money."

"My money, Harry. My money. Every cent he spends is one more I'll never inherit. What kind of hunt? What's he up to now?" She turns her head and raises her eyes at me like only I can understand what she really means by anything.

"He's got the Lost Horizon stocked with game animals," Mr. Harry says, getting a serious expression on his face now he's talking hunting. All the men in Miss Crystal's family got that look. They put their elbows on their knees and their chins in their hand and put on that look whenever they got to talk about hunting anything, whether it's animals or King the time he ran away to the hippie commune. Scare me to death when they look like that. "He's got antelope and water buffalo and Russian boar. Well, the water buffalo aren't there yet but they're on their way. He's arranging African safaris for people that don't have time to go to Africa. It could be big, Crystal. He could get back all the money he lost in the duck decoy factory. He could make up for that land deal in Joburg."

"He's having safaris at the Lost Horizon? That little scraggly piece of land? There aren't even any trees. I don't believe anybody would pay two thousand dollars to go down there for anything."

"You'd be surprised what people will do. I put some of my own money into it. So I think I'll just drive the car on down there for him, to protect my investment."

"Russian boar?" she said, like she couldn't believe she heard right. "He's importing Russian boar?"

"We better be getting Crystal Anne on home now," I say from the back seat. "I need to be putting her down for a nap." We were out in Jefferson Parish, almost to the lake, cruising along, it's like riding in a big green cloud, air conditioning so quiet you can hear yourself breathe, big old tires going thump, thump.

"I think I'll go with you to Texas," Miss Crystal says. "I'll take Traceleen and Crystal Anne and go along. It's a perfect time. Manny's out of town and King's in Meridian with Big King. I want to see this operation. This boar hunt. Honest to God, Harry, Phelan's outside the limits. He really is, you know he is."

"You just can't resist the car," Mr. Harry says, laughing and smiling, laying his hand on her knee. "You want to keep riding in it as much as I do."

"Let's don't forget to stock the bar," she says. "I want to really fill it up. Fix it the way it ought to be."

So the upshot of it is the very next morning Miss Crystal and Crystal Anne and Mr. Harry and me are driving out of town on I-10 headed for San Antonio. "I've never been to Texas in my life," I said to Mark, getting my permission to go. Mark's my husband, sweetest man you'll ever know. He don't stand in anybody's way. "Go ahead," he says. "See the country. I'll be right here when you get back, right where you left me." That's how it always is with Mark and me. Miss Crystal, she can't believe my luck in men. My first husband was just as sweet as Mark. I've had two since Miss Crystal knew me, one just as sweet as the other. "Your turn'll come," I tell her when she gets low. "You'll find your true love before it's over." Well, it didn't happen on this trip to Texas.

The first thing that happened was we stopped on the outskirts of Baton Rouge and stocked up the bar. They must have put two hundred dollars' worth of whiskey in the car. One hundred ninety-six, seventy-eight, to be exact. I saw it on the cash register when Mr. Harry paid the bill. Crystal Anne, she picks up a plastic lemon and starts sucking on the cap so he bought that too. I started getting worried when I saw all that whiskey. Mr. Harry, he's got a bad head for whiskey and much as I hate to say it Miss Crystal's not much better. They started mixing drinks in these little silver cups that come with the car and by the time we're to Lafayette I'm driving. Miss Crystal and Mr. Harry in the back seat drinking and singing country songs and me up front with Crystal Anne strapped in her seat sucking on the lemon. "Don't let her swallow the cap, Traceleen," Miss Crystal said. "Keep an eye on her." As if I didn't have enough to do driving the number six hundred down the road and it starting to rain. I mean rain. We were just outside of Crowley when it started coming down. Coming down in sheets!

People from other parts of the country they see us on television having our rains and floods and sometimes I wonder what they think it's like. Because the thing the television can't show them is the smell. Not a bad smell, a cold clean smell like breathing in water. We're below the sea in south Louisiana and when the rains come we're in the sea. The rain that day was the worst I've ever seen. I hadn't been driving ten minutes outside of Crowley when I knew we'd have to stop. "I can't see a thing," I said. "I can't see the road before me."

"Pull over," Mr. Harry said. "Let me take the wheel. Pull over on the side." I tried to. Crystal Anne was screaming and standing up in her seat belt. And the rain was coming straight at us like a hurricane. I thought I saw a place to pull over beside a bridge. I turned the wheel and the next thing I knew we were sliding down a wall of mud headed for an oak tree. We hit it broadside and came to a stop not ten feet from a river. "It's the Lacassine!" Mr. Harry yelled. "Goddamn, I've fished this river."

"Oh, my God," Miss Crystal said. She set down the glass she was holding and pulled Crystal Anne into the back seat. I'll say one thing for Miss Crystal. She's a good mother when she wants to be. "What are we going to do now, Harry?" she said. "What in the name of hell are we going to do?"

"I bet that door'll cost a couple of grand," he said. "At least two."

"To hell with the door," she said. "How are we getting out of here?"

"I'm not sure," he said. "Fix me another drink and let me think it over." So, there we were and it kept on raining. Every now and then I'd feel the car squench down in the mud, like it was settling. You could see me shudder every time it did it. Miss Crystal, she fixed me a bourbon and Coke. That helped a little. Crystal Anne had fallen asleep on her momma, just screamed a few minutes and went on off.

I guess this would be as good a time as any to tell you about the inside of the car. It was all made of leather, everything was leather. There wasn't anything that wasn't covered with leather but the dials. Even the refrigerator had a leather cover, softest, sweetest-smelling leather you could dream of in a million years, dark tan with here and there a black stripe.

Every place you turned there was a little hidden mirror. One

beside each seat. I couldn't help but think of Mr. Phelan looking himself over while he'd be driving. The bar was in the middle so you could fix drinks from the front or the back and
underneath was this nice little refrigerator that makes cubes the
size of table dice. Net bags on the back of the seats for holding things. Just like on a Pullman. Oh, it was some car. And there
we were, rammed up against a live oak and the rain coming down
and no one knowing what to do next. "I'm for getting out and
trying to make it up the bank," I said. "It's too big a chance to
take, getting washed into the Lacassine inside a car."

"This car's not going anywhere," Mr. Harry said. "It weighs
a ton. The best thing we can do is stay right here. Just sit tight
till it stops raining."

"I think he's right," Miss Crystal said. "Let's just make another drink and eat some of this lunch you had the sense to
bring." It *was* thanks to me there was anything to eat. I'd fixed a
lunch of cream cheese sandwiches on Boston bread and radish
roses and a little pie made of chicken scraps. Food tastes so good
when you're in danger. We ate it every bite.

The highway patrol finally came and got us out. I never have been
so glad to see a policeman. A black man, black as me, not coffee colored. "How you doing, ma'am," he said in the sweetest
voice, sticking his head into the car. It was still raining but it was
passing. "You hold on. We're bringing a rope for you all to hold
on to going up the hill. We'll have you out of here before you
know it." Then they came with ropes and took us one by one up
the hill, Crystal Anne first, awake now and screaming her head
off and in a while we're all up on the road and the policemen
are writing everything down. The rain's slacking up but it's still
falling.

Getting the car out was something else. They had to send for a
wrecker and when that didn't pull it they had to get a tractor and

lay boards on the hill and I don't know what all. Crystal Anne and I were sitting in the policeman's car watching and talking to him about everything. His people are from Boutte where Mark's from. Know everybody we know. Finally they got the wrecker and the boards all lined up and here come the car inching up the hill and back out onto the highway. Everybody clapping and cheering. The side that hit the tree didn't look too bad after all. Not as bad as I thought it was going to. Of course the doors won't open. All the men and policemen they're walking around the car, admiring it and commenting on it, talking about how much it cost and after a while Mr. Harry got into the driver's seat and turned the key and it started right up. Everybody cheered. "They make these things out of old tanks," Mr. Harry said, laughing up at the policeman. "Those Krauts can make a car. You got to hand it to them. They can make a car."

"Let's get going then," Miss Crystal said. She was starting to look pretty bad, her hair all coming out of her pageboy and her pants covered with mud. I can't stand to see her like that, hard as I work ironing everything she owns.

"Get in," Mr. Harry called out. "We're back on the road. We're on our way." So we all piled back into the car, this time I'm in the back with Crystal Anne and they're up front and as soon as we're out of sight of the policeman Miss Crystal tells me to reach in the refrigerator and hand her a bottle of wine. "No more hard liquor till we get to Texas," she said. "We've had enough trouble for one day."

Then it seem like we're driving forever. Like driving into a dream. First Beaumont, then Liberty, then Houston and we got to stop and let Mr. Harry get some Mexican food and call Mr. Phelan and tell him what's going on. Then someplace called Clear Lake where Crystal Anne went to sleep for the third time, this time for good. Then Almeda, then Salt Lick, then Seville. I'm memorizing the names to tell Mark. Then we're only six miles away on

an asphalt road, then we turn onto gravel, then to dirt and we're
there. Country as flat as a pancake and dry, hardly a tree in sight.
It's the middle of the night and we're at this Mexican-style house
all sprawled out in the moonlight, must have twenty rooms. Mr.
Phelan's waiting for us in the yard, about six dogs with him. These
big red dogs with skinny faces, like the ones Judge Winn have
over on Henry Clay, look like they'd take your arm off. The minute
I saw them I just held Crystal Anne closer to me.

"There he is," Miss Crystal said. "Wearing black. Look at
those pants, Harry. Can you believe he's kin to us?"

Mr. Phelan always wears black. Every time he come up to New
Orleans he's got on black. Look like that's his only style. This
night he's got on a long-sleeve shirt with a big collar and his
pants are sewn up the side with white stitching. His hair all cut
off real short. Look like it's been shaved, and he's standing with
his hands in his pockets, standing real still and not letting anything show on his face. If he's seen the side of the car he's not
letting on. Mr. Harry, he turn off the motor and get out and
hug his cousin. "Goddammit, Phelan," he says. "Put those dogs
up. I've had enough trouble for one day without fooling with your
dogs."

"They won't hurt you, Harry. They won't move unless I tell
them to. Sit," he says to the dog pack. "Show Uncle Harry your
manners." Every last one of them sit down on their hindquarters
the second he say it.

"Hello, Phelan," Miss Crystal says, getting out. "Look in the
back seat. There's your niece. Well, come on, stop acting like a
movie star and look at what we did. It isn't all that bad." She
walked around to the bashed-in side and he followed her.

"Who was driving?" he says. He still hasn't let on that he even
cares.

"Traceleen," Miss Crystal says. "And Crystal Anne was in
the front seat with her. It's a wonder she didn't crack her head

open. It's a wonder we aren't all at the bottom of the river."

"You were letting Traceleen drive?" He let out his breath and moved in to put his hand on the bashed-in door. I moved back deeper into the back seat, keeping Crystal Anne between me and him. "Holy Christ, Crystal. You let the nigger maid drive my car? This goddamn car isn't even insured. Well, Jesus fucking H. Christ . . . I don't believe it . . . I can't understand . . ." He stopped and stuck his hands back into his pockets. He looked off into the sky, this look coming onto his face like he is surrounded by a bunch of people that don't know what to do and he is tired of fooling with it and might just disappear into the night some day. "Never mind," he says. "I guess I'm lucky that it drives. I've got to use it tomorrow to pick up a party in San Antonio." He bent over and tried to stick a piece of chrome back on that was falling off. I felt sort of sorry for him for a moment. He'd been having a rough time lately from all I hear Mr. Harry and Miss Crystal say. Up to his ears in debt and all like that.

"Well, come on in," he was saying. "Come in and see the place." We all went in together. You've never seen such a sight as was in that house. No words will describe it. Every animal you ever heard of was in there. A full-sized baby giraffe, that's one thing. A big pile of elephant tusks. I don't know how many. Lion heads and leopards and some kind of curved-horn sheep and several deer and this caped buffalo that almost killed him when he shot it. In between the animal heads was pictures of Mr. Phelan on his hunts. He's kneeling over animals in every picture. Like a preacher. Every way you'd turn there's another picture of him kneeling over something. I was thinking maybe if he was so broke he might think of starting him a museum.

"I want to go with you on the hunt tomorrow," I heard Miss Crystal saying. "I want to watch you hunt a Russian boar."

In the morning some new troubles started. Miss Lauren Gail. They were all around this big Mexican table eating breakfast and

Miss Lauren Gail's with them now. She's Mr. Phelan's new wife. And her little girls, Teresa and Lisalee. Miss Lauren Gail's in a bad mood about the car. "He told me he bought a secondhand car over there," she's saying to Mr. Harry. "He didn't tell me he bought it from the president of Mercedes-Benz. All he does is lie to me. He lies when he could tell the truth. Crystal, remember that ring I wanted in that antique store in New Orleans, that I called you about? It was only eight hundred dollars. Eight hundred dollars, that's all, and he said we couldn't afford it and now he turns up with this car. How much did it cost, Phelan? I want to know how much it cost."

"I don't want to hear any more about the car," Mr. Phelan said. "That's a business car, Lauren Gail. And anytime you don't like what's going on around here you just take your feet out from underneath my table and hit the road . . . I mean it, Lauren . . . and take that expression off your face. I'm not going to watch you pout all day. That's it . . . start crying . . . because then I'll just go pack for you myself."

She straightened up her face and Mr. Harry tried to change the subject. He always is the peacemaker. "How many groups you had down here, Phelan?" he said. "Enough to start paying expenses?"

"We're doing okay. Rainey's got so much work he can't get caught up. He's got four heads waiting in the freezer. It's going to go, Harry, don't worry about that . . . I mean it, Lauren Gail," he says, looking her way again. "Don't pull that stuff on me when I have company." He's looking at her with his mouth set in a line.

Miss Lauren Gail she don't say any more after that and it all passes. In a little while she take her little girls and go off to her end of the house and Mr. Phelan he leads the way to show us around the ranch. We got to go see the stables and the cisterns and the lookout tower and then he takes us to see the hunt animals. First we got to go look at the antelope. They're in this corral with a barn behind it. "Haldeston shipped them from

Wyoming," Mr. Phelan's saying. "We lost three on the truck and a couple since they got here. But they're all right. I think this crowd's going to make it. See that stallion over there. That's the horse. That's the ringleader. I'm saving him for myself."

"I thought you were letting them run," Mr. Harry said. "You told me you were going to keep them on the range."

"In time," Mr. Phelan said. "All in good time. Got to get them fattened up first. Come on, let's go look at the boar. That's the cash crop this year." He had the Russian boars in a special pen about a mile from the house. We got to drive across a field to get there. It's this pen behind a stand of pine trees, all surrounded by barb wire with some dogs outside and another fence around them. These dogs called mastiffs, all dusty and mean looking. Russian boar on the inside and mastiffs on the outside.

There are six boar altogether. Two real small looking, the other ones look okay. They're all milling around. They don't look like anything worth two thousand dollars to me, dead or alive. Just look like old wild pigs anybody can see up around Crowley. Only these boar got gray fur, with black hair around their faces and legs. Where you get them from? I kept wanting to ask but I don't say it, I just hold on to Crystal Anne and keep my eyes and ears open.

"You're charging people two thousand dollars to shoot one of those things?" Miss Crystal says. "You've got to be kidding."

"It costs a lot to keep them," he says. "Have to air-condition the shed and God knows what else. They're very delicate. It's hard to keep them healthy."

"You've lost your mind, Phelan," she says. "Do you realize that?"

"Well, Sister," he says, shutting the door to the pen and turning around to take us back. "Nobody asked you to come down here and tell me how to live my life. I don't come up to New Orleans and stick my nose in your business, do I?"

"You've gone too far, Phelan. These pigs are just too far." She

was right up to him now, almost touching. There couldn't have
been an inch between them. It's busting loose, I thought. It's getting out of hand. I held on to the baby, holding in my breath.
It was terrible, those mean-looking dogs leaning up against the
fence and Miss Crystal, she's got this bad hangover anyway, she's
right up in his face threatening him on his own ranch.

"I'm not the same person you used to kick around, Phelan,"
she says. "I'm a powerful woman, strong and powerful. I wouldn't
mess around with me if I was you. I'm a different person than
the one you used to know."

"That may all be so, little sister," he says. He hasn't moved an
inch. He is still as he can be. "On the other hand, it's the same
wall you're up against." I looked at him then and he did sort of
look like a wall. I guess Miss Crystal thought so too because she
took the baby out of my arms and started walking back to the
car, holding up her head and swaying from side to side kind of
devil-may-care.

We weren't in the big car this time. We were in a little steel-
covered jeep made in England. It was fitted out with all kinds of
hunting things. We all squeezed back into it and headed back to
the ranch. Jack was driving. He's this black man Mr. Phelan took
off to college with him when he was young. Call himself a chauffeur but he ain't no better than a slave. "Jack was the first black
man to go to Ole Miss," Mr. Phelan's saying. "He was there a
long time before James Meredith, weren't you, Jack? Jack was a
KA, lived in the house with me. We even had him a pin made.
Jack, you still got your KA pin? I want you to show it to Traceleen
when we get back." Jack didn't say a word, just grinning from ear
to ear.

Then Mr. Phelan and Mr. Harry took the new car and drove off
to San Antonio to get the men for the hunt and the rest of us
spent the afternoon in the air-conditioning listening to Miss
Lauren Gail talk about Mr. Phelan won't buy her anything. "Don't

say anything to the visitors about the pen with the boars in it," he had said to me, taking me aside when he was leaving. "We pretend the boar just comes charging out of nowhere. It makes it more exciting."

"Don't worry about me," I said. "I just came along to ride in the car."

Later that afternoon Mr. Phelan and Mr. Harry come back with these two men and they all sit around and have drinks and hot pepper cheese and then they have this Mexican dinner. You ought to see that dining room. Forty feet long, fireplace on either end. Every wall covered with animal heads, this big brown bear standing in one corner with his teeth showing and his claws out. Mr. Phelan's third wife shot it in Tennessee. Got her picture in a gun magazine for doing it. They got the story framed beside the bear in this glass frame that's really for holding recipe books. "Lauren Gail thought that up," Mr. Phelan said. "She should have been a decorator. Then she could have been in stores buying things all day long." He hugged her to his side and she put on this sad look like what's she supposed to do but take it.

In the middle of the room there's this big mahogany table and hand-carved chairs with chairseats embroidered with Mr. Phelan's coat-of-arms. He had a picture of it on the wall too, painted to match the chairseats. He kept asking Mr. Harry didn't he want him to get him a coat-of-arms for his house but Mr. Harry said no, he already had everything on his walls he needed.

These two men from Jackson they're having the time of their lives. One of the men was in the shoemaking business. He'd been playing chess with Mr. Phelan before dinner and he kept talking about how smart Mr. Phelan was. That he hadn't ever played anybody could beat him so fast. The other man, he used to have a tent factory but the government closed it down by driving him crazy telling him what all to do. He kept complaining about the gov-

ernment doing different things to him and getting drunker and
drunker and Mr. Phelan kept pouring him wine and egging him
on. "So I just closed the goddamn place and went to Vegas," he
kept saying. "Fuck 'em. Fuck 'em. I just closed it down and went
to Vegas. Fuck 'em. That's all I've got to say. Fuck 'em all."

I took Crystal Anne and went off to bed as soon as I could.
I don't like her listening to talk like that. "Fock em, fock em,
fock em," she's saying. "Fock em, fock em, fock em." She parrot
everything she hear. What's going to happen when she shows up
at nursery school talking like that? I could still hear them yelling
while I'm walking down the hallway, talking all about the government and hunts they'd been on and what a wild Russian boar
will do to you if you only wound it and don't kill it right and
how you have got to shoot it just so or you'll mess it up for
being stuffed. Mr. Phelan he was standing up when I left showing them a Russian boar nailed to a board, showing them where
you have to make the bullets go in so you won't mess up the face.

"We're going on that hunt tomorrow, Traceleen," Miss Crystal
said when she came to get in bed with Crystal Anne and me. She
just climbed right in with us. First time I'd ever sleep with a lady
I work for. That's how Miss Crystal is. Just act like she thinks
she can make up the world. So she and Crystal Anne and me
snuggle down into the covers. "Tomorrow you will see me in action, Traceleen," she said. "Crystal Anne, I want you to remember what's going to happen next." I thought it was the whiskey
talking.

Now morning comes and they all have a breakfast of tequila and
lemons and bread and butter. Mr. Phelan insist that's the right
thing for hunters to have before they start a hunt. Miss Crystal,
she's drinking it with them. Then she and Mr. Harry and one of
the men from Jackson get into the English truck and Mr. Phelan
and the other man and this one named Rainey that's the one
stuffs the animals, they're next in the jeep and Jack and me and

Crystal Anne bringing up the rear in the number six hundred. Jack, he's got on his cowboy hat and an African hunter's vest and he's been working on the bar. Got it fixed up more Mexican than we had it. Beer and tequila and some homemade drinks I never did learn the name of. So then we're ready and the sun's lighting up this big Texas field, looked like they hadn't had any rain in a year. Crystal Anne she's real excited to be going somewhere so early in the morning and she's reaching up in the front seat trying to get Jack's attention and pulling on his hat.

Off we go down that dirt road and out onto the asphalt and then back onto dirt and up in front I can see Mr. Phelan standing up behind the wheel pointing out things and talking. We come to a little used-up house by the road and we all stop and they come back to our car to get some more to drink and he's talking all about the boar and how tricky they are. Them men from Jackson hanging on to his every word. He should have been a preacher. I've thought that before.

So we pack back up and this time we take off across a stubble-covered field and cross a little ditch on top of some two by fours don't look like they'd hold a man much less a car, then we follow the ditch, it's supposed to be a creek but there's no water in it. It looks to me like we're just driving around the ranch. I can't see that we've gone three miles from home. We have another stop beside an old chimney that used to be a house and Mr. Phelan's got the binoculars out now, sighting through them and letting the men use them and they're sweeping the country he calls it. Then Mr. Phelan keeps on looking and looking at a spot over near a stand of pine trees and finally he takes down the binoculars and looks around on the ground for a while walking around and around in a circle looking for tracks. After a while he puts his arm around the tent man's shoulders and the two of them come over to our car and fix a drink. "We'll use that stand over there by the ridge. They've got to come this way sooner or later to get to water." He pointed east. "Over there's the only water source,

a pond about a mile away. So we'll lay for them on the rise." He
licked his finger and stuck it up into the air. "Yeah, the breeze
is with us. They won't be able to smell us until they're here. They'll
come before too long. They've got to have water. The only tracks
are two days old. You're lucky, Charlie. This breeze is going to
win you a shot. You're a lucky man. I can tell that. I feel lucky
just being with you." He leaned into the car. "Jack, you come over
when we get set. Traceleen, you and the baby stay in the car. We're
going up to the stand." His voice is real low now and he's pointing over to the east where the sun is getting up above the ground.
There's this little rise of land look like it was pushed up by a
tractor. With a board screen like for a bullfight in a movie. They're
all real quiet now and put all the tequila glasses back in the car
and take out all the guns and the men and Miss Crystal go walking off to the rise. Miss Crystal, she's at the edge, look like she's
holding back. Off in the distance is the stand of pine trees in
front of the wild Russian boar pen. I'm just hoping nobody will
make a mistake and shoot at the car. "Now what's going to happen?" I ask Jack.

"Now the boys will let 'em wait awhile and get all hot and
bothered. Then they'll let one of the boars go, back behind the
trees, and it'll come charging out and as soon as it sees people
it'll come running at them. Them boars go crazy when you let
'em loose, they'll run at anything."

"Then what?" I said.

"Then Mr. Phelan'll let somebody shoot and he'll shoot too
in case they miss and then they'll keep letting them loose till
everybody that paid gets to shoot one. Then they'll be through
and Rainey'll put the boars in a tarp and take them off to be
stuffed unless somebody wants to drive home with it tied to the
hood of the jeep. Sometimes they do that." He stretched his arms
and opened up the door. "Well, let me get my rifle out the trunk.
He likes me to be standing by in case he should miss. You excuse me, Miss Traceleen. I got to get my gun out the trunk and

load it up. I forgot to have it loaded." Then Jack pushes a button to open the trunk and he get out and goes around the back of the car to get his gun.

"Here's what's going to happen," I say to Crystal Anne, thinking I'd better tell her what it's going to sound like when they start shooting. So she won't be surprised. But I never got time to tell her because about that time it all busted loose. Someone at the pen has let a boar loose and he's coming across that field like a baseball. He's coming so fast my heart almost stopped. I feel Jack jump into the trunk of the car. He let out a big yell and jump right in on top of his gun and here comes Miss Crystal running down off the hill and she jump into the driver's seat and starts honking the horn as loud as she can and starts the car and then the car's moving and she's chasing the pig. Trying to save him or run over him one, I can't decide. Then the pig he takes off in the direction of the sun and we're chasing him in the car. Jack's in the back with the trunk top flopping up and down and Crystal Anne's laughing her head off, she thinks it's wonderful. I look out the window and there's Mr. Phelan, running after us with his gun in his hand. He's sprinting like a deer, heavy as he is. He's as mad as he can be.

Then we're on the asphalt and Miss Crystal's yelling. "Traceleen, roll up the window. Lock the doors." Jack's jumped out by then but the trunk top's still waving up and down and we're on the road. "Where're we going?" I say. "What's happening now?"

"We're going for the antelope pen," she says. "We're going to ram it down." Sure enough, she press her foot down on the pedal, lean into the wheel, the seat's too far back for her but she doesn't even stop to adjust it, and we're headed for the ranch. Mr. Phelan's still running after us, then I see him stop and help Jack up off the ground. We bust on down the road and turn on the gravel, one tire's sliding off in the ditch but Miss Crystal, she holds it on the road. I wish you could have seen her, sitting there behind the steering wheel in her fringed vest and her hunting pants with sandpaper on the knees and her khaki-colored hunting shirt, her hair all messed up and wild looking. If I live a million years I won't ever forget the look on her face that morning or the ride we had.

First we come to the automatic gate. What you call a Kentucky gate, you have to stop and pull a chain and it opens, then you got to close it by hand from the other side, but we don't close it this time. We bust on down the road over the cattle gaps and go on past the house without even slowing up, almost run over a couple of dogs, then we're to the antelope pen and Miss Crystal she just drive the car right into the gate, just ram it down. Then she backs up and rams it again. I could see it giving in and the radiator on the front of the car starting to smoke. This is no way to treat a Mercedes-Benz number six hundred that cost twenty-six thousand dollars I couldn't help thinking. It would have been just as good to do it with the English truck. "Don't hit it on the front," I said, but she wasn't listening. "Hit it more to the side, with the fender." She don't even hear me. She just back up and ram it one more time. This time the whole gate and half the fence fall forward like they was made out of paper.

Then antelope are everywhere, all around us. For a minute it seem like the windows are covered with antelope faces, then they're gone, spreading out in every direction, their little white tails waving behind them.

The biggest one, the one Mr. Phelan call the horse, is taking off across the field behind the boar pen, two more following him. It's a field that stretches way off and ends in a wood beside where that little dry river runs. I watched those ones until they disappeared into the trees.

Then we're backing out over the boards and Miss Lauren Gail and her little girls and all the kitchen help are running out into the yard to see what's happened. The radiator's really smoking now, but Miss Crystal she backs and turns and pulls up in front of the kitchen stairs to yell to Miss Lauren Gail. "Send my clothes to New Orleans," she yells out the window. "Tell Harry I'm sorry I had to leave him here." Then we're barreling back down the dirt road and through the gate and onto the asphalt.

"You think we ought to drive it with that steam coming out in front?" I said.

"It will run," she says. "If we don't stop it will get us where we're going." We make it through the gate and turn onto the main road and here comes Mr. Phelan in the jeep headed right at us. "God in Heaven," I'm yelling. "Here he comes. What if he shoots?"

"I'll run over him if he shoots at me," she says. "I'll knock his goddamn jeep off the road." She was gripping the wheel like it was a horse she was riding. She was *driving* that car. I held Crystal Anne in my lap. When we passed Mr. Phelan I laid my head down so I wouldn't have to see him. I was sure he would shoot out our tires but I guess even Mr. Phelan knows better than to shoot at people. We passed him on that narrow road with a swoosh, so close I could hear him screaming. I guess he could see the steam coming out the radiator. I was wondering if Miss Crystal caught his eye.

She had planned it all before it happened. Well, not the exact way but near enough. She had put a bag for Crystal Anne into the car and had her pockets stuffed with money and credit cards and we drove to San Antonio at ninety miles an hour and cruised into the parking lot at the airport and got out and left the car sitting there with steam coming out the bottom and the top. It had made it to San Antonio but I heard later that all it was good for after that was to sell in Mexico. I sure hated to leave that car like that. I ran my hand across the leather dashboard as I was getting out, admiring one last time the way the leather parts fit into the steel so fine you couldn't tell where one began and the other ended. Even the button on the dashboard looked special, like it had grown there. Look like a navel on a baby, I was thinking. Or a navel orange.

We got a ticket on a United Airlines 747 and started for home. We were traveling first class, traveling in style. That's how Miss Crystal does things. She's always saying she's going to stop and save some money but she can't ever seem to find the right place to stop.

We strapped ourselves into these nice big seats, with Crystal Anne sitting in the middle, and Miss Crystal leaned back and took a moment's rest for the first time since she'd opened her eyes that morning. She still had on her hunting clothes. Looked like some famous actress that had been on a location shot. She reached over and touched me on the arm. "We're going home in triumph, Traceleen. What a trip. I could never have followed my conscience today if you hadn't been there to help, you know that, don't you?"

I accepted the compliment. I knew it was the truth. Nobody can get anything done all by theirself. That's not the way the world is set up.

"It is very sad," she said to me later, when the plane was in the air, and we had been served some French Columbard wine and were having our lunch. "When you cannot love your one and only brother. It breaks my heart, Traceleen, here he is in the modern world and still killing things all the time. Like he was from another century. He was such a smart little boy. He was destined for better things."

"I wouldn't waste too much time feeling sorry for Mr. Phelan," I said. "He looks to me like he does about what he wants to do."

"You're right," she says. "That wine was making my mind soft. Listen, Traceleen, let me tell you a story about what he did to me one time. I was thinking about it this morning while I was getting up my courage, waiting for the boar to come. This was a long time ago, when I was eight years old and he was twelve."

She took a big sip of her French Columbard wine and started telling the story.

"It was one Sunday, in Indiana, right in the middle of the Second World War. It was in this Spanish house we had. There was this living room, with very high cathedral ceilings, and I came downstairs one Sunday and there was Phelan, sitting at Momma's card table driving an airplane. There were foot pedals for his feet and a steering wheel and a dashboard with all sorts of dials on it. It was a special kind of plane where the pilot is also the bombardier and Phelan was flying over Japan, dropping bombs on cities and ammunition dumps.

"Ack, ack, ack, his guns would roar. Ziiiiiinnnnnnnggggg, as the bombs fell. Then he would lift up into the clouds barely escaping the zeroes. I almost fainted with envy when I saw him. It drove me crazy. Finally I went over and asked him if I could fly it and he said no, it was against the law because I wasn't a pilot.

"So I went to my room and got my new Monopoly set and brought it out and offered to trade. 'No,' he said. Then I went back into my room and got my butterfly collecting kit and I brought that out and still he wouldn't let me have a turn.

"All day I kept adding to the pile of things beside the fireplace and still Phelan flew on and on as if I wasn't even there. Ack, ack, ack, the guns would roar. Ziiiinnnnnnngggggggggg.

"Finally I went to my room and came out with the binoculars my great-uncle Philip Phillips had used in World War I and I said, 'Phelan, I will trade you these binoculars for the plane.'

"He got up from the pilot's seat and took the binoculars and the Monopoly set and my rubber printing stamps and several other things that interested him and we shook hands on the deal. At our house a deal was a deal forever. If you shook hands it was over. So Phelan took my stuff and I sat down at the plane and reached for the steering wheel. It was only an old piece of cardboard he had painted. I put my feet down on the pedals. They were two old shoeboxes with cardboard springs. Traceleen," she said. Her voice was rising. "Traceleen, are you listening? Can you hear me? This is everything I know about love I'm telling you. Everything I know about everything."

"Momma," Crystal Anne said, laying her hand on her momma's cheek to calm her down. "Momma's talking."

DRUNK WITH LOVE

FREDDY HARWOOD sat in his office at his bookstore in Berkeley, California, with his feet up on the desk and chewed the edge of his coffee cup. Frances came to the door three times to see if he would talk but he wouldn't even look at her. "You've got to send back those calligraphy books," she said. "We haven't sold a single one. I told you not to get that many."

"I don't want to send them back," he said. "I want them right where they are. Don't talk to me now, Frances. I'm thinking."

"Are you okay?"

"No. Now go on. Close the door."

"What's wrong?"

"Nora Jane's pregnant."

"Oh, my God."

"Leave me alone, Frances. Please shut the door."

"You need someone to talk to. You need —"

"Go run the bookstore, Frances. Please don't stand there."

She left the door open. Freddy got up and closed it. He laid his feet on a stack of invoices and stuck the edge of his thumb into his mouth. Manic-depressive, he decided. I was perfectly all right five minutes ago, a normal average neurotic walking down the street on my way to do my share of the world's work, on my way to add my light to the store of light, on my way to run the single most financially depressed bookstore in northern California and maybe the world. Perfectly, absolutely all right. Normal. And the minute I came in this room I started thinking about her and all she ever did in this room in my life was try to rob me. My God, I love her.

He raised his hands to his face. He made a catcher's mitt out of his hands and laid his face into that container. This is it, he decided, what all the science and art and philosophy and poetry and literature and movies were supposed to deliver me from and they have failed. A baby inside of her and it might not even be mine. A curved universe, low and inside, coming at me below the knees.

The first shock passed up the desk and through his hands and into his jaw. Books fell from their shelves, a chair slid into a window, there were crashes downstairs. She's in the car, he thought. She's in that goddamn convertible. He got up and pulled the door open and moved out into the hall. The stairway was still there. He ran down the stairs and found Frances in the History section holding on to a man in a raincoat. Several customers were huddled around the cash register. Willis and Eileen were on the floor with their arms over their heads. "Get out in the street," Freddy yelled. "For Christ's sake, get out of here. There's too much to fall. Let's go. Let's get outside." He pushed a group of customers through the turnstile. The second shock came. A section of art books fell across Children's Fantasy.

"Out the door," he was screaming. "For Christ's sake get out the door. Frances, get over here. Get out that door before it shatters." He dragged the customers along with him. They were barely out the door when the third shock came. The front window collapsed around the sign *Clara Books, Clara For Light.* His baby. The whole front window caved in upon a display of photography books. It moved in great triangular plates right down on top of Irving Penn and Ansel Adams and Disfarmer and David Hockney and Eugene Smith. A five-thousand-dollar print of "Country Doctor" fell across the books. "Is anyone else in there?" Freddy yelled. "Willis, where is Allison? Was she in the storeroom?"

"She's here," Willis said. "Right here by me." Telegraph Avenue was full of people. They were streaming out of the stores. A woman in a sari was running toward them. She grabbed Freddy's arm and pulled him toward a door. "In there," she was screaming. "My babies in there. You save them. In there." She pulled him toward the door of a restaurant. "In there," she kept saying, pointing to the door, pulling on his arm. "My babies in there. In the kitchen. In there." He pushed her behind him and walked into the restaurant. He moved between the tables, past the barstools and the bar, and turned into a narrow hall. He went down a hallway and into a kitchen and pushed a fallen counter out of his way and there they were, huddled beneath a sink, two little boys. He covered them with wet tablecloths and picked them up, one under each arm, and walked back out the way he had come. He handed them to a policeman and sank down onto the pavement on top of a tablecloth and began to cry. He rolled up in a ball on the wet tablecloth and cried his heart out. Then he went to sleep. And into a terrible dream. In the dream Nora Jane's retreating back moved farther and farther away from him through the length of Golden Gate Park. Come back, he yelled after her, come back, I'm sorry I said it. I'm sorry. You goddamn unforgiving, Roman Catholic bitch, come back. Don't you dare break my heart, you heartless uneducated child. Come back to me.

He woke up in a hospital room with his best friend, Nieman Gluuk, standing beside his bed. Nieman was a film critic for the

San Francisco Chronicle. On the other side of the bed was his mother. His hands were bandaged and there were newspapers piled up on a tray. "You're a hero," Nieman said. "Coast to coast. Every paper in the U.S.A."

"My hands hurt," he said. "My hands are killing me."

"It's only skin," his mother said. "Stuart's been here all night. He said they're going to heal. You're going to be all right."

"Where is Nora Jane? Nieman, WHERE IS NORA JANE?"

"She's on her way. She was on a bridge. She's in Sausalito with some plastic surgeon's wife."

"What day is it?"

"It's Friday. The city's a mess. It's the worst quake in fifty years. Do you want some water?"

"She's pregnant. Nora Jane's going to have a baby. Where is she, Nieman? I want to see her."

"She's coming. It's hard to get around right now, Freddy. She's on her way."

"Get me something for my hands, will you? Goddammit, where is Stuart? Tell him to get me some butter. You have to put butter on it, for Christ's sake. Mother, get Stuart in here. That bastard. Where is he? If he was all burned up I wouldn't be wandering around somewhere. Tell him to get me some butter for my goddamn hands." Stuart was a heart surgeon. He was Freddy's older brother. "I want some butter, for God's sake. Go tell him to get in here." A nurse appeared and slipped a needle out of a cone and put it into Freddy's arm and he drifted back down into his dreams. These dreams were better. It was the beach at Malibu on a windy day, the undertow signs were up and the sun was shining and everyone was sitting around under umbrellas drinking beer. Nieman was filming it. It was a movie about Malibu. They were going to make a million dollars by just being themselves on a beach telling stories and letting Nieman film it.

"She's pregnant?" Mrs. Harwood said, looking at Nieman. "His little girlfriend's pregnant?"

"It's been quite a day," Nieman said. "Well, your son's a hero," he added.

"Do you think his hands will be all right?"

"Medical science can do anything now."

Nora Jane Whittington was on the Richmond–San Rafael bridge when the earthquake moved across the beautiful city of San Francisco, California. She got out of her car and made her way around the front and climbed into a station wagon full of babies being driven by one Madge Johnson of Sausalito, California. After Nora Jane and Madge were rescued by the Coast Guard they went to Madge's house in Sausalito and Madge's husband, who was a plastic surgeon, took everyone's pulse and the maid fed them supper and Nora Jane told the Johnsons the story of her life, up to and including the fact that she was pregnant and wasn't sure if the father was Freddy Harwood or her old boyfriend, Sandy. "You can have an amnio," Doctor Johnson suggested. "That way you'll at least know if it's a girl or a boy." He laughed at his joke.

"My God, Arnold, that's incredible you would joke at a thing like this," Madge said. "I am really upset with you."

"That is how men face the facts of conception." Doctor Johnson straightened his shoulders and went into his lecture mode. "Men always get dizzy and full of fear and hilarity at the idea of children being conceived. It's a phenomenon that has been documented in many cultures. They have photographed men everywhere, including some very remote tribes in New Guinea, being presented with the fact that a conception has taken place and they uniformly begin to joke about the matter, many going into this sort of uncontrolled smiling laughing state. In much the same way people are often filled with laughter at funerals. It seems to be a clue to the darkness or fear of death hiding in us all. . . .'"

"Oh, please," Madge said. "Not now. About this amnio. I think you should consider it, Nora. It would at least tell the blood type."

"What exactly do they do?" Nora Jane said. "They stick a needle down where the baby is? I don't like that idea. How do they know where it is? I don't see how that could be a good idea, to make a hole in there, a germ might get in."

"Oh, they've got it all on a sonar screen while they're doing it," Doctor Johnson said. "There's no chance a good technician would injure the baby. For your own peace of mind you ought to go on and clear this up. It's the modern world, Nora Jane. Take advantage of it. Well, it's up to you."

"Of course it's up to her," Madge said. "Let's turn on the television again. I want to see what happened in the city."

The television came on. Scenes of downtown San Francisco, followed by shots of firemen escorting people from buildings. There were broken monuments, stretchers, smashed automobiles. Then Freddy Harwood's face appeared, a shot Nieman had taken years ago at a Berkeley peace rally. "Bookstore owner walks into burning building," the announcer was saying. "In an act of unparalleled daring and courage a Telegraph Avenue bookstore owner walked into a Vietnamese restaurant and carried out two small children through what firemen described as an inferno. He was taken to Mount Sinai Hospital where he is being treated for burns of the hands and legs. The governor has sent greetings and in a press release the President of the United States said . . ."

"It's Freddy," Nora Jane said. "Oh, my God, Madge, that's him. How can I call him?"

Now Nora Jane stood at the foot of the hospital bed. Madge and Doctor Johnson were with her. Nieman had moved back. Mrs. Harwood was still stationed by her son's head. "He said you were going to have a baby," she said. "I think that's wonderful. I want you to know I will do anything I can to help." She lifted her hands. She held them out to the girl.

"How is he?" Nora Jane said. "Are his hands going to be okay?"

"They'll heal," Nieman said. "He's a hero, Nora Jane. He's gone the distance. That's the important thing. After you do that you can fix the rest."

"I don't know what to say," Nora Jane said. "I never knew a hero." She moved closer to the bed. She lay her head down on Freddy's crazy hairy chest. She very softly lay her head down upon his heart. He was breathing. No one spoke. Mrs. Harwood looked down at the floor. Madge rolled her hips into Doctor Johnson's leg. Nieman closed his mind.

"Nora Jane was a hero too," Madge said. "She helped me so much on the bridge. I never would have made it without her. I had a whole carpool with me."

"I didn't do anything," Nora Jane said. "I just came over there because I was afraid to be alone." She stood up, put her hand on Freddy's head, looked at his mother. She was thinking about something he did when he made love to her. He pretended he was retarded. "Oh, Missy Nora Jane, you so good to come and see us at the home," he would say. "Miss Dater, she say we should be so good to you. You want me to do what I do for Miss Dater? Miss Dater, she say I'm so good at it. She say I get all the cookies and candy I can eat. She say —"

"Shut up," Nora Jane would say whenever he started that. "I won't make love to you if you pretend to be retarded." Now that he was a hero she wished she had let him do it. She giggled.

"I'm sorry," she said. "I was just thinking about something he does that's funny. He does a lot of real crazy things."

"Don't tell me," Mrs. Harwood said. "I'm his mother."

"He's waking up," Nieman said. "Don't talk about him. He can hear." Freddy opened his eyes, then closed them again, then waved his hands in the air, then moaned. He opened one eye, then the other. He was looking right at her. Nora Jane's heart melted. "Oh, Freddy," she said. "I'm so glad you're here."

"You're going to marry me," he said. He sat up on his elbow. "You are going to marry me, goddammit. You can't play with

somebody's affections like that. I'm a serious man and SERIOUS
PEOPLE GET MARRIED. Goddammit, my hands are killing
me. Mother, would you get Stuart to come in here. That GOD-
DAMN STUART, THEY OUGHT TO TAKE HIS LICENSE
AWAY . . . NORA JANE."

She put her hands on his chest. It seemed the best place to
touch him. "I'll get a test," she said. "Doctor Johnson's going to
fix it up."

"I don't want a test," he said. "I want you to marry me." He
sank back down on the pillows. He was starting to cry again.
Tears were starting to run down his face. His mother looked away.
Nieman was writing it. I admire your passion, he was writing. I
always admire passion. Freddy kept on crying. Madge and Doctor
Johnson clutched each other. Nora Jane moved her hands up onto
his shoulder. "Please don't cry anymore," she said. "You have a
good time. You have a happy life. You watch movies all the time
and read books and go up to Willits and camp out and build
your solar house. Freddy, please stop crying. We're alive, aren't we?
I mean, we're lucky to be alive. A lot of people got killed." He
stopped at that.

"Wipe off my face, will you, Mother? And tell Stuart to get
in here and put something on my hands. Oh, shit. Could I have
another shot? I really want another shot."

"I love you," Nora Jane said. "I really love you, Freddy. I'm
not just saying that. You are the best friend I've ever had."

"Good," he said. "I'm glad you do." Then the nurse came in
the room with Freddy's brother right behind her and they moved
everyone out into the hall and put him back to sleep.

Twelve injections of Demerol, seven days on Valium and Tylenol
Number Three, four days on Bayer aspirin, failed attempts at tran-
scendental meditation, self-hypnosis, and positive thinking, three
days of walking all over the Mount Sinai Hospital behind the
bookmobile, and Freddy was dismissed, with his hands still bandaged, to resume his normal life. Nora Jane picked him up at the

emergency entrance. Three nurses helped him into the car, piling the back seat with flowers and plants.

"Stop off somewhere and get rid of these goddamn flowers," Freddy said, as soon as they pulled out onto the freeway. "I had to take them."

"I never saw anybody get that many flowers in my life, even when the archbishop died."

"Let's go to Peet's. I want a cup of real coffee so goddamn much."

"I made an appointment to get an amnio. They said I could come in tomorrow. I, well, never mind that."

"What? Never mind what? Cut down Redwood."

"I know. I was going to. Listen, I think you'll be sorry I did it. Well, anyway, what difference does it make?"

"It makes a difference to me."

"It might not even tell me anything. I don't even know what blood type Sandy is. Well, never mind it. I don't know how we got into this." She parked the car across from Peet's and turned around in the seat and put her hands on his bandages. "I like you the most of anyone I've ever made love to or run around with. That's true and you know it. You're the best friend I've ever had. But I am not in love with you and that is also true." Her black curls were violet in the sun. Her shoulders were bare beneath the straps of her sundress. If he could not have her there was no reason for anything. If he could not have her there was no reason in the world, all was madness and random evil and stupid jokes being played by the galaxy and all its real and imagined gods. Gods, yes, if he could not have her there must be gods after all, only something in the image of man could be so dumb, mistaken, ignorant, and cruel. The sun beat down on Nora Jane's blue convertible, it beat down on her head and shoulders and Freddy Harwood's bandaged hands. "You don't have to love me, Nora Jane. As long as that baby belongs to me."

"I don't think it does."

"Well, get out and let's go see if I can figure out a way to drink a cup of coffee without making a goddamn fool of myself." He knocked the door open with his elbow and stepped out onto Telegraph Avenue. Seven people were around him by the time Nora Jane could come around the other way. Three people who already knew and loved him and four more who wanted to. He's a hero, Nora Jane was thinking. Why would anybody like that want to like me anyway?

The next morning Nora Jane went down to the Berkeley Women's Clinic and had the amniocentesis. Afterwards she was going to meet Nieman and Freddy for lunch. She got up early and dressed up in a jade green silk dress, which was beginning to be too tight around the hips, and she screwed her face together and walked into the clinic determined to go through with it.

The first thing she had to do was take off the dress. Next she had to lie down on a bed surrounded by machinery, and in a moment she was watching the inside of her uterus on a television screen. "Oh, oh," the technician said. The doctor laughed.

"What happened?" Nora Jane said. "What's wrong?"

"There're two of them," the doctor said. "I thought so by the heartbeats. You've got twins." He squeezed her hand. The technician beamed, as delighted as if he had had something to do with it.

"What do you mean?" Nora Jane sat up on her elbow.

"Two babies in there. Identical by the looks of it. I think it's one sac. Can't be sure."

"Oh, my God."

"Be still now. Lie back. We're going to begin the amnio. It won't take long. It's all right. Don't worry. Hold Jamie's hand. Oh, that's a good girl." Then Nora Jane squeezed her eyes and her fists and the needle penetrated her skin and moved down into the sac Lydia and Tammili were swimming in and took one ounce of amniotic fluid and withdrew. The doctor secured the test tube, rubbed a spot on Nora Jane's stomach with alcohol and patted her on the leg. "You're a good girl," he said. "Now we'll get you out of here so you can celebrate."

"I can't believe it," she said. "I just don't believe it's true."

"We'll give you a picture to take home with you. How about that?" An hour later Nora Jane left the clinic carrying in her purse an envelope containing a photograph of Tammili and Lydia floating around her womb. This is too much knowledge, she decided. This is more than I need to know.

"What's this all about?" Nieman said. He was at an upstairs table at Chez Panisse holding Freddy's hand while the test went on. "Stop chewing your bandages, Freddy. Talk to me."

"She fucked this crazy bastard she used to go with in New Orleans. One afternoon when she was mad at me, so she doesn't know if the baby's mine. I should have killed him the minute I saw him. He's a goddamn criminal, Nieman. I ought to have him put in jail. Well, never mind, he isn't here anyway. So she's having this amniocentesis and she won't get the results for about a month anyway. I'm going crazy. You know that. Everything happens to me. You know it does. I'm probably going to lose my left hand."

"No you aren't. Stuart said it was healing. Besides, you're a hero. It was worth it."

"That's easy for you to say."

"So when will she find out?"

"I don't know. Who knows anything anymore. Well, I'm marrying her anyway if I can talk her into it. I can't live without her. You wouldn't believe how goddamn much my hands hurt at night. That goddamn Stuart won't give me a thing."

"Have you heard from the kids, the ones you saved?"

"Of course I have. They write me every other day. They've written me about ten letters. I'm going to get them into Camp Minnesota next year. I was thinking about that this morning. I'll take them up there as soon as they're old enough." Freddy still went to his old camp every summer. He was a senior counselor. Nieman looked away. Freddy's friends never mentioned his camp to him. They liked to talk about that behind his back. "Well," Nieman said. "Here she comes. You want me to leave?"

"Of course not, Nieman. This is Berkeley. Not Ohio. What's happening?" He stood up and held out a chair for Nora Jane and gave her a small quick kiss on the side of the face. Freddy was in extremely high gear this morning. Even for him he was running very tight and hot. He handed Nora Jane her napkin, laid it in her lap. "What did they say?"

"It's two babies. It's going to be twins. I have a picture of them if you'd like to see it." She fished it out of her purse and Freddy held it up to the light and looked at it.

"A month?" Freddy said. "Well, let's eat lunch. A month, huh? Thirty days."

"I don't think they're yours," she said. She was looking straight at him. "The right time of month when I was with Sandy. You never listen when I tell you that." Nieman coughed and drank his wine and signaled to the waiter for some more.

"The role of will is underrated in human affairs," Freddy said. "To tell the truth, Miss Whittington, you have driven me crazy. Have I told you that today?"

"I didn't mean to," she answered. "You're the one that thought up sleeping with me." Nieman rose a few inches from his chair and caught the waiter's eye. Nothing human is foreign to me, he said to himself, as he did about a hundred times a day.

II

Sandy, the beautiful and mysterious Sandy George Wade of Louisiana and Texas and nowhere. Abandoned when he was six years old, after which he roamed the world playing out that old scenario, doing things to please people and make them love him, then doing the things to make them desert him. It was all he knew. One of the people he talked into caring for him was a poet who taught English at his reform school in Texas. The poet taught him to love poetry and to wield it with his voice and eyes. Nora Jane was a sucker for poetry. When they lived together in New Orleans Sandy had been able to get her to forgive him anything by quoting Dylan Thomas or A. E. Housman or a poem by Auden called "Petition," which ends with a plea to "Look shining at, new styles of architecture, a change of heart." Nora Jane always took that to mean she was supposed to think anything Sandy did was all right with advanced thinkers like poets.

Now, on the same day that Nora Jane was having her amniocentesis, Sandy was sitting alone in his room in Mirium Sallisaw's tacky West Coast mansion thinking of ways to get Nora Jane to forgive him and take him back as her mate and child and live-in boyfriend. Sandy worked for Mirium Sallisaw in her cancer business. She sold trips to Mexico for miracle cures. She had made several million dollars collecting the life savings of terminal cancer patients and she paid Sandy well to be her driver.

In his spare time Sandy had been talking to Mirium's psychoanalyst and he was beginning to see that some of the things he had done might actually be affecting the lives of other people, especially and specifically Nora Jane, who was the best thing that had ever happened to him. He paced around his room and lay down on his bed and thought up a thousand tricks to get her back. Finally he decided to sit down and write out his frustration in a poem and have Mirium's Federal Express service deliver it. By the time he had finished it he was so excited he abandoned the Federal Express idea and drove into town and delivered it himself. She was not there, so he left it in the mailbox.

Nora Jane found the poem when she got home from lunch at Chez Panisse. She had spent the afternoon arguing with Freddy about whether they should get married and finally, when she left

him at his house, she had agreed to consider a trial marriage for
the duration of her pregnancy.

Now she walked up onto the porch of the beige and green
house where she had a room and saw the piece of paper sticking out of her mailbox. She knew what it was. No one in her
life had left her things sticking out of mailboxes except Sandy.
Sandy was one of the few young men left in the Western world
who understood the power of written communications. There it
was, sticking out and beckoning to her as she walked by the red
salvia and the madrone hedge and the poppies. She pulled it out
and sat down on the stairs to read.

> *Jane, Jane, where can you be?*
> *Flown so very far from me.*
>
> *The golden rain trees are blooming now*
> *Above the house where we once lived.*
> *Could we go there once again?*
> *Could we recapture the love we had?*

She folded it up and put it back into its envelope and went
into the house and called him up.

"Come on over," she said. "I have a lot to tell you."

"What is that?" he answered.

"You won't believe it, I'm going to have two babies about six
months from now."

"You mean that, don't you?"

"I think they're yours, but I'm not sure. Are you coming?"

"As fast as I can get there."

"Do you think it's funny?"

"No."

"Neither do I."

He arrived at eight o'clock that night, pulling up to the curb in
Mirium Sallisaw's white Cadillac Coupe de Ville. It was the car

he used to drive her clients down to Mexico to the Laetrile clinic and to Las Vegas to get their bootleg Interferon. It was weird and depressing work and Sandy had been saving his money so he could quit. He was up to about four thousand dollars in savings on the night Nora Jane told him she was pregnant. He sped along the freeway thinking what a small sum it was, wondering where in the world he would get some more.

Nora Jane was waiting for him on the steps. He took her into his arms and the old magic was as good as new. The poem he had written to her was true. Back in New Orleans the golden rain trees were covering their old roof with golden dust. "That stuff is made of stars," Sandy had told her once. "And we are too."

"I love you," he told her now. "God, I've been missing you."

"I miss you too," she answered.

"I'm sorry I've been such an asshole. I don't know what makes me act that way."

"It's okay. It was half my fault. Come on in. I've got a lot to tell you."

It was some hours later and the moon was shining in on her small white bed with her new lace-trimmed sheets and the lace-trimmed pillowcases and the yellow lilies in a vase she had run out and bought when she knew he was coming. She was wrapped up in his arms. She had told him all she knew. Now she was finishing her speech. "I'm going to have them no matter whose they are. It's all I know for sure. I don't care what anyone says. Or who gets mad at me."

"Don't sound like that. I want them. I want them to be mine so much I'd reach inside and touch them." He ran his hands across her stomach. "Listen, baby, we're going to get out of here and get a place together and start living like white people. I've had all I can take of loneliness. You can call the shots. You tell me what you want and I'll deliver. I'm quitting Mirium. I've got four grand saved up in the bank and that will tide us over. I'm going to an employment agency tomorrow and see what they can offer. I'll take anything they offer me." He got up from the bed and pulled a package of cigarettes out of his pants and lit one and stood in the window smoking. The moonlight was on his body. He was so graceful it broke Nora Jane's heart to look at him. He was the most beautiful and graceful person she had ever watched or seen. Everything he did made sense in the beauty of movement department. Watching him now, so beautiful and perfect, she thought about a terrible story he told her about being left somewhere when he was small and standing by the door for days waiting for his mother to come back but she didn't come. "Oh, Sandy," Nora Jane got up and stood behind him, holding him in her arms. "I will never leave you again no matter what happens or what you do. I will stick by you if you want me to." Then she was crying tears all over his beautiful graceful back.

Across the campus of the University of California at Berkeley Freddy Harwood was in his hot tub getting drunk. His bandaged hand was propped up on a shoe rack and a bottle of VVSOP Napoleon brandy was by the soap dish and he was talking on the remote-control phone. "She hasn't even called and she isn't there. It means she's with him. I know it. She's bound to be. I've had it, Nieman. Life's not doing this to me. I'm getting out. I mean it. I'm getting into dope or moving to New York or paddling up to Canada in a birchbark canoe. None of it is funny anymore. The whole thing sucks and you know it. The whole show. You goddamn well know it. I would take any age over this age. Fuck it all to goddamn bloody fucking hell. That's all I've got to say. I'm through."

Nieman said he would come over.

"Well, hurry up. I'm in deep, old buddy. I lost my sense of

reality a while ago. I mean, I didn't do anything to deserve this. This is fucking unfair. I don't know. I just don't know."

Nieman said he was on his way. He called up Freddy's old girlfriend, Buiji Dalton, and told her to meet him there. Then he called a friend of theirs named Teddy who was a psychotherapist and told him to get in his car. They converged on Freddy's house. It was a wooden house with great glass wings that swept the horizon for miles across San Francisco and the bridges and the bay.

It had cost three hundred and fifty thousand dollars. It had paintings by every major painter who had worked in the United States in the last twenty years. It had books in six languages and light and air and was full of food and wine and bottled water from Missouri that tasted like honey. In the middle of the patio, looking out on the bay, was the hot tub where Freddy was contemplating suicide or having a prefrontal lobotomy or taking heroin every day. "The pain," he was saying into his tape recorder. "This is real pain. This is not some figment of my imagination. This is not just trying to get something that's hard to get. I don't want her because she's hard to get. I want her because I like to look at her and if those aren't my babies in there it's all over, she will never marry me. I risked my life to save two small children. I walked into a burning building. It isn't fair. IT IS NOT FAIR. I'M MAD AS HELL AND I'M NOT GOING TO TAKE IT ANYMORE." He turned off the recording machine and called Nieman back. "You haven't left yet?"

"I was going out the door."

"Have you got a tape of *Network*, that movie with Peter Finch as the television announcer who gets all the people yelling out the windows?"

"I think so."

"Bring it over, will you?"

Freddy laid down the phone and turned the recorder back on. "Bitter," he said into the microphone. "Bitter, bitter, bitter, jaded, tired of life and cynical. No good for anything anymore. Nothing works. The system fucks."

Clouds of vapor were rolling in from the Pacific Ocean. In a petri dish near the Berkeley campus Tammili and Lydia Whittington's DNA began to give up its secrets to the Chinese student who was working overtime to make money to bring his sister to the United States from Singapore. "Very interesting," he thought. He added one drop of a chemical and watched the life below him form and re-form. *AB positive, universal donors,* he wrote on a pad. He translated it into Chinese with a few brief strokes of his pen. This case interested him very much. He wrote down the name, Nora Jane Whittington. Yes, when he got home he would cast the I Ching and see what else was in store for these baby girls with the lucky blood. Lin Tan, for that was his name, moved the dish to one side and picked up the next one.

Sandy got back into bed with Nora Jane and cuddled her up into his arms. He kissed her hair and then her eyes. He arranged their bodies so they fit against each other very comfortably and perfectly. He heaved a sigh. It was so fragile. It never stayed. It always deserted him. It always went away. It was here now. It would go away. It would leave him alone. "Calm down," she said. "Don't get scared. We don't have to be unhappy if we don't want to."

"When will you know?"

"They said a month. They're busy. So what kind of blood do you have anyway? I'm B positive."

"It's some weird shit. I've forgotten. I'll call and find out."

"Go to sleep. We'll make it."

"Do you love me?"

"Yes, I do."

"Well, I love you too."

*   *   *

Freddy got out of the hot tub. He was the color of a sunset at Malibu when there were plenty of clouds. Buiji Dalton took a big white towel and began to dry him off. She'd been trying to marry him for his money for five years and she wasn't giving up now. Not with all she had to offer. Not after she had divorced Dudley and only kept the house. "I couldn't believe it when I read it in the paper. I cut it out and showed it to everyone. I made a hundred copies and mailed them to people. I'm so proud of you."

"Hey, stop that, will you?"

"What?"

"Drying me. I'm okay. Come on. Let's go in the bedroom and watch this movie. It's the greatest movie made in the United States in four years and Nieman had to go and trash it. He trashed it. Wait till you see it. I want you to tell him what you think when it's over."

"Do you want anything to eat?"

"No, just get me that brandy, will you?" Freddy draped the towel over his shoulder and pulled the other part across his stomach to cover his reproductive organs and went into his bedroom and got into bed with his best friend and his old girlfriend on either side of him and pushed a button and the movie started. Freddy had changed his mind about suicide. After all, Nora Jane was practically illiterate. She had never even read Dostoevski. The copyright warning appeared on the screen. His psychiatrist friend, Teddy, came tearing into the room waving a bag from the deli. He took up the other side of Buiji Dalton and the movie began.

"This will go away," Sandy was saying. "It will disappear."

"It might not," Nora Jane answered. "Don't get scared. We don't have to be miserable if we don't want to be."

*   *   *

Down inside Nora Jane's womb Tammili signaled to her sister. "Nice night tonight."

"I wish it could always be the same. She's always changing. Up and down. Up and down."

"Get used to it. We'll be there soon."

"Let's don't think about it."

"You're right. Let's be quiet."

"Okay."

THE YOUNG MAN

THIS IS A STORY about an old lady who ordered a young man from an L.L. Bean catalog. He was a nice young man with wide shoulders and a worried smile. He had on a tweed coat and dark tan pants and a nice-looking tie with little squiggly things all over it. His fingernails were clean and his hair neatly combed. He liked to work but he was also a good companion on trips. His table manners were excellent but not noticeable. He liked to talk but knew how to let the other person have their turn. Mrs. Bradlee never did get around to asking him what his profession was, his line of work. There never did seem to be a polite way to ask.

All of Mrs. Bradlee's friends were getting young men. You could hardly find four for bridge anymore at the Recess Club. Fanny Hawkins had even started dressing like her young man, flat shoes and work pants. Carrie Hatcher pretended her young man was a chauffeur. All they did was drive around talking about themselves. Elsie Whitfield stayed on the coast with hers; they went fishing. It made Mrs. Bradlee sick at her stomach to think of it.

One night she dreamed a big Greyhound bus pulled up in front of the old courthouse on State Street and all these young men got out and started spreading out all over Jackson, moving out in all directions. Like a web that had fallen over the world.

Mrs. Bradlee wasn't having anything to do with it. They weren't eating dinner at her house. I've seen enough, she told herself. I've had enough to contend with. Mrs. Bradlee was a widow. She had buried two sons in two wars and a husband from smoking cigarettes. All I want to do from now on is live a normal life, she told her remaining children. So whatever you do, don't tell me about it. Just come over on Sunday after church while you're still covered up.

You shouldn't live alone, her friends were always telling Mrs. Bradlee. She still lived in her house on Lakefront Drive, with all her rooms. They wanted her to get an apartment where they were, at Westchester Arms, or Dunleith Court or Dunsinae Towers. Well, she wasn't going to move into an apartment. She wasn't joining the herd. She had been raised in the country. She had seen one cow lead the rest to water. Still, it was getting lonely in the big stone house. If only it could be like it used to be, with her friends coming over for cards. They had even started bringing the young men to Saint James. Right up to the prayer rail, and beyond. Alece Treadway was sending hers to divinity school.

It was too much. In the past Mrs. Bradlee had been known as the leader. She had been the first to cut her hair at college, the first to have a white cook, the first to get a face-lift (when the time came), the first to visit behind the Iron Curtain, when August, her husband, was still alive. Now, with their craze for young men, the crowd had left her behind.

It was all so, well, so messy. And the young men themselves, well, she hated to cast stones, but they were messy too. Well, they were.

They wore open-collar sport shirts and tennis sneakers and barely cut their hair. It was too much. It was just too much. Mrs. Bradlee's knitting needles clicked like a thousand crickets. She was alone in her living room. A beautiful sunset was covering the lake with her favorite shades of blue and pink. Elvie Howard had bowed out of their Wednesday night canasta game, now that she had her swimming pool maintenance friend. He has a degree in Philosophy, she told Mrs. Bradlee, from the East. It's television, Mrs. Bradlee decided. That's where they got the ideas. She switched off her own and went into the library to read.

A stack of catalogs was on a table by the windowseat. She began flipping through them, thinking of ordering some clothes for the grandchildren for Christmas. She took a piece of white chocolate from a dish and began to nibble on it, looking at the elegant clothes and shoes and hand-carved decoys, the scarves and ties and stacks of well-made shirts. One model began to catch her eye. He was in several different catalogs. The best picture was on page sixteen of the L.L. Bean catalog. He had such neat hair, his smile was so, well, just right, not too smiley, just enough so you would know he was friendly. His hands were in his pockets. He was standing so tall and straight. I ought to order him, she thought, laughing to herself out loud. She ate another piece of chocolate. Then another. Hello, she said to the photograph. What's your name?

It was growing dark outside. She pushed a light switch and carried the catalog over to a desk and sat down and took an order blank out of the back and began to fill it in. *One*, she wrote, page 16, number 331, color, white, she paused at where to fill in the amount. $10,000, she wrote and added her Merrill Lynch Visa Card number. There, that should be about right. She folded the order blank in halves, stuck it into its envelope, and carried it across the room to the marble table before the fireplace. She dropped it on a silver salver. Here, Mr. Postman, she said, as if

she were a child playing at things, take this letter to the warehouse.

A bell was ringing in the hall. The cook was calling her to
dinner.

In the morning the envelope was gone. "Have you seen an envelope I left in the library?" she said to the maid. "Well, yes, I did,"
the girl said. "I mailed it for you. In the morning mail."

"Oh, you can't mail that," Mrs. Bradlee said. "It was a joke.
Those people will think I'm crazy when they open that. They'll
say, here's a woman in Mississippi who's lost her mind."

"What was it, ma'am?" the maid said.

"I ordered something they don't sell," she said. The two of
them laughed together at that. Mrs. Bradlee liked the little maid.
An octoroon named Rivers, a sweet girl who was always neat and
clean and smelled good.

It was a week later when the young man came. It was nine in the
morning. A Sunday morning. Mrs. Bradlee had been up and
dressed for an hour, enjoying the fall colors out the windows. She
saw him coming up the walk. "You ordered me," he said. "And
here I am."

"Go away," she said.

"I can't," he said. "I belong here now. You asked for me. I
don't have anyplace else to be."

"Have you had breakfast?" she said.

"No," he said.

"Come in," she said. "I will feed you." It was warm in the
breakfast room, filled with morning sunlight. "Do you mind if I
take off my coat?" he said. "Oh, no," she answered. "Here, let
me take it for you." She took the lovely tweed coat and laid it
across an empty chair. It was the cook's day off. She fixed eggs
and toast and juice. When he was finished he laid his fork and

knife neatly along the edge of the plate. "If you'll excuse me now," he said. "I would like to use your bathroom."

She led the way to the guest room. When he returned she suggested that they go to church. "Mr. Biggs, our choir director, has a special musicale this morning. After morning prayer. You might enjoy that."

"It will be fine," he said. "I'm sure I'll think it's just right."

You should have seen the eyes when Mrs. Bradlee walked in with him, walked right up front to her regular pew and he helped her in and pulled down the prayer bench and knelt beside her. Thank you, she heard herself pray, you know I deserved this. The music was grand, clear and cold water running over stones. The whole church and all its people melded together by music, one big melodic pyramid. Afterwards, they stood outside and Mrs. Bradlee introduced him all around.

In the afternoon they took naps in their rooms, then went for a walk around the grounds, down to the lake, and back to the house. He walked at just the right rate of speed, not running ahead of her all the time like August did, saying can't you keep up, if you didn't talk so much you could keep up with me. Larry didn't mind how much Mrs. Bradlee talked. He was interested in everything she said.

"How long are you staying?" she asked finally. It was after dinner. They were having coffee in the den. It seemed like the proper thing to say.

"How long did you want me for?" he asked. He was looking straight at her out of his dark blue eyes. He was looking at her as if there were no wrong answers.

"Let me think about it," she said. "I'm still getting used to the idea."

"Fine," he said. "Whatever you say."

"Where would you go if you left here? Where else would you be?"

"I wouldn't be," he said. "There is only here."

"And you don't mind?" she said.

"Why should I mind?" he answered. "That's the way it is."

"I'm going to bed now," she said. "I need to sleep."

"Good night then," he said. "I'll see you in the morning."

In the morning it was Monday. She dressed before she went downstairs. They had breakfast. "Now you should go to work," she said. "It's Monday morning."

"Fine," he said. "I'll be back at five thirty."

"Take the blue car," she said. "I don't use it."

"I will," he said. "I like cars to be blue. It's my favorite color." After he was gone Mrs. Bradlee talked on the phone all morning. All her friends called her one by one. What's he like, they asked. He likes blue, she answered. His favorite color is blue. Go fishing with us, Elsie Whitfield said. We might, Mrs. Bradlee answered. I'll have to see. Do you want to? she asked him later. I don't know, he said. Do you? I don't think so, she said. It's so messy. Find a nice way to tell them, he said. Don't hurt their feelings.

Don't you need some other clothes, she said. You might grow tired of that coat. That will be nice, he said. We'll go shopping at the mall.

Many days went by. Many weeks. Christmas came and went. They gave each other gifts. He gave her a bracelet with her name inside. She gave him a bundle of fatwood sticks she ordered from Maine and a tiny sled containing a gold watch. He put it on. His wrist was so perfect. The hair lay so softly along the flesh. Mrs. Bradlee drew in her breath. For a moment she wanted to kiss his hand. God is love, she thought, and reached out to touch his hand instead. We might go to Switzerland for a month, she said. That would be nice, he said. I think that would be perfect.

✳   ✳   ✳

In January the rain fell and the Pearl River rose and the cold came and stayed. It got into Mrs. Bradlee's bones. She felt tired even in the mornings. Her appetite was not good. When she passed Larry in the hall she sighed. He was there every morning. He was there every afternoon. Every Friday she filled the blue car up with gasoline. Every month the bills came. Every morning after breakfast he disappeared into the guest room. It made her sick at her stomach to think what he did in there.

She began to be cold to him. She was quiet when they went on walks. She stopped telling him everything. After all, what had he ever told her? She was giving him all her stories. In return, all he knew was blue. Blue skies, blue, blue, blue.

"I think you should play the piano," she told him one evening. "It would be a good idea for you to play."

"I'm not a piano player," he said. "That isn't what you asked for."

"You could learn, couldn't you? You could take lessons."

"I'll try," he said. "I'll be glad to try."

"It should sound like this," she said. She took a Mozart sonata out of its cover and put it on the record player. It was sonata number 13 in B major, played by Wanda Landowska.

"But that's a woman playing," he said.

"It doesn't matter," Mrs. Bradlee said. "It's all the same thing."

He wasn't any good at the piano. He took lessons for three months but nothing happened. His hands were better in his pockets. His hands were better taking the Maine fatwood and using it to light the library fires at night. They were nice laying his knife and fork across his plate after meals. They were too large for the piano or too stiff or too short. Something was wrong. You're disappointed, aren't you, he said at last. Yes, she answered, to tell the truth I am. I think you will have to leave soon. It isn't a good idea anymore. You will have to find somewhere else to go.

How long should I stay, he asked. I don't know the right amount of time.

Until Easter weekend, she said. That should be about right.

Maundy Thursday came. They met for breakfast without speaking of it. He looked pale. Eat, she said. You should eat before your journey.

On Good Friday they went to communion. He looks tired, Fanny Hawkins said to her. He looks like he needs a rest.

On Holy Saturday he walked all around the house, all day, out into the yard, and down along the river. He looked very beautiful, and light. He had not gone into the guest room after breakfast. He had barely eaten anything at all. Mrs. Bradlee was beginning to enjoy him again. He seemed so light, so easy to support.

Perhaps I'll have him stay till summer, she thought, watching his progress across the yard; he was moving toward a line of dogwood trees set against the horizon. Three trees against a blue sky. Yes, I will tell him we will think it over.

The phone rang. It was the refrigerator repairman. What a time to call, she told him. Come Monday. Don't worry about it now. It broke her concentration. She went back to her afghan. She was knitting an afghan to sell at a church bazaar. When Larry came in he walked by without speaking. He did not come down to dinner. I'll talk to him later, she thought. The meal was heavy. She drank too much wine and fell asleep earlier than she expected.

In the morning she went to find him. Of course he was not there. She looked all over the house. She looked in all the closets. She looked in the basement and the wine cellar and the attic. She went out into the garage and looked in the blue car. She went to the guest room. She stood in the door. There was nothing there. The door to the guest-room powder room was open. I could look in there, she thought. But I'm not going to.

She went out into the hall and sat down on the stairs. She

listened for the sound of footsteps. She thought about the stars. She said the alphabet over and over to herself. It was a trick she had practiced as a child to pass the time. After a while she went down to the library and got out the new catalogs and began to look through them. I might get a young woman this time, she thought. It was a gay thought. How brave, they would all say. A young woman with all the things that can go wrong. I would like a tall one with a long waist, she decided. Long legs and a long waist. A singing voice. Piano skills.

TRACELEEN
AT DAWN

A LOT OF PEOPLE have asked me to tell the story of how Miss Crystal stopped drinking. It seems a number of other ones think it would be a good idea for them too. Miss Crystal is the lady I work for. I take care of the house and nurse Crystal Anne. I have nursed her since she was born and I have been with Miss Crystal ever since she married Mr. Manny and moved to New Orleans from Jackson, Mississippi, where her family is. She has a son from her former marriage and that has complicated things.

So we have all been here in the house on Story Street for six years. It seems longer. It seems like so many things could not have happened in so short a time. I have noticed time seems to pass in different ways at different times. Eighteen years since I graduated down at Boutte and that seems like a million years. Two years since Miss Crystal quit drinking and that seems like yesterday.

The reason she had to quit to begin with is that she is able to drink all night if she wants to. Every member of her family is the same way, especially the men. The men of Miss Crystal's family are not like men in New Orleans. They are more like men from a while ago.

Well, to begin with, Miss Crystal's decision not to take a drink was not some sudden decision, like you see on television or like that. No, it was a long time coming. Several incidents led up to it. First, her closest friend told her she thought it was time for her to stop. They were out running on the Tulane track. It was Miss Sister Laughlin that said it. She is Miss Crystal's oldest friend except for Miss Lydia who is out in California living on vegetables. She has become quite thin. Miss Sister stopped Miss Crystal dead on the track and told her she had been drinking too much and it was not good for Crystal Anne to have a mother that was that way. Miss Sister couldn't have said it at a better time. It was only a few weeks after the incident in the French Quarter when Miss Crystal and Mr. Deveraux were locked in the bordello trying to stop the child abuse ring. Mr. Manny had had to come and get them out and was so mad about it he had moved to Mandeville for good. That story was all over town so I guess Miss Sister had heard it.

Miss Crystal came home from the track very low. She stayed inside all day without combing her hair. Finally she decided she must quit taking a drink if it was the last thing she would ever do. "How can I do it, Traceleen?" she said. "I cannot join the AA. They are not my type of people."

"They might turn out to be nice," I said. "Judge Wiggins, that I used to work for, joined them. He is a very nice man."

"No, I went there once," she said. "They are so sad and try to cover it up with jokes and drink this goddamn coffee all the time instead of whiskey. No, I will do it cold turkey. I will do it on my own."

"Call Miss Sister and get her to come over and help you," I said. "She's the one that brought it up." So Miss Sister comes over and they sit in the kitchen drinking coffee and are real serious and Miss Sister calls her brother that is a psychiatrist. We were acquainted with him already. We took Crystal Anne to him once when she was acting crazy and would not wear shoes. I thought he was a very nice man and sensible. He said to let her keep them off until she stumped her toe and so we did.

So Miss Sister calls her brother and the upshot of it is he makes Miss Crystal an appointment and she puts on this light green dress with white flowers on it and goes over to find out how to quit. When she comes back she has this tape. She is supposed to lie down on the den floor with a pillow under her head and listen to it each morning and each night and it will put messages in her brain. Alcohol is your enemy. It is bad for your body and bad for your mind. Alcohol will kill you. Like that.

So Miss Crystal comes home and throws all the whiskey in the house down the sink, even Mr. Manny's wine that he orders from France, and then she goes in the den and lies down on the floor and listens to her tape.

Then about ten days go by. It is raining a lot and that didn't help. Miss Crystal, she don't let it get her down however and starts cleaning up the house, cleaning out all the closets and the basement and the attic and Crystal Anne's room. I was standing by all I could and even made an excuse to come in on Sunday so as to help her get through the weekend.

Saturday goes by and it is a long day. Miss Crystal, she is used to getting dressed up on Saturday afternoon and having people over. Now what is she supposed to do? The sun was shining. It might have been better if it had not been. By five o'clock she was pacing the floors. "Go to the park," I advised her. "Take Crystal Anne and push her on the swings. I will be here making you a caramel cake. When you get back there will be a cake with icing an inch thick." That cheered her up. I have never seen Miss Crystal turn down sugar. So she went out to the park and played with her daughter and came home and ate the cake and we made it until Sunday. I let myself in on Sunday morning about nine o'clock. I'd been up since dawn wondering what I'd find when I got there.

She was sitting in her robe reading a book, happy as she could be not to have a hangover. "What are you reading?" I said. "A story about a Kool-Aid wino," she said. She was laughing. "This crazy man out in California wrote it. It's about a little boy who is hooked on grape Kool-Aid. It could be me."

Then Sunday went by and I thought we were out of the woods when who should show up but Mr. Manny. He comes by pretending to need some shirts but as soon as he has a stack of them in his arms he turns around and demands to know why Miss Crystal has let Crystal Anne quit school. She is dressed by then, in some plaid wool walking shorts and one of his open-neck casual shirts. He have so few things. It never fails to make him mad when Miss Crystal and King just borrow anything they like of his without even asking. "Is that my shirt?" he says. Then, "I can't believe you let Crystal Anne quit school. Children can't just quit school."

"She is only three years old," Miss Crystal says. "Three-year-old children do not need to go to school."

"She'll never get in Newman if you let her get behind. She has to go somewhere, Crystal. I don't care where it is but she has to start back tomorrow. Tomorrow, do you understand?"

"She said a fat girl was trying to drown her. I don't know if I'll even get her to put her head under in the tub again. She'll probably never learn to swim."

"You are crazy, Crystal. Do you know that? And my daughter is going back to school. She can't sit in that tent all her life. There's a big world out there and my child is going to be prepared to meet it." They are facing each other in the hall now. Just like old times. Crystal Anne, she is eating it up, standing in the doorway of the den where she's been watching TV in her tent. I am tired of that tent myself to tell the truth. Can't even get in the den to vacuum.

So Mr. Manny has come over and started this ruckus and they fight it out for about fifteen minutes, calling each other Lawyer and Whore and White Liberal Bullshit and Crazy and Mother's Boy and Drunkard and Alcoholic and like that. Then Mr. Manny, he go get Crystal Anne and hug her and tell her not to worry he is going to get a court order and take her across the lake where she can live a normal life and go to school. As soon as he is out the door Miss Crystal she walk across the kitchen and call the airport and order a private plane. Then she pour herself a drink. I don't say a word. It is not me she has to answer to. Besides, it does not do the slightest bit of good to tell someone not to drink if they have set their mind to it. Pray is the best thing to do under those circumstances. Hide the car keys and pray.

Anyway, then she pack a bag for herself and Crystal Anne and say she is going to do what she should have done weeks ago, go up to Vail, Colorado, and get King. He is working in a ski village up there since he left school. This has not been an easy house to work for. We have shed our tears. I've told you that before.

So Miss Crystal pack their bags and dress Crystal Anne in a new white velvet dress and off they go. No sooner are they out the door than Mr. Manny call up and want to talk to her. He seem more reasonable than when he left, talking very sweet and polite.

"Traceleen, go find my wife and tell her I'm on the phone and would she pick up the receiver and talk to me." Like that, controlled I guess you'd call it.

"They're gone," I said. She had not told me not to tell. "She has got a plane to take her to see King. She has had a drink, Mr. Manny. I guess I should tell you that. To tell the truth she has had several." I felt bad about taking sides like that, nobody in the world could love anybody more than I love Miss Crystal but there comes a time when you must do what's right even if it could be misunderstood. "Thank you," Mr. Manny said. We hung up and I sat down at the table and put my head in my hands. I was trying to pray but no prayers came. It is too confusing to be alive sometimes, sometimes there are things that make me wish we were all back in Boutte sitting on my auntee's porch without a car. Why couldn't Mr. Manny and Miss Crystal just fall in love again and spruce up the bedroom and have Miss Sister over making bread and playing practical jokes on their cousins like they used to do when we were first setting up housekeeping? What has gone wrong around here that no one can love anyone anymore?

Then Mr. Manny is there and begging me to go with him and we get in his car and go out to the private airport. We got there just as they were taking off. A Queenaire, that's what she hired to take them to Colorado. Mr. Manny, he hired us a smaller plane, with just one engine, and the two of us got into it behind the pilot and we are chasing them through the skies. Our pilot has got Miss Crystal's pilot on the radio, trying to make him turn back on the grounds that Miss Crystal is drinking and unfit to charter an airplane. Miss Crystal's pilot, he won't do it, he says only the pilot must be sober. About that time I have remembered how to pray. I do not like the looks of the sky around us, there is lightning going off in all directions. I had never known what lightning looked like before that day. From down below you only see a very small part of what is going on in the clouds. I would have to draw it to describe it to you. I know airplanes with only one motor should not be up in that kind of weather. "Turn around," I said. "We have got no business flying into that lightning." About that time a big bolt of it went off out the window, a whole network of lightning streaks like a spiderweb or the veins on old people's hands. I thought I would throw up or start to scream. Mr. Manny he put his hand on my knee and squeeze it. Then he talks on the radio some more, then he confers with the

pilot and we begin to turn around. Miss Crystal's voice is on the
radio again and I hear Mr. Manny promise her that if she will
turn around too and come back home he will go get King himself and anything else she wants him to do, even quit his job.
The radio is crackling and crackling. These big lightning clouds
are almost touching the wings of the plane. It is the most terrible time I have ever had with the Weisses and even beats the day
Miss Crystal threw the television set out the window during the
Vietnam war. It is so terrible and the sky is so full of every kind
of thing and so many colors I could not describe what they looked
like, there is no paint or name for them.

Then I see the Queenaire turning around beside us and we
fly back to the New Orleans airport. I thought I must have been
gone a year. Mark had a fit when I got home and told him what
had happened. He told me never to let him know the details unless I wanted somebody killed.

Part two. Now it is the next morning and Miss Crystal is more
determined than ever to quit drinking. It has cost her twelve hundred dollars for that airplane ride. It is getting too expensive to
drink and besides, King will be coming home and she will need
her wits about her if we are to get him back into a school and
off of dope and everything. I wish Miss Crystal had some God
she could hold on to in times like these. But no, she prefers to
go it alone. So we got Crystal Anne fixed up with Adelaide
Simmons to play with and Miss Crystal gets dressed and goes
back to the drinking doctor. She is gone half the day. It turned
out she was having to have blood tests made.

So this time she come home with these white pills that do
something to your blood. If you drink when you have them inside your bloodstream you will become violently ill and think you
are going to die. It is called the aversion theory of stopping drinking. Miss Crystal, she thinks it is perfectly suited to her personality as it lets you decide ahead of time whether you are going

to drink and not at a party when you are not as likely to hate yourself for doing it.

I wish they could get something like that for the ones that like to eat. Anyway, we have got to wait three days for her to take a pill. You must wait until the slightest trace of alcohol has gone from your blood. So three days go by and meanwhile we are moving furniture. Mr. Manny had decided to move back in. They have made a truce. He is only moving into the guest room though. Not into the bedroom. He said they have had so many fights in there, including the time King tore the bedpost off the bed, that he is never sleeping there again. Besides, I think he suspects Miss Crystal has been sleeping there with Mr. Alan while he was across the lake. Of course, he is the one that left so he can't throw stones.

So we are moving a king-size bed into the guest room and Mr. Manny's big mahogany wardrobe that he takes everywhere he go. He has moved it five times since I have worked for the Weisses, once to Mandeville and once to an apartment on Exposition Boulevard and once down to the Pontalba for the summer. Every time there is a flare-up in this relationship I end up with my back out from moving furniture. I have learned my lesson by now though and have Mark's cousin, Singleton, over to do the heavy work.

So everything is going along fine for several weeks. Miss Crystal, she takes her big white pills and is writing an article for the *Times-Picayune* about how to stop drinking. She had been a reporter when she was young. I think I have told you that. Crystal Anne is in school every morning at Saint James where they do not have a pool. King is home and has a job working for a man that makes Mardi Gras floats. It is in this warehouse down on Tchoupitoulas and Miss Crystal goes down every day and takes him his lunch. It is beginning to seem like an army camp around our house, everybody on time and doing what they should.

* * *

There is this one float King was especially interested in that has
the king of the sea surrounded by mermaids and oysters and
shrimp and holding a shrimp boat in his hand. He drew it for
me on a tablet, then made me come down on my way home from
work and take a look in person. He looked smaller than sixteen,
in that big old warehouse with them grown men he works with.
I do not understand that boy although I love him and could look
at him all day, he is so beautiful and golden. Poor Miss Crystal.
She has been in for it since the day she had him when she was
only eighteen. That's too young to be a mother for someone as
high-strung as she is.

Anyway, she is taking her white pills and the children are coming along and Mr. Manny, he is just like always. He gets up early
and puts on his brown suit and goes downtown to make the
money. He is trying to be cheerful but I know he is just waiting
for the other shoe to drop. Also, I wish Miss Crystal would break
down and go sleep in the guest room. I think it is her place to
give in on that and I was on the point of telling her so. Miss
Crystal and Mr. Manny love each other. If they did not have a
strong love they could never have overcome their families and
made a mixed marriage. Still, love dies. We must admit that. The
problem with Miss Crystal and Mr. Manny is they are too smart
for each other and love excitement and love to argue. Sometimes
I think it is best if very smart people do not marry each other.
There is not enough room in one marriage for so many opin-
ions.

So the winter is going by at our house and it looks like Miss
Crystal is going to make her thirty-fifth birthday and maybe even
Mardi Gras without a drink. That is her goal. At that time she
could tell you to the day how long it had been since she took a
drink. She talked about it quite a bit, muttering to herself. Also,
she had been finding out about those pills. Antabuse, that is what

they are called. It seems that what they do is more complicated than we thought at first. Miss Crystal found this article in a medical magazine that says they might change the middle of your brain where the messages go through from one side to the other and keep the left working with the right. Miss Crystal is very particular about her brain. She was an exceptional student when she was in school and studied philosophy and the Greek language.

Anyway, back to those pills. Miss Crystal had become very worried over this article she read. Also there was an incident at a party she went to. Someone served her a dessert with sherry in it and she became very red in the face and had to leave the table. She was quite frightened by that and had been half afraid to swallow one since. She had been doing so well with not drinking and gotten all the way through Christmas and was enjoying not having any hangovers so she decided to throw the pills away and go back to the tape. Here is how complicated the pills became. We couldn't decide how to throw them away. If we flushed them down the toilet they might get back into the water supply and kill someone down the line. Anything can happen with chemicals. It seems to me that people should be very careful about making anything they cannot get rid of. Finally, we just crushed them up and put them in the attic marked poison, in a sealed can up high where no child could find them. I suppose they are still up there. I should check and see.

Part three. We had come down to the weekend of February 10. Miss Crystal is almost finished with her article for the newspaper and about to turn it in. She was worried about whether they would print it or not as she had not written anything for a long time and she thought she might have lost her touch. I thought it was very good, the part she let me read, but with too many big words. I like writing to stay simple myself, be more like talking so the reader doesn't get the idea they are being preached at. Anyway, Miss Crystal is on a diet on top of quitting drinking and she is nervous and can't sit still. She keep going out to the park and running around the lagoon. Every time she go out there she keeps running into this girl that has this disease that makes her think she is fat even though she is thin as a rail. She is married to this lawyer Miss Crystal knows and she has this six-month-old baby boy she pushes around the park all day while she runs. She is driving everyone that sees her crazy. Miss Crystal wants to get some exercise but every time she goes to the park there is this crazy girl pushing this baby and it makes her ask herself, Am I Crazy Too? Why would someone stop doing everything they like? Maybe I am as crazy as that girl, here I am, almost thirty-five years old and married to a rich man and I cannot even have a drink or a tuna fish sandwich. That is the type thing she would ask herself when she came home from exercising in the park. She had me doing it, wondering what I was giving up, not letting myself do. I am still thinking about that. Who is telling that girl she is fat? Why is she listening to what she hears?

So Miss Crystal is on this diet and she is depressed from being hungry and not being able to decide whether being on a diet is a good idea or something other people have put in her head. She is torn down the middle on that issue. Finally, she comes in the kitchen, it is two o'clock in the afternoon on February 10, I'll remember that day, and she starts making a lemon meringue pie, which is King's favorite. The next thing I know she has me getting out the freezer and Crystal Anne is sitting in the middle of the kitchen floor turning the crank on homemade chocolate ice cream and I am beating up a pound cake. Butter and eggs and sugar and flour and vanilla flavoring and on Miss Crystal's counter there is lemon and evaporated milk and lemon rind and crushed-up graham crackers. I don't know what all. It was spring in that kitchen. I felt like we had gotten somewhere, made some sort of opening. Begun to see the light. That sort of sentiment was in my head.

*   *   *

Life is not that simple. God has made it harder than that. Sometimes I get very mad at Him and think He is not a good judge of things.

Just about the time we are getting the kitchen straightened up and powdered sugar sprinkled on the cake Miss Crystal turns on the radio and this song comes on. A song she used to listen to with Mr. Alan last year when they were having their love affair. She stand very still, her meringue knife in her hand. "Oh, you came here with my best friend, Jim, and here I am, trying to steal you away from him. Oh, if I don't do it, you know somebody else will, if I don't do it, you know somebody else will."

It is a funny song to have for a love song. I remember Mr. Alan standing in this very kitchen dancing and singing along to it, making shrimp creole and being in love with her. That was when she split up with Mr. Manny the first time.

Miss Crystal listened to the whole song without saying a word. Then she reach up in a cabinet and take down a bottle of whiskey and pour herself a drink. "I am going to die when all this is over," she said. "And I have not had my share of the stuff I wanted. I am tired of being hungry. To hell with it. I'm starving to death for everything I need." She drank the glass of whiskey and poured herself another one. I did not say a word. I looked at the clock. It was four-thirty. What would the evening bring?

Part four. What happened next I had to piece together from re-ports. As soon as we cleaned up the kitchen I left. I was not stay-ing around. I put on my things and went on home. "Stop worrying about that woman," Mark said to me. "She can take care of her-self." But how was I to stop? If you are with someone you begin to love them, you hear their joys and sorrows, you share your heart. That is what it means to be a human being. There is no escaping this. Ever since the first day I went to work for her I have loved Miss Crystal as if she was my sister or my child. I have spread out my love around her like a net and I catch whatever I have to catch. That is my decision and the job I have picked out for myself and if Wentriss wants to call me a slave that is because she does not know what she is talking about. Miss Crystal always pays me back. She would go to battle for me. We know these things. We are not as dumb as we seem.

Anyway, back to the night of February 10. I was put out with her that night. She was going to ruin all our good work and there was nothing anyone could do to stop her. The Lord's will be done, I suppose I was saying something like that. That is the will of the Lord. I still think I was right to go on home. Of course, if it had turned out differently I would be feeling like it was my fault. That is also how we are, something we cannot change or do anything about.

The night of February 10. Miss Crystal kept on drinking and cooking and called up a number of her friends and ordered champagne. Mr. Manny was in Chicago for the night. Then everyone came over and ate and drank and talked but it did not last too long. Miss Crystal's heart wasn't in it and besides it had been so long since she had a drink she couldn't hold up like she used to. King had come home and grabbed his chance and gone off to play the machines at The Mushroom Cloud. Miss Crystal sent her friends home about nine and fell out on the sofa, just passed right out leaving Crystal Anne alone.

Crystal Anne was being real quiet, taking things in and out of her tent. Dishes of ice cream we found later and half the cake and a champagne bottle. All her dolls and her spacemen and Luke Skywalker and Pilot Barbie. I was the one that cleaned up the tent, what was left of the tent.

It had turned off chilly when the sun went down. None of the ones at the party had turned the heat on and Miss Crystal was asleep so Crystal Anne decided to build herself a campfire. She knew just how to do it. She had watched King do it at the beach. She carried some newspapers out of the kitchen and arranged them on the den rug right in front of her tent. Between the tent and the TV. Then she got some blocks and Tinkertoys and put them on. Then she went into the living room and got some of Mr. Manny's fat pine kindling he orders from Maine and she arrange it just so. Then she go get all her stuffed dolls and toys and set them up around the edge in a circle and then she took a cigarette lighter she found somewhere and set it on fire. The fire was between where she must have been and the door to the sun room. She was trying to jump from the sofa arm through the door when Miss Crystal woke up and heard her screaming. "Stay there," Miss Crystal says she remember yelling it over and over. "Go in the bathroom. Go in the bathroom, Crystal Anne. If you don't go in the bathroom I will kill you." Miss Crystal bust on through the fire and grab her up and run into the bathroom with her and out the back door onto the porch and there is no way down that way but the hanging ladder King got in New York at a fancy toy store. It has been there for years. Miss Crystal didn't know whether to risk it or just throw Crystal Anne off the balcony or try to make it down the hall. From the bedroom door it did not look like the hall was burning yet. She made the best decision that she could. She put Crystal Anne on her back and climbed down with that baby hanging on to her, clawing her face and pulling at her hair but hanging on like a little monkey, as Miss Crystal always described it later. "Arboreal we were, arboreal we are." That's how she puts it. It means we used to live in trees if you go along with that theory.

So finally they have made it to the ground on that rope ladder that's been hanging there five years in the sun and rain and then Miss Crystal breaks into a downstairs window to see if King is in his room but he is not there. Then, finally, she calls the fire department and they come and ruin all the upholstery and drapes in the upstairs not to mention the carpets. We were living in the

Pontchartrain Hotel for several months after that. It was quite a mess.

That was the end of Miss Crystal's drinking. I wish the story could be of more use to other people. It seems it takes something like a fire or falling down a flight of stairs or getting torn up in a drunk driving accident to separate people from their desire to have a drink with one another.

Of the things Miss Crystal tried the one I would recommend the most is that tape she had. It had some very nice things on it beside the ones dealing with alcohol. Your Body Is Your Temple, that is the one I liked. Whatever you put into it, the next day that is what you will be made out of. What would you rather look like in the end, a bottle of whiskey or a stalk of celery or a dish of chocolate ice cream? That's the question I'm asking myself right now. As soon as I finish ironing this shirt I am going to make today's choice. Today it will be one thing. Tomorrow it might be something else.

ANNA, PART I

IT WAS A COLD DAY in the Carolinas, drizzling rain that seemed to hang in the sky, that barely seemed to fall. The trees were bare, the mountains hazy in the blue distance, the landscape opened up all the way to Virginia. It was a big day for Anna Hand. It was the day she decided to give up being a fool and go back to being a writer. She called her editor.

"I want a contract. I can't stand it anymore. I'm going back to work."

"For a novel or a book of stories?"

"Stories. Stories will do."

"Are you all right?"

"May I have the contract or not?"

"You are spoiled rotten. Do you know that?"

"I want it today."

"You've got it."

"Good. I'm hanging up."

"Wait a minute. Are you all right?"

"I will be. I've wasted ten months of my life. Ten goddamn

months in the jaws of love. Well, I had to do it. It's like a cold. If you leave the house sooner or later it happens. Anyway, I'm through. Call David and get something in writing for me, will you? I'm hanging up."

"Call me if you need me. Anna, listen to me a minute. If you need me, call me."

"For ten months every meaningful or true thing in my life was a secret. Can you believe that? The main part of my life was secret and the junk was public. Imagine living like that. Try to imagine it, Arthur. Imagine living that way."

"Was it my fault? Did I do it?"

"You contributed. You were there. Well, I'll have you something by September. Something really good."

"What's it going to be called?"

" 'Light can be both wave and particle.' To make them think. If they can't think they can't be my readers."

"Don't get cynical."

"I am already. I'm cultivating it." She hung up the phone and went upstairs and into her small old-fashioned kitchen. The cupboards were bare. There was nothing on the shelves but some protein powder and crackers and several kinds of tea and four different brands of instant coffee. She put some water on to boil, thinking of her father. It's a wonder I could love anyone at all, even for ten months, she decided. Even a married man who was doomed to break my heart. Even a redhaired married baby doctor who looks like my twin brother.

She stared out the window at the hills, thinking of the places she had been. She had been in Stockholm and London and Zurich and Rome. In Boston and Seattle and New York City. Now she was home. Now she would find the pieces of herself, take herself back from the world. But I do not exist without the world, she thought. All of them are part of me. Quanta exist in the set of all existing quanta. They go in and out of existence as part of the whole. Still, they are discrete. Figure it out. Start with the tribe.

She closed her eyes and thought of her family. There were so many of them, wild and unpredictable and always getting married and having babies. Four brothers, six nephews, twelve nieces, a hundred cousins. Only Anna was childless.

The day before she had stood in her brother's living room watching her beautiful fourteen-year-old niece practicing a dance for her school variety show. "LIVING IN THE MATERIAL WORLD," Madonna was coming out of four speakers. "I'M LIVING IN THE MATERIAL WORLD AND I AM A MATERIAL GIRL." The beautiful niece stopped after the chorus and held out her hands toward her aunt. She was a shimmering hopeful girl, smiling a wonderful fourteen-year-old smile. She spread wide her long white fingers. "I'm going to be throwing dollars all over the place while I do it," she said. "I might get some printed up."

Anna smiled back. She was not offended. Poor nieces and nephews. They were living in the material world, surrounded by cars and sweaters and swimming pools and shoes and jackets and coats and shirts and toys and equipment.

This particular dancing niece, however, looked as if she might survive. "I love you," Anna said. "I think you're great."

Now she was in her kitchen making coffee and looking out the window. Her old corduroy robe was belted around her waist, her feet were in ski socks, her hips were thin and hollow from living in the city. She giggled, did a little dance of home. I'm back, she decided. I'm going to work and I'm not giving another interview of any kind or letting anybody take another picture of me. Fuck it, I'm taking that goddamn phone and putting it in the shed. I'm never answering that goddamn phone again as long as I live. She turned around and read the notes pinned to her refrigerator.

Fuck doubt, press on.

The dishes can wait.
Serve the whole.

She poured a cup of coffee, added sugar and cream, stuck some chocolate mint candies in the pocket of her robe, and went into her office. It would be many hours later before she remembered it was her birthday.

The married man, she decided, unwrapping one of the mints. I will tell the story of the married man. But how to plot it? How to make it happen? How to make it live? How to move the characters around so they bruise against each other and ring true? How to ring the truth out of the story, absolve the sadness, transmute it, turn it into art?

How to do it from the start, as the poet said. Notice everything. The stain on the ceiling. The way the candle burned all night that last night he slept with me. Scott Joplin on the stereo. "Solace" and "Red Flower Rag" and "Jasmine Blues."

The married man had made love to Anna as if there were no tomorrow. "It's like cancer," she said to him, rolling over to feel his chest against her breasts, then back again to feel his chest against her back, keeping an eye on the clock. Romeo and Juliet, star-crossed lovers, he had actually said that to her one night. She had written it on the mirror, thinking it would make her stop loving him.

Great swamps of sentimentality stretching out in three directions behind her. In front the sea of cliché, above, the maudlin skies, nothing to breathe, not a molecule of air that hasn't carried a million love songs from one radio station to another. Dance with Me, I Just Called to Say I Love You, Sail Away to Key Largo, Yes, It's Me and I'm in Love Again. Love Letters Straight from My Heart. We need Madonna, Anna thought. We need anything we can get. Anything anyone can teach us.

II

The married man had entered Anna's life at a party given by her editor in Brooklyn. A dinner party with rare roast beef and triple chocolate cake and cold spinach soup. Anna had arrived late. Her plane had fallen from the sky over Washington and made an emergency landing in New Jersey. For seven minutes the DC-9 had fallen from the sky at a severe angle of descent. Anna had breathed through an oxygen mask and wondered if she would die on impact or live to feel the skin burn from her body. *The Assumption,* she had been thinking. *Little Easters, Coming Over Jordan, Calvin Street, Psalm and Dream, Mariana.* She chanted the names of her books. She saw her unfinished manuscripts lying on her table and the new one that was put to bed in Boston waiting for the fall. Then the plane leveled off and made its bumpy landing.

"You never thought of God?" The man beside her at the dinner table unfolded his napkin and placed it on his lap. It was five hours later. Anna was sitting at her editor's dinner table. Her editor's gorgeous actress wife beamed at her. Her editor's good-looking blond son poured the wine. They were so glad she was here. So glad she was safe. The tall redheaded baby doctor was unfolding his napkin across his knee and asking if she had thought of God. His hands were beautiful and clean and freckled, like her own. Anna stared at his freckles. Ever since she had gotten off the plane her vision had been very intense, everything standing out in brilliant demarcations and colors. The tablecloth, the wine-glass half full of red wine, the baby doctor's freckled hands, his immaculate fingernails, his freckled nose. His hair, the exact color of her own. She smiled at him. She believed she had known him forever.

"No," she said. "I don't believe in God. I believe in man."

"Hmmmm," he said. He smiled deeper into her face, completely caught up in her. It occurred to Anna that the whole table must be watching them. It was too thick. She shook it off.

"I've never entertained the idea of God in my life. When I was a very small child the idea seemed ludicrous and stupid and I never believed it no matter how many hours I spent on my knees at the Episcopal church. I didn't trust the ministers. And I didn't like the idea of hell and I never put my money in the collection plate. The only thing I hated worse than ministers were the men passing the collection plate." She paused, then went on. "I did find out one very interesting thing on that plane ride. I discovered it's all right to die if you've done your work. I was saying the titles of my books over and over to myself." She looked at her editor. He smiled back. "Anyway, I said the titles of the books over to myself like a mantra, then I regretted not having children, then I was ready to die. It was all right. It really was. It seemed all right." She sat back. The baby doctor was still entranced. Well, he could take it or leave it. The whole thing. The wide brow, the scary, flaky intelligence.

"We never had children either," the baby doctor said. "My wife always wanted to adopt a child but I wouldn't let her."

"Oh, you're married," Anna said. They all laughed. Her editor's son caught her eye. They began to talk of other things. The party wore on to its conclusion. The baby doctor asked if she would share a cab and she said yes. She was full of wine and at four o'clock that afternoon she had seen her death so she took the baby doctor off to hear jazz in the Village and later she took off her raincoat and then her dress and took him to bed. So it began. It was everybody's luck that his wife was out of town.

"It's a good thing I learned my lesson about married men years ago," she said, sitting up in bed, watching him dress. The light was coming in around the edges of the drapes. It was a tall, old-fashioned hotel room. She had stayed there with both her husbands. Now she was here with this married man. This freckled, redheaded baby doctor, with his lanky bones and long, clean, immaculate freckled hands and his surprising libido and his gentleness. "I can tell you're a married man," she said. "Because you know how to make love. I have a theory that the only way to learn to make love is to be married a long time to one person. I've been meaning to do a piece about it if I ever get time." She pulled the bedspread up around her legs, settled her elbows on her knees, looked nice and normal and balanced and uninvolved. He buttoned his pants and zipped them up. He put on his tie without looking in the mirror. He was looking at her.

"I'll call you later," he said. "Where will you be?"

"God knows. I could be anywhere. I'll probably go by my agent's or the Metropolitan Museum of Art. It's my favorite place in New York City."

"I want to see you tonight." He sat down on the bed. He put his hands on her feet. His face was as clear and unmasked as one of the two-year-olds he treated. "I'm going to fall in love with you," he said. "It's already happened. It's already too late. Don't look away. You feel it too. I know you do."

"How old are you?"

"I'm forty-five years old. I don't do this, Anna. I don't cheat on my wife. This is brand-new."

"Well, I cheat on everyone," she said. She rolled off the side of the bed. She picked up the red silk shirt she had been wearing the night before and put it on. She stood before him with her gorgeous legs, playing it for all it was worth and denying it at the same time. "And I'm not having an affair with a married man. That is that." She moved into the bathroom and began to brush her teeth, talking around the toothpaste. "If you want to take me out to dinner, get a divorce and call me up. I've done that already." She spit out the toothpaste and wiped her mouth off with a towel. He had followed her. He was watching her. "I love myself too much to have an affair with a married man." She began to floss her teeth. "Stop liking me. I don't want you to like me."

"I can't get a divorce. She's mine. I love her. I take care of her."

"Well, that's your life then, isn't it?" She pulled the dental floss out of her teeth and threw it into the sink and went back into the room and opened the drapes and looked out on Fifth Avenue. "What a city. I tried to live here once but it didn't work. I might try again. A friend offered me an apartment for next winter. Where do you live? In what part of all this."

"Near the park. You could come see me if you go to the museum. You could come by my office and see where I work." He was offering her everything he could think of. He had never in his life wanted anything as much as he wanted this woman to see him again. It made no sense and he didn't try to make sense out of it. He wanted to know everything she had ever done and was going to do. He wanted to talk to her for hours, ask her a million questions. He had read the books before he met her and seen the photographs. She was more than the sum of the parts. She was so soft, so easy to reach. He stood away from the bed with his hands at his sides waiting for her to dismiss him.

"It wasn't even all that good," she said. "I'm not very good at making love anymore. I don't get excited like I used to. I think I'm bored with the whole thing."

"It was good." He put his hands in his pockets.

"Yes," she said. "It was good." He sat down on the bed and took her back into his arms. He held her there. "Anna, please see me tonight."

"All right. If you put it that way I will. I shouldn't, but I will." Then he took off his clothes and made love to her some more and then they were really in for it.

They went to dinner in a small restaurant on Madison Avenue. Afterwards they walked around the city talking of their pasts. Nothing they said now made any difference. Now it was too late for words. Now they were caught up, trapped, held. She took him to a bookstore on Madison Avenue where people knew her and kept her books in the window. She wanted it seen. She wanted it validated in the world.

He took her to his apartment and showed her where he slept with his wife. The apartment was white and green, like a greenhouse, the apartment was desperately cheerful.

"Where is she?"

"She's visiting her mother."

"When will she be back?"

"This weekend."

"Good. I'm leaving Saturday."

"When will you be back?"

"This winter, but not to see you. This is only for this week."

"You can't mean that."

"Of course I mean it. You're married. You couldn't even spend the night. To hell with it. It makes me mad to even think of it. It's terrible. It's the worst thing anyone can do. The worst and stupidest and most tragic fucking thing a woman can do. I am not going to do it."

"You are doing it."

"I'm going to stop." Then she took off her coat and made love to him in his wife's bed.

"Why did we do this?" she said later.

"Because the unconscious calls the shots."

"Not in my life it doesn't." She got out of bed and began to put on her clothes. "It's two days old and already we're crazy. Well, it isn't going to happen to me. I spent five years of my life on a married man and I'm never doing it again. The last time I married a perfectly nice human being on the rebound and ruined his life. I don't want this. I'm bailing out before it's too late."

"It's too late now. It's happened."

"No, it's not. When I'm gone it will go away. I'm going to

get a plane reservation and leave tomorrow. I'm getting out of here."

So Anna flew back to the mountains and it was nine months before she came back to New York City and it had done no good. The minute she saw the redhaired baby doctor it was exactly the same. Nothing had changed, not a freckle on his hand.

"It's life," he said. "Abundance, largess. You can't turn this down."

"It's a lot of bullshit," she answered. "If you like me so much, get a divorce."

"I love her."

"I don't believe you."

"Believe me. I want you to believe that so you won't get hurt."

"I'm already hurt. You're going to ruin my life for five years. It's the worst thing that ever happened to me. It's worse than the last time. It's like a groove I've worn in my brain."

"Come go to the park with me. Come see the castle they're redoing."

"It's not your fault. I'm not blaming you. I'm not blaming it on anyone. And I don't want to see the castle. Then I'd never be able to see a goddamn castle without thinking of you."

"It's my fault."

"Maybe it is. Goddammit, I was married and I got a divorce so that the next time I fell in love I'd be free to live with whomever I fell in love with. I'm not married. I'm free. Or whatever wiggle on space our small amount of freedom in the world consists of. Randolph says it's a wiggle in the petri dish. Maybe he's right. I was free until I fell in love with you. Until that plane fell from the sky and reminded me I was mortal."

"I'm sorry."

"No, you aren't. You love it."

"Go to the park and see the castle."

"Okay. I will."

That is how it went between them in the fall and winter when Anna was in New York City to have a reward and a change of scenery to liven up her work. The worst part was making sure the redhaired doctor was suffering as much as she was. She wanted him miserable. She thought she had every right to lie in bed and send him terrible messages across the city and hope they kept him up all night and made him drink.

III

Where was will in all of this? the married man wondered. He was waiting for a traffic light. It was raining. A dark evening in the rain. He was driving along Fifth Avenue. He turned on 65th into the hospital parking lot and gave the car to an attendant. He went into an office and called her apartment but the line was busy. Who was she, after all? he wondered. This woman who was doing this to him. With her short red hair as thin as a child's and her four pairs of glasses and her legs that fell apart beneath him as if there were no bones in them. "Don't read the books," she had told him. "Promise not to read my books."

It was a quirk that he never admitted he had read them. He had read them all before he knew her and one weekend he read them all again. Not that he learned anything from them. Not that they had anything to do, really, with the hand that lay across his leg or face or hand. He was not sleeping well.

Anna walked through the Metropolitan Museum of Art and stood for a long time before the half-built replica of the Parthenon trying to find some solace in the cold wisdom of the Greeks. She had been crying and it was certain that before the day was over she would cry again. She examined the gods on the frieze, in their passions and their furies. The furies, she decided, I am being pursued by the furies for wishing his goddamn wife was dead. To hell with it. I'm going out and buy some clothes or read a book or get drunk. That's it. I'll get drunk and get thrown in jail and he'll have to come and bail me out.

She left the museum and walked down to her favorite bookstore, a place on Madison between 81st and 82nd. Her friends were behind the counter. "How's it going?" they said. "How's life treating you?"

"Get me some books," she answered. "I need all the books I can carry. I need some books like a victim of the plague." They loaded her up with books to read, thinking she was suffering from fame.

IV

Thirteen blocks away from where Anna was trudging home through the city carrying her books the married man removed the needle from the baby's aorta and closed the incision. He wiped the blood from the arm. He handed the sponge to his assistant. He took off the great microscopic glasses and laid them on a table and looked down at the small thing that had been an eight-month-old baby boy until a moment ago. He gave an order to the nurse and walked out to the sink and pulled the gown off and washed his arms and got into his shirt and tie and suit and changed shoes and went out into the waiting room to tell the family. He waited with his hands folded while the mother consoled the father and the grandmothers held each other and the brother pulled the magazines down off a table. It was seven-fifteen in the evening of a cold wet December day. She would be gone by the time he got there and besides, she had told him not to come to her apartment or call her on the phone.

"You did what you could," the father said. The father patted his arm. The father looked into his eyes. "I thank you for trying."

"We don't get to keep them all," he told the father. "No matter what we do. I wish it wasn't so." What difference does it make? he told himself. What the fuck difference does any of it make?

They ought to let the sick ones die at birth. Like the Swedes. Dip them in a bucket of cold water and the ones that lived got to live. To hell with it. He took the man's hand and removed it from his sleeve. "I have to be somewhere where someone needs me. I'm sorry I can't stay."

"It's all right," the mother said. "It's not your fault. There was nothing you could do." He made his escape before she began crying again. Walked out the side door and across the street and the parking attendant got out his car and he slid into the driver's seat and began driving aimlessly down Fifth Avenue, then around the park, then down Lexington, then up Madison to 72nd. He parked the car illegally before a brownstone and got out and walked to her building and went in and rang the bell. "Please see me."

"Come on up. I look like hell." She was right. She did look like hell. She had on a white sweatshirt and some warm-up pants and a pair of white socks and her hair was flying all over her head. "What are you doing?" he said.

"I'm writing. What's wrong with you?"

"Nothing."

"Yes there is. Tell me."

"It's nothing. Nothing anyone can do. I miss you. That's the main thing." She went over to the fireplace and began to wad up pages of newsprint and throw them into the catch. She threw in four or five wadded-up pages, then added a whole section, then put two logs on top of that. She struck a match and the mess miraculously caught and began to flame. "This wood's incredible," she said. "I think they pump lighter fluid into it. So," she turned back to where he was watching her. "Sit down. Why did you have to see me if nothing's wrong?"

"I lost a baby."

"That's nice."

"Have you had dinner?"

"No."

"Go out with me." She poked at the fire some more. It blazed higher. She left the room. In a minute music came on. "I'll order something from the deli," she said. "I don't want to get dressed. Fix a drink. I'll set the table. Go on, let's play house. We'll be married people. You'll come home from a hard day where the babies die and I'll be groping around in an old sweatshirt and what the hell, we'll make a fire and eat and make love and go to bed and sleep and get up ready to face the world again. What do you want? They have some pretty good lobster salad if you like it."

"Anything will do. That's fine." He went into the dining room and poured a glass of scotch and carried it back to the sofa. He sank back against her embroidered pillows. She went to him and sat on her knees on the floor. She ran her hands up his legs and lay her head on his lap. "I love you," she said. "If that matters."

"It matters."

"We'll eat," she said. "Then we can cry."

He spent the night. The next day was Sunday. They lay in bed all morning. They listened to the radio and made love and only cried once. They looked at each other and they were crying and they didn't talk about it. What good does it do to talk about crying?

"We could go for a walk," he said. "We could see if my car's been towed away."

"You've got a car?"

"I had one last night."

"Would you let me drive it? I haven't driven a car since I got to New York City. I need to drive a car." She was laughing now. "You don't have a tape deck, do you?"

"I think there's one. I've never used it."

"Oh, God, that would make my day. If I could drive around New York listening to music I'd get well. I keep thinking this goddamn depression isn't about you at all, it's about missing my car." She was making up the bed and talking. When she was happy she looked sixteen. Then, suddenly, she would look her age. This year, for the first time in her life she sometimes looked old. She would pass a mirror and see it and it made her curious, as if it were some stranger she was observing, something far away and foreign to herself. Now, chattering and pulling on a pale blue sweater, she seemed sixteen and not a day older. She tucked the bedspread in around the pillows. He went into the next room and called his wife.

Anna listened. She had forgotten he was married. She had broken the first and most important rule she lived by, to always know exactly where she was and what she was doing. It was the ground of her existence, the stand she made. As long as I know exactly what is going on and who I am, she told herself. As long as I don't lie to myself or to them. As long as I know. As long as the cards are on the table. As long as I call it by its name. Now, here, in this old apartment in this cold city on this dark cold December weekend, she had forgotten.

Adultery. Pandora's box. You open it and all the furies come flying out, jealousy, rage, pain and sorrow, all the shades and furies of the world. They flew out now, lit upon the dresser, laughed down at her from the sconces and the chandelier.

He came back into the room. "Let's walk in the park," he said. "I'd like so much to walk with you."

The car was there but she didn't want to drive it now. They went into the park which was filled with people in bright scarves and gloves. They walked for a while, then came to rest on a bench beside a statue of a Polish general on horseback.

"Will you leave her?" Anna said.

"I can't. What would she do?"

"Well, that's that then. Let's get some breakfast. I'm starving."

"I can't leave her."

"Don't talk about it anymore. I don't want to hear it. Shut up."

*   *   *

That was the absolutely last time. When she said good-bye that afternoon she meant it. Still, there were obligations to be met. It would be three more weeks before she could leave the city. She began to dream of home. She dreamed of her grandfather's farm, the long fields of milo and wheat. She dreamed Philip's wife was in the middle of a field of wheat. Crows were all around her on the ground. She was feeding the crows from her hand. She was so gentle, so real. At least I never saw her, Anna thought. At least I was spared that.

That afternoon she ran into them at the Metropolitan beside the Greek and Roman statues. They stopped beside a huge black marble statue of a hero. The woman was very thin, very pretty, with alabaster skin. A cashmere shawl around her shoulders. There were introductions. The Greek hero looked down at them, holding his arrows and his bow.

"Have lunch with us," the woman said. "Phil has told me so much about you. We've loved your books. Do have lunch."

"I can't today," she said. "I'm researching something. For an article."

"In antiquities? I used to know a bit about them. What are you writing?"

"Oh, nothing very interesting. Just research. I'm sorry I can't stay. It's good to meet you. I have to go now. Good-bye, Philip. It's nice to see you. I mean, thank you. I'm sorry I can't stay." She escaped and went out into the sunshine and began to walk as fast as she could with her hands stuffed down into the pockets of her coat. Fists of hands, she was thinking. A fist of a heart. Yes, they were right to think it is the heart. It knots up and beats against itself and takes your breath away. Breathe, walk, run, as fast as you can down this cobbled street.

Museums went by, people in thick coats and bright Yankee hats. Anna walked all the way to 120th Street. The knot began to slacken in her breast. She stopped on a corner where a man was roasting chestnuts. His blackened jacket and his blackened face belonged to another century. A crow lit upon a bench. The sun fell between the buildings. Fuck love, she said to herself. How dare he do this to me? How did I get into this? Where am I? What on earth am I doing? It's too goddamn much. I won't stay in this town another day. I'm going home. This time for good.

v

There is a way to organize this knowledge, Anna decided. To understand what happened. This love affair, this very last love affair. In a minute I will get out of this bed and begin to understand what happened. I will pick up the telephone and call Arthur and then I will begin to write the stories and they will tell me what is going on.

I will create characters and they will tell me my secrets. They will stand across the room from me with their own voices and dreams and disappointments. I will set them going like a fat gold watch, as Sylvia said. I am in my house on the mountain and I will call Daniel and Judith and Matthew and Will and Ginny and Jim. I will gather my tribe around me and celebrate my birthday. There will be champagne and a doberge cake from the bakery that Cajun runs on the highway. Yes, all that for later. For now, the work before me, waiting to be served and believed in and done. My work. How I define myself in the madness of the world.

Anna rose from the bed and turned off the electric blanket and picked up all her clothes and threw them on the closet floor and went upstairs and opened a brand-new box of 25-percent cotton bond and set it on a table by her typewriter. She pushed her hair out of her face and began to write.

SOME BLUE HILLS
AT SUNDOWN

IT WAS THE LAST TIME Rhoda would ever see Bob Rosen in her life. Perhaps she knew that the whole time she was driving to meet him, the long drive through the November fields, down the long narrow state of Kentucky, driving due west, then across the Ohio River and up into the flat-topped hills of Southern Illinois.

If it had been any other time in her life or any other boyfriend she would have been stopping every fifty miles to look at herself in the mirror or spray her wrists with perfume or smooth the wrinkles from her skirt. As it was she drove steadily up into the hills with the lengthening shadows all around her. She didn't glance at her watch, didn't worry about the time. He would be there when she got there, waiting at the old corrugated building where he worked on his car, the radio playing, his cat sitting on a shelf by the Tune Oil, watching. Nothing would have changed. Only she was two months older and he was two months older and there had been another operation. When he got home from the hospital he had called her and said, "Come on if you can. I'll be here the rest of the semester. Come if you want to. Just let me know."

So she had told her mother and father that if they didn't let her go she would kill herself and they believed her, so caught up in their terrible triangle and half-broken marriage and tears and lies and sadness that they couldn't fight with her that year. Her mother tried to stop it.

"Don't give her a car to go up there and see that college boy," her mother said. "Don't you dare do that, Dudley. I will leave you if you do."

So her father had loaned her the new Cadillac, six thousand dollars' worth of brand-new car, a fortune of a car in nineteen fifty-three, and she had driven up to Southern Illinois to see Bob Rosen and tell him that she loved him. No, just to see him and look at his face. No, to watch him work on his car. No, to smell the kind soft whiteness of his cheeks. To see him before he died. Untold madness of the dark hour. "Now by this moon, before this moon shall wane, I shall be dead or I shall be with you."

He was waiting for her. Not working on the car. Not even inside the building. Standing outside on the street, leaning against the building, smoking a cigarette and waiting. One foot on top of the other foot, his soft gray trousers loose around the ankles, his soft white skin, his tall lanky body fighting every minute for its life.

"Hello," he said. "I'm glad to see you. Let me see this god-damn car. Where did you get this car? My God, that's some car."

"He's getting rich. Just like he said he would. Who cares. I hate it there. There isn't anything to do. No one to talk to. I think about you all the time." He slid into the driver's seat and turned around and took her into his arms. It was the first time in two months that she had been happy. Now, suddenly, it seemed as if this moment would be enough to last forever, would make up for all the time that would follow.

"I ought to just turn around and go home now," she said. "I guess I just wanted to make sure you were real."

"It wouldn't be a good idea to get in the habit of loving me. I shouldn't have let you come up here."

"I asked to come."

"So you did. Well, look here. Let's go to the Sweetshop and get a sandwich and see who's there. I'll bet you haven't eaten all day."

"I don't want to eat anything." She pulled away. "I want to do it. You said you'd do it to me. You promised me. You swore you would."

"When did I do that?"

"You know."

"Rhoda, Rhoda, Rhoda. Jesus. Exactly where did you envision this deflowering taking place?"

"In the car, I guess. Or anywhere. Where do people go?"

"I don't go anywhere with sixteen-year-old girls. I'd go to jail, that's where I'd go. Come here." He pulled her across his legs and kissed her again, then turned around toward the steering wheel and turned on the ignition. "Talk while I drive. I'll take you out to the roadside park. It's completely dark out there. You can see a thousand stars. Remember that night Doc Stanford was here from Louisville and we played music out there? You were having that goddamn slumber party and I had to take all your goddamn friends to get you out of the house. My friends still haven't let me stop hearing about that. That cousin of yours from Mississippi was there. Do you remember that night?"

"You won't do it?"

"Hell, no, I won't do it. But I want to. If it gives you any satisfaction you'd better believe I want to." They were cruising very slowly down a dark street that led upward through a field of poplars. There was one streetlight at the very top of the deserted street. "I drive by your house every now and then. It seems like the whole street died when your family left. Everyone misses you. So your father's doing well?"

"They're getting a divorce. He's having an affair and my mother acts like she's crazy. That's why I got to come. They're too busy to care what I do. They sent Dudley off to a boys' school and next year I'm going to Virginia. I'll never get to come back here. If we don't do it tonight, we never will. That's what's going to happen, isn't it?"

"No, we are going to the Sweetshop and get a malt and a ham sandwich and see who's there. Then I'm going to take you over to the Buchanans' house where you're supposed to be before someone calls out the state cops. Did you call and tell them you're in town?"

"No, they don't even know I'm coming. No one knows but Augusta. And Jane Anne. She had to tell Jane Anne." He shook his head and pulled her very close to him. She was so close to him she could feel him breathe. I'm like a pet dog to him, she decided. I'm just some little kid he's nice to. He doesn't even listen to what I say. What does he want me here for? He doesn't need me for a thing. It was dark all around them now, the strange quiet weekend dark of small midwestern towns in the innocent years of the nineteen fifties. Rhoda shuddered. It was so exciting. So terrible and sad and exciting, so stifled and sad and terrible and real. This is really happening, she was thinking. This feeling, this loving him more than anything in the world and in a second it will be over. It ends as it happens and it will never be again in any way, never happen again or stop happening. It is so thick, so tight around me. I think this is what those old fairy tales meant. This is how those old stories always made me feel.

"I want you to know something," he said. He had stopped the car. "I want you to know that I would have made love to you if I had been well. If you had been older and I had been well and things had been different. You are a wonderful girl, Rhoda. A blessing I got handed that I can't ever figure out. DeLisle loves you. You know that? He asks me about you all the time. He says he can't figure out what I did to deserve you writing me letters all the time."

"I don't want to talk about DeLisle."

"I'm taking you to the Sweetshop now." He put the brake on the car and kissed her for a very long time underneath the streetlight. Their shadows were all around them and the wind moved the light and made the street alive with shadows and they held each other while the wind blew the light everywhere and her fingers found the scars on his neck and behind his ear and caressed them and there was nothing else to say or nothing else to do and they expanded and took in the sadness and shared it.

After a while he started the car and they went to the sweetshop and ate ham sandwiches and talked to people and then drove over to the Buchanans' house and he left her there and walked the six blocks home with his hands in his pockets. He was counting the months he might live. He thought it would be twenty-four but it turned out to be a lifetime after all.

THE
STARLIGHT EXPRESS

NORA JANE was seven months pregnant when Sandy disappeared again. *Dear Baby,* the note said. *I can't take it. Here's all the money that is left. Don't get mad if you can help it. I love you, Sandy.*

She folded up the note and put it in a drawer. Then she made up the bed. Then she went outside and walked along the water's edge. At least we are living on the water, she was thinking. I always get lucky about things like that. Well, I know one thing. I'm going to have these babies no matter what I have to do and I'm going to keep them alive. They won't die on me or get drunk or take cocaine. Freddy was right. A decent home is the best thing.

Nora Jane was on a beach fifty miles south of San Francisco, beside a little stucco house Sandy's old employer had been renting them for next to nothing. Nora Jane had never liked living in that house. Still, it was on the ocean.

The ocean spread out before her now, gray and dark, breaking against the boulders where it turned into a little cove. There were places where people had been making fires. Nora Jane began to pick up all the litter she could find and put it in a pile beside a fire site. She walked around for half an hour picking up cans and barrettes and half-burned pieces of cardboard and piled them up beside a boulder. Then she went back to the house and got some charcoal lighter and a match and lit the mess and watched it burn. It was the middle of October. December the fifteenth was only two months away. I could go to Freddy, she was thinking. He will always love me and forgive me anything. But what will it do to him? Do I have a right to get around him so he'll only love me more? This was a question Nora Jane was always asking herself about Freddy Harwood. Now she asked it once again.

A cold wind was blowing off the ocean. She picked up a piece of driftwood and added it to the fire. She sank down upon the sand. She was carrying ten pounds of babies but she moved as gracefully as ever. She wiggled around until her back was against the boulder, sitting up very straight, not giving in to the cold or the wind. I'm one of those people that could go to the Himalayas, she decided. Because I never give in to cold. If you hunch over it will get you.

Freddy Harwood stood on the porch of his half-finished house, deep in the woods outside of Willits, California, and thought about Nora Jane. He was thinking about her voice, trying to remember how it sounded when she said his name. If I could remember that sound, he decided. If I could remember what she said that first night it would be enough. If that's all I get it will have to do.

He looked deep into the woods, past the madrone tree, where once he had seen a bobcat come walking out and stop at the place where the trees ended and the grass began. A huge yellow cat with a muff around its neck and brilliant eyes. A poet had been visiting and they had made up a song about the afternoon called "The Great Bobcat Visit and Other Mysteries of Willits." If she was here I could teach it to her, Freddy thought. So, there I go again. Everything either reminds me of her or it doesn't remind me of her, so everything reminds me of her. What good does it do to have six million dollars and two houses and a bookstore if I'm in love with Nora Jane? Freddy left his bobcat lookout and walked around the side of the house toward the road. A man was hurrying up the path.

It was his neighbor, Sam Lyons, who lived a few miles away up an impassable road. Freddy waved and went to meet him. He's coming to tell me she's dead, he decided. She died in childbirth in the hands of a midwife in Chinatown and I'm supposed to go on living after that. "What's happening?" he called out. "What's going on?"

"You got a call," Sam said. "Your girlfriend's coming on the train. I'm getting tired of this, Harwood. You get yourself a phone. That's twice this week. *Two calls in one week!*"

In a small neat room near the Berkeley campus a young Chinese geneticist named Lin Tan Sing packed a change of clothes and his toilet articles, left a note for himself about some things to do when he returned, and walked out into the beautiful fall day. He had been saving his money for a vacation and today was the day it began. As soon as he finished work that afternoon he would ride the subway to the train station and get on board the Starlight Express and travel all the way up the California coast to Puget Sound. He would see the world. My eyes have gone too far inside, Lin Tan told himself. Now I will go outside and see what's happening at other end. People will look at me and I will look at them. We will learn about each other. Perhaps the train will fall off cliff into the ocean. There will be stories in the newspapers. Young Chinese scientist saves many lives in daring rescues. President of United States invites young Chinese scientist to live in White House and tutor children of politicians. Young Chinese scientist adopted by wealthy man whose life he saves in train wreck. I am only a humble scientist trying to unravel genetic code, young Chinese scientist tells reporters. Did not mean to be hero.

Do not know what came over me. I pushed on fallen car and great strength came to me when it was least expected.

Lin Tan entered the Berkeley campus and strolled along a sidewalk leading to the student union. Students were all around. A man in black was playing a piano beneath a tree. The sky was clear with only a few clouds to the west. The Starlight Express, Lin Tan was thinking. All Plexiglas across the top. Stars rolling by while I am inside with something nice to drink. Who knows? Perhaps I will find a girl on the train who wishes to talk with me. I will tell her all things scientific and also of poetry. I will tell her the poetry of my country and also of England. Lin Tan folded his hands before him as he walked, already he was on the train, speeding up the California coast telling some dazzling blonde the story of his life and all about his work. Lin Tan worked at night in the lab of the Berkeley Women's Clinic. He did chemical analyses on the fluid removed during amniocentesis. So far he had made only one mistake in his work. One time a test had to be repeated because he knocked a petri dish off the table with his sleeve. Except for that his results had proved correct in every single instance. No one else in the lab had such a record. Because of this Lin Tan always kept his head politely bowed in the halls and was extra-nice to the other technicians and generous with advice and help. He had a fellowship in the graduate program in biology and he had this easy part-time job and his sister, Jade Tan Sing, was coming in six months to join him. Only one thing was lacking in Lin Tan's life and that was a girlfriend. He had what he considered a flaw in his character and wished to be in love with a Western girl with blond hair. It was only fate, the *I Ching* assured him. A fateful flaw that would cause disaster and ruin but not of his own doing and therefore nothing to worry about.

On this train, he was thinking, I will sit up straight and hold my head high. If she asks where I come from I will say Shanghai or Hong Kong as it is difficult for them to picture village life in

China without thinking of rice paddies. I am a businessman, I will say, and have only taken time off to learn science. No, I will say only the truth so she may gaze into my eyes and be at peace. I will buy you jewels and perfume, I will tell her. Robes with silken dragons eating the moon, many pearls. Shoes with flowers embroidered on them for every minute of the day. Look out the Plexiglas ceiling at the stars. They are whirling by and so are we even when we are off the train.

Nora Jane bought her ticket and went outside to get some air while she waited for the train. She was wearing a long gray sweat-shirt with a black leather belt riding on top of the twins. On her legs were bright yellow tights and yellow ballet shoes. A yellow and white scarf was tied around her black curls. She looked just about as wonderful as someone carrying ten pounds of babies could ever look in the world. She was deserted and unwed and on her way to find a man whose heart she had broken only four months before and she should have been in a terrible mood but she couldn't work up much enthusiasm for despair. Whatever chemicals Tammili and Lydia were pumping into her bloodstream were working nicely to keep Nora Jane in a good mood. She stood outside the train station watching a line of cirrus clouds chug-ging along the horizon, thinking about the outfits she would buy for her babies as soon as they were born. Nora Jane loved clothes. She couldn't wait until she had three people to dress instead of only one. All her life she had wanted to be able to wear all her favorite colors at one time. Now she would have her chance. She could just see herself walking into a drugstore holding her little girls by the hand. Tammili would be wearing blue. Lydia would be wearing red or pink. Nora Jane would have on peach or mauve or her old standby, yellow. Unless that was too many primaries on one day. I'll start singing, she decided. That way I can work at night while they're asleep. I have to have some money of my own. I don't want anyone supporting us. When I go shopping and buy stuff I don't want anybody saying why did you get this stuff and you didn't need that shirt and so forth. As soon as they're born I'll be able to work and make some money. Nieman said I could sing anyplace in San Francisco. Nieman should know. After all, he writes for the newspaper. If they don't like it then I'll just get a job in a day-care center like I meant to last fall. I'll do whatever I have to do.

A whistle blew. Nora Jane walked back down the concrete stairs. "Starlight Express," a black voice was calling out. "Get on board for the long haul to Washington State. Don't go if you're scared of stars. Stars all the way to Marin, San Rafael, Petaluma, and Sebastopol. Stars all the way to Portland, Oregon, and Seattle, Washington. Stars to Alaska and points north. Stars to the North Pole. Get on board this train. . . ."

Nora Jane threw her backpack over her shoulder and ran for the train. Lin Tan caught a glimpse of her yellow stockings and reminded himself not to completely rule out black hair in his search for happiness.

Freddy Harwood was straightening up his house. He moved the wooden table holding his jigsaw puzzle of the suspended whale from the Museum of Natural History. He watered his paper-white narcissus. He got a broom out of a closet and began to sweep the floor. He found a column Nieman did about *My Dinner with André* and leaned on the broom reading it. It was two o'clock in the afternoon and there was no reason to leave for the station before five. They aren't my babies, he reminded himself. She's having someone else's babies and they aren't mine and I don't want them anyway. Why do I want her at all? Because I like to talk to her, that's why. I like to talk to her more than anyone in the world. That's that. It's my business. Mine and only mine. I like to look at her and I like to talk to her. Jesus Christ! Could I have a maid? I mean would it violate every tenet if I had a maid once a week?

He threw the broom into a closet and pulled on his boots and walked out into the yard to look for the bobcat.

The house Freddy was stamping out of was a structure he had been building on and off for years. It was in Mendocino County near the town of Willits and could only be reached by a long winding uphill road that became impassable when it rained. Actually, it was impassable when it didn't rain but Freddy and his lone neighbor put their four-wheel jeeps in gear and pretended the rock-covered path was a road. Sometimes it even looked like a road, from the right angle and if several trips had been made in a single spell of dry weather.

The house sat on high ground and had several amazing views. To the west lay the coastal ranges of northern California. To the east the state game refuge of the Mendocino National Forest. In any direction were spruce trees and Douglas fir and Northern pine. Freddy had bought the place with the first money he ever earned. That was years ago, during the time when he stopped speaking to his family and smoked dope all day and worked as a chimney sweep. He had lived in a van and saved twelve thousand dollars. Then he had driven up the California coast until he found Douglas fir on land with no roads leading to it. He bought as much as twelve thousand dollars would buy. Two acres, almost three. Then he set up a tent and started building. He built a cistern to catch water and laid pipes to carry it to where the kitchen would later be. He leveled the land and poured a concrete foundation and marked off rooms and hauled stones for a fireplace. He planted fruit trees and a vineyard and put in root plants and an herb garden for medical emergencies. He had been working on the house off and on for twenty-three years. The house was as much a part of Freddy Harwood as his skin. When he was away from Willits for long stretches of time, he thought about the house every day, the red sun of early morning and the redder sun of sundown. The eyes of the bobcat in the woods, the endless lines of mountains in the distance. The taste of the air and the taste of the water. His body sleeping in peace in his own invention.

Now she's ruined my house for me, he was thinking, leaning against the madrone tree while he waited for the bobcat. She's slept in all the rooms and sat on the chairs and touched the furniture. She's used all the forks and spoons and moved the table. I'm putting it back where it goes today. Well, let her come up here and beg for mercy. I don't care. I'll give it to her. Let her cry her dumb little Roman Catholic heart out. I guess she looks like hell. I bet she's as big as a house. Well, shit, not that again.

He turned toward the house. A redbird was throwing itself against the windows. Bird in the house means bad luck. Well, don't let it get in. I'll have to put some screens on those windows. Ruin the light.

The house was very tall with many windows. It was a house a child might draw, tall and thin. Inside were six rooms, or areas, filled with books and mattresses and lamps and tables. Everything was white or black or brown or gray. Freddy had made all the furniture himself except for two chairs by Mies van der Rohe. A closet held all of Buiji Dalton's pottery in case she should come to visit. A shelf held Nieman's books. On a peg behind the bathroom door was Nora Jane's yellow silk kimono.

When she comes, Freddy was saying to himself as he trudged back up the hill to do something about the bird, I won't say a word about anything. I'll just act like everything is normal. Sam came over and said you'd be on the train and it was getting into Fort Bragg at eight and would I meet you. Well, great. I mean, what brought you here? I thought you and the robber baron had settled down for the duration. I mean, I thought I'd never see you again. I mean, it's okay with me. It's not your fault I am an extremely passionate and uncontrollably sensitive personality. I can tell you one thing. It's not easy being this sensitive. Oh, shit, he concluded. I'll just go on and get drunk. I'm a match for her when I'm drunk. Drunk, I'm a match for anyone, even Nora Jane.

He opened the closet and reached in behind one of Buiji Dalton's hand-painted Egyptian funeral urns and took out a bottle of Red Aubruch his brother had sent from somewhere. He found a corkscrew and opened it. He passed the cork before his nose, then lifted the bottle and began to drink. "There ain't no little bottle," he was thinking. "Like that old bottle of mine."

At about the same time that Freddy Harwood was resorting to this time-honored method of acquiring courage, Lin Tan Sing was using a similar approach aboard the Starlight Express. He was drinking gin and trying not to stare at the yellow stockings which were all he could see of Nora Jane. She was in a high-backed swivel chair turned around to look out the glassed-in back of the train. She was thinking about whales, how they had their babies in the water, and also about Sandra Draine, who had a baby in a tub of saltwater in Sausalito while her husband videotaped the birth. They had shown the tape at the gallery when Sandra had her fall show. It won't be like that for me, Nora Jane was thinking. I'm not letting anyone take any pictures or even come in the room except the doctor and maybe Freddy, but no cameras. I know he'll want to bring a camera, if he's there. He's the silliest man I have ever known.

But I love him anyway. And I hate to do this to him but I have to do what I have to do. I can't be alone now. I have to go somewhere. The train rounded a curve. The wheels screeched. Nora Jane's chair swiveled around. Her feet flew out and she hit Lin Tan in the knee with a ballet shoe.

"Oh, my God," she said. "Did I hurt you?"

"It is nothing."

"We hit a curve. I'm really sorry. I thought the chair was fastened down."

"You are going to have a baby?" His face was very close to her face. It was the largest oriental face Nora Jane had ever seen.

The darkest eyes. She had not known there were eyes that dark in all the world, even in China. She lowered her own.

"Yes," she said. "I am."

"I am geneticist. This interests me very much."

"It does me too."

"Would you like to talk with me?"

"Sure. I'd like to have someone to talk to. I was just thinking about the whales. I guess they don't even know it's cold, do they?"

"I have gone out in kayak to be near them. It is very mysterious. It was the best experience I have had in California. A friend of mine in lab at Berkeley Women's Clinic took me with him. He heads a team of volunteers to collect money for whales. Next summer I will go again."

"Oh, my God. That's where I go. I mean, that's my doctor. I'm going to have twin baby girls. I had an amnio at your clinic. That's how I know what they are."

"Oh, this is very strange. You are Miss Whittington of 1512 Arch Street, is it not so? Oh, this is very strange meeting. I am head technician at this lab. Head technician for night lab. Yes. I am the one who did the test for you. I was very excited to have these twin girls show up. It was an important day for me. I had just been given great honor at the university. Oh, this is chance meeting like in books." He stood up and took her hand. "I am Lin Tan Sing, of the province of Suchow, near Beijing, in Central China. I am honored to make your acquaintance." He stood above her, waiting.

"I am Nora Jane Whittington, of New Orleans, Louisiana, and San Jose, California. And Berkeley. I am glad to meet you also. What all did the tests show? What did they look like under the microscope? Do you remember anything else about it?"

"Oh, it is not in lab that I learn things of substance. Only chip away at physical world in lab. Very humble. Because it was a memorable day in my own life I took great liberty and cast *I*

Ching for your daughters. I saw great honors for them and gifts of music brought to the world."

"Oh, my God," Nora Jane said. She leaned toward him. "I can't believe I met you on this train." Snowy mountains, Lin Tan was thinking. Peony and butterfly. Redbird in the shade of willows.

Later a waiter came through the club car and Lin Tan advised Nora Jane to have an egg salad sandwich and a carton of milk. "I am surprised they allow you to travel so far along in your pregnancy. Are you going far?"

"Oh, no one said I could go. I mean, I didn't ask anyone. They said I could travel until two months before they came." She put her hand to her mouth. "I guess I should have asked someone. But I was real upset about something and I needed to come up here. I need to see this friend of mine."

"Be sure and get plenty of rest tonight. Very heavy burden for small body."

"My body's not so small. I have big bones. See my wrists." She held out her wrists and he pretended to be amazed at their size. "All the same, be sure and rest tomorrow. Don't take chances. Many very small babies at clinic now. I am worrying very much about so many months in machine for tiny babies. Still, it is United States and they will not allow anything to die. It is the modern age."

"I want my babies no matter what size they are." She folded her hands across her lap. "I guess I shouldn't have come up here. Well, it's too late now. Anyway, where did you learn to speak English so well? Did you have it in school?"

"I studied your writers. I studied Ernest Hemingway and William Faulkner and John Dos Passos. Also, many American poets. Then, since I am here, I am learning all the time with my ears."

"I like poetry a lot. I'm crazy about it to tell the truth."

"I am going to translate poetry of women in my country for

women of America. I have noticed there is much sadness and menustation in poetry of women here. But is not sadness in life here. In my country poetry is to overcome sadness, help people to understand how things are and see beauty and order and not give in to despair."

"Oh, like what? Tell me some."

"Here is poem by famous poet of the T'ang Dynasty. The golden age of Chinese poetry.

"A branch is torn from the tree
The tree does not grieve
And goes on growing"

"Oh, that's wonderful."

"This poet is called the White Poppy. She has been dead for hundreds of years but her poems will always live. This is how it is with the making of beautiful things, don't you find it so?"

"Whenever I think of being on this train I'll remember you telling me that poem." She was embarrassed and lowered her eyes to be talking of such important things with a stranger.

"A poem is very light." Lin Tan laughed, to save the moment. "Not like babies. Easy to transport or carry." Nora Jane laughed with him. The train sped through the night. The whales gave birth in the water. The stars stayed on course. The waiter appeared with the tray and they began to eat their sandwiches.

Freddy was waiting on the platform when the train arrived at the Noyo–Point Cabrillo Station. He was wearing his old green stadium coat and carrying a blanket. Nora Jane stepped down from the train and kissed him on the cheek. Lin Tan pressed his face against the window and smiled and waved. Nora Jane waved back. "That's my new friend," she said. "He gave me his address in Berkeley. He's a scientist. Get this. He did the amnio on Lydia and Tammili. Can you believe it? Can anybody believe the stuff that happens?"

Freddy wrapped the blanket around her shoulders. "I thought you might like to see a movie before we go back. *The Night of the Shooting Stars* is playing at the Courthouse in Willits."

"He ran off and left me," she said. "I knew he would. I don't think I even care."

"You met the guy on the train that did the amnio? I don't believe it."

"He knew my name. I almost fainted when he said it."

"Look, we don't have to go to a movie unless you feel like it. I just noticed it was playing. It's got a pregnant woman in it."

"I've seen it three times. We went last year, don't you remember? But I'll go again if you want to."

"We could eat instead. Have you eaten anything?"

"I had a sandwich on the train. I guess we better go on to the house. I'm supposed to take it easy. I don't have any luggage. I just brought this duffel bag. I was too mad to pack."

"We'll get something to eat." He took her arm and pulled her close to him. Her skin beneath her sleeve was the same as the last time he had touched her. They began to move in the direction of the car. "I love the way you smell," she said. "You always smell just like you are. Listen, Freddy, I don't know exactly what I'm doing right now. I'm just doing the best I can and playing it by ear. But I'm okay. I really am okay. Do you believe everything that's happened?"

"You want to buy anything? Is there anything you need? You want to see a doctor or anything like that?"

"No, let's just go up to the house. I've been thinking about the house a lot. About the windows. Did you get the rest of them put in?"

"Yeah, and now the goddamn birds are going crazy crashing into them. Five dead birds this week. They fight their reflections. How's that for a metaphor." He helped her into the car. "Wear your seat belt, okay? So, what's going on inside there?"

"They just move around all the time. If I need to I can sell the car. I don't want anybody supporting us, even you. I'm really doing great. I don't know all the details yet but I'm figuring things out." He started the motor and began to drive. She reached over and touched his knee. They drove through the town of Fort Bragg and turned onto the road to Willits. Nora Jane moved her hand and fell asleep curled up on the seat. She didn't wake again until they were past Willits and had started up the long hill leading to the gravel road that led to the broken path to Freddy's house. "He said they were going to give great gifts to the world, gifts of music," she said when she woke. "I think it means they won't be afraid to sing in public. I want to call Li Suyin and talk to her about it. I forgot you didn't have a phone. I need to call and tell her where I am. If she calls San Jose she'll start worrying about me."

"You can call tomorrow. Look, how about putting your hand back on my leg. That way I'll believe you're here." He looked at her. "I want to believe you're here."

"You're crazy to even talk to me."

"No, I'm not. I'm the sane one, remember, the control in the modern world experiment." She was laughing now so he could afford to look at her as hard as he liked. She looked okay. Tired and not much color in her face, but okay. Perfect as always from Freddy Harwood's point of view.

II

"I want to take them on the grand tour as soon as they're old enough," Freddy was saying. They were lying on a futon on top of a mattress in the smallest of the upstairs rooms. "My grandmother took me when I was twelve. She took my cousin, Sally, and hired a gigolo to dance with her in Vienna. I had this navy blue raincoat with a zip-in lining. God, I wish I still had that coat." Nora Jane snuggled down beside him, smelling his chest. It smelled like a wild animal. There were many things about Freddy Harwood that excited her almost as much as love. She patted him on the arm. "So, anyway," he continued. "I have this uncle in New Orleans and he's married two women with three children. He's raised six children that didn't belong to him and he's getting along all right. He says at least his subconscious isn't involved. There's a lot to be said for that. . . . What I'm saying is, I haven't lived in Berkeley all my life to give in to some kind of old worn-out masculine pride. Not with all the books I've read."

"All I've ever done is make you sad. I always end up doing something mean to you."

"Maybe I like it. Anyway, you're here and that's how it is. But we ought to go back to town in a few days. You can stay with me there, can't you?" He pulled her closer, as close as he dared. She was so soft. The babies only made her softer. "I ought to call Stuart and tell him you're here."

"He's a heart doctor. He doesn't know anything about babies."

"Wait a minute. One of them did something. Oh, shit, did you feel that?"

"I know. They're in there. Sometimes I forget it but not very often. Tell me some more about when you went to Europe. Tell me everything you can remember, just the way it happened. Like what you had to eat and what everyone was wearing."

"Okay. Sally had a navy blue skirt and a jacket and she had some white blouses and in Paris we got some scarves. She had this scarf with the Visigoth crowns on it and she had it tied in a loop so a whole crown showed. She fixed it all the time she wore it. She couldn't leave it alone. Then they went somewhere and got some dresses made out of velvet but they only wore them at night."

"What did you wear?" She had a vision of him alone in a hotel room putting on his clothes when he was twelve. "I bet you were a wonderful-looking boy. I bet you were the smartest boy in Europe."

"We met Jung. We talked to him. So, what else did you talk about to this Chinese research biologist?"

"A genetic research biologist. He's still studying it. He has to finish school before he can do his real work. He wants to do things to DNA and find out how much we remember. He thinks we remember everything that ever happened to anyone from the beginning of time because there wouldn't be any reason to forget it, and if you can make computer chips so small, then the brain is much larger than that. We talked all the way from Sausalito. His father was a painter. When his sister gets here they might move to Sweden. He believes in the global village."

"He says they're musicians, huh?"

"Well, it wasn't that simple. It was very complicated. He had the biggest face of any oriental I've met. I just love him. I'm going to talk to him a lot more when we both get back to San Francisco." Her voice was getting softer, blurring the words.

"Go to sleep," Freddy said. "Don't talk anymore." He felt a baby move, then move again. They were moving quite a bit.

"I'm cold," she said. "Also, he said the birth process was the worst thing we ever go through in our life. He told me about this boy in England that's a genius, his parents are both doctors and they let him stay in the womb for eighteen months for an experiment and he can remember being born and tells about it. He said it was like someone tore a hole in the universe and jerked you out. Get closer, will you. God, I'm tired."

"We ought to go downstairs and sleep in front of the fire. I'm going to make a bed down there and come get you."

Freddy went downstairs and pulled a mattress up before the fireplace and built up the fire and brought two futons in and laid them on top of the mattress and added a stack of wool blankets and some pillows. When he had everything arranged, he went back upstairs and carried her down and tucked her in. Then he rubbed her back and told her stories about Vienna and wondered what time it was. I am an hour from town, he told himself, and Sam is twenty minutes away and probably drunk besides. It's at least three o'clock in the morning and the water's half frozen in the cistern and I let her come up here because I was too goddamn selfish to think of a way to stop it. So, tomorrow we go to town.

"Freddy?"

"Yes."

"I had a dream a moment ago . . . a dream of a meadow. All full of light and this dark tree. I had to go around it."

"Go to sleep, honey. Please go to sleep."

When she fell asleep he got up and sat on the hearth. We are here as on a darkling plain, he thought. We forget who we are. Branching plants, at the mercy of water. But tough. Tough and violent, some of us anyway. Oh, shit, if anything happened to her I couldn't live. Well, I've got to get some air. This day is one too many.

He pulled on a long black cashmere coat that had belonged to his father and went outside and took a sack of dogfood out of the car and walked down into the hollow to feed the bobcat. He spread part of the food on the ground and left the open sack beside it. "I know you're in there," he said out loud. "Well, here's some food. Come and get it. Nora Jane's here. I guess you know that by now. Don't kill anything until she leaves." He listened. The only sound was the wind in the trees. It was very cold. The stars were very clear. There was a rustle, about forty yards away. Then nothing. "Good night then," Freddy said. "I guess this dog food was grown in Iowa. The global village. Well, why not." He started back up the hill, thinking the bobcat might jump on him at any moment. It took his mind off Nora Jane for almost thirty seconds.

At that moment the Starlight Express came to a stop in Seattle, Washington, and Lin Tan climbed down from the train and started off in search of adventure. Before the week was over he would fall in love with the daughter of a poet. His life would be shadowed for five years by the events of the next few hours but he

didn't know that yet. He was in a wonderful mood. All his philosophical and mystical beliefs were coming together like ducks on
a pond. To make him believe in his work, fate had put him on
a train with a girl whose amnio he had done only a few months
before. Twin baby girls with AB positive blood, the luckiest of all
blood. Not many scientists have also great feeling for mystical
properties of life, he decided, and see genetic structure when they
gaze at stars. I am very lucky my father taught me to love beauty.
Moss on Pond, Light on Water, Smoke Rising Beneath the Wheels
of Locomotive. Yes, Lin Tan concluded, I am a fortunate man in
a universe that really knows what it is doing.

Freddy let himself back into the house. He built up the fire, covered Nora Jane and lay down beside her to try to sleep. This is
not paranoia, he told himself. I am hyper-aware, which is a different thing. If it weren't for people like me the race would have
disappeared years ago. Who tends the lines at night? Who watches
for the big cats with their night vision? Who stays outside the
circle and guards the tribe?

He snuggled closer, smelling her hair. "What is divinity if it
can come only in silent shadows and in dreams?" Barukh atah
Adonai eloheinu, melekh ha-olam. Praised be thou, Lord our God,
King of the Universe, who has brought forth bread from the
earth. Nora Jane, me. Jesus Christ!

It was five-thirty when she woke him. "I'm wet," she said. "I think
my water broke. I guess that's it. You'd better go and get someone."

"Oh, no, you didn't do this to me." He was bolt upright,
pulling on his boots. "You're joking. There isn't even a phone."

"Go use one somewhere. Freddy, this is serious. I'm in a lot
of pain, I think. I can't tell. Please go on. Go right now."

"Nora Jane. This isn't happening to me." He was pulling on
his boots.

"Go on. It'll be okay. This Chinese guy said they were going to be great so they can't die. But hurry up. How far is it to Sam's?"

"Twenty minutes. Oh, shit. Okay, I'm going. Don't do anything until I get back. If you have to go to the bathroom, do it right there." He leaned fiercely down over her. His hands were on her shoulders. "I'll be right back here. Don't move until I come." He ran from the house, jumped into his car, and began driving down the rocky drive. It was impossible to do more than five miles an hour over the rocks. The whole thing was impossible. The sun was lighting up the sky behind the mountains. The sky was silver. Brilliant clouds covered the western sky. Freddy came to the gate he shared with the other people on the mountain and drove right through it, leaving it torn off the post. He drove as fast as he dared down the rocky incline and turned onto gravel and saw the smoke coming from the chimney of Sam Lyons's house.

Nora Jane was in great pain. "I'm your mother," she was pleading. "Don't hurt me. I wouldn't hurt you. Please don't do it. Don't come now. Just wait awhile, go back to sleep. Oh, God. Oh, Jesus Christ. It's too cold. I'm freezing. I have to stop this. Pray for us sinners." The bed filled with water. She looked down. It wasn't water. It was blood. So much blood. What's going on? she thought. Why is this happening to me? I don't want it. Holy Mary, Mother of God, pray for us sinners now and at the hour of our death, Amen. Hail Mary, Mother of God, blessed art thou among women and blessed is the fruit of your womb, Jesus. Oh, Christ, oh, shit, oh, goddammit all to hell. I don't know what's so cold. I don't know what I'm going to do. Someone should be here. I want to see somebody.

The blood continued to pour out upon the bed.

✳   ✳   ✳

Sam came to the door. "A woman's up there having babies," Freddy said. "Get on the phone and call an ambulance and the nearest helicopter service. Try Ukiah but call the hospital in Willits first. Do it now. Sam, a woman's in my house having babies. Please." Sam turned and ran back through the house to the phone. Freddy followed him. "I'm going back. Get everyone you can get. Then come and help me. Make sure they understand the way. Or wait here for them if they don't seem to understand. Be very specific about the way. Then come. No, wait here for them. Get Selby and tell him to come to my house. I'm leaving." He ran back out the door and got back into his car and turned it around and started driving. His hands burned into the wheel. He had never known anything in his life like this. Worse than the earthquake that ruined the store. He was alone with this. "No," he said out loud as he drove. "I couldn't love them enough to let them call me on the phone. No, I had to have this goddamn fucking house a million miles from nowhere. She'll die. I know it. I have known it from the first moment I set eyes on her. Every time I ever touched her I knew she would die and leave me. Now it's coming true." The car hit a boulder. The wheel was wrenched from his hand but he straightened it with another wrench and went on driving. The sky was lighter now. The clouds were blowing away. He parked the car a hundred yards from the house and got out and started running.

Lydia came out into the space between Nora Jane's legs. Nora Jane reached for the child and held her, struggling to remember what you did with the cord. Then Freddy was there and took the baby from her and bit the cord in two and tied it and wrapped the baby in his coat and handed it to her. Tammili's head moved down into the space where Lydia's had been. Nora Jane screamed a long scream that filled all the spaces of the house and then Nora Jane didn't care anymore. Tammili's body moved out into

Freddy's hands and he wrapped her in a pillowcase and laid her beside her sister, picking up one and then the other, then turning to Nora Jane. Blood was everywhere and more was coming. There was nothing to do, and there was too much to do. There wasn't any way to hold them and help her too. "It's all right," she said. "Wipe them off. I don't want blood all over them. You can't do anything for me."

"I want you to drink something." He ran into the kitchen and pulled open the refrigerator door. He found a bottle of Coke and a bottle of red wine and held them in his hands trying to decide. He took the wine and went back to where she lay. "Drink this. I want you to drink this. You're bleeding, honey. You have to drink something. They'll be here in a minute. It won't be a minute from now."

She shook her head. "I'm going to die, Freddy. It's all right. It looks real good. You wouldn't believe how it looks. Get them some good-looking clothes ... get them a red raincoat with a hood. And yellow. Get them a lot of yellow." He pulled her body into his. She felt as if she weighed a thousand pounds. Then nothing. Nothing, nothing, nothing. "Wake up," he screamed. "Wake up. Don't die on me. Don't you dare die on me." Still, there was nothing. He turned to the babies. He must take care of them. No, he must revive Nora Jane. He laid his head down beside hers. She was breathing. He picked up the bottle of wine and drank from it. He turned to the baby girls. He picked them up, one at a time, then one in each arm. Then he began to count. One, two, three, four, five, six, seven, eight. He laid Lydia down beside Nora Jane, and, holding Tammili, he began to throw logs on the fire. He went into the kitchen and lit the stove and put water on to boil. He dipped a kitchen towel in cold water, then threw that away and took a bottle of cooking oil and soaked a rag in it and carried Tammili back to the fire and began to wipe the blood and mucous from the child's hair. Then he put Tammili down and picked up Lydia and cleaned her for a while. They were both crying, very small yelps like no sound he had ever heard. Nora Jane lay on the floor covered with a red wool blanket soaked in blood and Freddy kept on counting. Seven hundred and seventeen. Seven hundred and eighteen. Seven hundred and nineteen. He found more towels and made a nest for the babies in the chair and knelt beside them, patting and stirring them with his hands until he heard the cars drive up and the helicopter blades descending to the cleared place beside the cistern. Barukh atah Adonai eloheinu, melekh ha-olam, he was saying. Praised be thou, Lord our God, King of the Universe, who has brought forth bread from the earth. Praised be thou, inventor of helicopters, miner of steel, king of applied science. Oh, shit, thank God, they're here.

When Nora Jane came to, the helicopter pilot was on top of her, Freddy was doing something with her arms, and people were moving around the room. A man in a leather jacket was holding the twins. "They're going to freeze," she said. "I want to see them. I think I died. I died, didn't I?" The pilot moved away. Freddy propped her body up with his own and Sam tucked a blanket around her legs. "The ambulance is coming," he said. "It's okay. Everyone's okay."

"I died and it was light, like walking through a field of light. A fog made out of light. Do you think it's really like that or only shock?"

"Oh, honey," Freddy crooned into her hair. "It was the end of light. Listen, they're so cute. Wait till you see them. They're like little kittens or mice, like baby mice. They have black hair. Listen, they imprinted on my black cashmere coat. God knows what will happen now."

"I want to see them if nobody minds too much," she said. The man in the leather jacket brought them to her. She tried to reach out for them but her arms were too tired to move. "You just be still," the pilot said. "I'm Doctor Windom from the Sausalito Air Emergency Service. We were in the neighborhood. I'm sorry it took so long. We had to make three passes to find the clearing. Well, a ground crew is coming up the hill. We'll take you out in a ground vehicle. Just hold on. Everything's okay."

"I'm holding on. Freddy?"

"Yes."

"Are we safe?"

"For now." He knelt beside her and buried his face in her shoulder. He began to tremble. "Don't do that," she whispered. "Not in front of people. It's okay."

Lydia began to cry. It was the first really loud cry either of the babies had uttered. Tammili was terrified by the sound and began to cry even louder than her sister. Help, help, help, she cried. This is me. Give me something. Do something, say something, make something happen. This is me, Tammili Louise Whittington, laying my first guilt trip on my people.

LIGHT CAN BE BOTH WAVE AND PARTICLE

Lin Tan Sing was standing on the bridge overlooking Puget Sound, watching the sea gulls (white against the blue sky) caught in the high conflicting winds. He was trying to empty his mind, even of pleasant memories like his talk with Miss Whittington on the train.

Just Lin Tan, he was thinking. Just sunrise, just sea. Sometimes I go about in pity for myself, and all the while, a great wind is bearing me across the sky. He sighed. Lin Tan was very wise for his age. It was a burden he must bear and he was always thinking of ways to keep it from showing, so that other people would not seem small or slow-witted by comparison. All men have burdens, he decided. Only mine is greater burden. I am like great tanker making waves in harbor, about to swamp somebody. This is bad thinking for early morning. I am on vacation now, must enjoy myself. He sighed again. The sun was moving up above the smokestacks on the horizon. The first day of his vacation was ending and the second was about to begin.

A girl stepped out onto the bridge and stood very still with her hands in the pockets of her raincoat. She was looking at him.

Just beautiful girl, Lin Tan thought. Just karma. Twin fetuses inside Miss Whittington and now this girl comes like a goddess from the sea.

"Are you lost?" he said. "Have you lost your way?"

"No," she answered. "I just wanted to see the place where my cousin committed suicide. Isn't that morbid?"

"Curiosity is normal mode of being," he said. "I am Lin Tan Sing of San Francisco, California, and China. I am candidate for doctor of medicine at University of California in San Francisco. Third-year student. I am honored to make your acquaintance on lucky second day of my vacation."

"I'm Margaret McElvoy of Fayetteville, Arkansas. Look down there." She leaned far out over the rail. "My God, how could anybody jump into that."

"Water is not responsible for man's unhappiness."

"Well, I guess you're right about that. My father says religion is."

"What!"

"Oh, nothing. I didn't mean to say that." She straightened her shoulders, leaned down and looked again into the deep salty bay. Now the sun threw lines of brilliant dusty rose across the water. On a pillar of the middle span someone had written "Pussy" with a can of spray paint. Margaret giggled.

"Please continue," Lin Tan said. He thought she was thinking of the dark ridiculous shadows of religion.

"Oh, it's nothing. My father thinks he can find out what got us in all this trouble. He thinks we're in trouble." She turned and really looked at him, took him in. He was tall for an oriental, almost as tall as her brothers, and he was very handsome with strong shoulders and a wide strong face. His eyes were wise, dark and still, and Margaret completely forgot she wasn't supposed to talk to strangers. Something funny might be going on, she thought, like kismet or chemistry or magnetism or destiny and so forth.

"Great paradox of religion must be explored by man," Lin Tan said. "In its many guises it has brought us where we are today, I agree with your father. We must judge its worth and its excesses. I am Buddhist, of Mayany Timbro sect. I am more scientist than Buddhist however."

"I'm nothing. My mother's Catholic and my father's a poet. Well, the sun's coming up and the gulls are feeding." Margaret pushed her bangs back with her hand. She smiled into Lin Tan's eyes. She wasn't doing anything on purpose. She was just standing there letting him fall in love with her.

"I am very hungry after night on supertrain called Starlight Express. It would be great honor for me if you would accompany me to breakfast. I am alone in Seattle on first morning of my vacation and need someone to ask about problem I have just encountered."

"Oh, what is that?"

"I am working part-time in women's clinic in Berkeley, near to campus of University of California. I am in charge of test results from amniocentesis, do you know what that is?"

"Sure."

"Some months ago I made analysis of amniotic fluid from one Miss Nora Jane Whittington of Berkeley. Was auspicious day in my life as I had been given honor by university for my work in fetal biology. So I remember date. Also, this test was unusual as it revealed twin female fetuses with AB positive blood, very special kind of blood, very rare. Often found in people whose ancestors came from British Isles, especially Scotland and Wales. So I wrote out the report and later I found I had made a mistake on it. I made a notation that the blood type is that of universal donor. I should have written universal recipient. Now, last night, in coincidence of first order, if you believe theory of random events and accidents, last night on the train I meet this Miss Whittington, now seven and a half months pregnant and in the course of our conversation she tells me how happy she is that her daughters will be able to give blood to whole world if needed. She has in her pocketbook a copy of the report, with this false notation signed with my name. I am not in habit of making even slightest mistake. Now I must decide whether to tell my superiors at the lab and spoil my record of unblemished work."

"Could anyone be hurt by this?"

"No."

"Then let it lay. Let sleeping dogs lie, that's what my mother says."

"Very wise, very profound saying."

"Well, I'm a teacher. I'm supposed to know things. I teach first grade." She pushed the hood back from her hair. A cascade of golden curls fell across the shoulders of her raincoat. Her eyes were beautiful, large and violet colored and clear. "I was on my way to school when I stopped by here."

"I will walk you there." His throat constricted. His voice was growing deeper. He heard it as if from a great distance. Just love, he was thinking. Just divine madness.

"Well, why not." She looked out across the water, thinking of her cousin, dead as he could be. "I don't pick men up usually, but I'm a linguist. I can't miss a chance like this. I already speak French and Russian and Italian and some Greek. No Chinese, so far. What's your name?" She began walking down from the bridge. Lin Tan was beside her. The fog was lifting. The sun rising above the waters of Puget Sound. The dawn of a clear day.

"My name is Lin Tan Sing. Here, I give you my card." He pulled a card out of his pocket, a white card embossed in red. Down the center ran a curved red line. To remind him in case he should forget.

"I have to go to the launderette and get some clothes I left in the dryer," she said. "Then we'll go and get some breakfast."

Soon they were sitting in a small restaurant by the quay. They were at a table by a window. The window had old-fashioned panes and white lace curtains. A glass vase held wildflowers. A waiter appeared and took their orders.

"So this is the Tao on your card," she said. "I read a lot of Zen literature. And I try meditating but it always fails. My dad says the Western mind is no good for meditation. He writes books of philosophy. He's wonderful. I bet you'd love him if you met him."

"I would be honored to do so. I have wondered where the poets of United States were living. Where is he now? This father of yours?"

"In Arkansas. Do you have any idea where that is?"

"No. I am ashamed to say I do not understand geography of United States yet. I have been very busy since I arrived and have had no time to travel."

"It's a small state on the Mississippi River. We have wild forests and trees and chicken farms, the richest man in the world lives there, and we have minerals and coal. In the Delta we grow cotton and sometimes rice." She was enchanted by the foreignness of his manner. This is just my luck, she was thinking, to run into a Chinese doctor and get to find out all about China on my way to school.

"Oh, this is strange coincidence," he was saying. "In province where I come from, we are also growing cotton. Yes, I have heard of this Mississippi Delta cotton. Yours is very beautiful but no longer picked by hand, is it not true."

"Yours is?"

"Oh, yes. I have picked it myself when I was a small boy. The staple is torn by machine. The cloth will not be perfect. Perhaps I could invent a better cotton picking machine. I have often thought I should have been an inventor instead of a scientist but my mother died when I was thirteen so I have lived to save lives of others. I had meant it as an act of revenge against disease, now see it as finding harmony for life in its myriad forms. So you know the Tao?"

"I know of it. I don't know how to do it yet." The light of morning was shining on her face. Just face, he thought. Just light of sun. Just Tao. "It is the middle way, the way of balance and of harmony." He picked up a napkin, took a pen from his pocket and drew a diagonal line down the center of it. "This is the life we are living, now, at this moment, which is all we ever have. This is where we are. It is all that is and contains everybody." He looked at her. She was listening. She understood.

"I want to see you a lot," she said. "I want us to be friends." Her voice was as beautiful as the song of birds, more beautiful than temple bells. Her voice was light made manifest. Now Lin Tan's throat was thick with desire. He suffered it. There was nothing in the world as beautiful as her face, her voice, her hands, the smell of her dress. She took a small blue flower from the bouquet on the table and twisted it between her fingers. She looked at him. She returned his look. This was the moment men live for. This was philosophy and reason. Shiva, Beatrice, the dance of birth and death. If I enter into this moment, Lin Tan knew, I will be changed forever. If I refuse this moment then I will go about the world as an old man goes, with no hope, no songs to sing, no longing or desire, no miracles of sunlight. So I will allow this to happen to me. As if a man can refuse his destiny. As if the choice were mine. Let it come to me.

He closed his eyes for a second. Wait, his other mind insisted. Get up and leave. Get back on the train and ride back down the coast and enter the train station at San Francisco. Go to the lab. Work overtime on vacation. Catch up on all work of lab. Take money and increase holdings of gold coins in lockbox at Wells Fargo Bank of San Francisco, California. Spend vacation time at home. Go with friends to the beach, there is no destiny that holds me in this chair. Here is where I could prove free will, could test hypotheses. If not for all mankind, at least in my case.

"I would like very much if you would have dinner with me when you finish teaching for the day," he said. "I will be finding the greatest restaurant in all Seattle while you bestow gift of knowledge on young minds. I will tell you about my home and language and you will tell me of Romance languages and Arkansas."

"There's a Japanese movie at the Aristophanes. It's by Kurosawa. We could get a sandwich somewhere and go to the movie. I don't need to go to great restaurants." The waitress had appeared with their waffles and orange juice. "To think I started out this morning to go see where somebody committed suicide." She raised her orange juice. "This table reminds me of a painting I saw last year at the Metropolitan Museum of Art in New York City. It was by Manet. It was just incredible. I almost died. A painting of a bar with a barmaid. This sad-eyed blond barmaid standing behind a bar filled with glasses and bottles of colored liquid. The light was all over everything and her face was shining out from all that. It was real primal. My father loves paintings. We couldn't afford the real thing, but there were always wonderful prints and posters all over our house, even on the ceiling. This waffle is perfect. Go on and eat yours."

She took a bite of golden waffle soaked in syrup, then wiped her mouth daintily, with a napkin. A queen is inside of this girl, Lin Tan thought. She is a princess. He laughed with delight at everything she had said, at the light on the table, the syrup soaking into the waffle, the largess, bounty, divinity of the day.

"We will go and see what the barbaric Japanese have done with your film," he said. "Or anything that will seem nice to you."

"What time is it getting to be?" she answered. "I've got to hurry up. I'm going to be late to school."

They never made it to the movie. They walked for miles after dinner talking in all the languages they knew and telling their stories. She talked of the origins of language, how she wished to study man's speech and was teaching six-year-olds so she could investigate their minds as they learned to read and write. As they formed the letters and grew bold and turned the letters into words.

He told her of physics, of quantum mechanics and particle physics, the quark and chaos, a vision of reality as a swirling mass of energy bound into forms that are always changing. The greatest mystery is time, he insisted. Energy is held for a moment in form, then flung back into chaos, re-formed, captured again, undone, done and undone, an endless dance which we glimpse when we hear music. "Man is the inventor of time," he said. "Only man has need of it."

"You don't care if it is meaningless?"

"Is even more beautiful that way. I think I am falling in love with you, Margaret."

"I was afraid you would say that." She stopped by a stone wall and allowed him to take her hands. "It excites me, the way you talk. But we have to be careful. I could just be getting you mixed up with my dad. He talks like that all the time. It's sort of made me older than a lot of people. It has made me older." She pulled her hands away. "I don't want to fall in love with someone just because he talks like my father. Even if you are Chinese. I mean, he is Scotch-Irish. His father was all Irish. We have a lot of Irish blood."

"The blood of poets."

"How did you know that?"

"Because I read your literature."

"Well, I'm not going to bed with you tonight."

"Oh, no." Lin Tan bowed his head. "I was not expecting you to. I will take you home now. In the morning I will come and propose marriage. But not until I know you better." He laughed a great hearty laugh, a laugh he had forgotten he possessed. It was the best laugh he had ever laughed in the United States. He leaned back against the wall and laughed for several minutes and Margaret McElvoy laughed with him.

"This is the strangest night I ever spent in my life," she said. "Come on, let's go home."

✳   ✳   ✳

She took him to visit her school. On the fourth day of his vacation Lin Tan found himself lecturing on Chinese education to a combined first- and second-grade class. He told them everything he knew about grade school in rural China, then showed them a dance Chinese children learn to help them remember their multiplication tables. He had gone to Seattle's Chinatown and borrowed a traditional Chinese teacher's costume to wear to the school. Margaret sat in the back of the class and watched the muscles of his back as they moved his arm up and down on the blackboard. The soft blue cloth of his jacket rippled as his muscles moved his hand, and Lin Tan knew she was watching him and kept his body as graceful and supple as a dancer's as he taught. That night she went to bed with him.

"This might be too soon," he said, when she suggested it.

"It's too soon but I haven't done it with anybody in a year, so that makes up for it."

Then, in a rented room in a small hotel, with a lamp burning on the table and the sounds of Seattle outside the windows, they offered their bodies to each other, as children would, with giggles and embarrassment and seriousness, with shame and passion and a very large amount of silliness they searched each other out and made love, not very well at first, then better. "Here is where my knowledge of anatomy and obstetrics should come in handy," Lin Tan said. "Here is where the doctor comes in."

"I used to play doctor with my cousin, but we always got caught. We would put baby oil on each other because her mother was always having babies and we'd get it on the sheets, then they would catch us and take us off to the living room and tell us not to do it. You should have seen my mother's face when she'd be telling me not to. The smell of baby oil would be everywhere. She was a girl but we were only four so I don't think that means I'm a lesbian, do you?"

"What would you do with the baby oil?" They were lying side by side on the bed, talking without looking at each other.

"We would put it on and then stick this toy thermometer in each other. I guess that really was dangerous, wasn't it? Maybe that's what made them so mad." She sat up on one elbow and looked at him. "I wonder if it was made of glass. We could have killed each other sticking glass up our vaginas."

"Perhaps made of wood," Lin Tan said. "Many toys are made of wood."

"We could have gotten splinters. No wonder they got so mad, but I think they were really mad because we had found out about sex. They were so protective. They still are, to tell the truth."

"What would you say to one another when you would stick this thermometer into your hollow places? Did you say, 'I will diagnose you now'?"

"We said, 'This will make you feel better.'" She started giggling and Lin Tan laughed his great lost belly laugh again and they rolled back into each other's arms.

"Will you stay the night with me," he asked, "or shall I take you to your home?"

"I'll stay. When I do this I always do it right. My dad told us not to sleep with anybody unless we liked them enough to spend the night."

"And what else?"

"To call up the next day and talk about it. I mean, say something. Because it's pretty important, you know. It's not nothing, making love to another person."

"What did your mother say?"

"She said not to do it until you get married. She says it's for making babies, not some game."

"I would like to meet these parents of yours. I would like to talk with them."

"Well, if things keep going like this I guess you'll get to." She touched his hand. She was falling asleep. She left the waking universe and entered the world of sleep. Once we were always asleep, Lin Tan remembered. Slowly man has awakened. Oh, let the awak-

ening proceed. Let us rouse to clarity and not blow up the world
where Margaret sleeps. He stilled his mind then with a mantra
of wind and water and slipped down into the ancient mystery of
sleep himself.

In the morning they woke very early and talked for a while.
Then Margaret dressed and Lin Tan walked her down to the car.
"It is very awkward to leave someone after making love," he said.
"It is very hard to know what to say."

"I know," she answered. "Well, say you'd like to see me again.
That's the main thing anyone wants to hear."

"Oh, I want to see you many more times."

"Then come over tonight. Can you remember the way?"

"I will be there," Lin Tan answered. He helped her into the
car and stood watching as she drove away. He shook his head. It
amazed him that Americans worried about him finding his way
from one place to another when the country was filled with maps
and street signs. At the place where her car had been, several pi-
geons flew down from a roof and began to peck at the sidewalk.
Lin took that for a sign and went back into the hotel and sat in
meditation for an hour, remembering the shape of the universe
and the breathtaking order of the species. He imagined the spirit
of Margaret and the forms of her ancestors back a hundred generations. Then he imagined Margaret in the womb and spoke to
her in a dream on the day she was conceived. Then he dressed
and walked around the city of Seattle, Washington, all day long,
bestowing blessings in his mind and being blessed.

A soon as Margaret got home from school that afternoon she sat
down at her desk and wrote the first of what her family would
later refer to as the Chinese Letters.

Dear Mom and Dad, Jane and Teddy and Len,
    I have met THE MAN. I'm not kidding you. This one is
too much. I don't know where to begin. In the first place I met

him on *the exact place* on the bridge where Sherman jumped off.
He was standing there when I got there. He is Chinese. Dad,
don't go crazy. Listen to this. He is the smartest person I ever
met in my life except for you. He reminds me a lot of Professor
Levine. I mean he has the same kind of penetrating black eyes
that just bore into you and *like* you so much you feel like you
have known him always. He is twenty-five. He's a medical student (third year) at the University of California at San Francisco
and has a job besides. He runs a diagnostic lab and he is going
to graduate with high high honors, then go back to China to
help his people. Please don't worry about this. I had to tell
you, but not if I get a lot of phone calls at seven in the morning telling me what to do. Momma, thank you for sending the
sweater and the blouses. They will come in handy with the laundry problems. Love and kisses. I love you,

Margaret

She sat back, read over what she had written, drew a few trees
on the leftover paper on the bottom, addressed and stamped an
envelope and stuck the letter in. Then she left her apartment and
went down to the mailbox to mail the letter. While she was gone
Lin Tan tried to call four times. Each time he left a message on
her answering machine. The last time he left a poem.

> *Miracle of seven redbirds*
> *On snow-covered bamboo*
> *What brings them here on such a day?*
>
> *Miracle of a tall woman*
> *Watching beside me*
> *She bends her head my way.*

"By the poet Wang Wei from Qixion County in Shaanxi. I am
counting the moments until I am with you again."

❊   ❊   ❊

That night he stayed at her home. A small apartment overlooking the bay. A balcony was on the back. They sat with their feet on the railings and he told her about his work. "Then I will see into the heart of life, the very heart of the beginning of life, and, for my specialty, I am studying the beginning and formation of the human brain. At a moment soon after conception one cell of the zygote splits off and decides to become brain. After that moment, that cell and all its progeny become the brain stem and the brain, the miraculous brain of man. This happens, oh, a million times a minute. Everywhere on earth new people are being created. Inside women this miracle is going on and inside miracle, second miracle of brain formation is happening. Oh, problem is how to feed and care for them. There is so much work, it must be done. Must be done. It is very presumptuous to wish to do such important work but so my dreams are. Dreams often come true. If something is not within human grasp we can not conceive of it. Think of Thomas Edison with his dream of electricity. Light up the world. Yes, and my friend, Randal Yung of Pisgah, New Jersey, only this very week, has captured atoms in a prison of laser beams and is watching them grow. They are growing because he is watching. Is called the Bose-Einstein condensation and was only a theory until this week. I have been invited to go and view this experiment. Would you care to fly to New Jersey sometime to see miracle of captured atoms?"

"You know the guy in New Jersey who did that?" She had been taking a roasted chicken from the oven to baste it. Now she closed the oven door and walked over to the table where he was sitting. "You know that guy?"

"He is a friend of mine from boyhood. From village next to mine. His Chinese name is difficult to pronounce in English so he has taken the name of Randal. We were sent to the advanced school together from our province. He is very advanced about everything, is very smart, is great scientist. Randal wishes to live in the stars. He is a beautiful man. All the girls are ready to die for him."

"And we could go up there and really look at this?"

"Yes, we could."

"Then we have to go. My God, this is the chance of a life-time. I can get a substitute to teach for me. I'll tell them where I'm going. Oh, God, my father will have a fit when he finds out. He adores physicists. He says they are doing things they don't even understand. My God." She threw her hair back from her face. A pot of green beans was boiling over on the stove. Lin Tan got up and took the pot holder from her and saved their dinner.

Later, they made love again. This time it was better than it was the first time since they were no longer afraid of each other.

It is a strange thing to make love to a member of another race. Exciting and strange, curious and amazing. The amazing thing is that nothing unusual happens. The foreign person doesn't turn into a demon or begin to speak in pagan incantations or turn out to be automatically unsound. They just get in bed and make love with the same old set of moves and pleasures that have stood all the races in good stead for many centuries. This is me with this beautiful goddess, Lin Tan was saying to himself now, as he watched Margaret pulling a pink satin petticoat over her head. Just Lin Tan. Just Margaret. Just fantastic sexual activity of species. Oh, if she will only love me I will solve riddle of can-cer and also learn to operate on fetal heart.

"What are you thinking about?" she said. The petticoat was across her legs.

"I am thinking of the fetal heart. Sometime the valves develop in bad sequence. If the mother has been smoking or not eating properly or very nervous and worried. You must come sometime to my lab and see the sonograms. Very beautiful to watch babies like fish swimming." He was quiet. When he raised his head there were tears in his eyes. "Sometimes, by the time they are in our laboratories, they are not happy swimmers. Sometimes they are in trouble. Last week, we thought we had triplets on the screen. Much excitement. It was two little boys fighting to live. They had transfused each other through the common umbilical cord. So tragic. The mother was struggling and in pain. We delivered them by cesarean section and did all that was possible but they were gone by the time we got them to the incubator. Poor little mother. Thinking of this makes me wonder what has been happening with Miss Whittington." He got up. He was wearing a terry cloth robe that had belonged to one of Margaret's brothers. He walked over to where he had left his clothes and found his billfold and searched in it for the phone number Miss Whittington had given him on the train. "She should not have been traveling so late in her pregnancy. I should have left the train to see that she made it safely to a place of rest, but if I had done that I would not have been standing on bridge when you came out of fog bank. Like a goddess."

"You are crying over a stranger."

"All the world is one reality. Each man or woman is exerting many influences every moment of day. This is the night I meant to show you my great zen lovemaking I read about today in a book while you were in school. Instead, I tell you this sad story." He stood by the bedpost holding his billfold, the drapes of the terry robe falling open across his chest and stomach. Margaret crawled across the bed and pulled him into her arms. She stretched him out on the bed and began to count his ribs. "I never had this much fun knowing anybody," she said. "I can't believe you left a poem on my phone."

"I must find a more romantic poem for you. I will translate modern Chinese poetry for you so you can know my country through its poets."

"You are going back there to live?"

"I am not certain yet." He closed his eyes. She will think me ignoble, he decided, if I tell her that I wish to stay in the United States and make money. She is daughter of poet, very romantic upbringing. "I wish to go heal my people," he added. "I wish to be noble physician so that Margaret McElroy will think I am a wonderful man and care for me."

"I do," she said. "What do you think I'm doing here?"

"Would you go with me to live in China?"

"I don't know," she answered. "I've never been there."

Her father called at seven the next morning. "What's going on?"

"Nothing's going on. I only met him a week ago."

"Your mother's worried. Here, talk to her."

"Margaret."

"Yes."

"Don't do anything foolish."

"I'm not writing to you anymore if you call me up this early."

"Come home and bring this Chinese doctor with you. Your father wants to meet him."

"He's on his vacation. He doesn't want to come to Fayetteville, Arkansas." She looked across the bed at Lin Tan. He was nodding his head up and down. His mouth was saying, Yes, I will. Yes, I do. "He wants to," Margaret added. "He's here."

"In your apartment? At seven o'clock in the morning?"

"It's nineteen eighty-six, mother. Look, I'm hanging up. I'll call you later."

"We'll pay for the plane ticket. Get down here this weekend, Margaret Anne."

"Mother, I have company now. I'll call you later."

"Your father and I want you to come home this weekend. You can bring your friend with you. I don't know what you are doing out there, Margaret. If you don't come here, we are coming out there."

"I'll try. Wait a minute." She put her hand over the receiver and turned to Lin Tan. "You want to go visit them? Momma works for a travel agency. She'll send us some tickets. You want to go?"

"I would be honored to go meet your mother and father. But I can pay for my own airplane ticket."

"We'll come. Send me some tickets. Oh, okay. We'll do that. I'll call you tomorrow." She hung up and turned back to Lin Tan. "Well, here we go. Now you'll see the real me, I guess. My parents are wonderful but they boss us all around like crazy. You sure you want to do this?"

"Of course. It will be great honor and also allow me to see interior of United States. But I must pay for my own airplane fare."

"Don't worry about that. It's her perks, you know, she gets a certain number of tickets free. She gets mad if we won't use them. Well, I guess we're going then, aren't we? Imagine you meeting my dad. Just imagine." She moved closer to him and it was several hours before they finished their other plans.

Two thousand miles away Big Ted McElvoy was sitting at his desk trying to write a poem. He had been reading *The Seven Pillars of Zen.* The poem was subtly but not greatly influenced by that reading.

> *Hostages to fortune, what does that mean?*
> *A man should bow his head and watch his children*
> *Disappear? Has given hostages, a conscious act? . . .*

He studied the lines, tore the page from the tablet, laid it on a stack. He went back to the tablet, drew several parallelograms, then four isosceles triangles, then a cone. He got out a compass, measured the angles of the triangles, then laid the compass down and picked up the phone. He called a close friend who was a doctor and asked him to come by on his way home from work.

"I'm writing a poem about daughters. You might want to see it. Where's Drew?"

"She's still in Tulsa. She changed jobs. So what's up? I take it you heard from Margaret. How is she?"

"She's out in Seattle seeing some Chinese doctor she met on a bridge. It's too hard, Ken. It's too goddamn hard to do."

"She'll be okay."

"I don't know. I don't know about letting them go off to goddamn cities and start screwing anybody they meet on a bridge. Well, she's bringing him here Saturday. Jane sent them tickets."

"I'd like to meet this Chinese doctor."

"Damn right. That's why I'm calling. Come give me a printout. She says he plays chess. Come Saturday night."

"Sure, and Ted, I'll be over as soon as I finish up here."

"Good. Hurry up."

The beautiful and awesome scene when Margaret and Lin Tan arrived in Fayetteville, Arkansas. The progress of the car that carried them from the airport to the house where she was born. The embraces at the baggage claim, father and daughter, mother and daughter, mother and Lin Tan. They drove home through the campus of the University of Arkansas. The oaks and maples were golden and red and the Ozarks were a dark dusty blue on the horizon. The marching band was practicing in the Greek amphitheater. "Sweet Georgia Brown" filled the brisk fall air. Big Ted steered the old Buick slowly past the buildings that housed his life's work. Twenty-seven years of English students had floundered beneath the gaze and searing intelligence of Big Ted. But he was not teaching now. His face was straight ahead. His hands were on the wheel. His mind was concentrated on one thing and one thing only. To get to know this Chinese man before he pronounced judgment on him. He had been up since dawn reading the late poems of William Butler Yeats to fortify himself.

"Where were you raised?" he asked. "Tell me where you come from."

"My father owns small plot of land. He was doctor for our section for many years. Not member of party but looked on with favor by party. I am the oldest son. I was chosen to come here and learn Western medicine. There are many medicines and tools here that we need." Lin Tan paused. He folded his hands together. "I will graduate with highest honors. Perhaps at head of class. At least in number-two spot."

"How do you know Randal Yung?"

"Is cousin and boyhood friend from school. Same age as me."

"Have you talked to him since he did it?"

"Oh, yes. Several times."

"What did he see?"

"Atoms swimming in thick honey of light. Very confused activity. Random and unpredictable. Entropy setting in. Disequilibrium. Atoms are moving very slowly now. Like death of organism, he says."

"We'll talk when we get home." Big Ted shook his head, as if to say, Don't talk about this in front of the women. In the back seat Jane McElvoy gave her daughter a look and Margaret McElvoy returned the look.

They pulled into the driveway of the house. A frame house painted blue with white trim. An old-fashioned screened-in porch with two porch swings ran across the front of the house. Gardens with chrysanthemums blooming bordered the porch and the sidewalk leading from the driveway. A silver maple in full fall color commanded the yard. A sleepy old fox terrier guarded the stairs. "This is it," Margaret said. "This is where I live."

"Come on in," Big Ted said to Lin Tan. "We'll talk in my office."

*   *   *

They brought the suitcases inside and put them on the beds in the downstairs bedrooms, then the two men walked down a hall and out the back door to a small building beside a vegetable garden. "Office," it said on the door, and Big Ted formally and with graciousness escorted Lin Tan into his place of business. Held the door open for him, then waved him to the place of honor in a brown leather chair beside a desk. The office had been made from an old double garage. The walls of the room were lined with books, poems in glass frames, posters from museums. Propped against the books were other poems, framed and glued to pieces of cardboard or attached to the spines of books by paper clips. This is part of one of the poems Lin Tan could read from where he was sitting.

> They flee from me that sometime did me seek
> With naked foot, stalking in my chamber.
> I have seen them gentle, tame and meek,
> That now are wild, and do not remember
> That sometime they put themselves in danger
> To take bread at my hand; and now they range,
> Busily seeking with a continual change,
> > Thanked be to fortune it hath been otherwise,
> Twenty times better; but once in special,
> In thin array, after a pleasant guise,
> When her loose gown from her shoulders did fall,
> And she me caught in her arms long and small,
> Therewithal sweetly did me kiss,
> And softly said, "Dear heart, how like you this?" . . .

"So you are going back to China when you finish your degree?" Big Ted said.

"No, first I have to do my residency."

"Where will that be?"

"I am not certain yet. Perhaps on East Coast or in Seattle."

"If you're one or two you ought to have your choice."

"Perhaps. They have not written to me yet."

"Then what? After you finish your residency?"

"It will take several years. I wish to operate on fetal heart. Also, to pursue studies of child development."

"You've got that pretty well knocked in your culture. Why study it here?"

"I might remain in this country. Perhaps mental aspects of child rearing are key to all health, or perhaps all is genes, chromosome charts of children with lymphomas are very interesting. Perhaps we can teach body of child to heal itself. If mothers can be taught to carry babies in their arms for one year after birth. But this is all theory of mine."

"No, it's common sense. Difficult to teach in the United States in nineteen eighty-six." Big Ted sighed. He looked across the desk at the young man. The energy flowed from Lin Tan's body, made an aura around him. It was going to be okay. I did good, Big Ted thought. Goddammit, I raised a girl with a brain in her head, hitting on all cylinders the morning she plucked this one from the sea. So, we'll let go. Let her go. Lose her. Maybe never see her again. Goddammit, she could wind up in a rice field or a prison. No, not with this man. He could take care of her.

Big Ted sighed again. He reached into a drawer of the desk and took out a bottle of whiskey and two small glasses. "You want a drink of whiskey?"

"You are worried about something? Tell me what you are thinking."

"I'm thinking you'll take my daughter to a communist country and I can't protect her there. Convince me I'm wrong."

"I might not return to my country. I have done a wrong thing. I have allowed her to think I am hero who would give up opportunity to stay in the United States and be a wealthy man to go back and serve my people. It was unworthy subterfuge." Lin Tan looked Big Ted straight in the eye. Outside someone was knocking on the door. "Lin Tan." It was Margaret's voice. "Come to the phone. It's a man at Johns Hopkins calling you. It's the dean of Johns Hopkins."

"There goes your noble subterfuge," Big Ted said. "Go and answer it."

They were offering Lin Tan the moon and he said yes, he would be glad to come and take it. Later that night he asked Margaret very formally to be his wife and she accepted and Big Ted and Jane got on the phone and started calling their friends.

"Do we still have to sleep in separate rooms now that we're engaged?" Margaret asked her mother, later, when the two of them were down in her mother's room. "I mean, is it all right if I go in Teddy's room and sleep with him?"

"Oh, my darling, please don't ask that. I'm not ready for that."

"We're going to be married, Mother. Think how strange it must be for him, being here in this country, with us. I mean, after all."

"If you want to sleep with him go on and marry him then. We could have a wedding. You could get married while you're here." Her mother sank back against the pillows of the bed. It was a huge four-poster bed made from cypress logged on her grandfather's land. It had been a wedding gift from her parents, a quarter of a century ago, in another place, another time. Margaret's mother had been the most beautiful girl in that world. She was beautiful still, serene and sure, elegant and kind. Margaret hugged the bedpost. She was always a child in this room. All her life she had come in and hugged this bedpost while she asked questions and made pleas and waited for answers. Never once in her life had she been treated unfairly or unkindly in this room. So she looked upon the world as a place that could be expected to be kind and to be fair.

"It's too late to get married tonight," she said. "May we sleep with each other if we're going to get married tomorrow?"

"I don't want to discuss this any further," her mother said. She picked up a magazine and pretended to read it. "We'll talk about it tomorrow."

Margaret went to her bedroom and bathed and put on her best nightgown and unbraided her hair and brushed it. She put perfume on her wrists and knees and behind her ears. She opened the door to her brother's old room which adjoined her own. She gathered all of her old fashion magazines from around the room and sat down crosslegged on the bed and began to read. It was ten-fifteen.

Outside in the office Lin Tan and Big Ted were talking context. "It's got to be seen in the scheme of things," Big Ted was saying. "Bateson's got a nice little book on it. Trying, for God's sake, to make them comprehend they are part of nature. Poor babies. They've lost that in our cities. Poor goddamn babies. Makes me want to cry." He filled a glass with ice from a cooler, added two small jiggers of whiskey, and signaled Lin Tan to hand his over for a refill.

There was a knock on the door. Big Ted got up, opened it, let his friend Kenneth Felder in. "This is Doctor Felder, Lin Tan. He's our heart man around here. His daddy did it before him. This is Lin Tan, Ken. He got the big fellowship at Johns Hopkins handed him today. You two have plenty to talk about." He took Ken Felder's coat, motioned him to a red leather chair beside the brown one.

"So how do you like it here?" Ken said. "Have you figured out where you are yet?"

"Oh, yes, we studied a map on the airplane flying here. Margaret is very good guide. This country is larger than can be imagined from maps. We flew over mountains of the west. Very beautiful country. Here in your home is very beautiful also."

"Your own country's doing good. My wife and I were there

last summer. We were impressed with the schools. She's a teacher, like Ted here. She had Margaret. She had all these kids. Well, we're all glad to have you here."

"They want to get married," Big Ted said. "Margaret's down there with Jane making plans. And I don't mind." He raised his glass in Lin Tan's direction. "The global village. Jesus, imagine the kids. And tomorrow we're going up to New Jersey to look at his buddy's atoms before they condense any further. You want to go along? It's Saturday. Call and see if you can get a plane ticket."

"Oh, yes," Lin Tan said. "Please go with us. My friend, Randal, is very lonesome for someone he knows to come and share triumph with him. He has been surrounded by reporters for many days now. We would be honored if you would go along."

"I can't do that," Ken said. "Well, Johns Hopkins. That's fine, Lin Tan. Really fine. You must have worked hard."

"Very hard. Also, very lucky. There are many fine students in class with me." He glanced at his watch. He sipped his whiskey. He stretched out his legs from the brown chair until they met Doctor Felder's legs, sticking out from the red one. Just Chinese man being enveloped by the culture of the West, he decided. Just one more adventure on the road of life.

"I brought the portable chess board out," Big Ted said. "If you're ready, we can play."

TRACELEEN
TURNS EAST

IT WAS LAST MAY when Miss Crystal gave up on her diet
and exercise program. She had completely lost heart and stopped
caring. She began wearing loose shirts and Mexican wedding
dresses. Caved in to fat. I had never seen her that way. Miss Crystal
is the kind that never believes the handwriting on the wall, that
always says, No way, José.

Why? I was asking myself. Why would she give up after all
these years of keeping herself in shape? Why give up now? Well,
the answer wasn't hard to find. After all, even Miss Crystal is not
prepared to trade her teeth for a smaller waist.

Here is how the problem developed. First it became harder
and harder to lose weight. No matter what Miss Crystal did or
how many nights she went to bed hungry or how many break-
fasts she skipped, still, the pounds would creep back on. One
spice cake for Mr. Manny's birthday. One roast beef on the first
cold day. One loaf of Mrs. Diaz's salt-rising bread and there
would go all her work.

⁎ ⁎ ⁎

Finally, Miss Crystal was frantic. She went down and spent two weeks at a health spa in Texas and came home thin as a rail. Then her teeth started falling out. She had gone too far in the diet craze. First two of her molars became very loose. She went down to her dentist and the dentist said, You have been grinding your teeth to powder while you were starving yourself to death down at that crazy spa. This is terrible. We are going to have to send you to an expert and have him operate on your gums and no telling what all. It is going to cost eleven thousand dollars to undo the damage you have done.

She came home from the dentist and went to work flossing her teeth. I will make my teeth stay in my head, she said to me. The force of the human brain has never been measured. Anything the brain wishes, it can make come true. Only you must concentrate your powers on the thing you want. I am not ready for surgery on my gums. I am not ready to lie down and let my mouth be cut open. I will not take drugs and have surgery when my own brain can do anything it wants to do if I can only reach its ultimate power.

I was in agreement with her. You are right, I said. It only happened because you were determined to get your waist back. You just settle down and let a few pounds climb back on you and everything will be just fine. Look at all the problems we have solved this year. Crystal Anne learned to roller skate so she won't be left out of birthday parties and King is off of coke and has been accepted in a college and is madly in love with that girl in North Carolina. You and Mr. Manny have settled your differences and made a happy home. You will also solve this problem of your teeth. I know you will. I am sure of it.

Oh, Traceleen, she said, and threw her arms around me. You are right. A few pounds won't matter all that much. She pulled me over to a gilded mirror above the sideboard in the dining room. It is a very harsh mirror in a harsh light but we looked straight into it. "The body ages," Miss Crystal said. "We must learn resignation or die worse fools than we were born."

So we made a sour cream devil's food cake with icing full of chocolate chips and sprinkled cut-up chocolate pieces on the top and cut a piece and ate it while we prepared fried chicken for the Saint James Auction and Picnic for the Benefit of the Home for the Incurables. Every year we fry ten chickens for them no matter how busy we are that day. By the time we finished the chickens and wrapped them in red and white checked cloths and put them into baskets and delivered them to the home Miss Crystal was in a better mood. She had decided to go on and let the dentist try to help her. One look at the old people sitting in their chairs with their jaws caved in was enough to make her decide to go with modern science. I have never seen it fail that charity always pays off. This is not the first time I have seen almost immediate results from a charitable act.

While we waited for November we decided to try yoga. Miss Crystal found this young woman named Ruthie Horowitz who agreed to come on Tuesday and Thursday mornings and teach us how to do it. It is the ancient art of India and the kind Miss Horowitz teaches is called Mahayana yoga. These postures, as they are called, are like very slow exercises. They stretch out parts of your body you didn't know you had and call attention to the fact that you are made of flesh and blood. Most people walking around now never give that a thought. They have forgotten they are breathing and think the main thing they are here for is to drive cars and go to the mall. This yoga gets you back to thinking about what you are really made of.

At first I didn't want to do it with them but Miss Crystal insisted that I give it a try. She is always worrying about my blood pressure so the first thing I knew there I was pulling myself into postures and breathing into my chakras, which is what you call the different parts of the spiritual development. This is all from the Hindu religion. My pastor at my church said not to worry, it wouldn't hurt me to see some heathen practices and might give me something to tell my Sunday school class about.

I have had to be at my church quite a bit lately, as I am a youth counselor in my spare time. We are fighting the dope as hard as we can down here but it looks like a losing battle. When I go down to the Saint Thomas Street project to visit people I know, these very small children come up to the car trying to sell us things.

This yoga teacher turned out to be more interesting than I thought she would be. I began to look forward to her visits. Began to worry that she might not come. We would take the telephone off the hook and go into the living room and light some incense and put on some very quiet slow music and then we would lie down on these sticky green mats Miss Horowitz brought with her and begin to do these postures, breathing all the time as deeply as we could to remind ourselves that we are not alone in the world but are breathing in the whole world every time we inhale. Out go the old things we don't need anymore. In come the new things for us to think about. In and out, in and out, in and out. They might be able to use some of this in the project, I kept thinking. We could get Miss Horowitz to tell the young people some of her theories. Miss Horowitz thinks young girls should not have babies. She believes in the early works of a woman named Margaret Mead. Mrs. Mead said that people should have to take a test to have a baby. They would have to take a test and pass it and then take out a special license to become a parent. She said no babies should be born to young girls who don't know how to take care of themselves, much less a baby. Miss Crystal was all ears since she had King when she was only nineteen and doesn't think she has been a good enough mother for him because of that.

Everything he does she blames it on herself for being so young when he was born.

So we are doing this yoga for the months of September, October, November, and December and it was wonderful for our bodies and our minds. Miss Crystal returned to a size ten and I got my blood pressure down to one hundred and twenty over ninety which is low for me. Also, we had many wonderful conversations with Miss Horowitz about her theories and where she thinks the world is going and how to do yoga even when you are in a crowd or walking around the house. I learned to do a headstand and Miss Crystal mastered the Heron pose, where you stand on one leg for fifteen minutes without moving. We also gave up sugar, since Miss Horowitz is so against it, and we found we did not need it with our minds at ease. The fall moved into winter. Breathe in, breathe out, breathe in, breathe out. Miss Crystal had her gum surgery and recovered without mishap using the yoga to help speed up her recovery. We were getting so good at the postures that Miss Horowitz said we might become samurai before too long. Samurai are people who have become warriors and know that you must struggle and suffer to live and don't mind it or complain.

There was one other thing Miss Horowitz taught us that is interesting enough to mention. She had this idea that she could be a medium for passing along power from the universe into mine and Miss Crystal's chakras. It was the only thing she did to us that I worried about. She said not everyone can do it and not everyone is able to take it in but that when the right two people get together the one that is the go-between can take this stuff out of the air and pass it through her chakras into the chakras of the one that is lying on the floor. I watched her do it to Miss Crystal and then to one of Miss Crystal's friends that is a poet. The one that is getting the stuff lies down on the sticky mat (that is the name for the green mats we do the postures on) and Miss Horowitz goes into a trance to get the power to protect herself from being drained and then she passes her hands above the chakras of the person on the floor and very powerful information goes from her hands into the other person's spiritual centers. If she does it exactly right it fills up the subject's chakras without taking anything from Miss Horowitz but in the hands of the wrong person it could make the person doing it quite sick.

Miss Crystal and her friend, Miss Buchanan, swore they had never felt better in their life than after Miss Horowitz filled them up so finally I lay down on the floor and let her do mine too. I know it sounds crazy but I think something happened to me while I was lying there. I felt like I had grown an inch but my husband Mark says that only proves once again there is a fool born every minute.

Mark was leery of this yoga from the start but he was wrong to be. It turned out to be a good thing we took that yoga and learned about being samurai. Who would have thought we would need to know so soon? Who would have thought an armed robber would show up on Story Street with a kidnap victim in the trunk of his car? It was three minutes until two on a Tuesday afternoon in January. I had gone down to the Rug and Flooring Company that morning and rented a machine to clean the orientals. I was in the process of cleaning up the mess when he came in, which is why white cleaning powder was spread from one end of the house to the other by the time the police finally got there.

I was vacuuming up the mess. Miss Crystal was in her office with a secretary dictating letters about the March of Dimes Celebrity Chef Dinner. She is the chairman of that this year. Dr. Phillips and his wife are going to participate and a famous physicist from here is returning to make Gumbo File and several others you would have heard of. The doors were unlocked, of course. Miss Crystal was born in the country and so was I. Neither of us are in the habit of thinking we are always about to be hit in the head.

Our doors will be locked from now on. You can be sure of that. We do not want to go through what we went through last Tuesday again. Although it was nice to have a photograph of ourselves on the front page of the *Times-Picayune* and the story was good publicity for the Celebrity Dinner.

Still, if I live to be a hundred I will not forget what it felt like to be running the vacuum sweeper and hear a footstep and turn around and there is an armed robber with his gun pointed at me. "Who else is here?" he asked, but I did not answer. I remembered the course in self-defense I took at the police department and I began to scream. I screamed as loud as I could scream. I was also looking around for something to throw out the window, hoping someone on the street would see a window breaking and call for help.

The robber listened to me scream for just a second, then he ran across the white powdered dry cleaner and grabbed me by the arm and put the gun to my head. About that time Miss Crystal and her secretary, who is really Miss Bitsy Schlesinger, a tennis player, came running into the room and when they saw us they began to scream. Miss Bitsy had taken a course similar to mine at Tulane and knew what to do. They screamed at the top of their lungs. Then the robber pushed the gun deeper into my head and told them to shut up or he would kill me. He made us sit down on the dining-room chairs and tied us onto them and then he went to the garage and opened it and drove his car in and got his kidnap victim out of his trunk and brought her upstairs.

It was horrible to behold. She was a lady almost seventy-five years old, as sweet as she could be. She had been kidnapped at one o'clock from a shopping mall and she was being held for one million dollars in ransom money. "But what do you want with us?" Miss Crystal said to the armed robber. "We have done nothing.

We can't help you. You can't kill us all, can you? Who are you? What is wrong with you? Let us convince you to set this woman free and go away. Take my car. It's yours. There are the keys in my pocketbook. Take the pocketbook. It's got credit cards and money and a bank card. You can draw money from my account. You can take out two hundred dollars if you want to. The number is five five five. That's the secret number at any branch of the Hibernia Bank. There is one only two blocks from here."

"Shut up, lady," he said. "I don't want to hear any more out of you." Then all was very quiet for what seemed like several minutes. You could hear the refrigerator hum and the air-conditioning unit next door in Mrs. Diaz's yard. You could see the dust settling down through the light beams onto the table and I reminded myself how short a stay there is on the earth under the best of circumstances.

"I'll bet you're hungry," I said. "Why don't you let me make you a sandwich. You can't think straight when you are starving to death."

He waved the gun my way, then sank down into the easy chair where he was sitting.

"What's this white shit all over the place?" he asked. "What's this all about?"

"It's cleaner for the dry cleaning system we rented to clean the orientals," I said. "If you want to steal something you should take them. Miss Crystal's brother sent them here from Turkey. They are original oriental rugs from Istanbul."

"What time is it?" the armed robber asked. "Where's a clock around this house?"

"Right there in the kitchen," I answered. "You can see through the door." We were sitting around the rosewood dining table. Myself and Miss Crystal and Miss Bitsy and Mrs. Allison Romaine, which was the name of the kidnapee, tied to the chairs with package wrapping twine. The armed robber was sitting in the door to the front hall on an easy chair he had dragged in from the living room after he tied us up. He was a big man, wearing a nice open-neck blue shirt and work pants. He was a little overweight so his face was not as handsome as it might have been but he was still a nice-looking man. I couldn't tell how life had bent and shaped him into a criminal. It did not seem to fit with his appearance. I read quite a bit and at one time I made a specialty of murder mysteries so I know how to search the face of criminals to see if there is a clue to their motivations.

"You certainly don't look like a criminal," I said at last. "Also, I can see no point in us sitting here all day. What is the point of this?"

"I'm waiting to make a phone call," he said. "I have to wait for her husband to get back to his office so I can sell her back." He took a pack of cigarettes out of his pocket and lit one. No one said a word but in a minute Miss Crystal gave a little cough. I had never seen her that quiet for that long. I supposed she was terrified he'd still be here when King and Crystal Anne came home. This gun he had in his hand was a very terrible-looking weapon but somehow it seemed to me he would never really shoot it. Even when he had it pointed at my head I did not think he would pull the trigger. I guess I was having a denial. That's what Miss Horowitz said later when she heard the story. She said Miss Crystal was being samurai and I was having a denial. But later I also became a samurai when I had the brainstorm to fake a heart attack. She said the reason we were saved is that Miss Crystal and I are so used to working together and have honed the skills of cooperation so well that we knew how to read each other's minds when we had to. She said it is very interesting to understand the diametrics of a situation like that. She said what it looks like on the surface is very often not what is really going on. What it looked like that Tuesday was that everyone was scared to death. Miss Bitsy was breathing in little gulps, in, in, in, out, out, out. (She had not been doing any yoga.) Mrs. Romaine, the kidnapee, had begun to cry.

"Why me?" she kept asking. "Why did you pick out me?"

"Because your husband stole my racehorse," he said. "Because your husband owns the track and he owes me for ten years of my life if he wants to see you again. A hundred thousand dollars a year."

"I didn't do it," she said. "I didn't take anything from you." At that she began to cry louder than ever. Sobbing until I thought she might choke. She was tied up hand and foot onto a chair with a handmade petit-point seat cover of the coat of arms of the Manning family. She was too old to be tied up like that. I decided no matter how nice looking he was this robber must be the meanest man alive, perhaps a psychopath.

"Let me get her something to eat," I suggested. "She might get sick and have a heart attack. You might have a murder on your hands."

"Okay," he said. "Get some food ready. Make some sandwiches." He untied my feet and hands and I went into the kitchen and made five lovely little sliced turkey sandwiches with lettuce and tomato and mayonnaise and added some potato chips and brought it back on a tray. I set a place at the table for Mrs. Romaine and turned her around and untied her hands. So she could eat. I was thinking of things to poison him with. I thought of ways to grab the phone and dial nine for emergencies. I thought of how long until King would be coming home and how Crystal Anne would be waiting at her school with no one to pick her up. I thought of the time the bookcases in the den fell on me and Miss Crystal held them off with superhuman strength while I escaped. It might be possible to make them fall on him if we could get him in there. I thought of every weapon within my reach as I made another round of sandwiches. I thought of the dogs in the back yard. Three English sheepdogs that weighed more than a hundred pounds apiece. They were right out there in the back yard. How to get them in?

"Come on back in here," he said. "Stop fooling around." So

I brought in the second tray of sandwiches and the iced tea and passed them around and then got back into my chair.

It was a quarter to three. The robber got up and made a phone call from the kitchen phone. Then he came back in. "I think I'll take that pocketbook you offered," he said. "Where did you say it was?" I looked at Miss Crystal. She was so quiet. She was breathing in and out, in and out, in and out.

"It's in my bedroom on the dresser," she answered. "Look, could I go to the bathroom? I need to urinate. Also, my children will be coming home. If you let me make a call I can keep them from coming here. I don't know how long you plan to stay, but surely you don't want my children coming over with their friends. You can't hold a dozen people at gunpoint, can you? What is wrong with you anyway? Why don't you let us help you? You don't look like you're insane."

"All right," he said. "You can go to the bathroom. I'll go with you and we'll get that purse. I'll need your car." He tied me back to a chair and undid Miss Crystal.

He and Miss Crystal went back toward the bedroom. Miss Bitsy and Mrs. Romaine and I were still tied to dining room chairs. Miss Bitsy was where he had put her to begin with, beside the sideboard. Mrs. Romaine was facing the dining table. Her feet were tied but her hands were free. He had forgotten to tie her hands back together. I was beside the rubber plant near the French doors that open onto Story Street. Behind the doors is a small balcony with a row of red geranium plants. It was almost three o'clock. Children would be coming home from school. If I could break through the French doors I could get the attention of schoolchildren and call for help. Of course the sidewalk is quite a way from the house. I didn't know what to do. I was thinking as hard as I could. Here is how a samurai decides what to do. One, he sees the situation as a whole. Two, he gauges his own strength. Three, he figures out the strength of his enemy.

Then he fits it all together in his mind like a puzzle and finds the part that no one else can see. He must find the place where his strength fits into a hole in his enemy. Cutting my arms to pieces on the French doors did not seem to be a good enough plan. I thought harder. Who was this armed robber? What was he afraid of?

Miss Crystal came back in, carrying her pocketbook. She looked at me. I looked right back. I sent stuff to her chakras and she sent stuff to mine. "My heart," I screamed. "Oh, no, not my heart again." I pulled my chair forward with the weight of my body. I fell upon the floor taking my chair with me. "My pills," I gasped. "Miss Crystal, get my pills."

Mrs. Allison Romaine thought it was for real. She let out a scream. Then she picked up her sandwich plate and threw it at the robber. Miss Bitsy screamed too. "Heart attack," she screamed. "Call an ambulance. Get the pills for her. Untie me. I know CPR."

"Pills," I gasped. "Got to have my pills."

"I'll get them, Traceleen," Miss Crystal yelled. She ran from the room. The armed robber fell on his knees beside my chair to look at me. Just then the front door opened and King came in with his friend, Matthew Levine, beside him.

The dogs came bounding up the stairs. Tiger and Stoner and Boots. They ran into the room and started licking everyone in sight. Old English sheepdogs are the worst-smelling dogs you can ever imagine having. They are the last dogs in the world you want to let into your house and so kind they would never hurt a flea but the robber did not know that. I guess his guilt was so bad over kidnapping a woman old enough to be his grandmother that he thought the dogs had been sent from hell. He was screaming now. The harder he screamed the more the dogs licked and jumped on him. They sensed his fear and stopped being gentle.

Meanwhile, as soon as she opened the basement door for the dogs, Miss Crystal had climbed the fence and run into Mrs. Diaz's house to use the phone and call the police. They were not the first law enforcement to reach the scene, however. Our neighborhood guard came tearing in and disarmed the robber before the police drove up in three cars with their sirens running.

Mrs. Romaine was returned to her husband, who is a nice man who has never cheated anyone and ended up giving fifteen thousand dollars to the Celebrity Chef March of Dimes Fund. It put Celebrity Chef over the top and made them the most profitable charity event of the year. Miss Bitsy has been interviewed by three different publications concerning her role in the affair, including the *Tulane Alumni Newsletter.* They used a full-length photo of her wearing a white and green knit tennis outfit with a matching sweater. We are hoping it will help her catch a husband. She is so good at tennis it scares men off.

Miss Crystal and I have gone back to yoga. We are doing it for two hours every Tuesday and Thursday morning. No matter how busy we get we are in the living room with the phone off the hook two mornings a week doing our yoga postures. Both of us have many people depending on us. We must be strong enough to face the challenges. The strength to live your life and help other people begins in your own body. You must strive to make your body a strong thing that never forgets its place in the universe. Breathe in, breathe out. This is what Miss Horowitz is teaching us as we do the plough and the headstand. We must be ready, she keeps saying. It is every person's duty to be prepared. Breathe in, breathe out. Just because we have faced one challenge doesn't mean there won't be another.

MEXICO

JULY THE TWENTY-SECOND, nineteen hundred and eighty-eight, Agualeguas, Mexico, on the road to Elbaro, a Las Terras de Los Gatos Grandes.

It was the last day of the trip to Mexico. Another six hours and Rhoda would have been safely back in the United States of America where she belonged. Instead she was on the ground with a broken ankle. She was lying down on the hard stubble-covered pasture and all she could see from where she lay was sky and yellow grass and the terrible tall cages. The cats did not move in the cages. The Bengal tigers did not move and the lionesses did not move and the black leopard did not move. My ankle is torn to pieces, Rhoda thought. Nothing ever hurt this much in all my life. This is real pain, the worst of all pains, my God. It's karma from the bullfight, karma from the cats, lion karma, oh, God, it's worse than wasp stings, worse than the fucking dentist, worse than anything. I'm going to die. I wish I'd die.

Then Saint John was there, leaning over her with his civilized laconic face. He examined her ankle, turned it gently back into alignment, wrapped it in a strip of torn cloth. A long time seemed to go by. Rhoda began to moan. The Bengal tigers stirred in their cage. Their heads turned like huge sunflowers to look at her. They waited.

Dudley stood beside the fence. The lion was sideways. He was as big as a Harley-Davidson, as wide as a Queen Anne's chair. Dudley kept on standing beside the flimsy fence. No, Dudley was walking toward her. He was walking, not standing still. My sight is going, Rhoda decided. I have been blinded by the pain.

"Now I'll never get back across the border," she moaned. She pulled on Saint John's arm.

"Yes, you will," he said. "You're a United States citizen. All you need is your driver's license."

He carried her to the porch of the stone house. The caretaker's children put down the baby jaguar and went inside and made tea and found a roll of adhesive tape. Saint John taped up Rhoda's ankle while the children watched. They peered from around the canvas yard chairs, their beautiful dark-eyed faces very solemn, the baby jaguar hanging from the oldest boy's arm. The youngest girl brought out the lukewarm tea and a plate of crackers which she passed around. Saint John took a bottle of Demerol capsules out of his bag and gave one to Rhoda to swallow with her tea. She swallowed the capsule, then took a proffered cracker and bit into it. "Yo soy injured," she said to the child. "Muy triste, no es verdad?"

"Triste," the oldest boy agreed and shifted the jaguar to his left arm so he could eat with his right.

Then Dudley brought the station wagon around and Rhoda was laid out in the back seat on a pillow that she was sure contained both hookworm larvae and hepatitis virus. She pulled the towel out from under the ice chest and covered the pillow with the towel, then settled down for the ride back through the fields of maize.

"Well, Shorty, you got your adventure," Dudley said. "Old Waylon didn't raise a whisker when you started screaming. What a lion."

"I want another one of those pills, Saint John," she said. "I think I need another one."

"In a while," he said. "Wait a few minutes, honey."

"I'll never get back across the border. If I don't get back across the border, Dudley, it's your fault and you can pay the lawyer."

"You'll get across," Saint John said. "You're a United States citizen. All you need is your driver's license."

It is nineteen eighty-eight in the lives of our heroes, of our heroine. Twelve years until the end of the second millennium, A.D. There have been many changes in the world and many changes in the lives of Rhoda and Dudley and Saint John since the days when they fought over the broad jump pit in the pasture beside the house on Esperanza. The river they called the bayou was still a clean navigable waterway back then, there was no television, no civil rights, no atomic or nuclear bomb, no polio vaccine. Still, nothing has really changed. Saint John still loves pussy and has become a gynecologist. Dudley still likes to kill things, kill or be killed, that's his motto. Rhoda still likes men and will do anything to get to run around with them, even be uncomfortable or in danger.

Details: Dudley Manning runs a gun factory in San Antonio, Texas, and is overseeing the construction of Phelan Manning's wildlife museum. Saint John practices medicine on Prytania Street in New Orleans, Louisiana. His second wife has just left him for another man to pay him back for his legendary infidelities. She has moved to Boston, Massachusetts, and is fucking an old hunting buddy of his. She was a waitress in Baton Rouge when Saint John aborted her and fell in love. A bartender's daughter, a first-class, world-class, hardball player. Saint John has met his match. He is licking those wounds and not in top shape in nineteen eighty-eight. Rhoda Manning is in worse shape. She is fifty-three years old and she has run out of men. That's how the trip to Mexico began. It began because Rhoda was bored. Some people think death is the enemy of man. Rhoda believes the problem is boredom, outliving your gonads, not to mention your hopes, your dreams, your plans.

Here is how the trip to Mexico began. It was two in the afternoon on a day in June. Rhoda was in her house on a mountain overlooking a sleepy little university town. There was a drought and a heat wave and everyone she knew had gone somewhere else for the summer. There was nothing to do and no one to go riding around with or fuck or even talk to on the phone. Stuck in the very heart of summer with no husband and no boyfriend and nothing to do. Fifty-three years old and bored to death.

She decided to make up with Dudley and Saint John. She decided to write to them and tell them she was bored. Who knows, they might be bored too. Dudley was fifty-six and Saint John was fifty-eight. They might be bored to death. They might be running out of things to do.

Dear Dudley [the first letter began],

I am bored to death. How about you? Why did I go and get rid of all those nice husbands? Why did I use up all those nice boyfriends? Why am I so selfish and wasteful and vain? Yesterday I found out the IRS is going to make me pay twenty-four thousand dollars' worth of extra income tax. My accountant's computer lost part of my income and figured my tax wrong. So now I am bored and broke. How did this happen to me? I think I have been too good and too sober for too long. Let's get together and get drunk and have some fun. I miss you. Where is Saint John? I bet he's as bored as I am. I bet he would like to get drunk with us. I heard that beastly woman he married was up in Boston fucking one of his safari club buddies. Is that true? I'm sorry I've been so mean to everyone for so long. It was good to see you at Anna's funeral. You looked great. Considering everything, we are lucky to be alive. Write to me or call me. Your broke and lonely and undeserving sister, Rhoda Katherine.

Dear Saint John [the second letter began],

Let's get Dudley and go off somewhere and get drunk. I'm tired of being good. How about you? Love, Rhoda.

In five days Rhoda heard back from Dudley. "Hello, sister," the message said on the answering machine. "It's your brother. You want to go to Mexico? Come on down to San Antonio and we'll go to Mexico."

Rhoda stood by the answering machine. She was wearing tennis clothes. Outside the windows of her comfortable house the clean comfortable little town continued its easygoing boring life. *Why did I start this with Dudley?* Rhoda thought. *I don't want to go to Mexico with him. Why did I even write to him? My analyst will have a fit. He'll say it's my fascination with aggression and power. Well, it's all I know how to do. I wrote to Dudley because he looked so great at Anna's funeral, so powerful and strong, immortal. The immortal Eagle Scout who lived through polio and scarlet fever and shot a lion, ten lions, a thousand lions.*

Now Saint John will call me too. I shouldn't do this. I have outgrown them. I have better things to do than go down to Mexico with Saint John and Dudley. What else do I have to do? Name one thing. Water the fucking lawn? I can get out the sprinklers and waste water by watering the lawn.

Rhoda slipped on her sandals and walked out the door of her house into the sweltering midmorning heat. She set up the sprinklers on the front lawn and turned them on. Then reached down and began to scratch her chigger bites. *Fucking Ozarks,* she decided. Why in the name of God did I come up here to live in this deserted barren cultural waste? What in the name of God possessed me to think I wanted to live in this little worn-out university town with no one to flirt with and nowhere to eat lunch?

She pulled the last sprinkler out from under the woodpile and set it on the stone wall of the patio. Scientific method, she was thinking. Germ theory. I'll go down there with them and the next thing I know I'll have amoebic dysentery for five years. Saint John will bring his convertible and I'll get skin cancer and ruin the color of my hair and then Dudley will get me to eat some weird Mexican food and I'll die or spend the rest of my life in the hospital.

Rhoda stared off into the branches of the pear tree. She was afraid that by watering the lawn she might make the roots of the trees come up to the surface. World full of danger, she decided. How did I come to believe that?

She reached down to pick up the sprinkler. Her index finger closed down upon a fat yellow and orange wasp who stuck his proboscis into her sweat glands and emitted his sweet thin poison. "Oh, my God," Rhoda screamed. "Now I have been bit by a wasp."

An hour later she lay on the sofa in the air conditioning with a pot of coffee on the table beside her. Hot coffee in a beautiful blue and white Thermos and two cups in case anyone should come by and a small plate holding five Danish cookies and an ironed linen napkin. She was wearing a silk robe and a pair of white satin house shoes. Her head was resting on a blue satin pillow her mother had sent for her birthday. Her swollen finger was curled upon her stomach. She dialed Dudley's number and the phone in San Antonio rang six times and finally Dudley answered.

"What are you doing?" she said.

"Watching the boats on the lake. Waiting for you. Are you coming down? You want to go or not?"

"I want to go. Call Saint John."

"I already called him. He's free. Gayleen's up in Boston, as you noted. When do you want to go?"

"Right away."

"How about the fourth of July?"

"I'll be there. Where do I fly to?"

"Fly to San Antonio. We'll drive down. There's a hunting lodge down there I need to visit anyway. A hacienda. We can stay there for free."

"How hot is it?"

"No worse than where you are."

"I'm sorry I've been so mean to you the last few years."

"It's okay."

"No, it was mean as shit. I'll make it up to you."

"Let me know when you get a flight."

"A wasp bit me."

"You know what Kurt Vonnegut said about nature, don't you?"

"No, what did he say?"

"He said anybody who thinks nature is on their side doesn't need any enemies."

"I miss you, Dudley. You know that?"

"You know what a wedding ring is, don't you?"

"No. What?"

"A blow job repellent."

"Jesus," Rhoda answered.

"You know what the four most feared words in the United States are, don't you?"

"No. What?"

"I is your president."

"Jesus. Listen, I'm coming. I'll be there."

"I'll call Saint John. He'll be glad."

*   *   *

Rhoda hung up the phone, lay back against the satin pillow. My rubbish heap of a heart, she decided. I'm regressing. Well, they are my oldest compadres. Besides, where else will I find two men my own age who are that good-looking and that well-preserved and that brave? Where else will I find anybody to go to Mexico with in the middle of the summer? My ex-husbands are all snuggled down with their wifelets on little trips to Europe. Thank God I'm not sitting somewhere in a hotel room in London with someone I'm married to. About to make love to someone I've fucked a thousand times.

Well, I wouldn't mind having one of my old husbands here this afternoon. Yes, I must face it. I have painted myself into a corner where my sex life is concerned. I should get up and get dressed and do something with my hair and go downtown and find a new lover but I have run out of hope in that department. I don't even know what I would want to find. No, it's better to call the travel agent and go off with my brother and my cousin. Mexico it is, then. As Dudley always says, why not, or else, whatever.

Rhoda slept for a while, resigned or else content. When she woke she called Saint John at his office in New Orleans and they made their plans. Rhoda would fly to New Orleans and meet Saint John and they would go together to San Antonio and pick up Dudley and the three of them would drive down into Mexico. She would leave on July second. A week away.

During the week Rhoda's wasp sting got better. So did her mood. She dyed her hair a lighter blond and bought some new clothes and early on the morning of July second she boarded a plane and flew down to New Orleans. She took a taxi into town and was delivered to Saint John's office on Prytania Street. A secretary came out and took her bags and paid the taxi and Saint John embraced her and introduced her to his nurses. Then a driver brought Saint John's car around from the garage. A brand-new baby blue BMW convertible with pale leather seats and an off-white canvas top. "Let's take the top down," Saint John said. "You aren't worried about your hair, are you?"

"Of course not," Rhoda said. "This old hair. I've been bored to death, Saint John. Take that top down. Let's go and have some fun."

"We'll go to lunch," he said. "The plane doesn't leave until four."

"Great. Let's go."

They drove down Prytania to Camp Street, then over to Magazine and across Canal and down into the hot sweaty Latin air of the French Quarter. Tourists strolled along like divers walking underwater. Natives lounged in doorways. Cars moved sluggishly on the narrow cobblestone streets. Saint John's convertible came to a standstill on the corner of Royal and Dumaine, across the street from the old courthouse where one of Rhoda's lovers had written films for the Wildlife and Fisheries Commission. "Do you ever hear from Mims Waterson?" she asked.

"No," Saint John said. "I think he went back to North Carolina."

"If I hear North Carolina I think of Anna." They hung their heads, mourning their famous cousin.

"Anna," Saint John said, and moved the car a few feet farther down the street. "She was a strange one."

"Not strange, just different from us. Gifted. Talented, and besides, her father was mean to her. Her death taught me something."

"And what was that?"

"To be happy while I'm here. To love life. Tolstoy said to love life. He said it was the hardest thing to do and the most important. He said life was God and to love life was to love God."

"I don't know about all that." Saint John was a good Episcopalian. It bothered him when his cousins said things like that. He wasn't sure it was good to say that God was life. God was God, and if you started fucking around with that idea there wouldn't be any moral order or law.

"I thought we'd go to Galatoire's," he said. "Will that be all right?"

"That's perfect. Stop in the Royal Orleans and let me work on my face, will you? I can't go letting anyone in this town think I let myself go. I might have to come down here and scarf up a new husband if something doesn't happen soon with my life."

"What have you been doing?"

"Writing a travel book. Anna's agent is handling it for me. It might make me some money. At least pay my bills and get me out of debt."

"Will you write about this trip? About Mexico?"

"If there's anything I can use. Okay, there's the garage and they have space. Go on, Saint John, turn in there." He pulled into the parking lot of the Royal Orleans Hotel. The hotel was filled with memories for both of them. Secret meetings, love affairs, drunken lunches at Antoine's and Arnaud's and Brennan's. Once Rhoda had spent the night in the hotel with a British engineer she met at a Mardi Gras parade. Another time Saint John had had to come there to rescue her when she ran away from her husband at a ball. He had found her in a suite of rooms with one of her husband's partner's wives and a movie star from Jackson, Mississippi. Rhoda had decided the partner's wife should run off with the movie star.

"The wild glorious days of the Royal Orleans," Rhoda said now. "We have had some fun in this hotel."

"We have gotten in some trouble," Saint John answered.

"What trouble did you ever get in? You weren't even married."

"I was in medical school. That was worse. I was studying for my boards the night you had that movie star down here."

"I'm sorry," Rhoda said, and touched his sleeve. Then she abandoned him in the hotel lobby and disappeared into the ladies' lounge. When she reappeared she had pulled her hair back into a chignon, added rouge and lipstick, tied a long peach and blue scarf in a double knot around her neck, and replaced the small earrings she had been wearing with large circles of real gold.

"How do I look?" she asked.

"Wonderful," Saint John said. "Let's go." She took his arm and they walked down Royal Street to Bourbon and over to Galatoire's. Their cousin Bunky Biggs was standing outside the restaurant with two of his law partners. "Saint John," he called out. "Cousin Rhoda, what are you doing in town?"

"She's taking me to Mexico," Saint John said. "With Dudley."

"Oh, my Lord," Bunky said. "That will be a trip. I wish I was going."

"He's taking me," Rhoda said, very softly. It was all working beautifully, the universe was cooperating for a change. Now it would be all over New Orleans that she and Saint John were off on a glorious adventure. Bunky could be depended upon to spread the word.

"What are you going to do down there?" Bunky said. "There's no hunting this time of year."

"We're going to see some animals," Saint John said. "To have some fun." He was saved from further explanation. At that moment a delivery truck pulled up across the street and a tall black man emerged from the back of the truck carrying a huge silver fish. The man was six and a half feet tall. He hoisted the fish in his arms and carried it across the narrow crowded street. A small Japanese car squeaked to a stop. An older black man wearing a tall white hat opened a door and held it open and the fish and its bearer disappeared into the wall. We live in symbiosis with this mystery, Rhoda thought. No one understands it. Everything we think we know is wrong. Except their beauty. They are beautiful and we know it and I think they know it but I am far away from it now and get tired of trying to figure it out. Forget it.

The maître d' appeared and escorted them inside.

The restaurant was crowded with people. The Friday after-noon professional crowd was out in force. Women Rhoda had known years before were seated at tables near the door, the same tables they might have occupied on the day she left town with the poet. People waved, waiters moved between the crowded ta-bles carrying fabulous crabmeat salads and trout meunière and trout amandine and pompano en papillete and oysters Bienville and oysters Rockefeller and turtle soup and fettucini and marti-nis and whiskey sours and beautiful French desserts and bread pudding and flán.

"I should never have left," Rhoda exclaimed. "God, I miss this town."

Two hours later they emerged from Galatoire's and found the blue convertible and began to drive out to the airport.

"Dudley's been looking forward to this," Saint John said. "I hope we don't miss that plane."

"If we do there'll be another one along."

"But he might be disappointed."

"What a strange thing to say."

"Why is that? Everyone gets disappointed, Rhoda. Nothing happens like we want it to. Like we think it will."

"Bullshit," Rhoda said. "You're getting soft in the head, Saint John. Drive the car. Get us there. You're as rich as Croesus. What do you have to worry about? And take off that goddamn seat belt." She reached behind her and undid her own and Saint John gunned the little car and began to drive recklessly in and out of the lanes of traffic. This satisfied some deep need in Rhoda and she sat back in the seat and watched in the rearview mirror for the cops.

The plane ride was less exciting. They settled into their seats and promptly fell asleep until the flight got to Houston. They changed planes and fell back asleep.

*   *   *

Rhoda woke up just before the plane began its descent into San Antonio. She was leaning against the sleeve of Saint John's summer jacket. My grandmother's oldest grandson, she thought. How alike we are, how our bodies are shaped the same, our arms and legs and hands and the bones of our faces and the shape of our heads. Apples from the same tree, how strange that one little grandmother put such a mark on us. I was dreaming of her, after she was widowed, after our grandfather was dead and her hair would stray out from underneath its net and she gave up corsets. Her corsets slipped to the floor of her closet and were replaced by shapeless summer dresses, so soft, she was so soft she seemed to have no bones. Her lovely little legs. "Tell me again the definition of tragedy, I always forget." In my dream she was standing on the porch at Esperanza watching us play in the rain. We were running all over the front lawn and under the rainspouts, barefooted, in our underpants, with the rain pelting down, straight cold gray rain of Delta summers, wonderful rain. How burning we were in the cold rain, burning and hot, how like a force, powerful and wild, and Dan-Dan standing on the porch watching us, worrying, so we were free to burn with purpose in the rain. In the dream she is calling Dudley to come inside. Saint John and Floyd and I may run in the rain and Pop and Ted and Al but Dudley must come in. She holds out a towel to wrap him in. He was the sickly one, the one who had barely escaped with polio. And yet, he was stronger than we were. He was stronger than Saint John, stronger than Bunky Biggs, stronger than Phelan even. How could being sick and almost dying make you strong? Gunther told me once but I have forgotten. It was about being eaten and fighting, thinking you are being eaten and becoming impenetrable. Anna seemed impenetrable too but she turned out not to be. Rhoda shook off the thought. She got up very gingerly so as not to wake Saint John, and wandered down the aisle to the tiny bathroom to repair her makeup. She went inside and closed and locked the door. She peered into the mirror, took out her lipstick brush and began to apply a light peach-colored lipstick to her lips. A sign was flashing telling her to return to her seat but she ignored it. She added another layer of lipstick to her bottom lip and began on her upper one. How did being sick when he was little make Dudley so powerful? What had Gunther said? It was some complicated psychological train of thought. Because a small child can imagine himself being consumed, eaten, burned up by fever, overwhelmed by germs, taken, as children were taken all the time before the invention of penicillin and streptomycin and cortico-steroids. Before we had those medicines children died all the time. So Dudley must have lain in bed all those terrible winters and summers with Momma and Doctor Finley holding his hand and waged battle because they begged him to live, because they sat with him unfailingly and held his hand and gave him cool cloths for his head and sips of water from small beautiful cups and shored him up, because they won, because he won and did not die, he became immortal. Nothing could eat him, nothing could make him die.

Rhoda blotted the lipstick on a paper towel. So, naturally, he likes soft-spoken blond women who hold his hand and he likes to take small sips of things from beautiful cups and he likes to hang out with physicians. He is always going somewhere to meet Saint John, they have hunted the whole world together. It is all too wonderful and strange, Rhoda decided, I could think about it all day. It's a good thing I don't live near them, I would never think of anything else.

She put the lipstick away and took out a blusher and began to color her cheeks. The plane was descending. The sign was flashing. He loves the battle, Gunther had said. And he thinks he will always win.

"He never gets sick," Rhoda had said. "They were jaguar hunting in Brazil and three people died from some water they drank and Dudley didn't even get sick. Everyone got sick but Dudley."

"He can't lose," Gunther said. "Because your mother held his hand."

"Sometimes they lose," Rhoda said. "My grandmother lost a child."

"But Dudley didn't lose."

"He thinks he is a god."

"What about you, Rhoda? Do you think you are a god?"

"No, I am a human being and I need other human beings and that is what you are trying to teach me, isn't it?"

"I don't have any plans for you."

"So you say."

Rhoda finished her makeup and returned to her seat just as the stewardess was coming to look for her. "I'm sorry," she said, and slipped into the seat beside her cousin. He was shaking the sleep from his head. "We slept too long," he said. "We must have drunk too much at lunch. Don't know what's wrong with me." He squinched his eyes together, squirmed around. "It's okay," Rhoda said.

"Where have you been?"

"I was in the rest room. I figured out Dudley. Want to hear?"

"Sure. Put on your seat belt."

"He has to kill or be killed."

"What does that mean?"

"He hunts to keep from dying because he was sick when he was a child."

"Rhoda." He gave her his bedside look. Indulgent, skeptical, maddeningly patronizing.

"Never mind," she said. "I know you don't like psychiatry."

"Well, I'm not sure it applies to Dudley." Rhoda gave up, began to leaf through an airplane magazine. Outside the window the beautiful neighborhoods of San Antonio came into view, swimming pools and garages and streets and trees and trucks, an electric station, a lake. The modern world, Rhoda decided, and I'm still here.

Dudley was waiting for them, standing against a wall, wearing a white shirt and light-colored slacks, beaming at them, happy they were there. They linked arms and began to walk out through the airport, glad to be together, excited to be together, feeling powerful and alive.

They stopped at several bars to meet people Dudley knew and danced at one place for an hour and then drove in the gathering dark out to the lake where Dudley's house sat on its lawns, filled with furniture and trophies and mementos of his hunts and marriages. Photographs of his children and his wives covered the walls, mixed with photographs of hunts in India and France and Canada and the Bighorn Mountains of Wyoming and Africa and Canada and Tennessee. Rugs made from bears were everywhere. Four rhinoceros heads were on one wall. Jaguar, tigers, lions, cougars, mountain sheep. He should have been a biologist, Rhoda thought. He wouldn't have needed so much room to hang the trophies on.

They cooked steaks on a patio beside the lake and ate dinner and drank wine and played old fifties music on the stereo and went to bed at twelve. Rhoda had an air-conditioned room on the second floor with a huge bearskin rug on the floor and a leopard on the wall. She cleaned her face and brushed her teeth and put on a gown and fell asleep. At three in the morning she woke. Most of the lights in the house were still on. She wandered out onto the sleeping porch and there were Dudley and Saint John, stretched out on small white enamel beds with a ceiling fan turning lazily above them, their long legs extended from the beds. If I had one chromosome more, she decided. One Y chromosome and I'd be out here on this hot sleeping porch in my underpants instead of in an air-conditioned room in a blue silk dressing gown.

I'm glad I am a girl. I really am. They are not as civilized as I am, not as orderly or perfect. She turned off the lights they had left on and went back into her room and brushed her teeth some more and returned to bed. She fell into a dreamless sleep, orderly, perfect, civilized.

When she woke Dudley was in the kitchen making breakfast. "You ready to go to Mexico?" he asked. He handed her a tortilla filled with scrambled eggs and peppers. "Did you bring your passport?"

"No, I didn't think I needed it."

"You don't. It's all right. Well, we'll get off by noon, I hope. I have to make some phone calls."

"Where exactly are we going, Dudley?"

"To see a man about a dog." They looked at each other and giggled. It was the thing their father said when their mother asked him where he was going.

"Okay," Rhoda said. "When do we leave?"

It was afternoon before they got away. They were taking a blue Mercedes station wagon. Rhoda kept going out and adding another bottle of water to the supplies.

"How much water are you going to need?" Saint John asked. "We'll only be there a few days."

"We can throw away any we don't want," she answered. "But I'm not coming home with amoebic dysentery."

"Take all you want," Dudley answered. "Just leave room for a suitcase and the guns."

"Guns?"

"Presents for Don Jorge. You will like him, Shorty. Well, Saint John, are we ready?" They were standing beside the station wagon. Saint John handed him the small suitcase that contained their clothes. In a strange little moment of companionship they had decided to pack in one suitcase for the trip. Dudley had pulled a dark leather case from a closet and each of them had chosen a small stack of clothes and put them in. They stuck the suitcase in the space between the bottles of water. Dudley put the gun cases on top of the suitcase. They looked at one another. "Let's go," they said.

"You got the magical-gagical compound?" Saint John asked, as they pulled out of the driveway.

"In the glove compartment," Dudley answered. Saint John reached down into the box and brought out a little leather-covered bottle that had come from Spain the first time the two men went there to shoot doves, when Saint John was twenty-nine and Dudley was twenty-seven. Saint John held the bottle up for Rhoda to see. "The sacred tequila bottle," he said. Dudley smiled his twelve-year-old fort-building smile, his face as solemn as an ancient Egyptian priest. That's what the Egyptians did, Rhoda thought. Had strange bottles of elixir, went on mysterious expeditions and ritual hunts. The Egyptians must have been about twelve years old in the head, about Dudley and Saint John's age. Remember Gunther told me I was arrested at about fourteen. I don't think Saint John and Dudley even made it into puberty.

Saint John raised the little vial-shaped leather-covered bottle. He removed the top. Inside the leather was a very thin bottle of fragile Venetian glass. He took a sip, then passed the sacred bottle to Dudley.

"Exactly where are we going?" Rhoda asked. "I want to see a map." Saint John replaced the top on the sacred tequila bottle and restored it to its secret resting place in the glove compartment. Then he took out a map of Mexico and leaned into the back seat to show it to her. "Here," he said. "About a hundred and twenty miles below Laredo."

Then there was the all-night drive into Mexico. The black starless night, the flat fields stretching out to nowhere from the nar-

row asphalt road, the journey south, the songs they sang, the fathomless richness of the memories they did not speak of, all the
summers of their lives together, their matching pairs of chromo-
somes, the bolts of blue-and-white striped seersucker that had become their summer playsuits, the ancient washing machine that
had washed their clothes on the back porch at Esperanza, the
hands that had bathed them, the wars and battles they had fought,
the night the fathers beat the boys for stealing the horses to go
into town to meet the girls from Deer Park Plantation, the weddings they were in, the funeral of their grandmother when they
had all become so terribly shamefully disgustingly drunk, the people they had married and introduced into each other's lives, the
dogs they had raised, the day Saint John came over to Rhoda's
house to help her husband teach the Irish setters how to fuck,
the first hippie love-in ever held in New Orleans, how they had
gone to it together and climbed up a live-oak tree and taught the
hippies how to hippie. Their adventures and miraculous escapes
and all the years they had managed to ignore most of the rest of
the world. The way they feared and adored and dreamed each
other. The fathomless idiosyncrasies of the human heart. All of
which perhaps explains why it took all night to go one hundred
and eighty miles south of the place they left at three o'clock in
the afternoon.

First they goofed around in Laredo, then searched for diesel
for the Mercedes, then stopped at the border to get temporary
visas, then crossed the border into Nuevo Laredo. They drove
around the boundaries of Boy's Town, then went to the Cadillac
Bar for margaritas, then had dinner, then found the car.

It was black night when they left Nuevo Laredo and began to
drive down into Mexico. "Why don't we spend the night here
and go on in the morning?" Rhoda asked a dozen times. "Why
drive into Mexico at night?"

"Nowhere to stop," Saint John and Dudley said, and kept on
going, taking sips out of the sacred bottle, which seemed to hold

an inexhaustible supply of tequila. Rhoda was curled up on the back seat using her raincoat for a pillow, trying to think zen thoughts and live the moment and seize the day and so forth. I could be getting laid, she kept thinking. If I had expended this much time and energy on finding a new boyfriend I could be somewhere right now getting laid. I could have called an old boyfriend. I could have called that good-looking pro scout I gave up because of the AIDS scare.

"We were the lucky ones," she said out loud. "We got to live our lives in between the invention of the birth control pill and the onslaught of sexually transmitted diseases. We lived in the best of times."

"Still do," Dudley said.

"There was syphilis," Saint John added.

"But we had penicillin for that," Rhoda answered. "I mean, there was nothing to fear for about twenty years. If someone wanted to sleep with me and I didn't want to, I apologized, for God's sake."

"That's changed?" Dudley asked.

"It changed for me," Rhoda said. "I'm scared to death to fuck anyone. I mean it. It just doesn't seem to be worth the effort. I guess if I fell in love I'd change my mind, but how can you fall in love if you never fuck anyone? I can't fall in love with some-one who has never made me come."

"Her mouth hasn't changed," Saint John said. "Rhoda, do you talk like that in public?"

"In the big world? Is that what you're saying? You're such a prick, Saint John. I don't know why we let you run around with us. Why do we run around with him, Dudley?"

"I like him. He's my buddy." The men laughed and looked at each other and Saint John handed Dudley the tequila bottle and Dudley handed Saint John the salt. They poured the salt on their folded thumbs and licked it off. They shared a lime. They re-placed the top and put the sacred tequila bottle away. Nothing

had changed. Dudley and Saint John understood each other perfectly and Rhoda sort of understood them, but not quite. "Unless
you are both just as dumb as fucking posts and there is nothing
to understand."

"What's she saying now?"

"I said I want to drive if you are going to get drunk and I
want you to stop the car and roll up the windows and let's sleep
until it's light. I don't like driving down through this desolate
country in the middle of the night. I thought we were going to
some hacienda. No one told me I was going to have to spend
the night in a car."

"We're going," Dudley said. "We'll be there in an hour."

"It's two o'clock in the morning and you've already been lost
twice and I don't think you have the slightest idea where you're
going."

"You want some tequila, sister?"

"No, I want to get some sleep."

"You stopped drinking too? You don't get laid and you don't
get drunk, that's what you're telling me?"

"That's what I'm saying."

"Then why do you want to be alive?" Dudley shook his head.
"Have some tequila, honey. We'll be where we want to be when
we wake up tomorrow. You'll be glad, you'll see."

"Why baby her?" Saint John said. "If you give in to her, she'll
bitch all week."

"Fuck you," Rhoda said. She sat up and straightened her skirt
and blouse and arranged her legs very properly in front of her.
He was right, what was she living for? "Hand me that tequila,"
she said. "Is there anything to mix it with?"

"Wasting away again in Margaritaville," Rhoda started singing.
Dudley and Saint John joined in. They worked on country and
western songs for a while, which are hard songs to sing, then
moved into hymns and lyrics from the fifties and back into hymns

and finally, because it was the fourth of July even if they were in Mexico, into God Bless America and oh, say can you see and oh, beautiful for spacious skies, for amber waves of grain.

"Wait till you see the maize fields in the daytime," Dudley said. "That's how they bait the pamplona blanco. Maize fields on one side and irrigation ditches on the other. The whitewings are moving this way, and Don Jorge Aquillar and Mariana have been buying up all the leases for miles around. We're going to have some hunting this fall. Right, Saint John?"

"Who are Don Jorge Aquillar and Mariana?" Rhoda asked.

"The people we're going to see," Saint John said. "Right, Dudley," he went on. "If enough birds come. I can't bring my friends down here if the birds are scanty."

"Jesus, you've gotten cynical," Rhoda said. "Why are you so negative about everything?"

"Why are you picking on me?"

"I don't know, because I'm sick of riding in this car."

"Have another drink," Dudley said. "We'll be there in a little while. It isn't far now." He was right. They went another fifteen miles and began to approach the outskirts of a town. "Agualeguas, 1000 Habitantes," the sign said. They drove past small adobe buildings, then around a curving dirt road, then past a two-story building and a store and through a darkened neighborhood and went down a paved road and drove another three miles and came to a long brick wall covered with bougainvillea. A tall wrought-iron gate was in the middle of the wall with painted white wooden doves on either side of the lock. Attached to the dove on the right and fluttering in the breeze was an extra wing. Dudley stopped the car and got out and pulled the wing from the dove. It was a billet-doux. "Dearest Dudley," he read out loud. "I am waiting for you with a worried heart. Ring the bell and we will let you in. Love, Mariana."

So this is why we couldn't stay at a hotel in Laredo, Rhoda thought. So this is why we had to drive all night in the goddamn car. Because his new girlfriend is waiting. I should have known. Well, who cares, I signed on for this trip and this is what is happening. Who knows, maybe she has a brother.

Dudley rang the bell and a girl in a white skirt came running out of a building and began to fumble with the lock. Then the gates were open and servants appeared and took Rhoda's bags and led her to a room with beautiful red stone floors and windows that opened onto a patio. They set her bag on one of two small beds and brought her water and turned down the other bed. Rhoda took off her clothes and lay down upon the small wooden bed and went immediately to sleep. Outside the window she could hear Dudley and Saint John and Mariana laughing and talking and pouring drinks. They never stop, Rhoda thought. Fifty-six years old and still spreading seed. "This is Mariana," Dudley had said when he introduced the girl. "Isn't she beautiful, sister? Wouldn't she make great babies with me?"

When Rhoda woke she was in a hacienda in Agualeguas, Mexico. Bougainvillea, red tile roofs, a parrot in a cage, rusty red stone floors, a patio with a thatched roof and an oven the size of a cave, ancient walls, soft moist air, beside the oven a bar with wicker stools. Above the bar, cages of doves, pamplona blanco and pamplona triste, whitewings and mourning doves, very hot and still. I am still, Rhoda thought, this is stillness, this is zen. A dove mourned, then another and another. The doves woke me, Rhoda decided, or I might have slept all day. It seems I was supposed to come here. It is the still point of the turning earth, like the center, the way I felt one time when Malcolm and I sailed into an atoll in the Grenadines below Bequia and I said, This is the center of the earth, we must stay here forever. Well, we can anchor overnight, he answered, but in the morning we have to push on. No wonder I divorced him. Who could live with someone as work-drugged and insensitive as that. Mother-ridden and work-drugged. My last millionaire. Well, now I'm broke. But at least I'm happy this moment, this morning in this lovely still place with red tiles and thatch and the doves in cages and Saint John and Dudley asleep next door in case I need protection.

The stillness was broken by the sound of a Mexican man putting chlorine in the pool outside Rhoda's window. She dressed and went out onto the patio to watch. The pool was a beautiful bright blue. The man had put so much chlorine into it that the vapors rose like a cloud above the water. The birch trees beside the pool had turned yellow from the chlorine fumes. They were like yellow aspens, beautiful against the green shrubbery and the red flowers of the bougainvillea. Death is beautiful, Rhoda thought, as long as it isn't yours. She remembered something. A bullfight poster they had seen in Laredo advertising a bullfight in Monterrey. Let's go, she had said. I'm in the mood for a bullfight. Of course, the men had answered. They were amazed. When last they messed with Rhoda she had lectured them for hours about going to football games and eating meat.

Mariana came out from the thatched kitchen carrying a tray with coffee and two cups. Brown sugar and cream.

"Will you have coffee?" she asked.

"Con leche, por favor," Rhoda answered.

"What will you do today? Have they said?"

"We are to go see the fields. And maybe to a bullfight. There's some famous matador fighting in Monterrey."

"What's his name?"

"Guillarmo Perdigo."

"Oh, yes, with the Portuguese. They fight the bull from horse-back. It's very exciting."

"Muy dificil?"

"Oh, yes."

"Your English is so good."

"I am from Acapulco. I just came here to help my uncle."

"Dudley said it would be a famous place soon. That everyone will be coming here."

"We hope it will come true. If the doves come. We have bought up all the leases. We will have a monopoly."

"And some fun?"

"Oh, yes. That too." Mariana smiled, poured the coffee, looked away.

"Maybe the shopping clubs will come," Rhoda said. She watched Mariana, hoping to make her smile. Dudley had told Rhoda that groups of women came down to meet the hunters in Brownsville and Laredo and McAllen. Busloads of women from Shreveport and Baton Rouge came to meet the hunters at the Cadillac Bar and the bars of the Hilton Hotel and the Holiday Inn. It had begun by chance. First the men started coming down to hunt the doves. Then a group of women happened to be shopping in the border towns the same week. There were the bars full of good-looking hunters from all over the United States. So the women went home and told their friends and soon busloads of bored housewives from all over the South were down in the border towns buying up all the Mexican wedding dresses and piñatas in the world and getting laid at night by the hunters.

"That would be nice," Mariana said. "Do you think I should wake your brother?"

"No. Let sleeping men lie, that's what I always say."

"He told me to wake him at ten so he'd have time to see the fields. Carlos is here to drive you."

"Then wake him up. As long as you don't make me do it."

"Excuse me then." Mariana got up and moved in the direction of the men's rooms. I can't tell if she's shacking up with him or not, Rhoda thought. How Spanish not to flaunt it one way or the other. Spanish women are so mysterious, soft, and beautiful. They make me feel like a barbarian. Well, I am a barbarian, but not today. Today I feel as sexy as a bougainvillea. Rhoda sat back. The sun shone down between the thatched roof and the pool. The servants moved around the kitchen fixing breakfast, the yellow leaves fell into the bright blue pool, the carved tray holding the white coffeepot sat upon the wrought-iron table. Rhoda drank the coffee and ate one of the hard rolls and in a while Mariana returned with melons and berries, and the chlorine in the pool rose to the trees and the breeze stirred in the bougainvillea. The still point of the turning world, Rhoda thought. And what of the bullfight? Of the carnage to come? Death in the afternoon. What would it be? Would she be able to watch? It was getting hotter. Rhoda was wearing a long white skirt and a green and white striped shirt tied around her waist. White sandals. She was feeling very sexy, enchanting and soft and sexy. She looked around. There was no one to appreciate it. I'll just think about it, she decided. It's beautiful here, very zen and sexy. This is a thousand times better than being at home in the summer, a lot better than being bored.

The servants brought more coffee. Mariana returned. Then Dudley appeared, buttoning his khaki safari shirt. Saint John was behind him, dressed in white duck pants and wearing a cap with a visor.

"Why the cap, Saint John?" Rhoda asked. "Not that I don't like it. I do, a lot."

"It's from the Recess Club's last outing." He took off the cap, handed it to her so she could see the design. It was a man and woman locked in an embrace. "A Rorschach test," he added.

"Fabulous," Rhoda said. "How amusing."

"Give me back my cap." He retrieved it and planted it firmly back on his head. He had decided to be adamant about his cap. Rhoda moved nearer to him and put her arm around his waist. Poor Saint John, she decided. He could never wear that cap in New Orleans. All the trouble he's had all his life over pussy, he ought to get to make a joke out of it when he's in Mexico. "I think you're the sexiest man your age I've ever seen in my life," she said out loud. "I bet the ladies you treat fantasize about you all day long."

"I hope not," he said, but he was pleased and looked to Dudley to save him from himself.

"I thought Saint John got in the business to do it in the examining room," Dudley said. "Saint John, do you do it in the examining room?"

"Only with the nurses," he said, and they laughed and were relieved.

A driver appeared and they all piled into a four-wheel-drive vehicle and headed out of town toward the maize fields where the whitewing doves were already arriving in small numbers. From July to October more and more would come. Flying from the orange-red tops of the maize plants across the road to the irrigation ditches and then into the bush. It was all there, everything they needed, water and food and cover. All I need, Rhoda was thinking. All any creature needs.

"It will be a great fall," Dudley said, and opened a bottle of wine and began to pour it into paper cups. "Pamplona blanco bastante, right, Mariana? Right, Pablo?"

"We have a monopoly all along the river and the ditches," Mariana said. "And twenty-three rooms and three vehicles. Now if Dudley brings us hunters we are happy." She reached across the seat and touched his knee. I can learn from these women, Rhoda thought.

"A great fall," Dudley said again. "A great year." He leaned out the window, admiring the maize and the doves flying back and forth across the road as the vehicle approached the trees.

"I think I'll come twice," Saint John said. "Once in August and once in September. Look at that maize, Dudley. This place is going to be spectacular. I've counted twenty whitewings since we passed the dam."

"This place is going to be dynamite," Dudley agreed.

"I hope we make some money," Mariana said. "Uncle Jorge has invested very much."

"I'm coming back too," Rhoda said. "I know how to shoot. Don't I, Dudley?"

"Tell us which ones are the pamplona blanco," he answered. "Start practicing."

On the way back to the hacienda they stopped at a native market and bought fruit and packages of orange tortillas. The tortillas were such a beautiful shade of orange that Rhoda forgot her vow not to eat native food and began to gobble them up.

"They are also good with avocado on them," Mariana suggested. "I will find you some when we get home."

"I like them like this," Rhoda said, and brushed orange crumbs from her skirt.

"If you get lost we can find you by the crumbs," Saint John suggested. "Like Hansel and Gretel."

"If I get lost I'll be with some good-looking bullfighter who fell for my blond hair."

"Dyed blond," Saint John said.

"Sunbleached. Don't you remember, Saint John, my hair always turns blond in the summer."

"Rhoda, you never had blond hair in your life. Your hair was as red as Bess's mane, that's why we said you were adopted."

"Is she adopted?" Mariana asked.

"No," Dudley answered. "She is definitely not adopted."

It was after one o'clock when they got back to the hacienda. Time to get ready to leave for the bullfight.

"It starts at four-thirty," Rhoda said.

"They are always late," Mariana answered. "If we leave here by three we'll be there in time."

"Time for a siesta," Dudley said.

"Siesta time," Saint John echoed.

There was an hour to sleep. A dove mourned, then another, a breeze stirred an acacia tree outside the window, its delicate shadows fell across the bed and danced and moved. Dance of time, Rhoda thought, light so golden and clear, and Zeus came to her in a shower of gold, clear, dazzling, and clear. Rhoda curled up into a ball and slept on the small white bed. She had not felt so cared for since she was a child. No matter how much I hated them, she thought, they protected me. They would throw themselves between me and danger. Why, I do not know. Taught or inherent, they would do it. How spoiled I am, how spoiled such men have made me.

The bullfight was in Monterrey, a hundred and twenty kilometers to the south and west. Mariana sat up front with Dudley. Rhoda and Saint John rode in back. They drove along through the afternoon heat. Dudley had the air-conditioner going full blast. Mariana had a flower in her hair. They talked of the countryside and what it grew and Rhoda asked Mariana to tell them who she was.

"My father is Portuguese," she began. "This is not unusual in the towns of the coast. The Portuguese are seafarers. There were seven children in our family. I am the second oldest."

"I'm the second oldest," Rhoda said. "We're the oldest of all our cousins. We used to rule the rest of them. The rest of them were like our slaves."

"Why does she say things like that?" Saint John asked.

"Because that's how she thinks." Dudley handed Saint John the leather-covered tequila bottle. "Whatever she does, that's the best. If she was the youngest, she'd believe the youngest child had the highest I.Q. She's the queen, aren't you, Shorty?"

"We did rule them. You used to boss Bunky and his brothers all around and I used to boss Pop and Ted and Al. We used
to stay all summer at our grandmother's house, Mariana. We had
a wild time. I guess those summers were the best times of my
life. There were all these children there. Because of that I always
thought a big family must be a wonderful thing."

"Give Mariana some of our Dudley-Juice," Dudley said. "Give
her some magical-gagical compound, Cuz. She needs a drink."

"It was nice to have the others," Mariana said. "But we ran
short of money."

"What did your father do?" Rhoda went on.

"He is a builder," Mariana answered. "A contractor. He helped
build the Viceroy Hotel in Acapulco. He will come for the hunts.
If you come back you will meet him."

"How old is he?"

"He is sixty. But he looks much younger. He is a young man."

"Let's sing," Dudley said. "How about this?" He reached for
Mariana's hand, began to sing. "When Irish eyes are smiling, sure
it's like a morn in spring." I wonder if that stuff works on young
girls, Rhoda thought. I wonder if that old stuff gets him anywhere anymore. I mean, it's clear the child likes him, but it may
be for his money. They used to like him for his basketball prowess.
No, maybe it was always for money. Why did boys like me? Maybe
that was only Daddy's money. Well, now I'm broke. No wonder
I don't have any boyfriends and have to run around with my
brother and my cousin. Rhoda, stop mindfucking. Love people
that love you.

"I can't wait to see this bullfight," she said out loud. "I saw
one on my second honeymoon but I was so drunk I can't remember anything about it except that my feet hurt from walking
halfway across Mexico City in high heels."

"It's how she thinks," Saint John said. He took a drink from
the tequila bottle and passed it to Dudley.

"How do you think?" Rhoda said. "What are your brilliant

thought processes? Hand me that tequila bottle. Where is all the tequila coming from? When are you filling it up?"

"Doesn't have to be filled," Dudley said. "It's magical-gagical compound. Up, down, runaround, rebound."

They arrived in Monterrey at four-fifteen, parked the car and found a taxi and told the driver to take them to the Plaza de Toros.

"Lienzo Charros," Mariana told the driver. "Pronto."

"I do not think it is open," he answered. "I don't think they are there today."

"It said on the poster they would be there. Guillarmo Perdigo is fighting."

"We'll see." The driver shifted his cigar to the other side of his mouth and drove through a neighborhood filled with people. He went down a hill and turned sharply by a stone wall and came to a stop. They could hear the crowd and see the flags atop the walls of the compound.

"I can't believe we're here," Rhoda said. She got out of the taxi and stood waiting by a tree while Dudley paid the driver. Her sandals settled into the soft brown dirt beneath the tree. The dirt moved up onto her toes and covered the soles of the new white sandals. She was being taken, the earth of Mexico was making her its own. The taxi driver waved and stuck his arm out the window and the little party weaved its way down the incline toward a wooden ticket booth beside a gate. Rhoda was very excited, drawn into the ancient mystery and the ancient sacrifice, the bull dancers of Crete and Mycenae, the ancient hunters of France, the mystery of the hunt and ancient sacrifice, and something else, the mystery of Dudley and Saint John. What allowed Dudley to hunt a jaguar in the jungles of Brazil? What allowed Saint John to don his robe and gloves and walk into an operating room and open a woman's womb and take out a baby and then sew it all back up? What was the thing these men shared that Rhoda did not share, could not share, had never shared. I could never cut the grasshoppers open, she remembered, but Saint John could. I could pour chloroform on them. Poison, a woman's weapon since the dawn of time. But not the knife. The knife is not a woman's tool. She shuddered. Women give life. Men take it. And the species lives, the species goes on, the species covers the planet.

She took a twenty-dollar bill out of her pocket and tried to buy the tickets but Dudley pushed her hand away and gave the ticket seller a handful of thousand-peso notes. Then they walked across a dirt enclosure to the entrance to the stands. Small boys played beneath the stands, chasing each other with toy pics, charging each other's outstretched arms. A blindfolded horse was led by, wearing padding and a double rein, a tall white Andalusian horse that looked quite mad. The excitement was very sexy, very intense. Four students wearing shirts that said Stanford University were in front of them on the stairs. They were drinking beer and laughing.

"These guys are just hairdressers," one student said. He was carrying a minicam video recorder.

"A high school football game," his companion added. Rhoda felt the urge to kill them. Rich spoiled brats, she decided. If they start filming this on that goddamn minicam, I'm going to throw up. How dare they come and bring that goddamn California bull-shit to this place of mystery, this remnant of ancient sacrifice and mystery, this gentle culture and these lithe sexy Spanish men, how dare these California rich boys spoil this for me. She looked at Saint John and Dudley and was very proud suddenly of their intelligence and quietness. Dudley held the arm of the young Spanish girl. Both Dudley and Saint John spoke intelligible Spanish to anyone they met. We are civilized, Rhoda decided. We are polite enough to be here, to visit another world. But those goddamn muscle-bound California pricks. Who would bring a minicam to a bullfight? Fuck them. Don't let them ruin this. Well, they're ruining it.

They found seats and arranged themselves. Mariana on the outside, then Dudley, then Rhoda, then Saint John. The music began, terrible wonderful music. Music that was about death, about sex and excitement and heat and passion and drama and blood and death. The music was about danger, sex was about danger, sex was the death of the self, the way men and women tried themselves against death. Ancient, ancient, Rhoda thought. Oh, God, I'm so glad to be here. So glad to be somewhere that isn't ironed out. "Without death there is no carnival." A long boring life with no carnival. That's what I've come down to, that's what I've been settling for. And will settle for, will go right back to. Well, fuck safety and security and fuck the fucking boring life I've been leading. She put her hand on Saint John's arm. Reached over and patted her brother on the knee. "Thank you for bringing me here," she said. "Thank you for this."

"You want a Coke?" Dudley said. "Do you want a beer or anything? You want a hat?" He motioned to a vendor and the man came over and Dudley bought a black felt matador's hat with tassels for Mariana and tried to buy one for Rhoda but she refused his offer. "I don't wear funny hats," she said, then looked at Mariana. "You have to have black hair to wear that hat. On black hair it looks great." Mariana pushed the hat back from her head so that it hung down her back on its black plaited cord. Her gold earrings dangled about her shoulders. It was true. She did look nice in the hat.

A vendor passed before them carrying a huge basket full of candy and cigarettes and packages of M&M's and sunflower seeds. His wares were spread out like a flower opening. It was a beautiful and heavy load and he displayed it as an artist would. Over his shoulder Rhoda could see the Stanford students standing side by side in their muscle shirts rolling film on the minicam and she hated them with a terrible and renewed passion.

"This is a small corrida," Mariana said. "Three bulls, but the matadors are good. Especially Guillarmo. I have seen him fight. He fought last year in Mexico City. And the last matador is Portuguese. Yes, you are lucky to get to see this. This is unusual for Monterrey."

"Como se dice in Español, lucky?" Rhoda asked. "No recuerdo."

"Fortunata," Dudley answered. "Benedecire and fortunata."

The music stopped for a moment and the vendor passed by again, this time carrying Cokes and beer in aluminum buckets. He was assisted by two small boys who looked like twins. "Gemelos?" Rhoda asked, and added, "Are they yours?" The vendor laughed and shook his head. He opened a Coke for Rhoda and one for Mariana and beer for the men. The minicam crew from Stanford had turned the camera Rhoda's way. She held up her hand before her face and waved them away. They kept on filming. "Tell them not to do that to me," she said to Saint John. "I mean it." Saint John waved politely to the young men and they turned the camera back toward the arena. Rhoda drank her Coke. The vendor and the twins moved on. The band picked up their instruments. They were wearing red wool jackets with gold buttons and gold trim. "They must be burning up in those uniforms," Rhoda said. She shook her head. They raised their tarnished brass instruments and the wild dangerous music began again.

"Look," Saint John said. "At the toriles, the bull pens, you can see the bulls." Rhoda looked to where he was pointing. She could see the top of a bull beyond a wooden wall, then the horns, then a second bull. They were very agitated. Very large, larger and more powerful and more agitated than she had imagined they would be. The blindfolded horse was led into an arena beside the toriles, a picador in an embroidered suit was sitting on the horse, another leading it. A bull charged a wooden wall, then disappeared out of sight. The door to the arena containing the blindfolded Andalusian horse was open now. The bailiff came in. He was wearing a tarnished gold uniform, riding a tall black horse with a plaited mane. Other men on horseback joined him. The paseo de cuadrillas was forming. Three small boys chased each other with paper pics across the barrera. "We could sit down there," Mariana said, "if you don't mind getting blood on your clothes."

Dudley and Saint John didn't answer. They were getting serious now, the homage athletes pay each other. "The seats near the arena are barrera," Mariana added, addressing her remarks to Rhoda. "The torero's women sit there." The women exchanged a look. In the bull pen a bull broke away from its keepers. There was a rush to corner it. Rhoda thought of Ferdinand, the old story of the bull that wouldn't fight. My sweet little mother, she thought, trying to deny all mystery and death for me. Except for the soft passing of Jesus into heaven, she would shield me from all older worlds.

But there are no Ferdinands, put out to pasture if they will not fight. The ones that won't fight go to the slaughterhouse. My sweet mother, smelling of talcum powder and perfume, reading to me of Ferdinand smelling the flowers. Then she would get up and go into the kitchen and cut the skin from a lamb, as happy as Saint John in the operating room. Contradictions, half-truths. But this is true. Death in the afternoon is real danger, real death.

One of the toreros came up the stairs toward where they were sitting. He stopped in the barrera and spoke to a group of men. Two men stood up and embraced him. They are his father and his brother, Rhoda decided. The torero was tall, and lithe, like a dancer. Beneath his white shirt his skin seemed soft and white. Rhoda wanted to reach out and touch him, to wish him luck.

He sat down between the men he had embraced. The one who appeared to be his brother put an arm around his shoulder. They talked for a while. Then the torero got up as swiftly as he had arrived and left and went back down the stairs. The music grew louder, rose to a crescendo, descended, then rose again. The gates to the arena opened. The alguaciles rode out in his tarnished suit, leading the paseo de cuadrillas. Then the matadors, the bande-rilleros, the picadors. The mayor threw down the key to the toril. The matador who had come into the stand was wearing a short black jacket now, a montera, a dress cape.

The procession filed back through the gate. The gate to the toril was opened and the bull ran out. The matador, Guillarmo Perdigo, walked out into the arena and the ceremony began. This was no hairdresser, no high school football game, this was the most exquisite and ancient ceremony Rhoda had ever seen. The matador spread his cape upon the ground, squared his shoulders, planted his feet. The bull charged across the arena. The matador executed a pass, then another, then turned and walked away, drag-ging his cape. The bull pawed the ground, was confused, walked away. The matador turned to face the bull again, spread out his cloak, called to the bull. The bull charged again, and then again. The matador passed the bull's horns so close to his body, to his balls, to his dick. Rhoda held her breath. It's amazing, Rhoda thought. Where have I been while this was going on?

Dudley and Saint John had not moved. Mariana was still. A second matador appeared. Then the third. The matadors each did a series of passes, then the picadors came out on horseback and stuck the pics into the shoulder muscles of the bull. Rhoda was sickened by the sight. Fascinated and repelled, afraid for the mata-dor and trying to hate the bull, but there was no way to hate him now since he was outnumbered. She turned her eyes from the bull's wounds, turned back to the matador who was alone with the bull again. This is so sexy, so seductive, she was thinking, the hips on that man, the softness of his face, of the skin beneath his white shirt. How many years has he worked to learn this strange art or skill? To allow that bull to move its horns so close to his hips, to his dick, then to turn his back and walk away.

Still, to torture the bull. Rhoda, don't fall for this meanness. It is mean. Still, it doesn't matter, not really, not in the scheme of things. It is how things are, how things have always been. Men learned these skills to protect themselves from animals, to protect their children and their women. And it's so sexy, so fucking wonderful and sexy. I would fuck that bullfighter in a second, AIDS scare of not. I bet they think everyone from the United States has it. I bet no one in a foreign country would fuck an American now. They probably wouldn't fuck an American for all the money in the world. Rhoda leaned into the arena. The matador spread out his cape and made four beautiful and perfect passes, then drew the cape behind him and turned his back to the bull and walked away. He walked over to the barrio and was handed an older, redder cape and a sword. He came back out into the arena and displayed the sword against the cape and then prepared the cape for the kill. The bull looked confused, hesitant, worried. Perhaps he smelled his death. He walked away. "Toro," the matador called, "toro, toro, toro." The bull pawed the ground, made a fake pass, then moved back. The matador prepared again, spread out the red cape upon the ground, displayed the sword upon it, then moved the sword behind the cape, moved his feet very close together, then waited. The bull charged, the matador stuck the sword between the spinal column, planted it all the way to the hilt, and the bull's lungs filled with blood and it fell to its knees.

"The sword goes in and severs the spinal column," Saint John said. It was the first time he had spoken in thirty minutes. "It punctures the lungs and the lungs fill with blood. An easy death."

"Compared to what?" Rhoda said.

"Anything you can think of."

"What would be the easiest one?"

"Anna's wasn't bad. The shock of the freezing water would cushion the shock of the cyanide."

"What would be the easiest thing of all?"

"Fifty Demerols. I have a jar at home in case I have a stroke. I don't want to recover from a stroke."

"Nor I," Dudley said.

"Well, you probably won't have to," Rhoda said. "You'll just ruin your liver getting hepatitis down here in Mexico and call me up and ask me to give you one. God, I hope I don't have to give you a liver."

"I hope so too."

"Kidney," Saint John put in. "They don't transplant livers."

The picador ran out onto the dirt floor, took out a silver dagger, delivered the coup de grace. The matador stared at the bull, then turned his face to the sky and walked back across the dirt arena. Rhoda rose to her feet with the crowd. This is what theater was trying to do, she decided. This is what plays aspire to but this is real death, real catharsis, real combat and real battle, and the thing I can not understand and my shrink can not understand. This is not subject to Freudian analysis because this is older than Freud and besides I am not a German Jew. I am from a culture more deadly and cold than even these Spanish people descended from Moors. She looked at the face of her brother and the face of her cousin. They were completely satisfied. She was satisfied. The young men from California were still sitting. They had put their camera away. Even they knew that something had happened. Later, Rhoda thought, they will get drunk and blow it off. Whatever the matador represents they will not allow it in. They are future people, remaking the genes. No second-rate Mexican bullfighter can impress them. Perhaps nothing can impress them. They will just get on a talk show and explain it all away. They are the future, but I am not. Rhoda stood up, extracted some dollar bills from her purse, excused herself, and walked down through the still cheering crowd toward the barrio. She wanted to be near the matador, to breathe the air he breathed, to experience the terrible sexiness of his skin, to look at him. She walked down the steps toward the concession stand underneath the stadium. He was standing with his back to her, his back was sweating underneath the soft white cotton of his shirt, his hair reminded her of a painting she had seen once of a Spanish child, so black it was no color, his neck was soft and tanned and the skin on his shoulders beneath his shirt seemed to her to be the sexiest thing she had ever seen in her life. He turned and handed something to a woman in a yellow blouse. Rhoda withdrew her eyes and walked on down the stairs and stood by a long concrete tub which held beer and Cokes. Two men were selling the drinks. "Un Coke," she said. "Por favor." The vendor extracted one from the depths of the icy water and removed the top with a church key. He handed it to her and took her dollar. The blindfolded horse stood against a fence. A few tourists walked toward the stand, two small boys chased each other with make-believe swords, the heat was all around her. She drank the cold sweet drink, felt her body melt into the heat. She stood there a long time. Finally the matador came out of a gate and walked toward two men in black suits who were awaiting him. The men embraced. The matador held one of the men for a long time. They were the same height and their arms slid around each other's shoulders. The black-suited man patted the matador's wet shoulder. The matador looked past his friend and saw Rhoda watching him. He met her eyes and received her tribute. I could fuck him, Rhoda thought. If I were still young enough to have hope, I would walk across this twenty feet of earth and hand him a paper with my name on it and tell him where to find me. He would find me. He is young and still has hope. She set the cold sweet Coca-Cola down on the waist-high concrete tub and walked toward the matador. He excused himself from the men and came to meet her.

"Esta noche," she said. "Donde? Where will I find you?"

"At the Inn of the Sun." His lips were as soft and full as the skin on his shoulders. His hips were so close to her. The smell of him was all around her.

"I will come there," she said. "When? At which hour?"

"A los siete. At seven." He reached out and took her arm. "I was watching you. I knew you wished to speak with me."

"I am called Rhoda. Se nombre Rhoda Katerina."

His fingers held her arm. "At seven," he said. "I will wait for you." He moved closer. "Will you sit with me now?"

"No, I am with my brother. I will come at seven." She turned to walk back to the stairs. He walked with her to the first landing. The tourists were watching them. The men at the concession stand were watching them. The children were watching them.

She walked back upstairs and rejoined Dudley and Mariana and Saint John. The afternoon grew hotter. Two more bulls were killed, including one from horseback. Then the corrida was finished. The band put up their tarnished instruments and recorded music began to play from the speakers. Rhoda and Dudley and Mariana and Saint John went out on the street to find a taxi but there was none so they began to walk toward the hotel where they had left the car. I have to ask Mariana how to get to the inn, Rhoda thought. I have to get her alone and get her to help me.

"There is too much violence in the world," Saint John said. They were walking along the uphill dirt street, following the crowd in the direction of the town.

"Too much violence," Rhoda answered him. "What do you mean? You're as bad as those goddamn Stanford boys."

"You're all fascinated by your father's violence," Saint John said. "Look what it's done to Dudley."

"What are you talking about, Saint John? Make yourself clear. Jesus, it's hot as noon." They had walked out from the shade of the hill. It was as hot as noon, hotter, for the earth had had all day to soak up heat. Rhoda shuddered, thinking of the earth soaking up the blood of the bulls, blood soaking down into the earth and turning black. The matador's soft hands, the silver sword, the red cape and blood soaking down into the earth, the heat.

I'm too old for him, Rhoda thought. But then, what difference would my age make? Remember when Malcolm gave that speech at the medical college and we went to the party with all the surgeons. The oldest man in the room was the most powerful. God knows how old he was, but he came across the room and took me. Just took me because he wanted me. And I allowed it. I left everyone else that I was talking to and followed him out onto the patio and he said, I want to take you somewhere tomorrow. Where was it he wanted me to go? To see a cadaver or something terrible or grim and Malcolm came and found me and brought me back inside because even Malcolm knew what was going on. So it has nothing to do with age or even violence although violence is one of its manifestations. It's power that matters, and in this Mexican town on this hot day power is killing bulls and Saint John knows it and is pissed off at the matador and pissed off at me.

"Goddamn, I wish we'd find a taxi," Saint John said. "I'm not sure this is the way to town."

"We can catch a bus," Mariana said. "If we go this way we will come to the main street and a bus will come by." They trudged up the dusty street and arrived at a main thoroughfare, and in a few minutes a dilapidated city bus picked them up and took them into town. She told them on the bus. First she told Saint John. "I'm going to meet the bullfighter," she said. "I'm going to his hotel."

"Of course you aren't," Dudley said. He turned around from the seat in front of her. "No, that's final."

"You don't tell me what to do. I don't take orders from you."

"He's right," Saint John said. "You can't go off with those people."

"Why not? Why can't I? What do I have to live for that's so important I'm supposed to be careful? My children are grown. I'm going to his hotel at seven o'clock tonight."

"You aren't going off with a Mexican bullfighter," Dudley said.

"That is that. You aren't going to do that to us, Shorty."

"Is not a good idea," Mariana put in. "He would not really expect you to come even if you said you would. Not if he saw you were with men. He would think they would not let you." She lowered her eyes. "Even American men."

The bus had stopped at the downtown square. They filed off with the other passengers and found themselves in the middle of a parade which was forming to circle the square. A young girl in a red dancing dress was seated on a throne on a car. Her attendants were around her. A band was getting out its instruments.

"Be a good sport," Saint John said. "Don't start something with a matador. Not tonight, please, Rhoda." He took her arm. They began to walk toward the hotel where they had left the station wagon. "It was such a nice day. Why spoil it?"

"It's about death," Rhoda said. "I can't stand to do nothing constantly but displacement activities, amusements, ways to pass the time, until we get into the ground to stay. What's happening to us, Saint John? We are getting so old. We haven't got enough sense to be alive and it's almost over. We'll be crippling around with a pacemaker soon. We'll be completely dried out and ruined and I've never slept with a bullfighter in my life and I've always wanted to."

"Stop and get her a margarita," Dudley said. "Let's go in there." They had come to a restaurant on the square and went in and ordered a round of margaritas. They drank to the bullring and the brave matadors and Dudley began to give toasts.

"I'm going," Rhoda said. "I'm going over there at seven o'clock."

"Here's to the girl from the Delta, who never would say you are right, who never gives in, please give in, Rhoda, your brother and cousin are begging and begging you tonight." Dudley raised his margarita and signaled the bartender to bring them another round.

"Here's to the girls growing old," Rhoda raised her glass. She was into it now. "Who think they didn't get laid enough. Lost

their youth and their puberty and their childbearing years being
good for Daddy and big brother and fucking Jesus."

"Rhoda, you've had all kinds of husbands and boyfriends.
What did you miss out on?"

"Normal relationships. Having one husband and loving him
forever. Getting laid on a regular basis. Remember, Saint John, I
missed from the time I was thirteen to nineteen. I never got laid
during the great primitive fertile years, thanks to no birth control and our Victorian upbringing."

"So you want to go fuck some Mexican bullfighter in a cheap
hotel to make up for not having a normal life?"

"Don't lawyer-talk me." Rhoda put down her margarita. She
had decided to take it easy and not get drunk. "And you're not
getting me drunk," she added. "So don't try that. It will just make
me go over there more."

"He won't expect you to be there." Mariana reached out a hand
and touched Rhoda's arm. This woman was so different from her
brother. This woman was not careful. It would not be good to
hunt with her.

"I want to go and fuck this guy. I'm fifty-three years old. It's
none of anybody's business. I don't mess around with your sex
lives."

"Hey, look," Dudley said. "Here come the musicians." Three
guitarists had come in the door and were gathering around a table.
The music began, beautiful, sexy, exciting music. A song Rhoda
had heard once coming over a wall at a resort in Acapulco. "I
heard that music in Acapulco at Las Brisas once," she said. "I was
having a terrible honeymoon with a man I didn't love. See, think
of the terrible life I have been forced to live because I only liked
power."

The music rose. Dudley motioned to the musicians to come
their way. "I was on a honeymoon," Rhoda went on. "But all I
did was get drunk and swim in this pool where you swam over

to the bar. It was New Year's Eve and the musicians on the boats in the harbor played that wonderful music but it was all feet of clay, feet of clay." Rhoda finished the first margarita and started in on the second. The musicians came nearer. Dudley gave them money. "Let's dance, Shorty," he said. "I want to dance with my baby sister." Then the two of them went out onto the dance floor and began to dance together. My closest, closest relative, Rhoda was thinking. My own big brother. My own hands and legs and arms and face. The gene pool, Jesus, what a fantastic mess.

"Que paso, mi hermano," she said. "We shall dance a little while and then go and see the bullfighter."

Dudley was a wonderful dancer and Rhoda loved to dance. He had Rhoda where he wanted her now and he knew it. They drank many margaritas and some wine and danced until the sun was far down below the horizon and seven o'clock had come and gone. "I have to go over to the Inn of the Sun," Rhoda kept saying. "What time is it?"

"Let me dance with her," Saint John said. "I never get to dance with Rhoda."

Sometime later they found a restaurant and ordered tortillas and frijoles and chili with mole verde sauce. They drank sangria and ate the wonderful gentle spicy food. "The food of a thousand colors," Rhoda said. "The food of orange tortillas and green avocado mashed and red peppers the color of the bull. I have to get over to the hotel, Dudley. I want to change clothes and go and see the matador."

"Let him wait," Saint John said. "The longer he waits the more he'll want you."

"You're just saying that," Rhoda said. But she was in a wonderful suggestive drunken state and so she began to picture herself as she had been at fifteen, sitting in her room for fifteen minutes while her date cooled his heels waiting for her to come down the stairs. Fifteen minutes, LeLe had always insisted. You have to make them wait at least fifteen minutes. Don't ever be on time. Don't ever be waiting for them.

When they had eaten all they could eat of the exotic dangerous food, they wandered back out onto the street where the parade had ended and the carnival had begun. There were street vendors selling food and musicians playing, children everywhere, young men and women walking in groups and couples, drinking beer and sangria and calling out greetings. Dudley and Saint John and Rhoda and Mariana walked back to the hotel where they had left the station wagon and took possession of the rooms Mariana's friends at the hotel had saved for them. There were two large adjoining rooms with big tiled bathrooms and a common sitting room. They carried their small amount of luggage up the stairs and went into the rooms and all fell down on one enormous walnut bed. Dudley was still making up limericks.

"There was a young girl from Brownsville, who always wanted to swill wine, and when they said no, she said, 'You know where to go,' and now she is there waiting for them."

"That's terrible," Saint John said.

"There was a young doctor from New Orleans, who always said, 'I am going to warn you, you'll get into trouble if you go out with me, for I won't marry you but I'll charm you.'"

"Worse."

"There was a young girl from the womb," Rhoda began. "Who barely got laid from there to the tomb. She said, 'Well, goddamn, so that's where I am, who did this to me. I must find a way to blame whom.' Sinking spell," she added. "I am having a sinking spell." She rolled up on the bed, cuddling into Saint John's shirt.

"Don't worry," he said. "It will pass."

A short while later Rhoda made a recovery. "Wait a minute," she said. "Where's my cosmetic kit? I have to do something about

my face." She got up and found the small leather kit and carried
it into the bathroom. She put the kit on the counter and examined herself in the dark mirror. I'll have to start all over, she decided. She took out a jar of Charles of the Ritz face cleanser
and began to apply it to her face. Then she decided it was going
to get all over her hair so she dug around in the bag until she
found a shower cap and she put that on. She went back into the
room and opened the suitcase and took out a clean blouse and
disappeared back into the bathroom. Dudley had gone downstairs
to procure a bottle of wine and some glasses. Saint John and
Mariana were propped up on the bed having a conversation about
whitewing dove hunting and how to get the birds to come to
Laredo instead of Brownsville.

Now Rhoda decided to take a bath in the stone bathtub. She
took off all her clothes and wrapped herself in a towel and took
her clothes back out to the room and hung them over the back
of a chair. "Don't mess these up," she said. "They're all I have
to wear."

"He won't expect you to come," Mariana said, in a voice so
low only Saint John could hear her.

"Don't talk about it," Saint John said. "Don't say anything. So
tell me, how much land has your uncle leased? Has he got it all,
all along the irrigation ditches?"

"Yes," she said. "Para ustedes solamente. All of it. All the
land."

Rhoda ran water in the tub and washed the tub out. Then she
filled the tub with hot water and got in. What was I going to
do? she was thinking. Oh, yes, I'm going over there and see the
matador. LeLe will have a fit. She'll die of jealousy. If Anna was
alive what would Anna say? Anna would say, Rhoda, you are drunk.
Rhoda giggled, the thought was very heavy, the thought would
sink the hotel. That's why you got cancer, Anna, she decided.
From always thinking shit like that just when I was about to

have a good time. Rhoda examined her legs as they floated in the water. They didn't look very good anymore. There was something wrong with the quality of the flesh, with the color of the skin. I hate my fucking body, Rhoda decided. I just fucking hate growing old. There isn't one single thing about it that I like. She got out of the tub and wrapped the towel around her and went out into the room.

"We should give all our money to young people," she said. "It is wasted on people as old as we are."

"What's wrong now?" Saint John asked.

"The skin on my legs looks like shit. I mean, the flesh. The flesh looks terrible. There's something wrong with it. It's mottled looking. I hate myself. I hate getting old, Saint John, it sucks to hell and back."

Dudley came in the door with a tray. A Mexican boy was behind him with the glasses. There was fruit and cheese and champagne and Dudley opened the champagne while the young boy tried not to notice that Rhoda was wearing a towel. She picked up her clothes from the chair and took them into the bathroom. Dudley brought her a glass of champagne and she drank it. Then she sat down at the bathroom stool and began to put on makeup.

Saint John turned on the radio beside the bed. Wild music began to play. United States music. It was a broadcast from Tom and Jerry's in Nuevo Laredo. They were interviewing people who had come there to party all night. The music rose and fell and the people who were being interviewed told where they were from and what they had come to find in the border towns. It was funny. It was hilarious. The people were drunk and the broadcast was from Nuevo Laredo on the Mexican side so the interviewees were saying anything they wanted to say. It was amazing to hear people telling the truth on the radio. "I came down to get laid." "I came down to get drunk and let it all hang out." "I came down to find chicks." "I came down to find some guys to party with." "I came down to get away from it all." "It's cheap here."

"You can find a party, you can have a good time." And so on.

Rhoda was getting back into a wonderful mood. The champagne had erased time. Her face was starting to look mysterious and beautiful. The bathroom was beautiful and mysterious. There were baskets of beautiful colored towels. There was a tile wall of fine blue and white figured tiles, each one different, each one made by hand. Everything in the room had been made by hand. The wicker stool was high and comfortable. The lights were soft. Rhoda applied more rouge, added some blue eye shadow, then a small single line of silver. She was beautiful, perhaps the most beautiful woman in the world. She thought of the matador pacing around the lobby of the hotel waiting for her. Waiting and waiting, thinking she wasn't going to come. Then she would appear. Fresh and lovely, his dream come true.

Dudley came into the bathroom and filled her champagne glass. He kissed her on the cheek. "I'm about ready to go," Rhoda said. "As soon as I finish my face."

"You're sure you want to go there?"

"I am sure. I have to have experiences, Dudley. I can't live my whole life in a straitjacket." She peered into the mirror, a deep line furrowed her brow. She was not quite as beautiful as she had been a moment before. "Don't back out on taking me. You said you'd take me. You promised me."

"I'll take you. We're going to see the matador. El matador." He was serious. He was playing the game. He wasn't making fun of her. One thing about Dudley, Rhoda decided. He never makes fun of me. Their eyes met. Yes, they were going to take the world seriously. Otherwise it wouldn't be worth ruling in case they were ruling it.

"What's going on in there?" Saint John called out. "I thought we were going to the Inn of the Sun God to see a matador. You better hurry up before I go to sleep instead."

"Let's go," Dudley said. "Come on if we're going."

*   *   *

It was eleven o'clock when they left the hotel and walked back to the square to look for the matador's inn. The fiesta was in full swing. The cafés were full. Mariachi music was playing. Music was coming out of the doors of the cafés. Drunks were falling off of benches on the square. People had been drinking all day. The car with the throne perched on top was parked sideways on a curb.

"Where is the Inn of the Sun?" Rhoda kept asking people.

"Keep going," someone said, "you will come to it."

"I'm just going over there," Rhoda kept saying. "I may not stay."

It was a square brick hotel on the corner of a street two blocks off the square. There was a lamp over a desk in the lobby. The light was dim and no one was behind the desk. They went into the lobby and waited. "Anybody here?" Rhoda called out. Dudley and Saint John didn't say a word. Mariana cuddled into Dudley's arm. A sleepy-looking man came out a door and asked what they wanted.

"I am looking for the torero, Guillarmo Perdigo," Rhoda said. "Is he staying here?"

"He was here," the proprietor said. "With his family. But he is gone now. He has been gone for a while."

"Will he be back?"

"I do not know. Perhaps in the morning. Perhaps not."

"Thank you," Rhoda said, and turned and led the way out of the inn and back out onto the street. They walked back to the hotel and went up to their rooms and told each other good night. Saint John was sleeping on a pull-out bed in the sitting room. After a while Rhoda got up and went into the room and got into the bed with him. "I'm lonely as shit," she said. "I want to be near you."

"Get in," he said. "It's okay. I love you. You're our little girl. Are you okay?" He reached over and pulled the cover up over her shoulder. He patted her shoulder. He patted her tired worn-out head. Her used-to-be-red, now sunbleached, hair which was not standing up very well under the trip to Mexico.

"No," she said. "I drank too much and besides I wanted to go and meet that bullfighter. I wasn't really going to sleep with him, Saint John, I just wanted to get to know him."

"But you might catch something, Rhoda. Kissing is worse than intercourse for some of the viruses. You should see what I see every day. It's really depressing."

"I never think of you getting depressed."

"Well, I do."

"I really wanted to go over there and meet him."

"We went there."

"No, you got me drunk to keep me from going."

"I was afraid for you, Rhoda. I love you." He patted her shoulder. He felt old suddenly, very old and far away from the world where he and Rhoda and Dudley had been alive and hot and terrible.

"I miss my children," Rhoda said. "I am lonesome for them."

"I know you are," Saint John said, and kept on patting until Rhoda settled down and was still.

"Thank God," he said out loud and moved his hand and went to sleep beside her.

In the morning they drove back to the hacienda. No one mentioned the matador or having gone to the inn to look for him. Rhoda folded her arms around herself and thought about the softness of his shoulders and his black eyes seeking out hers across the concrete concession stand. Win some, lose some, she was thinking. Outside the windows of the station wagon the hills were purple in the early light. I love this country, Rhoda decided. Any place that can produce a man like that is okay with me. Oh, God, I wish Anna were here. I could call up Anna and tell it to her

and she would say, What a wonderful story. What a lovely encounter. Remember when she fell in love with that tennis player
that summer in New Orleans and he fell in love with her? Some
enchanted evening, only it was afternoon at the New Orleans
Lawn Tennis Club right after they moved to the new club and
the next day she showed up at my house at about eight in the
morning so excited and horny and borrowed my makeup because
she had been up all night making love to him in his apartment
on Philip Street. God, what a summer. What a hot exciting world.
It's true, we got to live in the best of times. Now they have to
have rubbers and spermicides and be scared to death of catching
things. We weren't afraid of anything. Oh, God, Guillarmo's back
and arms are the most beautiful things I've ever seen in my life. I
would like to see him fight bulls from now till the dawn of time.

"Rhoda?"

"Yes."

"Are you all right back there?" It was Dudley speaking. Saint
John was asleep beside him in the front seat. Mariana was asleep
beside Rhoda.

"Let's stop and get something to eat," Rhoda said. "I didn't
have any breakfast."

"We'll be at the hacienda soon. Can you wait till then? I don't
think there's anywhere to stop between here and there, except
maybe a native market."

"No, it's all right. I forgot. I forgot where I am."

"I want to take you to a special place this afternoon. To meet
some friends of mine."

"Sure."

"They're Americans who live down here. The man's from Austin
and his wife is from Ireland. You'll like them. They have a really
interesting place. An animal farm. You've never seen anything
like it."

"Where do they get the bulls?"

"For the fights?"

"Yes."

"They raise them. It's quite an art, to keep the bloodlines pure and keep from overbreeding them. I'll take you sometime to one of the ranches where they are raised."

"I want to go back to Monterrey and see another bullfight."

"I bet you do."

"Okay, Dudley. Well, I'm going back to sleep." She closed her eyes. Went into a fantasy of meeting Guillarmo on an island off the coast of Spain. Having babies with him. Raising bulls.

They got back to the hacienda in Agualeguas at noon and had lunch and packed up and said their farewells to Mariana. Mariana was wearing a new gold bracelet with the teeth of a saber-toothed tiger embedded in the gold. Does he carry that stuff around with him in the glove compartment? Rhoda wondered. I mean, does he just have it ready in case he gets laid or does he go out at night and buy it? Maybe the fairies deliver it. God, what a man.

"I wish you could stay another night," Mariana said. "The rooms are free."

"We have to get back," Rhoda said. "Saint John and I have to catch a plane tomorrow. Look, Mariana, could you get me a poster of that bullfight we saw yesterday? I mean if you see one or if you get a chance." Rhoda held out a twenty-dollar bill. "Keep this in case you see one and buy it and send it to me."

Mariana refused the money. "I'll send you one if I am able to find it." The women's eyes met. "Well, come back," Mariana added. She took Rhoda's hand. I love Mexico, Rhoda decided. I adore these people. I wish they'd all cross the border. This lovely tropic heat, the bougainvillea, Guillarmo's shoulders, blood on the arena floor."

"I'll come back," she said. "When the doves are here." Then Dudley embraced Mariana and Saint John embraced her and Rhoda embraced her and they got into the station wagon and drove off.

"One more thing we need to see," Dudley said as he turned onto the asphalt road. "One more thing to show Shorty."

"What is that?" Rhoda asked.

"The cats," Saint John said. "Dudley wants you to see the cats."

It was two o'clock in the afternoon when they left the hacienda. They turned onto an asphalt road leading northwest to Hidalgo and Candela. A few miles outside of Candela they left the main road and followed the course of a stream until they came to a fence and a gate. Dudley stopped the car and got out and spoke into a microphone attached to the gate. In a few minutes a boy came on a bicycle and opened the gate with a combination and held it while they drove in.

A well-kept road made of crushed stone led uphill between acacia and scrub birch trees. Dudley drove the station wagon carefully up the road. The road grew steeper and he shifted into second gear. Rhoda was leaning up into the front seat now, trying not to ask questions. They had all slipped once again into their childhood roles. Dudley, the general and pathfinder. Saint John, the faithful quiet lieutenant. Rhoda, lucky to be there, lucky to get to go, interloper.

"You may see a lion along here," Dudley said. "Don't be surprised if you do. They get loose. Dave Hilleen and I had to shoot one last month. Hated to have to do it."

"A lion," Rhoda said. Very softly, very quietly. "He's kidding, isn't he, Saint John?"

"No, he's not," Saint John said. "You'll see."

The road wound down a small hill, then across a wooden bridge. The bridge covered a creek that crossed and recrossed the road.

"There's a springbok," Saint John said. "Oh, there's the herd." Rhoda looked and there beneath the trees was a herd of twenty or thirty African springbok. Their tall sculpted horns rose like lilies into the low hanging limbs of the scrub brush. They quivered, then disappeared like a school of fish.

"My God," Rhoda said. "How lovely. How divine."

"There are kudu and sheep and deer," Dudley said. "We're hoping to get some rhino in the fall."

"You're kidding."

"No, he's not," Saint John put in.

"They'll love it here," Dudley said. "It's exactly like parts of central Africa. Only safer and there is hay. It's conservation, Shorty. Someday, this may be the only place these creatures live. The African countries are destroying their herds. They're being hunted out and their preserves raped. They're beautiful, aren't they?"

"Do you hunt them?"

"Very little. We sell them to zoos. Sometimes we trade them for cats."

"All right. I'll bite. What cats?"

"You'll see," Saint John said. "Wait till you see."

"Cats that circuses can't train. Ones that go bad. The one Dave and I shot was an old lion that went bad. Ringling Brothers paid us to take him."

"Who does this belong to?" Rhoda asked. "Who pays for all of this?"

"It pays for itself. Dave paid five thousand to shoot the lion. He was scared to death. I didn't think he was going to pull the trigger when it charged. Jesus, I never saw a man get so white. Afterwards he said to me, I was scared to death, Dudley. How do you do that in the wild? Just like you did it here, I told him. It's him or you. It took him two shots." Dudley was talking to Saint John now. "One glanced off the ear and one went in an eye, ruined the head. I shot for the heart and lung when I saw his first shot miss. Old Dave. I never saw a man go so white."

"Who started all this?" Rhoda asked. "Who does this belong to?"

"These are nice folks here," Dudley said, suddenly stern.

"They're friends of mine. Be nice to them and try not to talk too much."

"Of course," she said. "I'm always nice to everyone." Saint John sniggered, and Rhoda started to tell him to go fuck himself but for some reason she didn't feel like making Saint John or Dudley mad at her right that minute.

They had come to the top of a rise. A Caterpillar tractor with a grader blade was parked beside the road. Two Mexican boys sat underneath an umbrella drinking from a stone jar.

A house was at the end of the road. An old stone house like something out of a nineteenth-century English novel. It was three stories high with turrets and a tower. In the field behind the house were structures that looked like huge greenhouses. They were tall cages, sixty feet wide by eighty feet long. There were three of them, at intervals of forty feet, constructed of steel bars three inches thick. Swings were suspended from the ceiling beams and some of the cats were sitting on the swings. A leopard, Rhoda thought. That's a leopard. And that's another one. She was struck dumb. Now she did not have to try to be quiet. Nothing could prepare you for this, she decided, no words could prepare anyone for this.

Dudley drove the car up to the house and parked it. Children appeared on the back porch. The caretaker's children. A tall girl, maybe twelve or thirteen, a boy a little older, a smaller girl, an even smaller boy. They were dark-skinned and dark-haired but did not look like Mexicans. "Are they Mexican?" Rhoda asked.

"Of course."

"They don't look it."

"Their mother is Italian. Where's your momma?" Dudley called out. He opened the door and got out. "Hand me that sack of rolls," he added. They had stopped at a bakery in Anahuac and bought sweet bread and raisin loaves for the children. Dudley handed the sack to the oldest girl. The boy smiled and held out an animal he was wearing on his arm. "Baby jaguar," the boy said. "They are all gone for the day, gone hunting with Redman."

"We just came by to see the cats," Dudley said. He patted the jaguar. He got back into the car. "We'll be back to the house. I want to show my sister the cats." Rhoda was half in and half out of the car. Now she got back in and shut the door.

"The momma killed the other one," the boy said. "We are raising this one on a bottle."

"We'll be back," Dudley said. He put the car in gear and backed out of the parking place. The children arranged themselves on the porch stairs, the boy held up the baby jaguar, flies buzzed around the porch and the car, the ground was dry and yellow. Rhoda sat on the edge of her seat. Behind them was a fourth cage. It was full of very large cheetahs, at least three cheetahs. "That cage isn't big enough for the cheetahs," Dudley said. "We have to do something about it. We didn't know we were going to have so many. The cougar need better cages, too. There are fourteen cougar now. Too many, but everyone keeps sending them and no one wants to hunt them."

"Embarrassment of riches," Saint John muttered. Dudley ignored him and drove the car from the driveway and out into the field where the cages rose like monuments in the hazy blue sky. We will get bogged down in the field, Rhoda thought. The car will stop and we'll have to get out. Why do the men in this family always have to drive cars into fields? Why do I always end up driving on a field or in a ditch? Why can't we stay on the road like other people? Don't talk. Don't say a goddamn word. If you object it will just make him do it more. You can't stop Dudley by telling him not to do something. Just be quiet and it will soon be over.

"How do you like it?" Dudley said, and laughed. He began to circumnavigate the cages. Tigers were in the first one. At least five tigers, four gold and white striped tigers and one black tiger lounging on top of a concrete shelter. As they passed the cage

Rhoda saw that a sixth tiger was inside the shelter, a huge black tiger twice as large as the others, taking up the coolest, most protected spot in the concrete shelter. She shuddered, tried to take it in. Dudley drove on. In the second cage were Bengal tigers, with faces as big as car windows. Three Bengal tigers sitting together on swings looking at her with their huge heads. In the third cage were lions. A lioness and three young cubs. Dudley drove down to a fourth cage, which could not be seen from the house. Jaguars were in that one. There were more cages in front of the house, protected by shrubbery and trees.

"What are in those?" she asked quietly.

"Leopards and cougar and some more lions," Dudley said. "We have three lionesses with cubs now and the ones in the pasture."

"What pasture?" But then she knew. Dudley had stopped the station wagon beside a flimsy-looking forty-foot-high fence. Inside the fence was a huge lion. Behind him in the tall grass were two lionesses with their cubs. The lion turned his head their way. Dudley rolled down the automatic windows and opened the sun roof. "Aren't they gorgeous, Shorty?" he said. "Aren't they something?"

"My God," she said. Dudley got out and walked over to the fence. "Hello, Waylon," he said. "Long time no see." The lion roared, a long deep rattling in the throat. Dudley turned his back to the lion and walked away.

"Don't worry, Shorty," he said. "He wants me but not badly enough to do anything about it today." Rhoda could hear him but she was only looking from the deepest part of the back seat. She had tried looking at the lion out the window but it was like staring over a precipice. Still, she could hear every word Dudley said, every sound of the world, suddenly she could hear every nuance, every blade of grass.

"Don't talk to him," she said. "Don't do anything else. Get back in the car." Dudley turned back to the lion.

"Get in the car," Rhoda called out. In a very soft voice. "Roll up those windows. Get in the car and get me out of here. Saint John, roll these windows up."

"The windows wouldn't stop him," Saint John said. "If he wanted to get in the car he could do it."

"Well, drive it then," Rhoda said. She called out the window in the loudest voice she could muster: "Dudley, get in the car. Get in this car and get me out of here. I don't like it. I don't like that lion. Or those cats. Get me out of here."

"I thought you were into violence now," Saint John said. "Bull-fighters and blood and all that."

"Not when I'm part of the ring. Roll the windows up, Saint John, this is madness. That fence isn't big enough to stop a dog, much less a lion. Get Dudley back in the car. Let's get out of here. I don't like it here."

Dudley spoke to the lion again. "You want me, don't you, Waylon. Show Rhoda what you need." He turned his back to the lion again and began to walk away from the fence. The lion moved toward the fence.

"Oh, shit," Rhoda said. "I'm driving off, Dudley. I'm leaving you here. Roll those windows up, Saint John. Roll them up this minute, do you hear me?"

"It's okay," Saint John said. "You're okay."

"I am not okay. I am scared to death." Rhoda pulled herself into a ball in the very middle of the back seat. She considered climbing into the trunk, but there was no trunk, it was a station wagon.

Dudley turned back to the lion. "Old Waylon," he said. "He hates me but he doesn't know why. You don't know why, do you, Waylon? Except you know I'm not afraid of you."

"Get in the car," Rhoda yelled. "Get in the car this very minute. Roll those windows up. Oh, God, why did I come down here to fucking Mexico in the middle of July. Have they closed the window yet? Please close the window, Saint John. Dudley, close the goddamn sunroof and get back in the car and get me out of here.

I have had all I can take of these goddamn terrifying unbelievable cats. I don't want to see them anymore. Take me to that
house." He was still standing by the lion. "It's bad karma," Rhoda
continued. "It's terrible karma to have these animals here. They
should not be here. They should be dead or else back where they
came from, where the Indians or Chinese or Africans or whatever
can kill them themselves. If they lived where I lived I'd kill them
all tonight. Get back in the car. Leave that lion alone." The lion
bounded for the fence. Dudley laughed. Saint John got back in
the car.

"Start the car," Rhoda said. "Saint John, start the car."

"Not yet. Go on up to the house if you're scared."

"Hell no."

"They can't get out, Rhoda. Oh, I guess the lion could get
over the fence, but he doesn't really want to."

"Okay, I'm going. I can't take any more of this." Rhoda opened
the car door. She looked toward the house. The children were
standing on the stone steps holding the baby jaguar. "I'm going
to the house," she said. "Fuck being out here with these goddamn
lions." She stepped down on the grass, shut the car door, and
began to run. "Don't get so excited," Dudley yelled. *Don't get them
excited*, she thought he said.

"Watch out," Saint John called. "Watch your step." Rhoda
sprinted toward the house, which seemed a mile away. She ran
faster and stepped into a gopher hole and turned her ankle and
went sprawling down across the dry yellow grass. Pain shot up
her leg, then something was on top of her. It was Saint John. He
knelt beside her and began to feel the bones in her foot. "Get
me into the house," Rhoda was yelling. "Carry me into that house
and lock the door."

Rhoda lay on a filthy horsehair sofa in the parlor of the stone
house. One-half of the sofa was covered with the skin of a mountain sheep. Her broken foot lay propped on the sheepskin. By her

side was a marble table with a statue of Mercury, wings on his feet. Saint John had gone into the kitchen to call the hospital in Laredo. Dudley was outside the window helping the young girls feed the jaguar. I am lying on this sofa catching ringworm, Rhoda decided. The worms are going into my ankle through my wound and into the soles of my feet from where that dreadful little abandoned jaguar shit upon the floor. The children will have ringworm too. They will be bald and dead from the bad karma in the place. Live by the sword, die by the sword. There's no telling what will happen now. I don't even know if Saint John is a good doctor. Being my cousin doesn't make him good enough to set my foot, even if we do think our genes are superior to everyone else's in the whole fucking world. "It hurts," she called out. Then yelled louder. "My goddamn foot is killing me, Saint John. Please come give me something for my foot."

Dudley stuck his head in the open window. "What's wrong, Shorty? What's wrong now?"

"My foot is broken. And I want to go to the hospital. I don't want to wait another minute. It's your fault for not taking me to the house when I asked to go. I didn't know we were going to see these lions. Who said I wanted to go see a bunch of real lions? That fence wouldn't hold a lion for a minute if it wanted to get out. It could get out and kill everyone in the place."

"We're going in just a minute," Dudley said. "As soon as Saint John gets off the phone."

"Then hurry up," she said. "It's killing me. It's about to kill me, Dudley."

Saint John entered the room carrying a glass of water and a bottle of Demerol pills and stood by while she swallowed one. The water will give me amoebic dysentery, she decided. But I can't help that for now. "Where did the water come from?" she asked. "What kind of pills are these?"

Then the pain was better and finally stopped, or, at least, Rhoda didn't have to suffer it any longer. They carried her out to the station wagon and laid her out in the back seat beside a box of frozen pamplona blanco and two cases of German wine and the guns. Saint John borrowed an embroidered pillow from the children and arranged it underneath her head and propped her injured foot on a duffel bag and then Dudley made long elaborate farewells and they drove off down the line of caged animals. The panthers scurried around their cages. The lionesses flicked their tails. The lion cubs played with their paws. The Bengal tigers turned their stately faces toward the car like huge Indian sunflowers. The kudu pricked up their ears, they moved like leaves before the wind. The peacocks flew up to the fence posts. The Mexican guards waved and opened the gate. Dudley returned their wave and drove on through. Then he reached down into the glove box and took out the secret leather-covered tequila bottle and passed it to his cousin.

"When was the first time you two ever went hunting together?" Rhoda asked drowsily.

"When Saint John was ten and I was eight," Dudley answered. "Remember, Saint John, Uncle Jodie lent us his four ten and that little rifle, that twenty-two, and we went bird hunting, across the bayou behind the store."

"We were quail hunting," Saint John added. "We scared up a covey but we missed and then you shot a rabbit. Back where Man's cabin used to be."

"We skinned it and Babbie cooked it for us that night for dinner." They leaned toward each other in the front seat of the car, remembering.

"I took my old harpoon out of my dirty red bandanna," Saint John began singing. "And was blowing sweet while Bobby sang the blues."

"Blowing soft while Bobby sang the blues," Rhoda corrected sleepily from the back seat. "Not blowing sweet." She sank back down into the Demerol. The hunters looked at each other and shook their heads. A hawk high above them in the air spotted the car and was blinded by the reflection of the sunlight in his eyes.

"From the coal mines of Kentucky," Saint John started again. "To the California hills, Bobby shared the secrets of my soul."

A few days later Rhoda was back in her own house, safe from spotted fever and hookworm and amoebic dysentery and adventure. Her ankle was in a cast. She had a pair of rented crutches and a rented wheelchair. She had a young girl from the nursing school who was coming by in the mornings to fix her breakfast. She had an old boyfriend who taught history who was coming over in the afternoons to cheer her up. She had accepted an offer to teach Latin during the fall semester, replacing a young man who had gone crazy in the summer and run off to California without telling his department chairman. He had sent a note. "I can't bear their wretched little faces," the note said. "What do they need with Latin?"

The department chairman had called Rhoda and asked her if she could fill in. He had gotten her on the phone the day after Dudley had delivered her to her house. "Yes," she had said. "I will teach your class. I need some order in my life."

Now she sat in the wheelchair on the patio and watched the robins picking up seeds on the freshly mowed lawn. Her hands lay on her legs. She thought about her boring boyfriend. She thought about the sweet little nursing student who was fixing her such boring sweet little meals. She thought about lying in the back of the station wagon all the way home from Mexico and Saint John's hopeful, grating, off-tune voice singing the collected works of Kris Kristofferson and the collected works of Willie Nelson.

She thought of Dudley and how long they had all managed to live and how strange that they still loved each other. We know each other, she decided. Nothing has to be explained. No questions asked. *I wish them well.* Even if they do think it is all right to fuck around with a bunch of lions and tigers and risk their lives and keep on hunting when it is the twentieth century and for a long time men have dreamed they could evolve into something less dangerous and messy and bloody. Still, there was that bullfight.

The sun came out from behind a cloud and flooded the patio. Rhoda sank deep into herself. Moved by the light.

She considered her boyfriend, who did good dependable useful work in the world and how boring and pointless it was to make love to him. With or without her foot in a cast she had no passion for the man. Her chin fell to her chest. We are not making progress, she decided. This is not progress.

I will go back with them in September. To kill the beautiful and awkward pamplona blanco and pluck them and cook them and eat them. Anything is better than being passionless and bored. There's no telling who might be down there this fall. No telling what kind of gorgeous hunters might shut me up for a few hours or days and make me want to buy soft Mexican dresses with flounces and rickrack and skirts that sweep around my ankles. Bullfighters are waiting and blood on the arena floor. Blood of the bull and fast hot music and Mexico. "I should have left a long time ago," she began humming. Progress is possible, she decided. But it's very, very slow.

Several weeks later, when her ankle had healed enough that she could walk, she drove downtown to the travel agency to buy her ticket back to San Antonio. At the corner of Spring Street and Stoner she changed her mind and went to her old hippie psychiatrist's office instead. She parked the car and went in and asked the receptionist to make her an appointment. Then she went home and began to write letters. It was a cool day. The first cool day in months. The light was very clear. The trees were just beginning to turn their brilliant colors. Fall was coming to the mountains. Life was good after all. Peace was possible. Ideals were better than nothing, even if they were naïve. Here I go again, Rhoda thought, one hundred and eighty degrees a minute. She stuck some paper in the typewriter and began to write the first of the know-nothing letters. The proto-wisdom papers of the fall of 1988.

Dearest Dudley [the first letter began],

We have been the victims of Daddy's aggression all our lives. The pitiful little victims of his terrible desire for money and power. All he understands is power. He doesn't have the vaguest idea how to love anyone and neither do you and I. We must save ourselves, Dudley. Don't go back to Mexico and drink tequila and run around with lions. Come up here and visit me and we will sit on the porch and drink coffee and try to think of things to do that are substitutes for always being in danger. We could play cards. I will play cards with you for money, how about that? *I don't know anything now. I don't know where to begin.*

We need to talk and talk and talk. Please come.

Love, Rhoda

Dear Saint John,

Don't go back to Mexico and catch amoebic dysentery. Come up here instead. We don't need to kill things in order to eat. All we need to do is stay alive and work and try to appreciate life and have a good time.

Come on up. Dudley and I are going to revive card games. We are going to play poker and drink a lot of coffee and I'll make biscuits for breakfast.

We'll have new times instead of old times.

Love, Rhoda

P.S. I'm sorry about that bullfighter. I really am.

P.P.S. I had this vision of the three of us huddled together on the floor at Esperanza sucking on each other for sustenance and love. Trying to get from each other what we couldn't get from the grown people. All those terrible years — our fathers at the war and our mothers scared to death and the Japs coming to stick bamboo splinters up our fingernails and you and me and Dudley trying to mother and father each other. Life is not easy for anyone. That's for sure. I don't think we really understand much yet and may be losing the little that we used to know. We don't need Mexico, old partner. We need something to hold on to in the dark and someone to remind us of where we really are. We are spinning in space on this tenuous planet. I won't let you forget that if you won't let me.

Love and love again, me.

Rhoda sealed the letters into envelopes and addressed them. Then she got into the car and drove down the hill and deposited them in the box at the post office. She was in a good mood. She even remembered to think it was miraculous that man had learned to write, not to mention invented a system to get letters from one place to another. Not to mention taming horses and fighting bulls and living to grow up. Every now and then someone grows up, she decided. I've heard about it. Why not, or else, whatever.

A STATUE
OF APHRODITE

IN NINETEEN EIGHTY-SIX I was going through a drought. I was living like a nun. I was so afraid of catching AIDS I wouldn't sleep with anyone, not even the good-looking baseball scout my brothers ran in one weekend to see if they couldn't get me "back into the swing of things." My brothers love me. They couldn't stand to watch me sit out the game.

My name is Rhoda Manning, by the way. I write for magazines. I've lived in a lot of different places but mostly I live in the Ozark Mountains in a little town called Fayetteville. "I live in a small city, and I prefer to dwell there that it may not become smaller still." Plutarch.

During nineteen eighty-six and nineteen eighty-seven, however, I lived in Jackson, Mississippi, in the bosom of my family. I had gotten bored with the Ozarks and I wanted to make my peace with my old man. "The finest man I've ever known," as I wrote in the dedication to a book of poems. I don't think he ever read them. Or, if he did, he didn't read them very hard. He reads the *Kiplinger Newsletter* and *Newsweek* and *Time* and books he orders from the conservative wing of the Republican Party. He has large autographed photographs of Barbara and George Bush and Nancy and Ronald Reagan and flies an American flag in the front yard. You get the picture. Anyway, I admire him extravagantly and I was riding out the AIDS scare by being an old maid and eating dinner nearly every night with my parents.

Then this doctor in Atlanta fell in love with me and started writing me letters. He fell in love with a piece I did for *Southern Living* magazine. It was all about how we used to sit on porches at night and tell stories and the lights would go out when it stormed and we would light candles and coal-oil lamps until the power company could get the lines repaired. One of those cute, cuddly "those were the good old days" pieces that you mean while you are writing them. Later, you remember that you left out mosquitoes and flies and how worried we were that it wouldn't rain and make the cotton or that it would rain at cotton-picking time. The reason I leave that out is that I was a child at that time and thought the world was made of gold. It was made of gold and my daddy came home from the war unscathed and mostly we were able to pick the cotton and the black people on Hopedale Plantation were not miserable or unhappy and were treated with love and respect by my deeply religious family. I will never quit saying and writing that no matter how much people who were not there want to rewrite my personal history.

Anyway, this doctor was recently widowed. He was the head of obstetrics for Emory University Hospital and he fell in love with my article and the airbrushed photograph of myself I was putting into magazines at that time. I guess I was still having a hard time admitting I was pushing the envelope of the senior citizen category. Anyway, I kept putting this soft, romantic photograph into magazines and I still think it was that goddamn photograph that caused all the trouble and cost me all that money. I figured up the other day what my affair with the widowed physician cost me and it is upwards of ten thousand dollars. Do you know how many articles I have to write for magazines to make ten thousand dollars?

Back to the letters from the doctor. They were full of praise for my writing and "an intense desire to have you come and speak at our hospital enrichment program. We are very interested in keeping our staff in touch with the finer things in life and have a series of programs featuring writers and painters and musicians. We could pay you two thousand dollars and all your expenses and would take good care of you and see to it that we don't waste too much of your valuable time. Anytime in April or May would be fine with us. If you are at all interested in coming to light up our lives with a short reading or lecture please call collect or write to me at the above address. You could read the fine piece from *Southern Living*. And perhaps answer a few questions from the audience. Yours most sincerely, Carter Brevard, M.D."

Can you imagine any fifty-year-old woman turning that down? I could read between the lines. I knew he was in love with me before I even got to the second paragraph. I've fallen in love with writers through their work. And here's the strangest thing. You don't care what they turn out to be. If you fall in love with the words on the page, you are hooked. They can be older than you thought they were, or messily dressed to live in a hovel. When their eyes meet yours all you hear is the siren song that lured you in.

Of course this doesn't work for romance or mystery writers or people whose main objective is to get on the *New York Times* best-seller lists. This only works for writers when they are singing the song the muse gives them. I don't sing it all the time, like my cousin Anna did, but sometimes I do. Sometimes I trust myself enough to "know the truth and to be able to tell the truth past all the things which pass for facts," and when I do, people who read it fall in love. Re: Carter Brevard, M.D. Actually, if you subtract the two thousand dollars he paid me, I guess he only cost me eight thousand dollars. Which isn't all that much, considering the fact that I was living in an apartment and eating dinner with my parents every night. I guess I could afford eight thousand dollars to remember how nice it is to come. Have an orgasm, I suppose I should say, since this might make it into a magazine. But not *Southern Living.* They don't publish anything about what happens after people leave the porches and go to bed. It's a family magazine.

So I gave Doctor Brevard a date in April and his secretary called and made travel plans and sent me a first-class airline ticket, which is an absurd waste of money between Jackson, Mississippi, and Atlanta, Georgia, and made me a reservation for a suite of rooms at a four-star hotel and in short behaved as though I were the queen of England coming to pay a visit to the provinces. It was "Doctor Brevard wants to be sure you're comfortable," and "Doctor Brevard will meet your plane," and "Oh, no, Doctor Brevard wouldn't hear of you taking a taxi."

So now there are two people in love. Doctor Carter Brevard in love with an airbrushed photograph and a thousand-word essay on porches and yours truly in love with being treated like a queen.

My parents were very interested in this visit to Atlanta. "You ought to be thinking about getting married, Sister," my father kept saying. "It would be more respectable."

"It's against the law for me to get married," I would answer, wondering how much money someone made for being the head of obstetrics for Emory University Hospital. "I have used up my allotment of marriages."

February and March went by and unfortunately I had gained several pounds by the time April came. I trudged down to Maison Weiss and bought a sophisticated black three-piece evening suit to hide the pounds and an even more sophisticated beige Donna Karan to wear on the plane. I was traveling on Friday, April the sixth, leaving Jackson in the middle of the morning and scheduled to speak that night to the physicians of Emory University and their significant others. I was an envoy from the arts, come to pay my respects to applied science. I put on the beige outfit and high-heeled wedge shoes and got on the plane and read Denise Levertov as we sailed through the clouds. "The world is too much with us . . . Oh, taste and see. . . ."

He was waiting at the gate. A medium-sized white-haired man with nice eyes and a way about him of someone who never took an order and certainly almost never met planes. I could tell I was not exactly what he had ordered, but by the time we had collected my luggage and found a skycap and started to the car he was taking a second look. Letters can always win out over science. Letters can articulate itself, can charm, entice, beguile. Science is always having to apologize, is hidden in formulas, statistics, inexact results, closed systems. An obstetrician can hardly say, "I saw a lot of blood this morning. Pulled a screaming baby from its mother's stretched and tortured vagina and wondered once again if there isn't a better way."

He tried. "I did three emergency C-sections in the middle of the night. I'm going crazy with this AIDS thing. I'm trying to protect an entire operating room and I'm not even allowed to test the patient. It's the charity cases that scare me. Fourteen- and fifteen-year-old drug addicts. My sons are doctors. I was covering for one of them last night. Sorry if I don't seem up to par." He opened the door to a Lincoln town car and helped me in.

"I know what you mean," I answered. "I haven't been laid in fourteen months I'm so afraid of this thing. My friends call from all over the United States to talk about it. We're all scared to death. I don't think there's anyone in the world I would trust enough to fuck." Except maybe a physician, I was thinking. I don't suppose a doctor would lie to me. He got behind the wheel and started driving, looking straight ahead. "My wife died last year," he said.

"That's too bad. What did she die of?"

He took a deep breath. He went down a ramp and out onto an expressway. "She died of lung cancer. You don't smoke, do you?"

"I haven't smoked since the day Alton Ochsner told my mother it caused cancer. She was visiting them one summer and came home and told us of his findings. I don't do things that are bad for me. I'm too self-protective. I'm the healthiest person my age I know and I'm going to stay that way. I can't stand to be sick. If I got cancer I'd shoot myself." There, that should do it, five or six birds with one paragraph.

"I hope you enjoy the evening. It's at the University Club. The staff will be there and the resident physicians and their wives. They're all very eager to meet you."

"I hope I won't disappoint them."

"Oh, I don't see how that could happen."

He delivered me to the hotel and three hours later picked me up. He was wearing a tuxedo and looked very handsome. I began to forget he was of medium height. In the last few years I have decided such concerns limit the field too much for the pushing the senior citizen category. After all, I don't want to breed with the man.

The dinner and reading went well but there were two incidents that in retrospect seem worth noting. Two things I did not give enough weight to when they occurred. There was a woman with him when he picked me up. A thin, quasi-mousy woman about my age who introduced herself as his interior decorator. "I'm doing his country house in English antiques," she told me.

"I used to have a house full of antiques," I answered. "Then one day I hired a van and sent them all back to my mother. I couldn't face another Jackson press or bearclaw chair leg. I like simple, contemporary things."

THE STATUE OF APHRODITE

"He likes antiques," the woman said. "In furniture, that is." She and Doctor Carter Brevard laughed and looked at each other with shy understanding and I felt left out. Later, in the ladies' room at the University Club she made certain to tell me that they were not "lovers." Did he tell her to tell me that, I wondered. Or did she think it up for herself.

Later, while we were drinking wine and eating dinner I was telling the people on my right about my father. "He's a heroic figure," I was saying. "He has never told a lie. He's too stuck up to lie to anyone. And he's very funny. When he was about seventy-five he decided he was getting impotent. He told everyone about it. He told my brothers the minute that he noticed it. They said he came down to the office that morning shaking his head and laughing about it. 'I can't do it anymore,' he told them. 'Imagine that.'"

"What?" Doctor Brevard said, turning fiercely toward me. "He told your brothers that? He thought that was funny?"

"He's a great man," I answered. "He doesn't have to worry about his masculinity. It's grounded in stuff much more imperishable than whether he can get it up or not." I was laughing as I said it but Doctor Carter Brevard was not laughing. Maybe this is Atlanta society, I decided. Or what happens when people climb into society on their medical degrees.

So that sort of soured the evening, although I partially made up for it by making the doctors laugh by reading them a story about a woman who tried to stop drinking by going to live in the woods in a tent. It's a really funny story, a lot funnier than you'd imagine just to hear me tell about it.

Anyway, after the reading the doctor and his quasi-mousy interior decorator friend drove me back to the hotel and he walked me through the lobby to the elevator and stood a long time holding my hand and looking sort of half-discouraged and half-sweetly into my eyes. Then, suddenly, he pulled me to him and gave me a more than friendly hug. "I have a check for you in my pocket but I'm embarrassed to give it to you."

"Give it here. I'm embarrassed to take it, but what the hell, I have to work for a living like everybody else." I kept on holding his hand until he withdrew it and reached into his tuxedo pocket and took out the check and handed it to me. "You were marvelous," he said. "Everyone was so pleased. I wish we could have paid you more."

"This is fine. It was a nice night. You were nice to want me here."

"Maybe I'll come and visit you sometime. I'd like to see where you live."

"Come sit on the porch. I'll take you to meet my parents."

"Your father really said that to your brothers?"

"He did indeed. Well, I guess I better go upstairs. Linda is waiting in the car."

"She's only a friend. She's my decorator."

"So she said." I left him then and went up to my suite and turned on CNN and C-Span. Then I took a Xanax and went to sleep. What a prick-teaser, I was thinking. Is this what I've come down to now? Flying around the country letting aging doctors flirt with me and give me terrified hugs in hotel corridors? I stuck my retainer in my mouth to keep my capped teeth in place and went off to sleep in Xanax heaven. I only take sleeping potions when I'm traveling. When I'm at home I don't need anything to make me sleep.

Well, I didn't forget about it. When you haven't been laid in fourteen months and a reasonably good-looking doctor who makes at least two hundred and fifty thousand dollars a year hugs you by the elevator, you don't forget it. You mull it, fantasize it, angelize it. Was it him? Was it me? Am I still cute or not? Could you get AIDS from a doctor? Maybe and maybe not. All that blood. All those C-sections on fourteen-year-old girls. There is always nonoxynol-9 and condoms, not that anyone of my generation can take that seriously.

So I was mind-fucking along like that and five or six days went by and I was back to my usual life. Writing an article on Natchez, Mississippi, for a travel magazine, exercising all afternoon, eating dinner with my parents. Then, one afternoon, just as I was putting on my bicycle shorts, the phone rang and it was Carter calling me from his office.

"I've been thinking about you. How are you? Are you all right?"

"Sure. I'm fine."

"You were a big hit. You did the series a lot of good. Several people told me they'd attend more of the events if all the speakers were as entertaining as you were."

"That's nice to hear. That cheers me up and makes my work seem worthwhile."

"I don't suppose you'd like to come and visit me. I mean, visit in the country at my country house. It's very nice. I think you'd like it."

"The one with the antiques?"

"Oh, you really don't like them?"

"I don't care if you like them. I just don't want to have to dust them."

"Oh, I see." Was I actually having this scintillating conversation? Was I actually going to buy an airline ticket to go see this guy and have conversations like that for three days when I could pick up the phone in Jackson, Mississippi, and talk to writers, actresses, actors, television personalities, National Public Radio disc jockeys, either of my brothers, any of my nine nieces and plenty of other people who would have talked true to me and gotten down and dirty and done service to the language bequeathed to us by William Shakespeare and William Faulkner and Eudora Welty.

You bet I was and that was not the worst of it. I was going

to a wedding. "I'll tell you what," he proposed. "I'm having a wedding for my daughter in June. Would you come and be the hostess? She's a lovely girl. I have four children. Two are my wife's from a previous marriage. Two are my own, also from a previous marriage. It's going to be a garden wedding in my country house."

"With the antiques?"

"Very old-fashioned. The girls will all wear garden hats. The gardens will be in bloom. Some other famous people are coming. You won't be the only famous person there."

"I'm not famous."

"Yes, you are. Everyone here has heard of you."

"Well, why not. Okay, I'll come and be your hostess. I won't have to do anything, will I?"

"No, just be here. Be my date."

"Your date?" I started getting horny. Can you believe it? Talking to this man I barely knew on the phone I started wanting to fuck him?

Oh, yes. After the wedding, after the guests went away singing my praises, we would go upstairs and with his obstetrical skills he would make me come. Oh, life, oh, joy, oh, fecund and beautiful old world, oh, sexy, sexy world. "With everything either concave or convex, whatever we do will be something with sex."

The next morning two dozen yellow roses arrived with a note.

I tried to lose a little weight. Every time he would call and do his husky can't-wait-to-see-you thing on the phone I would not eat for hours. Remember, it was late spring and the world was blooming, blooming, blooming, "stirring dull roots with spring rain."

I had my white silk shantung suit cleaned and bought some new shoes. It is a very severe white suit with a mandarin jacket and I wear it with no jewelry except tiny pearl earrings and my hair pulled back in a bun like a dancer's.

"I want you to have gorgeous flowers," he said on the phone one afternoon. It was raining outside. I was sprawled on a satin comforter flirting with him on the phone. "What are you going to wear?"

"A severe white suit with my hair in a bun. All I could possibly wear would be a gardenia for my hair and I'm not sure I'll wear that."

"Oh, I thought you might wear a dress."

"I don't like dresses. I like sophisticated suits. I might wear a Donna Karan pantsuit. Listen, Carter, I know what looks good on me."

"I thought you might like something like a Laura Ashley. I'd like to buy you one. Let me send you some dresses. What size do you wear?"

"Those tacky little-girl clothes? No grown woman would wear anything like that. You've got to be kidding."

"I thought. That picture in that magazine."

"In that off-the-shoulder blouse? I only had that on because I was in New Orleans and it was hot as hell. Then that photographer caught up with me. It was the year I was famous, God forbid."

"I wish you'd wear a flowered dress from Laura Ashley. I'll have them send you some. I know the woman who runs the store here. She's a good friend of mine."

Wouldn't you think I would have heard that gong? Wouldn't you think that someone with my intelligence and intuition would have stopped to think? Don't you think I knew he was talking about his dead wife? A size six or eight from smoking who let him go down to Laura Ashley and buy her flowered dresses with full skirts and probably even sheets and pillowcases and dust ruffles to go on the antique beds and said, Oh, Daddy, what can I do to thank you for all this flowered cotton?

Listen, was I that lonely? Was I that horny? Right there in Jackson, Mississippi, with half the old boyfriends in my life a phone call away and plenty more where they came from if only I could conquer my fear of AIDS and quit eating dinner every night with my parents.

"All right," I said. "Send me one or two. A ten will do. I can take it up if it's too big."

So then I really had to go on a diet. Had to starve myself morning, night, and noon and add three miles a day to the miles I ran and go up to six aerobic classes a week.

By the time the dress arrived I was a ten. Almost. It was blue and pink and green and flowered. It came down to my ankles. Its full skirt covered up the only thin part of my body. Its coy little neckline made my strong shoulders and arms look absurd. Worst of all, there was a see-through garden hat trimmed in flowers.

Was I actually going to wear this out in public? I had the hots for a guy who had to have everything I take for granted explained to him. In exchange for which he had given me a dead wife, three C-sections performed in the middle of the night wearing double gloves, two dozen roses, a check for two thousand dollars, and one long slow hug by the elevator. You figure it out. Women and their desire to please wealthy, self-made men. Think about that sometime if you get stuck in traffic in the rain.

I found a Chinese seamstress and we managed to make the dress fit me by taking material out of the seams and adding it to the waist. We undid the elastic in the sleeves and lengthened them with part of the band on the hat. I found an old Merry Widow in my mother's cedar chest. Strapped into that I managed to look like a tennis player masquerading as a shepherdess.

In the end I packed two suitcases. One with the Laura Ashley special and its accoutrements. The other with my white shantung

suit and some extremely high platform shoes, to make me as tall
as he was.

I left Jackson with the two suitcases, two hatboxes, and a cosmetic kit. An extra carry-on contained my retainer, my Xanax, a
package of rubbers and a tube of contraceptive jelly containing
nonoxynol-9, and a book of poems by Anne Sexton.

He was waiting at the gate, wearing a seersucker suit and an
open shirt. He was taking the weekend off. We went to his town
house first and he showed me all around it, telling me about the
antiques and where he and his wife had bought them. "My first
wife will be at the wedding," he said at last. "Don't worry about
it. She's very nice. She's the bride's mother."

"How many wives have you had?"

"Just those two. You don't mind, do you? There's a guest cot-
tage at the country house. She and her husband are staying there."

"Oh, sure. I mean, that's fine. Why would that matter to me?"

"You won't have to see her if you don't want to. I thought
we'd stay in town tonight and go out there tomorrow morning.
The weddings is in the afternoon. Everything's done. The caterer
is taking care of everything, and Donna is there to oversee him."

"Donna?"

"The bride's mother."

"And I'm your date."

"If you don't mind. I thought we'd go downtown and hear
jazz tonight. There's a good group playing at the Meridien."

My antennae were going up, up, up. This was turning into a
minefield. I had starved myself for two weeks to show off for
his ex-wife and tiptoe around this minefield? I could have been
in New Orleans with my cousins. I could have been in New York
City seeing the American Ballet Theatre. I could have been in San
Francisco visiting Lydia. I could have gone to Belize to go scuba-
diving. I could have driven to the Grand Canyon.

"I can't wait to see the country house," I said. "Since you've told me so much about it." But that was a thrill postponed. We went first to his town house.

He showed me to my room. A Laura Ashley special. Enough chintz to start an empire. So many ruffles, so many little oblong mirrors and dainty painted chairs.

"You want me to sleep in here?" I asked. "Where do you sleep?"

"You can sleep wherever you like. I just thought you'd like your own room. Would you like to see the other ones? To see if there is one you might like better?"

Always play your own game, my old man had taught me. Never play someone else's game. "The room's fine. I mean, aren't you going to sleep with me? I'm a grown woman, Carter. I didn't come down here to dress up like a shepherdess and let you show me off to your friends. I thought you wanted to make love to me. What was all that talk on the phone? I mean, what are we doing here?" I sat back on the chintz bed. It was not the sort of atmosphere in which a fifty-year-old woman can feel sexy, but I tried.

"I wanted to take you to dinner first. Then to hear some jazz."

"What's wrong with now? We are alone, aren't we?"

"Now?" He stood very still. I could see the receding hairline and the bags under his eyes and there was no spark, no tinder, sulfur, or electricity.

"Never mind," I said. "Well, if you'll leave me, I'll unpack. I wouldn't want my wedding clothes to be wrinkled."

"If you really want to . . ."

"Never mind. I just wanted to know what was going on. Go on, I'll unpack and freshen up and we can go out to dinner."

"I have reservations at the club at eight."

"Fine. I'll be ready."

I patted him on the arm and he turned and left the room. I opened the suitcases and hung up the dress and suit. I took a bath and put on a black silk Donna Karan with small pearl earrings and went downstairs and waited in the overstuffed living room. In a while he joined me and we went out and had dinner and he got drunk and then we heard some jazz and he got drunker and then we went home and he got into the chintz-covered bed with me and made me come with his fingers. I'll say this for him, he lived up to my expectations in that corner. He knew how to use his fingers. In maybe two minutes he made me have an incredible orgasm and he had done it with his fingers. "I can't make love," he moaned into my shoulder after it was over. "I can't desire women I admire. I can only desire young girls that I can't stand to talk to. I don't know what's wrong with me."

"It's okay," I said. "Go to sleep. Go on to sleep."

I woke up in a really good mood. An orgasm is an orgasm and it's a hell of a lot better than Xanax. By nine o'clock we were in the Lincoln headed for the country house. I had one suitcase in the trunk. The one with the white suit and extremely high platform heels.

The country house was very nice. Most of the chintz and printed cotton was green and white and there were plants everywhere and plenty going on in every room. His interior decorator was there and his first wife and her husband and all four of the children and their wives and husbands. The bride-to-be and the groom-to-be were busting around fixing flowers and watching the caterers set up the tents and the bandstand. The children were all loudly and publicly fighting over a diamond ring the bride-to-be was wearing. It had belonged to wife number two and her children claimed it and were angry that Carter had given it to his daughter. Since he had given it to wife number two Carter thought it was his to bestow and he had given it to the bride because her impecunious bridegroom couldn't afford one yet. "She'll give it back to you in time," he told the stepchildren. "Don't spoil her wedding day."

But it was being spoiled so there was no chance of my being

bored that morning. The hostility rose to fever pitch now that Carter was there to suffer it and I sat at the kitchen table with wife number one, who was sipping rum and tonic, and I thought, it's true I could be somewhere where the natives speak my language, still, nothing is ever lost on a writer. Notice everything, the older stepdaughter washing dishes in a fury. The grandchildren, the first wife smoking, the pool cleaners trying to clean the pool, the striped tent being raised, the lobster salad, the uncomfortable sofas, the yard full of BMWs, the permanent waves, the eyeliner, the way the ring has taken the heat off my being Daddy's date. "I have ten grandchildren," I told Donna and her dishwashing daughter. "Things won't always be this hectic in your family. It will settle down when you reach my age."

"How old are you?" they asked.

"I'm pushing sixty," I told them. "The older you get the better."

The day went from bad to worse. It got hot and hotter. The air conditioning couldn't deal with the doors being opened and slammed as the hour for the wedding drew near and the two-carat diamond ring belonging to the dead wife's children was still on the bride-to-be's hand.

I went upstairs and put on the white suit and heels. The guests arrived. An anorexic internist cornered me in the hall and told me about his addiction to running. Two of his colleagues joined the conversation, praising him for looking fatter. I talked to the interior decorator. I talked to the husband of the mother of the bride, who was getting drunk enough to be jolly.

The wedding party gathered. We all pressed around. A minister read the ceremony. Video cameras were everywhere. I hid behind a group of pedestals holding potted ferns. The guests went out to the tent and began to eat and drink and listen to the music. I went upstairs and lay down on a bed and read medical journals and a bestseller on the doctor's bedside table. I read his little black book, which was beside it. There was a list of women with their names checked off. Mine was at the bottom. I went back to the novel, *Russia House.*

After a long time Carter came upstairs to find me. "What's wrong?" he said drunkenly. "Aren't you having a good time?"

"Are you going to make me come again or not?" I asked. "I'm tired of waiting."

"Well, not right now," he said.

"Why not? What's wrong with now?"

"I don't know, Rhoda. I don't think this is working out, do you?"

"No. As a matter of fact I was thinking of catching an earlier plane. I mean, now that we have them married and everything. There's a plane that leaves at nine. Could someone take me there? Or perhaps you could lend me a car." I got up off the bed. "You can mail the things I left at your house. Especially that nifty dress you bought me. Someday I might want it to wear to a Halloween party."

"I don't understand," he said. "What have I done wrong?"

"It's a class thing," I answered. "Your M.D. doesn't make up for the chintz."

Well, that isn't exactly what I said. I said something more subtle than that but probably equally mean. He didn't answer for a long time. Then he handed me the keys to the Lincoln and offered to have his son drive me to the airport but I refused. The band was playing Beatles' songs. I sneaked out the kitchen door and got into the Lincoln and drove myself to the Atlanta airport and flew on home.

Where did the rest of the ten thousand dollars come in? you might well ask. Well, that's what it cost to call up my old boyfriend in Fayetteville, Arkansas, and get him to fly down to Jackson and take me to New Orleans to make love and eat oysters and beignets. That's what it cost to spend a week at the Windsor Court getting nonoxynol-9 all over the sheets and then fly back to

Fayetteville, Arkansas, with him and make a down payment on a house on the mountain.

In a small city that needed me back so it wouldn't be smaller still. In a small, free city where no one I am kin to lives and where being respectable means getting your yard cut every two weeks in the summer and not smoking dope or getting your hair dyed blue.

Plus, three hundred and fifteen dollars for a reproduction of a statue of Aphrodite, which I belatedly mailed the bride and groom for a wedding present.

AMONG
THE MOURNERS

THE SPRING that I was thirteen years old a poet we knew died and we had to have the funeral. It was the most embarrassing thing that ever happened to me in my life. In the first place he killed himself and the police couldn't even get his briefcase open to find the suicide note, and in the second place it almost broke up my parents' marriage. Not that my mother minded my father offering to have the funeral. Somebody had to do it, I guess, and our house is always full of people anyway. She just goes back to her room and reads magazines until they go away. My dad is head of the English Department and there are always poets around telling Dad their problems. I'm used to them and so is she. But this was different. All those police cars pulling up in front of the house and my little sister running around in her pajamas in the front yard and everybody over there smoking cigarettes like it was going out of style. This was several years ago when a lot of people still smoked inside the house.

How would you feel if you had just gotten the first boyfriend you ever had and every time his parents drove by your house there were cars parked all over the yard and police cars in the driveway? I was mortified. His name is Giorgio and his mother is from Peru and his father is Jewish and they don't have things like that at their house. They are very religious. Giorgio goes to the Catholic church with his mom and goes to the temple with his dad. They teach in the Foreign Language Department and they don't always have to have crazy people around like you do if your father is head of the English Department.

Giorgio speaks about fifteen languages and he is so good-looking you wouldn't believe it. He's pretty short but I'm glad he is. I couldn't stand it if he was playing football and I had to get out there and cheer for him getting his nose broken or his teeth cracked. I'm on the Pep Squad. I didn't want to go out but my mother made me. She's always trying to make me have a normal life. Only how can I? With all my dad's crazy friends coming over all the time and my crazy little sister running around naked and failing the first grade. I think they got her mixed up in the nursery. I don't believe she's kin to me.

Anyway, this poet that used to come over all the time and talk to Dad shot himself because his girlfriend had talked his wife into divorcing him and the next thing I knew there were about a hundred cars parked all over the yard on the day after Giorgio finally told me he liked me. My cousin bet him ten dollars he wouldn't tell me, and he called me up that night and told me. I don't think he got the ten dollars but he didn't care. He was so glad to have me for a girlfriend. He's in Gifted and Talented and so am I. I've been liking him for ages but I didn't know it until he called me up. That was about six o'clock one afternoon. That night the poet shot himself and the people started showing up.

"Aurora," my dad says, when he called me into his office to tell me what was going on. "Mr. Alter has killed himself and the widow is going to stay here until we can figure out a way to bury him."

"Why'd he do that?" I asked.

"We don't know. We'll need your room if Mr. Seats comes in

from Saint Louis. You remember Mr. Seats? He used to teach here."

"He can't have my room. I'm making a project for Swim Team. It's the decorations for the banquet next week." I backed off toward the door. If you get into my dad's office he can talk you into things. It's like there's not enough oxygen in there when he really gets something on his mind. "Take Annie's room. It's filthy anyway. She's such a pig."

"Aurora."

"Yes, sir."

"A man has killed himself. We have a civilized duty to mourn when someone dies. If Mr. Seats comes we will need your room."

"I didn't kill him. Why should I give up my room?"

"Aurora, I am deeply disappointed in you. It makes me very sad to hear you talk that way. Mr. Alter was a guest in this house. He was a friend of mine and your mother's. We are going to pay him the respect that's due."

"If someone kills themself they don't get my respect."

"Alice Armene! Come in here!" So he starts screaming for my mother. He always blames her when he gets mad at me. As if she can stop it. Sometimes I think I'm the one who was switched in the hospital. Here's what they do that drives me crazy. They preach all the time about reason. *Dharma*, my dad calls it. He is so big on dharma. Then the first time something happens they start acting like these big Christians or something and having all these rituals.

By ten o'clock the next morning the house was full. Mr. Seats caught the first plane he could get and came on down and put his suitcase in my room. I will say this, he didn't touch anything. He just put his suitcase down and went into the living room and started watching television with Mother. He used to be a poet but he had just got this job sending in dialogue for *Days of Our Lives* so he had to watch all the soap operas all day even while he was mourning. He was the best friend of Mr. Alter and had just seen him a few weeks ago. Also, he was suffering a broken heart because the person he loved in Saint Louis wouldn't get a divorce and marry him. He was telling Mother all about it the first day he was there and she's sitting on the sofa with him patting him on the hand. That's what almost broke up my parents' marriage, not to mention almost got the television taken out of our house for good.

So here they are, all sitting around the house drinking beer and iced tea and eating all the food everyone kept bringing over and waiting for the police to finish their investigation so they could bury the body. Giorgio's mother said she thought they should stop making a big deal out of someone young and in good health who would kill themself. "It ees an unholy act," she kept saying in this beautiful accent she has. They only live three blocks from us so I started staying over there all the time. I couldn't stand it at my house with all those people coming in and out the doors and Momma sitting in the living room with Mr. Seats holding his hand.

My dad is insanely jealous of my mother. He won't let anyone near her. He fell in love with her at first sight. She was second runner-up for Miss Tennessee and he met her when his roommate at the University of Kentucky had him up to visit one Thanksgiving vacation. She was good friends with his roommate's sister and she came walking into a room and he was instantly in love with her. Then he swept her off her feet and married her and brought her to Fayetteville, Arkansas, to live. As soon as they got here they had me on a freezing cold January night. I'm an Aquarius, born in my own time, only my parents don't like for me to talk about astrology. They say it's lower-middle-class superstition and not worthy of me. They are afraid I'll get into a coven or something when I grow up if I start believing in astrology.

They had Annie seven years later, although they didn't mean to. My mom is a sculptor although she hasn't had time to do it since Annie was born. Annie wouldn't even go to kindergarten half the time. Then she failed the first grade. All she wants to do is ride her stupid bike or run around with hardly any clothes on or just hang on Dad like some kind of monkey. She adores him.

So what does she do while this funeral is going on but run around in these little pink nylon pajamas that are about ten years old and too short for her and go from person to person being cute and getting people to talk about her to Dad. She's a slut if I ever saw one. She'll do anything for attention. That's why she failed the first grade. Just to get attention.

"It makes me sick," I told Giorgio. We were sitting on the front wall looking at the house. You've never seen so many people going in and out of a house in your life. Mom's going to have to throw the carpets away. There won't be any way to clean them. "He thinks it is his job," Giorgio says. He's sitting right next to me and I can smell the Peruvian perfume his mother puts on everything he wears. Just to think I waited all these years to have a boyfriend and the minute I get one they start having this six-day funeral at my house.

"A wake," my dad told me. "This is the wake."

"When are they going to bury him?" I ask. I don't say another word about Mr. Seats living in my room. He has barely opened his suitcase the whole time he's been here. He thinks Mr. Alter has been appearing to him. Like a ghost. But does my father start screaming and say don't start getting into that lower-middle-class superstition? No, of course not. He just gets this really serious look on his face and lets Mr. Seats talk all he wants about seeing Mr. Alter's ghost behind the rocking chair in the living room and also in the front yard near the maple tree. I bet Mr. Seats told that story about fifty times in one day. Every time I would walk through the room, trying to get something to eat or take a bath or finish my decorations for the Swimming Team banquet, there he would be, telling about the ghost behind the rocking chair.

"Are you coming to my banquet?" I asked my mother finally. She and Mr. Seats were in the living room watching *The Young and the Restless*. Mr. Snider was with them. He's my father's student assistant. Dad told him not to let them watch the television alone. I heard Mr. Snider laughing and telling that to the widow like he was trying to cheer her up. Anyway, I believed it because every time they were in there with the TV on, Mr. Snider was there too.

"They should not have eenvolved you in thees death," Giorgio's mother said to me. "Thees murder."

"I can't even take a bath," I told her. "It's a good thing I'm on the Swim Team. I might get impetigo or something. I was late to practice yesterday because my mother couldn't back out of the driveway. They had this man there from the radio station. They've been playing a special program of all the dead guy's favorite music on the student radio station. He was there getting everyone to tell him what to play."

"Thees ees so morbid, you poor baby girl." Giorgio's mother asked me to eat dinner with them that night so I called and they said I could and Giorgio and I went into his room and listened to music and played Scrabble. Just the two of us. No one bothered us or came in. Well, he's an only child, and his father is a workaholic so there wasn't anyone there but us and his mother and I could tell she wanted us to be in love. She was real excited because I'm in Gifted and Talented too.

"I want Giorgio to have friends who share hees interests so he won't get involved with thees football people." You should hear her say involved. She gives it about fourteen syllables. She grew up speaking French and Spanish and English and I could just live over there listening to her talk.

I guess you think we were in there kissing and making out but you are wrong. I would never take advantage of that woman. I wouldn't violate Mrs. Levine's trust for fifteen-carat diamonds in my ears. I wouldn't hurt that woman for all the money in the world. I love her with all my heart. Even if Giorgio did quit liking me I would never do one thing to make Mrs. Levine unhappy. If it hadn't been for her I would never have made it through that week.

Finally, on the Friday after he killed himself on Saturday, the police released the body and they all went up to the cemetery and buried him. He didn't have any parents. He was an orphan from the word go, which is what made it so tragic. The only one who had ever loved him was his wife and he betrayed her with another woman and then he couldn't face the consequences of what he had done.

"Thees happens every day in my country," Mrs. Levine told me. "We do not theenk these things are tragedies. Tragedy ees for the poor widow or the child who loses his mother or when there ees a war. Thees young man will have eternity to regret hees act. It would be better if the living walked off and forget hees selfish life."

"Can Aurora spend the night tonight?" Giorgio asked. "She can sleep in the guest room. She hasn't had any sleep in days, Momma. She has to sleep with her little sister."

"I'm an insomniac anyway," I added. "But that's okay. I can take it another night."

"Of course not. Of course you can stay here with us. I will call your mother and see if thees ees all right with her, then?"

* * *

So listen, my parents are so wrapped up in this funeral they said yes. They let me spend the night at a boy's house. I couldn't believe it. I was afraid to go home and get my pajamas and toothbrush. I was afraid my mom would change her mind if she saw me. Sometimes she can read my mind like a Gypsy.

I sneaked in the side door and grabbed some clothes and stuffed them in a bag and almost made it back out into the yard when Dad caught me. "Where are you going?" he says. By now they have buried Mr. Alter and are back at our house sitting around discussing the funeral. I'm in the back hall about four feet from the kitchen and Dad's blocking the way to the door.

"I'm going to church with the Levines," I said.

"You're doing what?" My father has spent his life listening to students. There is no fooling him. I raised my head and looked him in the eye. "I think they're going to the synagogue," I said. "Or maybe to St. Joseph's. I'm freaking out from this funeral, Dad. The Levines asked me to stay with them. Mom said I could."

"Mr. Harris?" It was this graduate student named Bellefontaine who's a big favorite of my dad's. He had a faded red corduroy shirt in his hand. "This was one of Francis's shirts. We thought you might like it for a souvenir. We cleaned out his closets like you said. We brought this to you. I don't know. Maybe you don't want it." He stood blocking the door to the kitchen with the dead poet's shirt in his hand. My dad reached out and took it. I went under their arms and made my escape. "I have to go," I said. "They're waiting for me in the car." I was out of the door. I had just told two lies in a row to a man who never forgets anything and is never fooled. I lit out across the patio and took the short cut to the Levines' house across the backyards of my piano teacher and some people from Indiana that no one ever sees.

Giorgio and his mother were waiting for me. They were making paella for dinner. Mr. Levine was going to be late. We weren't going to have to wait for him.

*　　　*　　　*

Everything went along just fine until Mr. Levine came home and
he and Mrs. Levine went to bed, leaving Giorgio and me alone.
"You want to go for a walk?" he asked. "They won't mind. They
don't care what I do."

"It's ten-thirty at night. Sure. I'd love it. We can walk up to
the store." I was about five feet away from him. He smelled like
that perfume. He reached out and took my hand and we just
walked on out the door. "We can go to the park," he said.
"Sometimes I go there at night. It's not too far."

"I can walk a hundred miles. Who cares how far it is." So we
started off down Washington Avenue. It was in between semesters at the college and the town was quiet. We walked down to
Highway 71 and crossed at the IGA. There wasn't anyone around
but old Donnie Hights, who is a lunatic that walks the streets all
the time saying hello to people. He gives me the creeps but Dad
says he is proof there is still freedom in the United States and
to count my blessings and be polite.

Anyway, he was standing on the corner by the Shell station
so I held on tighter to Giorgio's hand and we crossed 71 and
started up toward Washington Elementary School.

"That's where I learned to read," I commented. "Right there
in that corner room. Mrs. Nordan taught me. She's the sweetest
lady in the world. I adore her."

"I adore you," Giorgio says. He said that. Right there by the
corner of the school on Maple Street. He got real near me and
sort of breathed into my hair.

That's all that happened then. We walked up Maple and cut
over at Doctor Wileman's house and went on down to the park.
At the wooden bridge we stopped and sat down and started
kissing. We just started kissing without saying a thing. I bet
there wasn't a person left in the park. If it hadn't been for the
lights in the houses on the hill there wouldn't have been any
light except for the moon and stars. "This is just like the old
shepherds in the Bible," I said at last. "Or else the Druids. It

makes me think of death to be alone in the night. Does it you?"

But all Giorgio did was put his hand on my breast and keep it there. I would have made him move it but I wanted to know what it felt like. It felt good. I can tell you that much. If I hadn't had to think about what it would be like when my dad got me in his office and started screaming at me I might have just let him keep it there all night.

"We better get back," I said. I was kissing him as hard as I could in between talking but I still have my braces on and it hurts to kiss very hard with them. Besides, last week I got a free certificate to TCBY for not breaking any pieces off of them for a month and I was trying to get another one. "You better stop doing that," I added, and pushed his hand off of my breast.

He didn't fight me. He just ran it down my shorts and stuck his finger up inside my underpants. Just stuck it right up around the edge of my underpants. I don't know what would have happened but a car full of teenagers pulled up on Wilson Street and got out and started running for the swing sets which are only forty feet from the bridge where we were lying. Something crashed in the creek. It was probably just a beer can but it sounded like a hydrogen bomb.

I stood up and dusted myself off. I already had about five hundred chigger bites but luckily I wouldn't know that until morning.

That's all there is worth telling about that night. We walked back to the house. Giorgio was acting like he was mad at me. He was pouting if you want to know the truth. He was acting like he was about five years old. He's spoiled rotten, to tell the truth.

Besides, in another year he'll be too short for me. We're already the same height and my mom is five foot seven and my dad's six five. It wasn't going to last.

So I don't care if he told my best friend he doesn't like me anymore.

Mr. Seats has twin boys my age who live up in Minnesota. When he comes down next winter to be the Poet in Residence he's going to bring them with him. He thinks they will both fall in love with me. "They always fall in love together," he told me, while he was packing up his stuff to leave my room. "You can have them both, Aurora."

So what do you think? Do you think Giorgio quit liking me because I let him put his hand on my breast? Or because I didn't let him put it in my pants? Or because there were police cars outside my house for seven days?

My dad would say that's like trying to figure out why Mr. Alter killed himself. He believes in the theory of random acts. He thinks lightning strikes. He thinks we should just live every day and do the best we can.

Also, this is the last funeral we'll have to have. Before they left, Dad called all the people into the living room and told them this was the last time he was going to a suicide's funeral. If anyone else killed themself they were on their own for getting buried. "This has had a negative effect on my children," he said. He knew I was listening in the hall. "I am worried that I allowed them to witness it. Aside from that, I love you all and I wish you well." I noticed as soon as Dad made his announcement that Mr. Seats went into my room and took a shower and put on a shirt and tie and started acting like a grown-up. My dad has the power to do things like that to people but he usually saves it up and only uses it at the end.

My parents are very cool people to tell the truth. They aren't even going to make Annie go to summer school. They're just going to let her run around all summer in her bathing suit and try again

next year. This is very advanced behavior for academics and everyone was congratulating them on it when they were getting in their
cars and leaving. You're right about Annie, people were saying. Let
her be a child. Don't push her, and so forth.

Of course, why should they worry? They've got me. And I
have them again. More than I need. The television has a sign on
it that says, GOODBYE, SEQUENTIAL THOUGHT, and a
schedule of times when Annie and I are allowed to watch it.
Although I think the sign is really just to remind my mother that
Mr. Seats has whored himself by agreeing to write the dialogue
for a soap opera.

Now that I know what it is they do when they go into their
room at night I am looking at them with different eyes. I feel
sorry for them, to tell the truth. If I had to do that stuff every
night I might not be able to stay in Gifted and Talented or even
be on the Swim Team. Here's the way I look when I start thinking about it. Very soft around the mouth and chin, like Bambi,
sort of big-eyed and stupid, bowing my head to chew a little
piece of grass.

Very helpless and half-asleep, while all around me for all I
know the forest might be catching fire.

THE STUCCO HOUSE

TEDDY WAS ASLEEP in his second-floor bedroom. It was a square, high-ceilinged room with cobalt blue walls and a bright yellow rug. The closet doors were painted red. The private bath had striped wallpaper and a ceiling fan from which hung mobiles from the Museum of Modern Art. In the shuttered window hung a mobile of small silver airplanes. A poet had given it to Teddy when he came to visit. Then the poet had gone home and killed himself. Teddy was not supposed to know about that, but of course he did. Teddy could read really well. Teddy could read like a house afire. The reason he could read so well was that when his mother had married Eric and moved to New Orleans from across the lake in Mandeville, he had been behind and had had to be tutored. He was tutored every afternoon for a whole summer, and when second grade started, he could read really well. He was still the youngest child in the second grade at Newman School, but at least he could read.

He was sleeping with four stuffed toys lined up between him and the wall and four more on the other side. They were there to keep his big brothers from beating him up. They were there to keep ghosts from getting him. They were there to keep vampires out. This night they were working. If Teddy dreamed at all that night, the dreams were like Technicolor clouds. On the floor beside the bed were Coke bottles and potato-chip containers and a half-eaten pizza from the evening before. Teddy's mother had gone off at suppertime and not come back, so Eric had let him do anything he liked before he went to bed. He had played around in Eric's darkroom for a while. Then he had let the springer spaniels in the house, and then he had ordered a pizza and Eric had paid for it. Eric was reading a book about a man who climbed a mountain in the snow. He couldn't put it down. He didn't care what Teddy did as long as he was quiet.

Eric was really nice to Teddy. Teddy was always glad when he and Eric were alone in the house. If his big brothers were gone and his mother was off with her friends, the stucco house was nice. This month was the best month of all. Both his brothers were away at Camp Carolina. They wouldn't be back until August.

Teddy slept happily in his bed, his stuffed animals all around him, his brothers gone, his dreams as soft as dawn.

Outside his house the heat of July pressed down upon New Orleans. It pressed people's souls together until they grated like chalk on brick. It pressed people's brains against their skulls. Only sugar and whiskey made people feel better. Sugar and coffee and whiskey. Beignets and café au lait and taffy and Cokes and snowballs made with shaved ice and sugar and colored flavors. Gin and wine and vodka, whiskey and beer. It was too hot, too humid. The blood wouldn't move without sugar.

Teddy had been asleep since eleven-thirty the night before. Eric came into his room just before dawn and woke him up. "I need you to help me," he said. "We have to find your mother." Teddy got sleepily out of bed, and Eric helped him put on his shorts and shirt and sandals. Then Eric led him down the hall and out the front door and down the concrete steps, and opened the car door and helped him into the car. "I want a Coke," Teddy said. "I'm thirsty."

"Okay," Eric answered. "I'll get you one." Eric went back into the house and reappeared carrying a frosty bottle of Coke with the top off. The Coke was so cool it was smoking in the soft humid air.

Light was showing from the direction of the lake. In New Orleans in summer the sun rises from the lake and sets behind the river. It was rising now. Faint pink shadows were beginning to penetrate the mist.

Eric drove down Nashville Avenue to Chestnut Street and turned and went two blocks and came to a stop before a duplex shrouded by tall green shrubs. "Come on," he said. "I think she's here." He led Teddy by the hand around the side of the house to a set of wooden stairs leading to an apartment. Halfway up the stairs Teddy's mother was lying on a landing. She had on a pair of pantyhose and that was all. Over her naked body someone had thrown a seersucker jacket. It was completely still on the stairs, in the yard.

"Come on," Eric said. "Help me wake her up. She fell down and we have to get her home. Come on, Teddy, help me as much as you can."

"Why doesn't she have any clothes on? What happened to her clothes?"

"I don't know. She called and told me to come and get her. That's all I know." Eric was half carrying and half dragging Teddy's mother down the stairs. Teddy watched while Eric managed to get her down the stairs and across the yard. "Open the car door," he said. "Hold it open."

Together they got his mother into the car. Then Teddy got in the back seat and they drove to the stucco house and got her out and dragged her around to the side door and took her into the downstairs hall and into Malcolm's room and laid her down on Malcolm's waterbed. "You watch her," Eric said. "I'm going to call the doctor."

Teddy sat down on the floor beside the waterbed and began to look at Malcolm's books. *Playing to Win, The Hobbit, The Big Green Book.* Teddy took down *The Big Green Book* and started reading it. It was about a little boy whose parents died and he had to go and live with his aunt and uncle. They weren't very nice to him, but he liked it there. One day he went up to the attic and found a big green book of magic spells. He learned all the spells. Then he could change himself into animals. He could make himself invisible. He could do anything he wanted to do.

Teddy leaned back against the edge of the waterbed. His mother had not moved. Her legs were lying side by side. Her mouth was open. Her breasts fell away to either side of her chest. Her pearl necklace was falling on one breast. Teddy got up and looked down at her. She isn't dead, he decided. She's just sick or something. I guess she fell down those stairs. She shouldn't have been outside at night with no clothes on. She'd kill me if I did that.

He went around to the other side of the waterbed and climbed up on it. Malcolm never let him get on the waterbed. He never even let Teddy come into the room. Well, he was in here now. He opened *The Big Green Book* and found his place and went on reading. Outside in the hall he could hear Eric talking to people on the phone. Eric was nice. He was so good to them. He had already taken Teddy snorkeling and skiing, and next year he was going to take him to New York to see the dinosaurs in the museum. He was a swell guy. He was the best person his mother had ever married. Living with Eric was great. It was better than anyplace Teddy had ever been. Better than living with his real daddy, who wasn't any fun, and lots better than being at his grandfather's house. His grandfather yelled at them and made them make their beds and ride the stupid horses and hitch up the pony cart, and if they didn't do what he said, he hit them with a belt. Teddy hated being there, even if he did have ten cousins near him in Mandeville and they came over all the time. There was a fort in the woods and secret paths for riding the ponies, and the help cooked for them morning, noon, and night.

Teddy laid *The Big Green Book* down on his lap and reached over and patted his mother's shoulder. "You'll be okay," he said out loud. "Maybe you're just hungover."

Eric came in and sat beside him on the waterbed. "The doctor's coming. He'll see about her. You know, Doctor Paine, who comes to dinner. She'll be all right. She just fell down."

"Maybe she's hungover." Teddy leaned over his mother and touched her face. She moaned. "See, she isn't dead."

"Teddy, maybe you better go up to your room and play until the doctor leaves. Geneva will be here in a minute. Get her to make you some pancakes or something."

"Then what will we do?"

"Like what?"

"I mean all day. You want to go to the lake or something?"

"I don't know, Ted. We'll have to wait and see." Eric took his mother's hand and held it. He looked so worried. He looked terrible. She was always driving him crazy, but he never got mad at her. He just thought up some more things to do.

"I'll go see if Geneva's here. Can I have a Coke?"

"May I have a Coke." Eric smiled and reached over and patted his arm. "Say it."

"May I have a Coke, please?"

"Yes, you may." They smiled. Teddy got up and left the room.

The worst thing of all happened the next day. Eric decided to send him across the lake for a few days. To his grandmother and grandfather's house. "They boss me around all the time," Teddy said. "I won't be in the way. I'll be good. All I'm going to do is stay here and read books and work on my stamp collection." He looked pleadingly up at his stepfather. Usually reading a book could get him anything he wanted with Eric, but today it wasn't working.

"We have to keep your mother quiet. She'll worry about you if you're here. It won't be for long. Just a day or so. Until Monday. I'll come get you Monday afternoon."

"How will I get over there?"

"I'll get Big George to take you." Big George was the gardener. He had a blue pickup truck. Teddy had ridden with him before. Getting to go with Big George was a plus, even if his grandfather might hit him with a belt if he didn't make his bed.

"Can I see Momma now?"

"May."

"May I see Momma now?"

"Yeah. Go on in, but she's pretty dopey. They gave her some pills."

His mother was in her own bed now, lying flat down without any pillows. She was barely awake. "Teddy," she said. "Oh, baby, oh, my precious baby. Eric tried to kill me. He pushed me down the stairs."

"No, he didn't." Teddy withdrew from her side. She was going to start acting crazy. He didn't put up with that. "He didn't do anything to you. I went with him. Why didn't you have any clothes on?"

"Because I was asleep when he came and made me leave. He pushed me and I fell down the stairs."

"You probably had a hangover. I'm going to Mandeville. Well, I'll see you later." He started backing away from the bed. Backing toward the door. He was good at backing. Sometimes he backed home from school as soon as he was out of sight of the other kids.

"Teddy, come here to me. You have to do something for me. Tell Granddaddy and Uncle Ingersol that Eric is trying to kill me. Tell them, will you, my darling? Tell them for me." She was getting sleepy again. Her voice was sounding funny. She reached out a hand to him and he went back to the bed and held out his arm and she stroked it. "Be sure and tell them. Tell them to call the president." She stopped touching him. Her eyes were closed. Her mouth fell open. She still looked pretty. Even when she was drunk, she looked really pretty. Now that she was asleep, he moved nearer and looked at her. She looked okay. She sure wasn't bleeding. She had a cover on the bed that was decorated all over with little Austrian flowers. They were sewn on like little real flowers. You could hardly tell they were made of thread. He looked at one for a minute. Then he picked up her purse and took a twenty-dollar bill out of her billfold and put it in his pocket. He needed to buy some film. She didn't care. She gave him anything he asked for.

"What are you doing?" It was Eric at the door. "You better be getting ready, Teddy. Big George will be here in a minute."

"I got some money out of her purse. I need to get some film to take with me."

"What camera are you going to take? I've got some film for the Olympus in the darkroom. You want a roll of black-and-white? Go get the camera and I'll fill it for you."

"She said you tried to kill her." Teddy took Eric's hand and they started down the hall to the darkroom. "Why does she say stuff like that, Eric? I wish she wouldn't say stuff like that when she gets mad."

"It's a fantasy, Teddy. She never had anyone do anything bad to her in her life, and when she wants some excitement, she just makes it up. It's okay. I'm sorry she fell down the stairs. I was trying to help her. You know that, don't you?"

"Yes. Listen, can I buy Big George some lunch before we cross the Causeway? I took twenty dollars. Will that be enough to get us lunch?"

"Sure. That would be great, Teddy. I bet he'd like that. He

likes you so much. Everybody likes you. You're such a swell little boy. Come on, let's arm that camera. Where is it?"

Teddy ran back to his room and got the camera. He was a scrawny, towheaded little boy who would grow up to be a magnificent man. But for now he was seven and a half years old and liked to take photographs of people in the park and of dogs. He liked to read books and pretend he lived in Narnia. He liked to get down on his knees at the Episcopal church and ask God not to let his momma divorce Eric. If God didn't answer, then he would pretend he was his grandfather and threaten God. Okay, you son-of-a-bitch, he would say, his little head down on his chest, kneeling like a saint at the prayer rail. If she divorces Eric, I won't leave anyway. I'll stay here with him and we can be bachelors. She can just go anywhere she likes. I'm not leaving. I'm going right on living here by the park in my room. I'm not going back to Mandeville and ride those damned old horses.

Big George came in the front door and stood, filling up the hall. He was six feet five inches tall and wide and strong. His family had worked for Eric's family for fifty years. He had six sons and one daughter who was a singer. He liked Eric, and he liked the scrawny little kid that Eric's wife had brought along with the big mean other ones. "Hey, Teddy," Big George said, "where's your bag?"

"You want to go to lunch?" Teddy said. "I got twenty dollars. We can stop at the Camellia Grill before we cross the bridge. You want to do that?"

"Sure thing. Twenty dollars. What you do to get twenty dollars, Teddy?"

"Nothing. I was going to buy some film, but Eric gave me some so I don't have to. Come on, let's go." He hauled his small leather suitcase across the parquet floor and Big George leaned down and took it from him. Eric came into the hall and talked to Big George a minute, and they both looked real serious and Big George shook his head, and then Eric kissed Teddy on the cheek and Big George and Teddy went on out and got into the truck and drove off.

Eric stood watching them until the truck turned onto Saint Charles Avenue. Then he went back into the house and into his wife's workroom and looked around at the half-finished watercolors, which were her latest obsession, and the mess and the clothes on the floor and the unemptied wastebaskets, and he sat down at her desk and opened the daybook she left out for him, to see if there were any new men since the last time she made a scene.

June 29, Willis will be here from Colorado. Show him the new poems. HERE IS WHAT WE MUST ADMIT. Here is what we know. What happened then is what happens now. Over and over again. How to break the pattern. Perhaps all I can do is avoid or understand the pattern. The pattern holds for all we do. I discovered in a dream that I am not in love with R. Only with what he can do for my career. How sad that is. The importance of dreams is that they may contain feelings we are not aware of. FEELINGS WE ARE NOT AWARE OF. The idea of counterphobia fascinates me. That you could climb mountains because you are afraid of heights. Seek out dangers because the danger holds such fear for you. What if I seek out men because I want to fight with them. Hate and fear them and want to have a fight. To replay my life with my brothers. Love to fight. My masculine persona.

Well, I'll see Willis tonight and show him the watercolors too, maybe. I'll never be a painter. Who am I fooling? All I am is a mother and a wife. That's that. Two unruly teenagers and a little morbid kid who likes Eric better than he likes me. I think it's stunting his growth to stay in that darkroom all the time. . . .

Eric sighed and closed the daybook. He picked up a watercolor of a spray of lilies. She was good. She was talented. He hadn't been wrong about that. He laid it carefully down on the portfolio and went into her bedroom and watched her sleep. He could think of nothing to do. He could not be either in or out; he could not make either good or bad decisions. He was locked into this terrible marriage and into its terrible rage and fear and sadness. No one was mean to me, he decided. Why am I here? Why am I living here? For Teddy, he decided, seeing the little boy's skinny arms splashing photographs in and out of trays, grooming the dogs, swimming in the river, paddling a canoe. I love that little boy, Eric decided. He's just like I was at that age. I have to keep the marriage together if I can. I can't stand for him to be taken from me.

Eric began to cry, deep within his heart at first, then right there in the sunlight, at twelve o'clock on a Saturday morning, into his own hands, his own deep, salty, endless, heartfelt tears.

Big George had stopped at the Camellia Grill, and he and Teddy were seated on stools at the counter eating sliced-turkey sandwiches and drinking chocolate freezes. "So, what's wrong with your momma?" Big George asked.

"She fell down some stairs. We had to go and get her and bring her home. She got drunk, I guess."

"Don't worry about it. Grown folks do stuff like that. You got to overlook it."

"I just don't want to go to Mandeville. Granddaddy will make me ride the damned old horses. I hate horses."

"Horses are nice."

"I hate them. I have better things to do. He thinks I want to show them, but I don't. Malcolm and Jimmy like to do it. I wish they were home from camp. Then he'd have them."

"Don't worry about it. Eat your sandwich." Big George bit into his. The boy imitated him, opened his mouth as wide as Big George's, heartily ate his food, smilingly let the world go by. It took an hour to get to Mandeville. He wasn't there yet. He looked up above the cash register to where the Camellia Grill sweatshirts were prominently displayed — white, with a huge pink camellia in the center. He might get one for Big George for a Christmas present or he might not wait that long. He had sixty-five dollars in the bank account Eric made for him. He could take some of it out and buy the sweatshirt now. "I like that sweatshirt," he said out loud. "I think it looks real good, don't you?"

"Looks hot," Big George said, "but I guess you'd like it in the winter."

Teddy slept all the way across the Causeway, soothed by the motion of the truck and Big George beside him, driving and humming some song he was making up as he drove. Eric's a fool for that woman, George was thinking. Well, he's never had a woman before, just his momma and his sisters. Guess he's got to put up with it 'cause he likes the little boy so much. He's the sweetest little kid I ever did see. I like him too. Paying for my lunch with a twenty-dollar bill. Did anybody ever see the like? He won't be scrawny long. Not with them big mean brothers he's got. The daddy was a big man too, I heard them say. No, he won't stay little. They never do, do they?

Teddy slept and snored. His allergies had started acting up, but he didn't pay any attention to them. If he was caught blowing his nose, he'd be taken to the doctor, so he only blew it when he was in the bathroom. The rest of the time he ignored it. Now he snored away on the seat beside Big George, and the big blue truck moved along at a steady sixty miles an hour, cruising along across the lake.

At his grandparents' house in Mandeville his grandmother and grandfather were getting ready for Teddy. His grandmother was making a caramel cake and pimento cheese and carrot sticks and Jell-O. His grandfather was in the barn dusting off the saddles and straightening the tackle. Maybe Teddy would want to ride down along the bayou with him. Maybe they'd just go fishing. Sweet little old boy. They had thought Rhoda was finished having children and then she gave them one last little boy. Well, he was a tender little chicken, but he'd toughen. He'd make a man. Couldn't help it. Had a man for a father even if he was a chickenshit. He'd turn into a man even if he did live in New Orleans and spend his life riding on the streetcar.

Teddy's grandfather finished up in the barn and walked back to the house to get a glass of tea and sit out on the porch and wait for the boy. "I might set him up an archery target in the pasture," he told his wife. "Where'd you put the bows the big boys used to use?"

"They're in the storage bin. Don't go getting that stuff out, Dudley. He doesn't need to be out in the pasture in this heat."

"You feed him. I'll find him things to do."

"Leave him alone. You don't have to make them learn things every minute. It's summer. Let him be a child."

"What's wrong with her? Why's she sick again?"

"She fell down. I don't want to talk about it. Get some tea and sit down and cool off, Dudley. Don't go getting out archery things until you ask him if he wants to. I mean that. You leave that child alone. You just plague him following him around. He doesn't even like to come over here anymore. You drive people crazy, Dudley. You really do." She poured tea into a glass and handed it to him. They looked each other in the eye. They had been married thirty-eight years. Everything in the world had happened to them and kept on happening. They didn't care. They liked it that way.

Teddy's uncle Ingersol was five years younger than Teddy's mother. He was a lighthearted man, tall and rangy and spoiled. Teddy's grandmother had spoiled him because he looked like her side of the family. Her daddy had died one year and Ingersol had been born the next. Reincarnation. Ingersol looked like a Texan and dressed like an English lord. He was a cross between a Texan and an English lord. His full name was Alfred Theodore Ingersol Manning. Teddy was named for him but his real father had forbidden his mother to call him Ingersol. "I want him to be a man," his father had said, "not a bunch of spoiled-rotten socialites like your brothers."

"My brothers are not socialites," Teddy's mother had answered, "just because they like to dance and have some fun occasionally, which is more than I can say for you." Teddy always believed he had heard that conversation. He had heard his mother tell it so many times that he thought he could remember it. In this naming story he saw himself sitting on the stairs watching them as they argued over him. "He's my son," his mother was saying. "I'm the one who risked my life having him. I'll call him anything I damn well please."

Teddy's vision of grown people was very astute. He envisioned them as large, very high-strung children who never sat still or finished what they started. Let me finish this first, they were always saying. I'll be done in a minute. Except for Eric. Many times Eric just smiled when he came in and put down whatever he was doing and took Teddy to get a snowball or to walk the springer spaniels or just sit and play cards or Global Pursuit or talk about things. Eric was the best grown person Teddy had ever known, although he also liked his uncle Ingersol and was always glad when he showed up.

All his mother's brothers were full of surprises when they showed up, but only Uncle Ingersol liked to go out to the amusement park and ride the Big Zephyr.

Ingersol showed up this day almost as soon as Big George and Teddy arrived in the truck. Big George was still sitting on the porch drinking iced tea and talking to Teddy's grandfather about fishing when Ingersol came driving up in his Porsche and got out and joined them. "I heard you were coming over, namesake. How you been? What's been going on?"

"Momma fell down some stairs and me and Eric had to bring her home."

"Eric and I."

"I forgot."

"How'd she do that?"

"She said Eric tried to kill her. She always says things like that when she's hungover. She said to tell you Eric tried to kill her." There, he had done it. He had done what she told him to do. "If she divorces Eric, I'm going to live with him. I'm staying right there. Eric said I could."

His grandfather pulled his lips in. It looked like his grandfather was hardly breathing. Big George looked down at the ground. Ingersol sat in his porch chair and began to rub his chin with his hand. "You better go see about her, son," his grandfather said. "Go on over there. I'll go with you."

"No, I'll go alone. Where is she now, Teddy?"

"She's in bed. The doctor came to see her. He gave her some pills. She's asleep."

"Okay. Big George, you know about this?"

"Just said to bring the boy over here to his granddaddy. That's all they told me. Eric wouldn't hurt a flea. I've known him since he was born. He'll cry if his dog dies."

"Go on, son. Call when you get there." His grandfather had unpursed his mouth. His uncle Ingersol bent down and patted Teddy's head. Then he got back into his Porsche and drove away.

"I'm going to stay with Eric," Teddy said. "I don't care what she does. He said I could stay with him forever."

Ingersol drove across the Causeway toward New Orleans thinking about his sister. She could mess up anything. Anytime they got her settled down, she started messing up again. Well, she was theirs and they had to take care of her. I wish he *had* thrown her down the stairs, Ingersol decided. It's about time somebody did something with her.

Teddy's mother was crying. She was lying in her bed and crying bitterly because her head hurt and her poems had not been accepted by *White Buffalo* and she would never be anything but a wife and a mother. And all she was mother to was three wild children who barely passed at school and weren't motivated and didn't even love her. She had failed on every front.

She got out of bed and went into the bathroom and looked at how horrible she looked. She combed her hair and put on makeup and changed into a different negligee and went to look for Eric. He was in the den reading a book. "I'm sorry," she said. "I got drunk and fell asleep. I didn't mean to. It just happened. *White Buffalo* turned my poems down again. The bastards. Why do I let that egomaniac judge my work? Tell me that."

"Are you feeling better?"

"I feel fine. I think I'll get dressed. You want to go out to dinner?"

"In a while. You ought to read this book. It's awfully good." He held it out. *The Snow Leopard,* by Peter Matthiessen.

"Has the mail come?"

"It's on the table. There are some cards from the boys. Malcolm won a swimming match."

"I wasn't sleeping with him, Eric. I went over there to meet a poet from Lafayette. It got out of hand."

Eric closed the book and laid it on the table by the chair. "I'm immobilized," he said at last. "All this is beyond me. I took Teddy with me to bring you home. For an alibi if you said I pushed you down the stairs. I can't think about anything else. I took that seven-year-old boy to see his mother passed out on the stairs in her pantyhose. I don't care what you did, Rhoda. It doesn't matter to me. All I care about is what I did. What I was

driven to. I feel like I'm in quicksand. This is pulling me in. Then
I sent him to Mandeville to your parents. He didn't want to go.
You don't know how scared he is — of us, of you, of everything.
I think I'll go get him now." Eric got up and walked out of the
room. He got his car keys off the dining-room table and walked
out into the lovely hot afternoon and left her there. He got into
his car and drove off to get his stepson. I'll take him somewhere,
he decided. Maybe I'll take him to Disney World.

Teddy was sitting on an unused tractor watching his grandfather
cut the grass along the edge of the pond. His grandfather was
astride a small red tractor pulling a bush hog back and forth
across a dirt embankment on the low side. His grandfather nearly
always ran the bush hog into the water. Then the men had to
come haul it out and his grandfather would joke about it and be
in a good mood for hours trying to make up for being stupid.
Teddy put his feet up on the steering wheel and watched intently
as his grandfather ran the bush hog nearer and nearer to the water's
edge. If he got it in the water, they wouldn't have time to ride
the horses before supper. That's what Teddy was counting on. Just
a little closer, just a little bit more. One time his grandfather had
turned the tractor over in the water and had to swim out. It would
be nice if that could happen again, but getting it stuck in the
mud would do. The day was turning out all right. His uncle
Ingersol had gone over to New Orleans to get drunk with his
mother, and his cousins would be coming later, and maybe they
wouldn't get a divorce, and if they did, it might not be too bad.
He and Eric could go to Disney World like they'd been wanting
to without his mother saying it was tacky.

His grandfather took the tractor back across the dam on a
seventy-degree angle. It was about to happen. At any minute the
tractor would be upside down in the water and the day would be
saved.

*   *   *

That was how things happened, Teddy decided. That was how God ran his game. He sat up there and thought of mean things to do and then changed his mind. You had to wait. You had to go on and do what they told you, and pretty soon life got better.

Teddy turned toward the road that led to the highway. The Kentucky Gate swung open, and Eric's car came driving through. He came to get me, Teddy thought, and his heart swung open too. Swung as wide as the gate. He got down off the tractor and went running to meet the car. Eric got out of the car and walked to meet him. Crazy little boy, he was thinking. Little friend of mine.

THE UNINSURED

August 1, 1993

Dear Blue Cross, Blue Shield,

I got your letter advising me that you are redoing our health insurance plans. I guess this means you are going to be raising our rates again. I know you *want* to raise my rates since for the past ten years it has cost you more to pay my psychiatrist than you have collected from me. We may be getting tired of each other. It may be time to sever our relationship especially since I am about to cut down on the number of times I see him each week and aside from that am in perfect health.

Yours most sincerely,
Rhoda K. Manning

September 3, 1993

Dear Blue Cross, Blue Shield,

While I wait to see if you have figured out a way to make money from me instead of me making money from you I have done the following at your expense. Had a mammogram and a

Pap smear. Had a bone density evaluation and scan. Had an AIDS test. Had a blood profile and blood pressure check. Had ten small skin lesions removed from my hands and arm and lower legs. Had all my prescription drugs filled.

I have also driven up to Jackson, Mississippi, to visit my eighty-six-year-old parents and found them both in perfect health. From all these tests and the evidence of my genes it is clear that, barring accidents, I will live to be about ninety years old with no bone, heart, liver, lung, or brain disease. My blood pressure is ninety over sixty. My bone density is that of a thirty-year-old woman. It is obvious that if you raise my rates I will have to consider bailing out of your Flex-Plan.

> Yours most sincerely,
> Rhoda K. Manning

October 10, 1993

Dear Blue Cross, Blue Shield,

I have applied to the John Alden Insurance Company of Springfield, Illinois, for inclusion in their Jali-Care Program. I am going to let the two of you bid for my healthy body. A healthy body, I might add, that has been shored up by twenty years of psychotherapy which has taught me to love, care for, and value myself.

The John Alden representative in our area has come to visit me. He is a very nice man about my age who once was a forest ranger in Oregon. We chatted and drank bottled water and he took my medical history. He said that, with the exception of my twenty years of psychotherapy, he was certain my record would be well received at the John Alden Jali-Care Evaluation Center. "I am not mentally disturbed," I told him. "I am a writer. The reason I have never been blocked is because I have been in psychotherapy and therefore able to withstand the pres-

sures of society upon my artistic nature. It is also the reason
I have never been depressed or had accidents."

You people at Blue Cross may think the four hundred dollars a month it has cost you to pay my psychiatrist is a lot of
money but think of what it might have cost you if I had harmed
myself with food or drink or drugs or unhappy love affairs.
You are coming out ahead, I assure you.

Well, this is just to keep you updated while I wait for my
letter telling me about the restructuring of Farm Policy Group
Seven's Comprehensive Major Medical Coverage for the Future.

Yours most truly,

Rhoda K. Manning

November 7, 1993

Dear Blue Cross, Blue Shield,

I just got my flu shot. I didn't charge it to you since I just
ran by the Mediquik and it only cost five dollars so I thought
it wasn't worth the paperwork. I have been racking my brain
trying to think of something else I can have done to myself
before I bail out of the health insurance business and devote
myself to staying in perfect health until I am sixty-five and can
get some of my tax dollars back in Medicare.

The John Alden Insurance Company sent a sweet young
woman out to do a medical check on me. She called one afternoon at four and asked if she could come the next day at
noon. I guess that was to make sure I wasn't forewarned in case
I secretly smoke or drink. I told her to come on and she said
I had to fast from eight that night until noon. That was the
hard part. I never go eight hours without food as I believe in
controlling the blood sugar levels at all times.

She arrived promptly at noon. It turns out she lives in my
part of town. She said when she was ready to buy a house she

asked a policeman where the safest place in town was and he said these old neighborhoods on the mountain. The houses were built in the 'sixties and look like there would be nothing here to steal.

She came in and weighed me on a pair of scales she carries with her in a carpet bag. Then she drew blood and separated it in various little cylinders and sealed them up and put them in a pack to be taken by Federal Express to a lab in Kansas City. I had to sign a paper saying they could do an AIDS test. That's two in two months' time. I was glad to do it. As I told Sharon Cane, that's her name, if you aren't part of the solution, you are part of the problem. A gay friend of mine tells that to anyone who won't be tested for HIV.

Next I gave Sharon a urine specimen. She explained to me that they could tell from it if I had smoked a cigarette in the last ten days or had a drink. I have not had a drink in twenty years. A hypnotist in New Orleans talked me out of that years ago.

The way I feel now is that if the John Alden Jali-Care people don't have enough sense to want my $157.69 a month after all of this they can go to hell.

You may think from the tone of this letter that I am getting mad at you, but you would be wrong. I have appreciated all those checks for fifty percent of my psychotherapy. I don't blame you for trying to figure out a way to get your money back but I don't think there's any reason for me to give it to you.

> Yours sincerely,
> Rhoda K. Manning

December 4, 1993

Dear Blue Cross, Blue Shield,

John Alden Jali-Care is considering my application. I passed all my physical tests with flying colors but they are worried about the years of psychotherapy and have requested a letter from my psychotherapist, which he is drafting now.

I assume that the reason I haven't heard from you about my policy is that you have been busy with the lawsuit the Arkansas Senate is bringing against you for raising all the rates of people with preexisting conditions to such exorbitant amounts that they (we) are all going to have to quit. In the meantime I am pursuing other options as I have told you in our correspondence.

It said in the paper today that you had begun all this in order to get ready for the great Health Care Debate of 1994. Well, all I can say is I am losing interest in the whole thing. I have always paid for the things that made a real difference to my health, like eyeglasses, running shoes, good books, good music, movies, food. I know how to go to Mediquik and get shots. Not to mention the dentist, which you do not cover either.

Good luck with your lawsuit.

Yours sincerely,
Rhoda Manning

December 5, 1993

Dear John Alden Jali-Care,

Here is the letter from my psychiatrist which you requested. From it you will see that the only reason I have been going to him all these years is because I am a writer. It has nothing whatsoever to do with health problems. It is preventive medicine, and besides, I'm cutting down on my sessions and you won't be responsible for them anyway as they are a preexisting condition. Hope everything is clear now.

Yours most sincerely,
Rhoda K. Manning

December 15, 1993

Dear Blue Cross, Blue Shield,

I received your offer to continue to provide me with health insurance for $567.69 a month with a three-thousand-dollar deductible and a fifty-thousand-dollar stop-loss. I have decided to decline this offer. It's been nice doing business with you but I think I'll quit while I'm ahead.

Stay well,
Rhoda Manning

January 1, 1994

Dear Blue Cross, Blue Shield,

This is my first day of being uninsured. It feels great. I have had the snow shoveled from my sidewalk, am wearing my seat belt at all times, and have invested two thousand, three hundred dollars in a new Exercycle from the StairMaster people.

If I subtract the one thousand, seven hundred and three dollars quarterly payment I would have sent you that is only about seven hundred dollars for the Exercycle.

Looking ahead to the second quarterly payment I have bought a new fur jacket to keep me from catching cold. With the two hundred dollars I saved by having all my prescriptions filled in 1993 I bought a matching hat and muff.

Yours for a happy and healthy new year,
Rhoda Manning

February 1, 1994

Dear Blue Cross, Blue Shield,

Now that a month has passed and all is well I have decided to look ahead to the money I would be paying you the next few years and put in a lap pool. The pool people don't have much to do this time of year and have given me a twenty percent discount.

February 27, 1994   Sorry I didn't get this off sooner but they came and started digging the hole for the pool and it's been chaos around here. All is well now. The pool is nine feet wide and sixty-nine feet long. It has an electric cover that can be opened or closed from a switch in the kitchen. Talk about high technology.

Do you remember Sharon Cane, who came to draw blood for the John Alden Jali-Care Evaluation? Well, she is swimming with me three days a week. She starts at one end and I start at the other to make waves for each other to swim against. We usually bet five dollars on who can swim the most laps in an hour. A lot of times we lose count because we are having so much fun. I am down to seeing my analyst three times a month now that I have to pay for it. No ill effects so far, only I can tell I am not working as hard as I was when I had him to drive me to it. Why should I work seven days a week? It's almost spring. The long winter is over and I didn't catch the flu. That five-dollar flu shot may be the best money I spent all year.

Yours for a healthy America,
Rhoda Manning

March 19, 1994

Dear Blue Cross, Blue Shield,

I had a long talk with my ninety-year-old neighbor, Kassie Martin, yesterday. She praised me for letting my insurance run out. She said that if I have a stroke or a heart attack it is best to arrive at the hospital uninsured as that might lower the chances of them putting you on a life support machine. She has seen many unpleasant things happen to older people who arrive at the hospital fully insured. Greed is nothing new in the world but why should we be victims of it?

On another note I have only had one prescription filled since I left you. I drove around town doing some comparison shopping. That pharmacy that used to fill my prescriptions is twice as high as the one at Wal-Mart. You should look into this.

Yours in spring,
Rhoda Manning

March 21, 1994

Dear Blue Cross, Blue Shield,

Well, it looks like John Alden Jali-Care is going to come through with a cheap policy for me. Their representative called this morning to say all they needed now were some copies of my books with pages marked showing them where I used the information I got in psychotherapy to help my writing.

It's difficult to believe that health care professionals could be that unlettered and that dumb, isn't it? Now that I have gotten accustomed to being uninsured and dependent on myself it is going to be hard for me to pay anyone anything for health insurance. I'll let you know what I decide.

Stay well,
Rhoda Manning

March 26, 1994

Dear Blue Cross, Blue Shield,

I can't bring myself to take John Alden up on their offer. Why would I want to do business with people who are dumber than I am?

Instead, I have decided to go to Italy. A hotel near the Ponte Vecchio. I don't know where that is yet, but I will soon. A young man of my acquaintance who speaks perfect French and Italian is going with me. We are going to stay at a hotel in Roma where Sartre and Buckminster Fuller and Isamu Noguchi and lots of other artists stayed. If I get sick in Italy, who cares? What could I have that Italian pasta and Italian men couldn't cure? We are going to Rome for twelve days and then to Florence for seven.

> Arrivederci,
> Rhoda Manning

April 10, 1994

Dear Blue Cross, Blue Shield,

Well, here we are in Florence after a heavenly time in Rome. The sun is shining and the world seems "to lie before us like a field of dreams, so various, so beautiful, so new." We arrived yesterday morning and walked around for a while. Then we slept awhile and ate dinner in a piazza. Tomorrow we will go to see the Uffizi Gallery. There are paintings there by Botticelli, Titian, and Raphael, to name a few. I'll probably faint, but don't worry, it won't cost you any money.

It's pretty amazing to step off an airplane and be in Italy. Thanks so much for making this possible by raising my rates so much that I couldn't keep my insurance.

I picked up a paper as I was leaving Fayetteville and noticed that you had made a deal with State Farm to keep everyone's group policies in effect another year with only a twenty percent increase. I started to call my insurance agent and see if I could get in on that but then I decided to hell with it. Why should I pay you three thousand dollars a year? That's ten more nights in first-class hotels in Tuscany. Well, stay well. This is the last letter I am going to write to you. I'm going to see paintings, eat Italian food, then rent a sports car and drive up to the mountains to go skiing. My young lover and I have a motto. We'll take today. I know we aren't the first to think of that but it still works.

> Arrivederci,
> Rhoda

PERHAPS A MIRACLE

IT WAS THE WORST argument they had had in months. Nora Jane almost never argued with Freddy Harwood. In the first place she thought he was smarter than she was and in the second place he always went rational on her and in the third place there were better ways to get what she wanted. The best way was to say she wanted something and then not mention it for a week or two. All that time he would be arguing with himself about his objection and in the end he would decide he didn't have the right to impose his ideas on any other human being, not even his wife. Freddy had not gone to Berkeley in the sixties for nothing. *The Greening of America* and *The Sorcerer of Bolinas Beef* were still among his favorite books. Once a reporter had asked Freddy to name his ten favorite books and he had left out both those books because this was the nineties and Freddy was famous in the world of publishing and independent bookstores and he didn't want to seem too crazy in public. If someone had asked him the ten things he regretted most, leaving *The Greening of America* and *The Sorcerer of Bolinas Beef* off his list would have been right up there with the butterfly tattoo on his ankle.

"It doesn't matter what you take," he said out loud. "It's none of my business."

"You don't care what I take?"

"All I said is that sociology is a pseudoscience and you're too good for that kind of mush. I didn't mean you shouldn't take it. I should never have asked what you are going to take. I'm embarrassed that I asked. All I care about is that you be home by three so the girls won't come home to an empty house."

"You don't want me to go to college. I can tell."

"I want you to go to college fiercely. I wish I could quit work and go with you. My biology is about twenty years behind the field."

"Freddy." She climbed down off the ladder. She had been putting up drapes while Freddy read. She was wearing a white cashmere sweater and a pair of jeans. She was wearing ballet shoes.

"You wear that stuff to drive me crazy," Freddy said. "If they sold that perfume Cleopatra used on Caesar, you'd wear it every day. How can I let you go to college? Every man at Berkeley will fall in love with you. Education will come to a grinding halt. No one will learn a thing. No one will be able to teach. It's my civic duty to keep you at home. I owe it to the culture." He pulled her across the room and began to dance with her. He sang an old Cole Porter song in a falsetto voice and danced her around the sofas. One thing about Nora Jane. She could move into a scenario. "Where are the girls?" she asked.

"In the den doing homework. I told them I'd take them down to Berkeley to get an ice cream cone when they were finished."

"Meet me in the pool house. Hurry." She smiled the wild, hard-won smile that worked on Freddy Harwood better than all the perfumes of the East.

"Yes, yes, yes," he answered, and let her go and she walked away from him and out of the room and down the stairs and across the patio to the guest house beside the swimming pool. She went into the bedroom and took off her clothes and waited.

In a moment he was there. He turned off the lights to the pool with a switch on the wall. He locked the door and lay down beside her and began to make love to her.

It was Freddy's theory that the way you made love to a woman was to worship every inch of her body with your heart and mind and soul. This was easy with Nora Jane. He had worshiped every inch of Nora Jane since the night he met her. He loved beauty, had been raised to know and worship beauty, believed beauty was truth, balance, order. He worshiped Nora Jane and he loved her. Ten years before, on a snow-covered night in the northern California hills, he had delivered the twin baby girls who were his daughters. With no knowledge of how to do it and nothing to guide him but love, he had kept them all alive until help came. Nora Jane had another lover at the time and no one knew whose sperm had created Lydia and Tammili. Most of the time Freddy Harwood didn't give a damn if they were his or not. They lived in his home and carried his name and gave his life meaning and kept Nora Jane by his side. The other man had disappeared before they were born and had not been heard from since. It was a shadow, but all men have shadows, Freddy knew. Where it was darkest and there was no path. This was Freddy's credo. Each knight entered the forest where it was darkest and there was no path. If there was a path, it was someone else's path.

Freddy ran his hand up and down the side of Nora Jane's body. He trembled as he touched her small round hip. I cultivate this, he decided. Well, some men gamble.

II

A four-year-old boy named Zandia, who was visiting his grandmother in the house next door, had been trying all week to get to the Harwoods' heated swimming pool. He didn't necessarily want to get in the water. He wanted to get the blue-and-white safety ring he could see from his grandmother's fence. All these days and his grandmother had not noticed his fascination with the pool. Perhaps she had noticed it but she hadn't given it enough weight. She trusted the lock on the gate, and besides, Zandia was such a wild little boy. He could have four or five plans of action going at the same time. His latest fascination was with vampires, and Clyda Wax, for that was his grandmother's name, had been occupied with overcoming his belief in them. "Where did you ever see a vampire?" she kept asking. "There is no such thing as a vampire, Zandia. There are vampire bats. I'll admit that. But they live in caves and they are very stupid and blind and I could kill a hundred of them with a broom."

"They would fly up and eat your blood. They can fly."

"I'd knock them down with the broom. They are blind. It would be easy as pie. I'd have a bushel basket full of them."

"They'd fly up and stick to the trees. What would you do then?"

"I'd get a giraffe to eat them."

"But giraffes live in Africa."

"So what? I can afford to import one."

"What about Count Dracula? You couldn't kill him."

"There isn't any Count Dracula. There's just that vulgar, disgusting, imbecile Hollywood trash that you are exposed to in L.A. I shudder to think what they let you watch down there. Did the baby-sitter show it to you? Did the baby-sitter tell you about vampires? Vampires are not true. Now go and play with your Jeep for a while. I want to rest." Clyda closed her eyes and lay back on the lawn chair. She didn't mean to go to sleep but she was exhausted from taking care of him. She had volunteered for one week. It had turned into three. He had been up that morning at five rummaging around in her kitchen drawers. "When your mother comes to get you I'm going to a spa," she said sleepily. "I'm going to Maine Chance and stay a month."

As soon as he saw she was asleep he walked over to the fence and undid the latch. He pushed the latch open and disappeared through the gate. There it was, shimmering in the moonlight, the swimming pool with all its chairs and the red rubber raft and the safety ring. He walked under the window of the bedroom where Nora Jane and Freddy lay in each other's arms. He walked around the chairs and up to the edge of the water. He bent over and saw his reflection in the water. Then he began to fall.

"Something's wrong." Nora Jane sat up. She pushed Freddy away from her. She jumped up from the bed. She tore open the door and began to run. She got to the pool just as Zandia was going under. She ran around the edge. She jumped in beside him and found him and they began to struggle. She pulled and dragged him through the water. When she got to the shallow end she pulled him up into the air. Then the lights were on and Freddy was in the water with her and they lifted him from the water and turned him upside down and Freddy was on the mobile phone calling 911.

"How did you know?" they asked her. After it was over and Zandia was in his grandmother's arms eating cookies and the living room was full of uniformed men and Tammili and Lydia had seen their naked parents performing a miracle and were the most cowed ten-year-old girls in the Bay Area.

"I don't know. I don't know what I knew. I just knew to go to the pool."

"You've never even met this kid?" one of the men in uniform asked.

"I've seen him in the yard. He's been in the yard next door."

Later that night, after Zandia and his grandmother had been walked to their house and Tammili had been put to bed reading *The Voyage of the Dawn Treader* and Lydia had been put to bed reading a catalog from *American Girl* and they were alone in their room, Freddy had opened all the windows and the skylight above the bed and they had lain in each other's arms, awed and pajamaed, talking of time and space and life at the level of microbiology and wave and particle theory and why Abraham Pais was their favorite person in New York City and how it was time to take the girls to the Sierra Nevada to see the mountains covered with snow. "We need to do something to mark it. Plant some trees at Willits. Lay bricks for a path."

"You could rearrange the books in the den. It's such a mess in there Betty won't even go in to clean. It's unhealthy to have that many books in a room. It's musty. It's like a throwback to some other age. It doesn't go with the rest of the house."

"Go on to sleep if you can."

"I can. You're the one who doesn't sleep."

"We should both sleep tonight. Something's on our side. I never felt that as strongly as I do right now." He patted her for a while. Then he began to dream his old dream of building the house at Willits. The solar house he and Nieman had built by hand to prove it could be done and to prove who they were. Our rite of passage into manhood house, Freddy knew. The house to free us from our mothers. In the recurrent dream it was a clear, cold day. They had finished the foundation and were beginning to set the posts at the sides. The mountain lions came and sat upon the rise and watched them. "You think I'm nuts to go to all this trouble to make a nest," he told the lions. "Well, you're wrong. This is what my species does."

In that magical house Tammili and Lydia were born and sometimes Freddy thought the house had been built to serve that purpose. To make them so much his that nothing could sever the bond. So what if one or both of them were Sandy George Wade's biological spawn? So what if maybe Tammili was his and Lydia was not? So what in a finite world if there was love? Freddy always ended up deciding.

✳   ✳   ✳

Next door, it was Zandia's grandmother who couldn't sleep. She was talking to Zandia's mother on the phone. "You just come up here tomorrow afternoon as soon as they finish shooting and spend the night. He's lonely for you. Four-year-old boys shouldn't be away from their mother for this many days."

"I can't. We have to look at rushes every night. It's the first time Sandy and I have had a chance to be in a film together. I'm a professional, Mother. I have to finish my work, then I'll come get him. There's no reason you can't hire a baby-sitter for him, you know. He stays with baby-sitters here."

"He almost died, Claudine. I don't think you understand what happened here. You never listen to me, do you know that? You only half listen to anything I say. The child almost died. Also, he is obsessed with vampires. Who let him see a movie about vampires? That's what I'd like to know. I'm taking him to my psychiatrist tomorrow for an evaluation."

"All right then. I'll send someone to get him. I thought you wanted him, Mother. You always do this. You say you want him, then you change your mind in about four days."

"He almost drowned."

"Could we talk in the morning? I'll call you at seven."

Claudine hung up the phone, then went into the bedroom to find Sandy. He was in bed smoking and reading the script. He put the cigarette out when he saw her and shook his head. "Where have you been?" he asked. "What took you so long?"

"Zandia fell in a swimming pool and Mother's neighbor had to fish him out. They're acting like it was some sort of big, big deal. God, she drives me crazy. This is the last time he's going up there. From now on if she wants to see him she can come down here."

"We'll be finished in a week or ten days. It can't drag on much longer than that. You think we ought to send for him?"

"She can bring him. I'll tell her in the morning. I'll line up a sitter and he can go back to the Montessori school in the mornings. I knew better than to do this."

"How'd he fall in a pool?"

"Mother's neighbors left the gate open or something. The police came. He's fine. Nothing happened to him. It's just Mother's insanity."

Then Sandy George Wade, who was the father of Lydia Harwood, as anyone who looked at them would immediately know, began to flip channels on the television set, hoping to find a commercial starring either Claudine or himself, as that always cheered him up and made him think he wouldn't end up in a poor folks home. He reached for Claudine, to believe she was there, and sighed deep inside his scarred, motherless, fatherless heart. His main desire was to get a good night's sleep so he would be beautiful for the cameras in the morning.

Claudine pulled away from him. She got up and went into the other room to call her mother back. When she returned she had a different plan. "We have to go to San Francisco and pick him up. She won't bring him. Well, to hell with it. She wants me to meet the woman who pulled him out of the pool. I probably ought to sue them for having an attractive nuisance. Anyway, we have to go. Will you take me?"

"Of course I will. As soon as we have a break. Come on, get in bed. I like San Francisco. It's a nice drive. We'll take the BMW. It's driving good since I got the new tires. Get in bed. Let's get some sleep." Then Claudine gave up for the day and climbed into the bed and let Sandy cuddle up to her. Their neuroses fit like gloves. They were really very happy together. They hated the same things. They liked to make love to each other and they liked to sleep in the same bed. It was the best thing either of them had ever known. They even liked Zandia. Neither one of them liked to take care of him but they didn't hate or resent him. Sometimes they even thought he was funny.

LUNCH AT THE
BEST RESTAURANT
IN THE WORLD

"SO WHY WAS I CHOSEN for this? That's what I keep asking myself. It's like a tear in the fabric of reality. Maybe I heard him walking by the window. I have a perfect ear for music. Well, I do. Maybe I saw him by the fence and knew he'd be wanting to get to the pool. All mothers are wary of pools. I've been watching to make sure no one drowns in our pool for years. Maybe there's a logical explanation. I'm sure there is. It only seems like a miracle." Nora Jane was talking. She and Freddy and Freddy's best friend, Nieman Gluuk, were at Chez Panisse having lunch. Nora Jane was wearing yellow. Freddy had on his plaid shirt and chinos. Nieman wore his suit. It was the first time the Harwoods had been out in public since the night Nora Jane pulled the child from the swimming pool. Nieman had been with them almost constantly since the event. Actually he had been with them almost constantly since they were married ten years before. Nieman and Freddy saw each other or talked on the phone nearly every day. They had done this since they were five years old. No one thought anything about it or ever said it was strange that two grown men were inseparable.

"Three knights were allowed to see the Grail," Freddy said. "Bors and Percival and Galahad. They were pure of heart. You're pure of heart, Nora Jane. And besides, you're an intuitive. The first time Nieman met you he told me that. He says you're the most intuitive person he's ever known."

"Maybe this means I shouldn't go to college. It means something, Freddy. Something big."

"You think I don't know that? I was there, too, wasn't I? I watched it happen. What it means is that there's a lot more going on than we are able to acknowledge. Thought is energy. It creates fields. You picked up on one. You're a good receiver. That's what intuitive means. Maybe I'll go to school with you. Just dive right into a freshman science course and see if I sink or swim."

Nieman sighed and shook his head from side to side. "I can't believe you had this experience just when you were getting ready to try your wings at Berkeley. It's a coincidence, not a warning. It doesn't mean the girls are in danger or that we are in danger. No, listen to me. I know you think that but you shouldn't. The point is that you saved his life, not that his life was in danger. You will always save lives in many ways. It's all the more reason to go back to school and gain more knowledge and more power. Knowledge is power, even if it does sound trite to say it."

"I wish they hadn't put it in the papers." Nora Jane turned to Nieman and touched his hand. She was one of the three people in the world who dared to touch the esteemed and feared Nieman Gluuk, the bitter and hilarious movie critic of the *San Francisco Chronicle.* "The whole thing only lasted about six minutes. I can barely remember any of it except the moment I knew to do it. Freddy remembers pulling him out better than I do."

"We must never forget it," Nieman said.

"A man who had it happen to him last year called last night. He went through a glass door to get to a pool and saved his nephew. He thinks it has something to do with water. Water as a conductor."

"It proves a lot of theories," Freddy added. "I was there too, Nieman. I witnessed it. I was in bed with her."

"Excuse me." They were interrupted by a waiter, who took their orders for goat cheese pie and salads and wine. "It was the single most profound thing that ever happened to me in my life," Freddy went on. "I will be thinking about it every day for the rest of my life. A tear in the cover, a glimpse of a wild, or perhaps exquisitely orderly, reality that is lost to us most of the time. Think of it, Nieman. The brain can't stand to consciously process all it senses and knows. We'd go crazy. The brain is a filter and its first job is to keep the body healthy. Occasionally, perhaps by accident, it sees a larger reality as its domain. Altruism. Well, it's so humbling to be part of it." He looked down, afraid they would think he wanted them to remember what he had done in the earthquake of 1986. But they knew better. He had forbidden his friends ever to speak of that. "Well, let's don't talk it all away. It's Nora Jane's miracle. I want to take her up to Willits for a while to think it over but she can't go. She starts school in three days, you know."

The waiter put bread down in front of them, the best French bread this side of New Orleans. Nieman held out a loaf to Nora Jane and they broke the bread. They ate in silence for a while.

"Fantastic about Berkeley." Nieman said at last. "Brilliant. I wish I could go. I feel like a dinosaur with my old knowledge. My encyclopedia is twenty years old. Every year I say I'll get another one but I never do."

The waiter brought more bread. Nieman buttered a piece and examined it, calculating the fat grams and wondering if it mattered. "Our darling Nora Jane," he went on. "Loose on the campus in the directionless nineties. I should write a modern opera for you. The problem is the ending. Shakespeare knew what to do. He poured in outrageous action, tied up all the loose ends, piled up some bodies, and danced off the stage on the wings of language. Ah, those epilogues. 'As you from crimes would pardoned be. Let your indulgence set me free.' Oh, he could lift the language! The modern stage can't bear the weight of so much beauty, so much fun. It's too large an insult to the modern fantasy, boredom, and self-pity. I went to three movies last week that were so bad I didn't last for the first hour. I just walked out. They began hopefully enough, were well acted by fine actors, then you could see the money mold begin to grow, the meetings where the money people in group think begin to decide how to corrupt the script. Well, let's not ruin lunch with such thoughts. After lunch shall we go over to the campus and walk around and get you accustomed to your new domain, Miss Nora? I heard the brilliant translator Mark Musa is here for the semester to teach *The Divine Comedy.* You might want to take that. We could go by and see if he's in his office and introduce ourselves."

"There you go," Freddy said. "Trying to take over what she takes. I pray to God every day to make me stop caring what classes she takes."

"The only answer is for you to go with me. You too, Nieman. Why not? Life is short, as you both tell me a thousand times a month."

"Life is short," Nieman agreed. "We could do it, Freddy. We could think of it as a donation to the university. Pay tuition as special students, sign up for classes, and go as often as we are able. I could take Monday and Tuesday off. I'm going to list the names of seven movies and then leave a blank white space. Think of us back on the campus, Freddy. Freddy was valedictorian of our class, Nora. But you know that."

"His mother's told me a million times. I think it was the high point of her life."

"That's what she wants you to think. The high point of her life was when she flew that jet to Seattle in the air show. No, I guess it was when she played Martha in *Who's Afraid of Virginia Woolf?* You know who she's going out with now, don't you, Nieman?"

"I heard. It's a terrible shadow, Freddy, but you have survived so far. Well, shall we do it then? Register for classes?"

"Yes. I'm taking biology, physics, and a history course. I want to see what they're teaching. It can't be as bad as I've heard it is."

"I'll take Musa's Dante in Translation and a playwriting course. I'll go incognito and write the play for Nora Jane and we'll put it on next year as an AIDS benefit."

"I'll sing 'Vissi d'arte' from the side of the stage while twelve little girls in long white dresses run around the stage doing leaps. Would that be a conclusion? Then a poet can run out on the stage and read part of 'Little Gidding.' Imagine us all going to college together."

"Meeting for coffee at Aranga's. When I was a student I was touched by old people going back to school. We will touch their silly little hearts. At least, Freddy and I will. You'll drive them crazy. I don't know, Freddy, maybe she's overeducated already."

"I want a degree. I'm embarrassed not to have a college degree. I'm the first person in my family in three generations not to have one." She sat up very straight and tall and Nieman and Freddy understood this was not to be taken lightly.

"Then let's go," Freddy said. "If you will allow us, we will accompany you on this pilgrimage." She turned her head to look at him and he fell madly in love with the sweep and whiteness of her neck and Nieman watched this approvingly. After all, someone has to be in love and get married and continue the human race.

An hour later they were on the Berkeley campus, walking along the sidewalks where Freddy and Nieman had walked when they were young. Nora Jane had been on the campus many times but never as a student. It was very strange, very liberating, and she felt her spirit open to the world she was about to enter. "I'll be Virgil and you be Dante and Nora Jane can be Beatrice," Nieman was saying. "The possibility of vast fields of awareness, that's what this campus always says to me. I used to think I could get vibrations from the physics building when the first reactor was installed and all those brilliant minds were here. I used to feel the force of them would dissolve the harm my mother did to me each morning. She would pour fear and anxiety over me and I would step onto the campus and feel it eaten up by knowledge. She was enraged that I was studying theater. She was very hard on me."

"You had to live at home with her?" Nora Jane took his arm to protect him from the past.

"She wanted me to go to medical school and be a psychiatrist, as she was seeing one. I would say to her, Mother, theater is psychotherapy writ large. The actors on the stage do what people do in ordinary life, keep secrets, say half of what they're thinking, manipulate, lie. Because it's writ large on the stage or screen the audience is on to them. They leave the theater and go out into the world more aware of other people's behaviors, if not of their own. Still, she was not convinced. She still thinks what I do is frivolous."

"She can't, after all these years?"

"Can she not? I'm an only child, don't forget that."

"I am too and so is Freddy. We're the only-child league. Like the redheaded league in Sherlock Holmes."

They linked arms, coming down the wide sidewalk to the student union. "This is like *The Wizard of Oz*," Nieman said. "In *The Divine Comedy* they walked single file."

"Well, these are not the legions of the damned either," Freddy added, "although they certainly look the part." They were passing students, some with rings in their ears and noses and lips and some wearing chic outfits and some looking like they were only there because they didn't have anything better to do.

"Let's go to the registrar's office and get that over with," Freddy suggested.

"I will fill out any number of forms but I am not sending off for transcripts," Nieman decreed. "If they start any funny stuff about transcripts I'll drop my disguise and call the president of the university."

"We aren't pulling rank, Nieman," Freddy said. "We go as pilgrims or not at all."

"You go your way and I'll go mine, as always. Yes, it's beginning to feel like old times."

"Don't talk about the sixties or I'll hit you. I was in a convent school kneeling in the gravel before the statue of the Virgin and you were here getting to read literature and hear lectures by physicists. It isn't fair. You're too far ahead. I'll never catch up."

"No competition please. We're in this together."

By five that afternoon it was done. Freddy was signed up to audit World History and Physics I and Biology I. Nieman was taking Dante and had met Mark Musa and promised to brush up on his Italian and Nora Jane had her books and notebooks for English, History, Algebra, and Introduction to Science. They had sacks of books from Freddy's bookstore and the campus bookstore.

When they were through collecting all the books they went to a coffeehouse across the street from the campus and picked out a table where they could meet. "I don't know if this table will be large enough," Nieman said. "Students will be flocking to us, don't you think?"

"Don't scare me like that," Freddy said.

"Don't turn my education into an anecdote," Nora Jane decreed. "Or I'll get my own table and have my own following." She piled her books up in front of her and looked at them. She was proud of them. She was on fire at this beginning.

YOU MUST CHANGE
YOUR LIFE

⁂

IN JANUARY of nineteen hundred and ninety-five the esteemed movie critic of the *San Francisco Chronicle* took an unapproved leave of absence from his job and went back to Berkeley full time to study biochemistry. He gave his editor ten days' notice, turned in five hastily written, unusually kind reviews of American movies, and walked out.

Why did the feared and admired Nieman Gluuk walk out on a career he had spent twenty years creating? Was it a midlife crisis? Was he ill? Had he fallen in love? The Bay Area arts community forgot about the Simpson trial in its surprise and incredulity.

Let them ponder and search their hearts. The only person who knows the truth is Nieman Gluuk and he can't tell because he can't remember.

The first thing Nieman did after he turned in his notice was call his mother. "I throw up my hands," she said. "This is it, Nieman. The last straw. Of course you will not quit your job."

"I'm going back to school, Mother. I'm twenty years behind

in knowledge. I have led the life you planned for me as long as I can lead it. I told you. That's it. I'll call you again on Sunday."

"Don't think I'm going to support you when you're broke," she answered. "I watched your father ruin his life following his whims. I swore I'd protect you from that."

"Don't protect me," he begged. "Get down on your knees and pray you won't protect me. I'm forty-four years old. It's time for me to stop pacing in my cage. I keep thinking of the poem by Rilke.

> *"His vision, from the constantly passing bars,*
> *has grown so weary that it cannot hold*
> *anything else. It seems to him there are*
> *a thousand bars; and behind the bars, no world.*
>
> *"As he paces in cramped circles, over and over,*
> *the movement of his powerful soft strides*
> *is like a ritual dance around a center*
> *in which a mighty will stands paralyzed.*
>
> *"Only at times, the curtain of the pupils*
> *lifts, quietly—An image enters in,*
> *rushes down through the tensed, arrested muscles,*
> *plunges into the heart and is gone."*

"You are not Rilke," his mother said. "Don't dramatize yourself, Nieman. You have a lovely life. The last thing you need is to go back to Berkeley and get some crazy ideas put in your head. This is Freddy Harwood's doing. This has Freddy written all over it."

"Freddy's in it. I'll admit that. He and Nora Jane and I have gone back to school together. I wish I hadn't even called you. I'm hanging up."

"Freddy has a trust fund and you don't. You never remember that, Nieman. Don't expect me to pick up the pieces when this is over. . . ." Nieman had hung up the phone. It was a radical move

but one to which he often resorted in his lifelong attempt to escape the woman who had borne him.

Nieman's return to academia had started as a gesture of friendship. Nieman and Freddy had attended Berkeley in the sixties but
Nora Jane was fifteen years younger and had never attended college, not even for a day.

"Think how it eats at her," Freddy told him. "We own a bookstore and she never even had freshman English. If anyone asks
her where she went to school, she still gets embarrassed. I tell her
it's only reading books but she won't believe it. She wants a degree and I want it for her."

"Let's go with her," Nieman said, continuing a conversation
they had had at lunch the day before. "I mean it. Ever since she
mentioned it I keep wanting to tell her what to take. Last night
I decided I should go and take those things myself. We're dinosaurs, Freddy. Our education is outdated. We should go and
see what they're teaching."

"Brilliant," Freddy said. "It's a slow time at the store. I could
take a few weeks off."

"Here's how I figure it." Nieman stood up, got the bottle of
brandy, and refilled their glasses. "We sign up for a few classes,
pay the tuition, go a few weeks, and then quit. The university
gets the tuition and Nora Jane gets some company until she set-
tles in."

"We have spent vacations doing sillier things," Freddy said,
thinking of the year they climbed Annapurna, or the time they
took up scuba diving to communicate with dolphins.

"I need a change," Nieman confessed, sinking down into the
water until it almost reached his chin. "I'm lonely, Freddy. Except
for the two of you I haven't any friends. Everyone I know wants
something from me or is angry with me for not adoring their
goddamn, whorish movies. Some of them hate me for liking them.
It's a web I made and I've caught myself."

"We'll get applications tomorrow. Nora Jane's already registered. Classes start next Monday."

Nieman went to the admissions office the next day and signed up to audit Dante in Translation and Playwriting One. Then, suddenly, after a night filled with dreams, he changed the classes to biochemistry and Introduction to the Electron Microscope.

This was not an unbidden move. For several years Nieman had become increasingly interested in science. He had started by reading books by physicists, especially Freeman Dyson. Physics led to chemistry, which led to biology, which led to him, Nieman Gluuk, a walking history of life on earth. Right there, in every cell in his body was the whole amazing panorama that led to language and conscious thought.

The first lecture on biochemistry and the first hour with the microscopes excited Nieman to such an extent he was trembling when he left the building and walked across the campus to the coffee shop where he had agreed to meet Freddy and Nora Jane. A squirrel climbed around a tree while he was watching. A girl walked by, her hair trailing behind her like a wild tangled net. A bluejay landed on a branch and spread his tailfeathers. Nieman's breath came short. He could barely put one foot in front of the other. Fields of wonder, he said to himself. Dazzling, dazzling, dazzling. If they knew what they are carrying as they go. Time, what a funny word for the one-way street we seem to have to follow.

"This is it," he told Freddy and Nora Jane when they were seated at a table with coffee and croissants and cream and sugar and butter and jam and honey before them on the handmade plates. "I'm quitting the job. I'm going back to school full time. I have to have this body of information. Proteins and nucleic acids, the chain of being. This is not some sudden madness, Freddy. I've been moving in this direction. I'll apply for grants. I'll be a starving student. Whatever I have to do."

"We don't think you're crazy," Nora Jane said. "We think you're wonderful. I feel like I did this. Like I helped."

"Helped! You are the Angel of the Annunciation is what you are, you darling, you."

"Are you sure this isn't just another search for first causes?" Freddy warned. "Remember those years you wasted on philosophy?"

"Of course it is. So what? This isn't dead philosophical systems or Freudian simplicities. This is real knowledge. Things we can measure and see. Information that allows us to manipulate the physical world."

"If you say so."

"May I borrow the house at Willits for the weekend? I need to be alone to think. I want to take the textbooks up there and read them from start to finish. I haven't been this excited in years. My God, I am in love."

"Of course you can borrow the house. Just be sure to drain the pipes when you leave."

"It might snow up there this weekend," Nora Jane put in. "The weather station warned of snow."

Two days later Nieman was alone in the solar-powered house Freddy and his friends had built on a dirt road five miles from Willits, California. The house was begun in 1974 and completed in 1983. Many of the boards had been nailed together by Nieman himself with his delicate hands.

The house stood in the center of one hundred and seven acres of land and overlooked a pleasant valley where panthers still hunted. In any direction there was not a power line or telephone pole or chimney. The house had a large open downstairs with a stone bathroom. A ladder led from the kitchen area to a loft with sleeping rooms. There were skylights in the roof and a wall of glass facing east. There was a huge stone fireplace with a wide hearth. Outside there was a patio and a deep well for drinking water. "This well goes down to the center of the earth," Freddy was fond of saying. "We cannot imagine the springs or rivers from which it feeds. This could be water captured eons ago before the crust cooled. This water could be the purest thing you'll ever taste."

"It tastes good," his twin daughters, Tammili and Lydia, would always answer. "It's the best water in the world, I bet."

Nieman stood in the living room looking out across the valleys, which had become covered with snow while he slept. He had arrived late the night before and built up the fire and slept on the hearth in his sleeping bag. "It was the right thing to do to come up here," he said out loud. "This holy place where my friends and I once made our stand against progress and the destruction of the natural world. This holy house where Tammili and Lydia were born, where the panther once came to within ten yards of me and did not strike. I am a strange man and do not know what's wrong with me. But I know how to fix myself when I am broken. You must change your life, Rilke said, and now I am changing mine. Who knows, when I come to my senses, somebody will have taken my job and I'll be on the streets writing travel articles. So be it. In the meantime I am destined to study science and I am going to study science. I cannot allow this body of information to pass me by and I can't concentrate on it while attempting to evaluate Hollywood movies."

Nieman moved closer to the window so he could feel the cold permeating the glass. Small soft flakes were still falling, so light and small it seemed impossible they could have turned the hills so white and covered the trees and the piles of firewood and the well. I can trek out if I have to, he decided. I won't worry about this snow. This snow is here to soothe me. To make the world a wonderland for me to study. Life as a cosmic imperative, de Duve says. I will read that book first, then do three pages of math. I have to learn math. My brain is only forty-four years old, for

Christ's sake. Mother taught math. The gene's in there somewhere.
It's just rusty. Before there was oxygen there was no rust. Iron ex-
isted in the prebiotic oceans in a ferrous state. My brain is like
that. There are genes in there that have never been exposed to air.
Now I will use them.

Nieman was trembling with the cold and the excitement of
the ideas in his head. Proteins and nucleic acids, the idea that all
life on earth came from a single cell that was created by a cosmic imperative. Given the earth and the materials of which it is
created, life was inevitable. Ever-increasing complexity was also inevitable. It was inevitable that we would create nuclear energy, inevitable that we would overpopulate the earth. It was not as insane
as it had always seemed. And perhaps it was not as inevitable once
the mind could recognize and grasp the process.

Nieman heaved a great happy sigh. He left watching the snow
and turned and climbed the ladder to the sleeping loft. There,
on that bed, in that corner beneath the skylight, on a freezing
night ten years before, Freddy and Nora Jane's twins had been
born, his surrogate children, his goddaughters, his angels, his dancing princesses. Nieman lay down upon the bed and thought about
the twins and the progress of their lives. Not everything ends in
tragedy, he decided. My life has not been tragic, neither has
Freddy's or Nora Jane's. Perhaps the world will last another
hundred years. Perhaps this safety can be stretched to include the
lives of Tammili and Lydia. So what if they are not mine, not
related to me. All life comes from one cell. They are mine because they have my heart. It is theirs. I belong to them, have pon-
dered over them and loved them for ten years. How can this new
knowledge I want to acquire help them? How can this new birth
of curiosity and wonder add to the store of goodness in the
world?

Well, Nieman, don't be a fool. It isn't up to you to solve the
problems of the world. But it might be. There were ninety-two
people in that lecture room but I was the only one who had this

violent a reaction to what the professor was saying. I was the only one who took what he was saying as a blow to the solar plexus. This might be my mission. It might be up to me to learn this stuff and pass it on. It is not inevitable that we overpopulate and destroy the world. Knowledge is still power. Knowledge will save us.

Nieman was crying. He lay on the bed watching the snow falling on the skylight and tears rolled down his face and filled his ears and got his fringe of hair soaking wet. He cried and he allowed himself to cry.

I had thought it was art, he decided. Certainly art is part of it. Cro-Magnon man mixing earth with saliva and spitting it on the walls of caves was a biochemist. He was taking the elements he found around him and using them to explore and recreate and enlarge his grasp of reality. After the walls were painted he could come back and stare at them and wonder at what he had created. Perhaps he cried out, terrified by the working of his mind and hands. I might stare in such a manner at this house we built. I could go outside and watch the snow falling on those primitive solar panels we installed so long ago. It is all one, our well and solar panels and the cave paintings at Lascaux and microscopes at Berkeley and this man in Belgium writing this book to blow my mind wide open and Lydia and Tammili carrying their back-packs to school each morning. The maker of this bed and the ax that felled the trees that made the boards we hammered and Jonas Salk and murderers and thieves and Akira Kurosawa and Abraham Pais and I are one. This great final truth, which all visionaries have intuited, which must be learned over and over again, world without end, amen.

Nieman fell asleep. The snow fell faster. The flakes were larger now, coming from a cloud of moisture that had once been the Mediterranean Sea, that had filled the wells of Florence, in the time of Leonardo da Vinci, and his royal patron, Francis, King of France.

✳   ✳   ✳

The young man was wearing long robes of dark red and brown. His hair was wild and curly and his feet were in leather sandals. His face was tanned and his eyes were as blue as the sky. He had been knocking on the door for many minutes when Nieman came to consciousness and climbed down the ladder to let him in. "Come in," Nieman said. "I was asleep. Are you lost? I'm Nieman Gluuk. Come in and warm yourself."

"It took a while to get here," the young man said. "That's a kind fire you have going."

"Sit down. Do you live around here? Could I get you something to drink? Coffee or tea or brandy? Could I get you a glass of water? We have a well. Perhaps you're hungry." The young man moved into the living room and looked around with great interest. He walked over to the window and laid his palms against the glass. Then he touched it with his cheek. He smiled at that and turned back to Nieman.

"Food would be nice. Bread or cheese. I'll sit by the fire and warm myself."

Nieman went into the kitchen and began to get out food and a water glass. The young man picked up the book by the biochemist de Duve, and began to read it, turning the pages very quickly. His eyes would move across the page, then he would turn the page. By the time Nieman returned to the fireplace with a tray, the young man had turned half the pages. "This is a fine book," he said to Nieman, smiling and taking a piece of bread from the tray. "It would be worth the trip to read this."

"You aren't from around here, are you?" Nieman asked.

"You know who I am. You called me here. Don't be frightened. I come when I am truly called. Of course, I can't stay long. I would like to finish this book now. It won't take long. Do you have something to do while I'm reading?" The young man smiled a dazzling smile at Nieman. It was the face of the Angel of the Annunciation in Leonardo's painting. It was the face of David.

"You knew me, didn't you?" the young man added. "Weren't there things you wanted to tell me?"

Nieman walked back toward the kitchen, breathing very softly. The young man's face, his hair, his feet, his hands. It was all as familiar as the face Nieman saw every day in the mirror when he shaved. Nieman let his hands drop to his sides. He stood motionless by the ladder while the young man finished reading the book.

"What should I call you?" Nieman said at last.

"Francis called me da Vinci."

"How do you speak English?"

"That's the least of the problems."

"What is the most?"

"Jarring the protoplasm. Of course, I only travel when it's worth it. I will have a whole day. Is there something you want to show me?"

"I want to take you to the labs at Berkeley. I want to show you the microscopes and telescopes, but I guess that's nothing to what you've seen by now. I could tell you about them. Did you really just read that book?"

"Yes. It's very fine, but why did he waste so many pages pretending to entertain superstitious ideas? Are ideas still subject to the Church in this time?"

"It's more subtle, but they're there. The author probably didn't want to seem superior. That's big now."

"I used to do that. Especially with Francis. He was so needy. We will go to your labs if you like. Or we could walk in this snow. I only came to keep you company. It's your time." He smiled again, a smile so radiant that it transported Nieman outside his fear that he was losing his mind.

"Why to me?"

"Because you might be lonely in the beginning. Afterward, you will have me if you need me." The young man folded the book very carefully and laid it on a cushion. "Tell me how cheese is made now," he said, beginning to eat the food slowly and carefully as he talked. "How is it manufactured? What are the cows named? Who wraps it? How is it transported?"

"The Pacific Ocean is near here," Nieman answered. He had taken a seat a few feet from the young man. "We might be able to get out in the Jeep. That's the vehicle out there. Gasoline powered. I don't know what you know and what you don't know. Do you want to read some more books?"

"Could we go to this ocean?"

"I guess we could. I have hiking gear. If we can't get through we can always make it back. I have a mobile phone. I'd like to watch you read another book. I have a book of algebra and a book that is an overview of where we are in the sciences now. There's a book of plays and plenty of poetry. I'd be glad to sit here and read with you. But finish eating. Let me get you some fruit to go with that."

"Give me the books. I will read them."

Nieman got up and collected books from around the room and brought them and put them beside the young man. Then he brought in firewood and built up the fire. He took a book of poetry and sat near the young man and read as the young man read. Here is the poem he turned to and the one he kept reading over and over again as he sat by the young man's side with the fire roaring and the wind picking up outside and the snow falling faster and faster.

> . . . *Still, if love torments you so much and you so much need*
> *To sail the Stygian lake twice and twice to inspect*
> *The murk of Tartarus, if you will go beyond the limit,*
> *Understand what you must do beforehand.*
> *Hidden in the thick of a tree is a bough made of gold*
> *And its leaves and pliable twigs are made of it too.*
> *It is sacred to underworld Juno, who is its patron,*
> *And it is roofed in by a grove, where deep shadows mass*

Along far wooded valleys. No one is ever permitted
To go down to earth's hidden places unless he has first
Plucked this golden-fledged growth out of its tree
And handed it over to fair Proserpina, to whom it belongs
By decree, her own special gift. And when it is plucked,
A second one always grows in its place, golden again,
And the foliage growing on it has the same metal sheen.
Therefore look up and search deep and when you have found it,
Take hold of it boldly and duly. If fate has called you,
The bough will come away easily, of its own accord.
Otherwise, no matter how much strength you muster,
You never will
Manage to quell it or cut it down with
The toughest of blades.

"Now," the young man said, when he finished the biochemistry textbook. "Tell me about these infinitesimal creatures, amoebas, proteins, acid chains, slime molds, white cells, nuclei, enzymes, DNA, RNA, atoms, quarks, strings, and so on. What an army they have found. I could not have imagined it was that complicated. They have seen these creatures? Many men have seen them?"

"We have telescopes and microscopes with lenses ground a million times to such fineness and keenness, with light harnessed from electrons. They can magnify a million times. A thousand million. I don't know the numbers. I can take you to where they are. I can take you to see them if you want to go."

"Of course. Yes, you will take me there. But it must be soon. There is a limited amount of time I will be with you."

"How much time?"

"It will suffice. Will your vehicle travel in this snow?"

"Yes. Perhaps you would like to borrow some modern clothes. Not that there's anything wrong with your clothes. They are very nice. I was especially admiring the cape. The weave is lovely. They're always worrying about security. I want to take you to the labo-

ratories at Berkeley. I can call the head of the department. He
will let us in."

"You may have the cloak since you admire it. It can remain
here." He removed the long brown garment and handed it to
Nieman.

"I'll give you a parka." Nieman ran for the coat rack and took
down a long beige parka Freddy had ordered from L.L. Bean. He
held it out to the young man. "I guess I seem nervous. I'm not.
It's just that I've wanted to talk to you since I was ten years old."

"Yes. You've been calling me for some time."

"I thought you would be old. Like of the time when you died.
Did you die?"

"I thought so. It was most uncomfortable and Francis wept
like a child, which was not altogether unpleasant." He laughed
softly. "It is better to come with my young eyes. In case there is
something to see."

"Where are you when you aren't here?"

"Quite far away."

"Will it matter that you came here? I mean in the scheme of
things, as it were?"

"It will matter to me. To read the books and see these instruments you are describing. I have always wished to have my
curiosity satisfied. That was always what I most dreamed of doing.
Francis never understood that. He could never believe I wouldn't
be satisfied to eat and drink and be lauded and talk with him. It
kept me from loving him as he deserved."

"I meant, will it change the course of anything?"

"Not unless you do it."

"I wouldn't do it. Could I do it by accident?"

"No. I will see to that. Do you want to go out now, in the
vehicle in the snow?" There it was again, the smile that soaked
up all the light and gave it back.

"Let's get dressed for it." Nieman led his guest upstairs and
gave him a warm shirt and socks and shoes and pants and long

underwear. While he was changing Nieman banked the fire and put the food away and set the crumbs out for the birds and locked the windows and threw his things into a bag. He forgot to drain the pipes.

"Well, now," he said out loud. "I guess I can drive that Jeep in this snow. Let's assume I can drive. Let's say it's possible and I will do it." He turned on the mobile phone and called the department at Berkeley and left a message saying he was bringing a senator to see the labs. Then he called the president of the university at his home and called in his markers. "Very hush-hush," he told the president. "This could be very big, Joe. This could be millions for research but you have to trust me. Don't ask questions. Just tell the grounds people to give me the keys when I come ask for them. I can't tell you who it is. You have to trust me."

"Of course, Nieman," the president answered. "After everything you and Freddy have done for us. Anything you want."

"The keys to everything. The electron microscopes, the physics labs, the works. We could use one of your technical people for a guide but no one else."

"There'll be people working in the labs."

"I know that. We won't bother anyone. I'll call you Monday and tell you more."

"Fine. I'll look forward to hearing about it." After he hung up the phone the university president said to his wife, "That was Nieman Gluuk. Did you know he's quitting writing his column? Took a leave of absence to go back to school."

"Well, don't you go getting any ideas like that," his good-looking wife giggled. "All he ever wrote about were foreign films. He'd gotten brutal in his reviews. Maybe they let him go. Maybe he just pretended that he quit."

There was a layer of ice beneath the snow. Nieman tested it by walking on it, then put Leonardo into the passenger seat and buckled him in and got behind the wheel and started driving. He drove very carefully in the lowest gear across the rock-strewn yard toward the wooden gate that fenced in nothing since the fence had been abandoned as a bad idea. "Thank God it's downhill," he said. "It's downhill most of the way to the main road. So, when was the last time you were here?" He talked without turning his head. The sun was out now. Birds were beginning to circle above the huge fir trees in the distance. "Have you been to the United States? To the West Coast?"

"Once long ago. I saw the ocean with a man of another race. I walked beside it and felt its power. It is different from the ocean I knew."

"We can go there first. It won't take long once we get to the main road. I'm sorry if I keep asking you questions. I can't help being curious."

"You can ask them if you like. I was visited by Aristotle in my turn. We went to a river and explored its banks. He was very interested in my studies of moving water. He said the flow of water would impede the mixture of liquids and we talked of how liquid forms its boundaries within a flow. He had very beautiful hands. I painted them later from memory several times. Of course everyone thought they were Raphael's hands. Perhaps I thought so too finally. After he left I had no real memory of it for a while. More like the memory of a dream, bounded, uncertain, without weight. I think it will be like that for you, so ask whatever you wish to ask."

"I don't think I want to ask anything now. I think we should go to the ocean first since we are so near. I forget about water. I forget to look at it with clear eyes, and yet I was watching the snow when I fell asleep. Also, I was crying. Why are you smiling?"

"Go on."

"I was thinking that when I was small I knew how to appreciate the ocean. Later, I forgot. When I was small I would stand in one place for a very long time watching the waves lap. Every day I came back to the same spot. I made footprints for the waves to wash away. I made castles farther and farther up the beach to see how far the tide could reach. I dug into the sand, as deep as it would allow me to dig. I was an infatuate of ocean, wave, beach. Are you warm enough? Is that coat comfortable?"

"I am warm. Tell me about this vehicle. What do you call it?"

"Automobile. Like auto and mobile. It's a Jeep, a four-wheel drive. We call it our car. Everyone has one. We work for them. We fight wars over the fuel to power them. We spend a lot of time in them. They have radios. We listen to broadcasts from around the world while we drive. Or we listen to taped books. I have a book of the Italian language we could listen to. You might want to see how it's evolved. It might be the same. It might be quite similar to what you spoke. Would you like to hear it?" Nieman shifted into a higher gear. The road was still steep but lay in the lee of the mountain and was not iced beneath the snow. "We'll be on the main road, soon," he added. "We're in luck it seems. I wouldn't have driven this alone. One more question. How do you read the books so fast?"

"I'm not sure." Leonardo laughed. "It's been going on since I quit the other life. It's getting better. At first it was not this fast. I'm very fond of being able to do it. It's the nicest thing of all."

"Where do you stay? When you aren't visiting? I mean, going someplace like this."

"With other minds."

"Disembodied?"

"If we want to be. Is that the main road?" It was before them, the road to Willits. Plows had pushed the snow in dirty piles on either side of the road. In the center two vehicles were moving in one lane down the mountain. A blue sedan and a white mini-van were bouncing down the road in the ripening sunlight.

"I believe this," Nieman said. "I'm in my red Jeep driving Leonardo da Vinci down from the house to see the ocean. My name is Nieman Gluuk and I have striven all my life to be a good man and use my talents and conquer resentment and be glad for whatever fate dumped me in Northern California the only child of a bitter woman and a father I almost never saw, and I never went into a movie theater expecting to hate the movie and was saddened when I did. Maybe this is payback and maybe this is chance and maybe I deserve this and the only thing I wish is that my friend, Freddy, could be here so it won't destroy our friendship when I am driven to tell him about it."

"You won't remember it." Leonardo reached over and touched his sleeve. He smiled the dazzling smile again and Nieman took it in without driving off the road and took the last curve down onto the highway. "You will have it," Leonardo added. "It is yours, but you won't have the burden of remembering it."

"I want the burden." Nieman laughed. "Burden me. Try me. I can take it. I'll write a movie script and publicize intelligence. *Nel mezzo del cammin di nostra vita mi ritrovai per una selva oscura, che la diritta via era smarrita. Ahi quanto a dir qual era e cosa dura esta selva selvaggia e aspra e forte.* That's the beginning of *The Divine Comedy.* That's what I went back to Berkeley to take. Instead, I'm in this forest of biochemistry. I'm dreaming the things I'm reading. They put literature into a new light. The artist intuits what the mind knows and the mind knows everything, doesn't it? Past, present, and forevermore."

"Some wake to it gradually. Some never know."

"I've worked for it," Nieman said. "I have worked all my life to understand, to see myself as the product of five hundred million years of evolution. You seem to have known it always."

"I was taken from my mother's house when I was four years old. On the walk to my father's house, the fields and the wonder of the earth came to console me. But I worked also. I always worked." He laid his hand on Nieman's arm. Nieman steered the Jeep across a pile of snow and turned onto the road leading down to Willits. Around them the snow-covered hills with their massive fir trees were paintings of unspeakable complexity. Neither of them spoke for many miles.

It was past noon when they drove through the small town of Willits and turned onto Highway 20 leading to the Pacific Ocean. "I'm going to stop for gasoline for the automobile," Nieman said. "We collect it in foreign countries. The countries of the Turks and Muslims, although some of it is under the ground of this country. We store it underneath these filling stations in large steel tanks. Steel is an alloy made of iron and carbon. It's very strong. Then we drive up to the pumping stations and pump the fuel into our tanks. Even young children do this, Leonardo. I don't know what you know and what you don't know, but I feel I should explain some things."

"I like to hear you speak of these phenomena. Continue. I will listen and watch."

Nieman spotted a Conoco station and stopped the Jeep and got out. He took down one of the gasoline hoses and inserted it in the fuel tank of the Jeep. Leonardo stood beside the tank watching and not speaking. "Don't smile that smile at anyone else," Nieman said. "We'll be arrested for doing hallucinogens."

"They never explode?" Leonardo moved in for a closer look, took a sniff of the fumes, then put both hands in the pockets of the jacket. There was a package of Kleenex in one pocket. He brought it out and examined it.

"It's called Kleenex. We blow our noses on it," Nieman explained. "It's a disposable handkerchief."

"Could one draw on it?" Leonardo held a sheet up to the light. "It's fragile and thin."

"Wait a minute." Nieman pulled a notepad and a black felt-tip pen out of the glove compartment and handed them to Leonardo. Leonardo examined the pen, took the top from it, and began to draw, leaning the pad against the top of the Jeep. Nieman put the hose back on the pump, then went inside and paid for the gasoline. When he returned, Leonardo had covered a page with the smallest, most precise lines Nieman had ever seen. Leonardo handed the drawing to him. It was of the mountains and the trees. In the foreground Nieman was standing beside the Jeep with the gasoline hose in his hand.

Nieman took the drawing and held it. "You are a microscope," he said. "Perhaps you will not be impressed with the ones we've made."

"Shall we continue on our way?" Leonardo asked. "Now that your tank is full of gasoline."

They drove in silence for a while. The sun was out in full violence now, melting the snow and warming the air. "The air is an ocean of currents," Nieman said at last. "I suppose you know about that."

"Always good to be reminded of anything we know."

"You want to hear the Italian tape? I'd like to hear what you think of it."

"That would be fine."

Nieman reached into a pack of tapes and extracted the Beginning Italian tape and stuck it into the tape player. "This Jeep doesn't have very good speakers," he said. "We have systems that are much better than this one." The Italian teacher began to teach Italian phrases. Leonardo began to laugh. Quietly at first, then louder and louder until he was shaking with laughter.

"What's so funny?" Nieman asked. He was laughing too. "What do you think is funny? Why am I laughing too?"

"Such good jokes," Leonardo answered, continuing to laugh. "What questions. What news. What jokes."

It was thirty-six miles from Willits to the Pacific Ocean. The road led down between mountains and virgin forests. They drove along at fifty miles an hour, listening to the Italian tape and then to Kiri Te Kanawa singing arias from Italian opera. Nieman was lecturing Leonardo on the history of opera and its great modern stars. Long afterward, when he had forgotten everything about the day that could be proven, Nieman remembered the drive from Willits to the ocean and someone beside him laughing. "Are you sure you weren't with me?" he asked Freddy a hundred times later in their lives. "Maybe we were stoned. But Kiri Te Kanawa didn't start recording until after we had straightened up so we couldn't have been stoned. I think you were with me. You just don't remember it."

"I never drove in a Jeep with you from Willits to the ocean while listening to Italian tapes. I would remember that, Nieman. Why do you always ask me that? It's a loose wire in your head, a precursor of dreaded things to come." Then Freddy would smile and shake his head and later talk about it to his psychiatrist or Nora Jane. "Nieman's fixated on thinking I drove with him in a Jeep listening to an Italian tape," he would say. "About once a year he starts on that. It's like the budding of the trees. Once a year, in winter, he decides the two of us took that trip and nothing will convince him otherwise. He gets mad at me because I can't remember it. Can you believe it?"

Outside the small town of Novo, Nieman found a trail he had used before. It led to a beach the townspeople used during good weather. He parked the Jeep in a gravel clearing and they got out and climbed down a path to the water. The ocean was very dramatic, with huge boulders jutting into the entrance of a small harbor. The snow was melting on the path. Even now, in the heart of winter, moss was forming on the rocks. "'The force that through the green fuse drives the flower,'" Nieman said.

"Dylan is happy now," Leonardo answered. "A charming man. I go to him quite often and he recites poetry. It makes the poetry he wrote when he was here seem primitive. I should not tell you that, of course. We try never to say such things."

"Look at the ocean," Nieman answered. "What mystery could be greater. Shouldn't this be enough for any man to attempt to understand? This force, this power, this place where land and air

meet the sea? '. . . this goodly frame, the earth . . . this most excellent canopy, the air . . . this brave o'erhanging firmament, this
majestical roof fretted with golden fire . . .' "

"Will loved the sea and wrote of it but had little time for it.
Plato was the same. He talked and wrote of it but didn't take
the time to ponder it as we are doing. Of course, in other ages
time seemed more valuable. Life was short and seemed more
fleeting."

They were walking along a strip of sand only ten to twenty
feet wide. It was low tide. Later in the day it would have been
impossible to walk here and they would have had to use the higher
path.

"We could just stay here," Nieman said. "We don't have to go
to the labs. I just thought you might want to see the microscopes."

"We have all day."

"They're leaving the labs open in the biochemistry building.
We can go to Berkeley or we can stay here. I saw you looking at
the atlas. Did you memorize it? I mean, is that how you do it?"

"I remember it. It is very fine how they have mapped the floor
of the oceans. Is it exact, do you think?"

"Pretty much so at the time of mapping. The sand shifts,
everything shifts and changes. They map the floor with sound-
ings, with radar. When you leave here, where do you have to be?
Is there some gathering place? Do you just walk off? Where do
you go?"

"I just won't be here."

"Will the clothes be here? I only wondered. That's Freddy's
coat. I could get him another one but he's pretty fond of that
one. He took it to Tibet."

Nieman moved nearer to Leonardo, his eyes shifting wildly.
The day had a sort of rhythm. Sometimes it was just beating
along. Then suddenly he imagined it whole and that made his
heart beat frantically. "I don't care, of course. You can take it if
you need to. You can have anything I have."

"I will leave the clothes. It would be a waste to take them."

"When will you go? How long will it be? You have to understand. I never had a father. No man ever stayed long enough. I was always getting left on my own. It's been a problem for me all my life."

Leonardo turned to face him. "This is not a father who leaves, Nieman. This is the realm of knowledge, which you always longed for and long for now. It is always available, it never goes away, it cannot desert you, it cannot fail you. It is yours. It belongs to whoever longs for it. If you desert it, it is always waiting, like those waves. It comes back and back like the sea. I am only a moment of what is available to you. When I am gone the clothes will be here and you can wear them when you are reading things that are difficult to understand. You will read everything now. You will learn many languages. You will know much more than you know now. Tell me about the microscopes."

"I haven't used one yet. But I can tell you how it works. It concentrates a beam of electrons in a tube to scan or penetrate the thing you want magnified. It makes a photograph using light and dark and shadow. The photograph is very accurate and magnified a million times. Then a portion of that photograph can be magnified several million more times. It's so easy for me to believe the photographs so I think it must be something I know. My friend, Freddy, thinks we know everything back to the first cell, that all discovery is simply plugging into memory banks. Memory at the level of biochemistry. Which is why I can't believe it took me so long to begin to study this. I had to start in the arts. My mother is a frustrated actress. I've been working her program for forty-four years. Now it's my turn. But this is plain to you. You're the one who saw the relationship between art and science. It never occurred to you not to do both."

"I am honored to be here for your birth of understanding. Where I am, the minds are past their early enthusiasms. I miss seeing the glint in eyes. I miss the paintbrush in my hand and the smell of paints. If you wish to show me this microscope we can go there now. The sea is very old. We don't have to stay beside it all day."

It was a two-and-a-half-hour drive to Berkeley. They drove along the western ridge of the Cascade Range, within a sea breeze of the Mendocino Fracture Zone. Beside the Russian River. They drove to Mendocino, then Littleriver, then Albion. At Albion they cut off onto Highway 128 and drove along the Navarro River to Cloverdale. They went by Santa Rosa, then Petaluma, then Novato, and down and across the Richmond–San Rafael Bridge and on to Berkeley.

It was six o'clock when they arrived at the campus. It was dark and the last students were mounting their bicycles as they left the biochemistry building. Nieman nosed the Jeep into a faculty parking space and they got out and entered the building through iron doors and went down a hall to an elevator.

"Have you been on one of these?" Nieman asked, holding the elevator door with his hand. "It's a box on a pulley, actually. It's quite safe. When they were new sometimes they would get stuck. Some pretty funny jokes and stories came out of that. Also, there were tragedies, lack of oxygen and so forth. This one is thirty years old at least, but it's safe."

"Arabic," Leonardo said, touching the numbered buttons with his finger. "I thought it would continue to be useful."

"The numbers? Oh, yes. Everyone uses the same system. Based on the fingers and toes. Five fingers on each hand. Two arms, two legs. Binary system and digital system. We run our computers on the binary system. It's fascinating. What man has done. There's one playwright dealing with it, a man named Stoppard." Leonardo stepped back and stood near Nieman. Nieman pressed 2 and the box rose in space on its pulley and the door opened.

Waiting for them on the second-floor hall was the head of university security. He was wearing a blue uniform with silver but-

tons. "Hello," he said. "If you're Mr. Gluuk they have a lady waiting for you. President Culver said to tell you she'd show you the
machines."

"Oh, that wasn't necessary. We only wanted to look at them."
He took Leonardo's arm. So he looks like a genius who has spent
a thousand years on a Buddhist prayer bench. So the smile is so
dazzling it hypnotizes people. No one would imagine this. No
one would believe it.

"Don't I know you from when I was a student?" Nieman asked.
"I'm Nieman Gluuk. I used to edit the school paper. In the sev-
enties. Didn't you guard the building when we had the riots in
seventy-five?"

"I thought I knew you. I'm Abel Kennedy. I was a rookie that
year and you kept me supplied with cookies and coffee in the
newspaper office. I'm head of security now." Captain Kennedy
held out his hand and Nieman shook it. He was trying to decide how to introduce Leonardo when a door opened down the
hall and a woman came walking toward them. She was of medium
height with short blond hair. She was wearing a pair of blue jeans
and a long-sleeved white shirt. Over the shirt was a long white
vest. There were pencils and pens in the pockets of the vest. A
pair of horn-rimmed glasses was on her head. Another pair was
in her hand.

"I was wondering if one could wear bifocals to look into the
scope," Nieman said. "I was afraid I'd have to get contact lenses
to study science."

"It's a screen." She laughed. "I'm Stella Light. My parents were
with the Merry Pranksters. Some joke. I meant to have it changed
but I never did." She held out her hand to Nieman. Long slen-
der fingers. Nails bitten off to the quick. No rings. She smiled
again.

"I'm Nieman Gluuk. This is our distinguished guest, Leo
Gluuk, a cousin from Madrid. I mean, Florence. Also from
Minneapolis."

"Make up your mind. Nice to meet you. I've read your stuff. I'm from Western Oregon. Well, what exactly can we do for you?"

"Just let us see the microscopes. Leo is very interested in the technology. It's extremely nice of you to stay late like this. I know your days are long enough already."

"I was here anyway. We've had an outbreak of salmonella in the valley. We're trying to help out with that. It gets on the chicken skin in the packing plants or if they are defrosted incorrectly. Well, I'll let you see slides of that. They're fresh."

They walked down a hall to a room with the door ajar. Inside, on a long curved table, was the console. In the center, covered with a metal that looked more like gold than brass, was the scanning electron microscope. The pride of the Berkeley labs.

They moved into the open doorway. Leonardo had been completely quiet. Now he gave Stella the smile and she stepped back and let him precede her into the room. She and Leonardo sat down at the console. She got out a box of slides and lifted one from the box with a set of calipers. She slid it into a notch and locked it down. Then she pushed a button and an image appeared on the screen. "To 0.2 nanometers," she said. "We can photograph it and go higher."

Nieman leaned over their shoulders and looked into the screen. It was a range of hills covered with cocoons. "A World War I battlefield," he said. "Corpses strewn everywhere. Is that the salmonella?"

"Yes. Let's enlarge it." She pushed another button. The hill turned into crystal mountains. Now it was the Himalayas. Range after range of crystals. Nieman looked down at his own arm. In a nanometer of skin was all that wonder.

Leonardo began asking questions about the machine, about the metal of which it was made, about the vacuum through which the electrons traveled, how the image was created. Stella answered the questions as well as she could. She bent over him. She put pieces of paper in front of him. She put slides into the microscope. She asked no questions. She had been completely mesmerized by the smile. She would remember nothing of the encounter. Except a momentary excitement when she was alone in the room at night. She thought it was sexual. She thought it was about Nieman. There I go, she would scold herself, getting interested in yet another man I cannot understand. The daddy track, chugging on down the line to lonesome valley.

They stayed in the laboratory for half an hour. Then they wandered out into the hall and found a second microscope and Stella took the thing apart and let Leonardo examine the parts. Then she let him reassemble it. She stood beside Nieman. She sized him up. He was better looking than his photograph in the paper. His skin was so white and clear. He was kind.

"You really quit your job?" she asked.

"A leave of absence. I was burned out."

"Who is he?" she asked. "I don't think I've ever met anyone I liked as much."

"We all love him. The family adores him. But it's hard to keep track of him. He travels all the time."

Leonardo put everything back into its place. He laid Stella's pencil on top of the stack of papers and got up from the chair. "We are finished now," he said. "We should be leaving. We thank you for your kindness."

Stella walked them to the elevator. They got on and she stood smiling after them. When they had left she went back into the laboratory and worked until after twelve. Two children had died in the salmonella outbreak. Twenty were hospitalized. The infected food had reached a grade school lunchroom.

When they left the building there was a full moon in the sky. There was so much light it cast shadows. Leonardo walked with Nieman to the Jeep. "I am leaving," he said. "You will be fine." He kissed Nieman on the cheek, then on the forehead. Then he was gone. Nieman tried to follow him but he did not know how.

When he got back to the Jeep, the clothes Leonardo had been wearing were neatly stacked on the passenger seat. On top of the clothes was a pencil. A black and white striped pencil sharpened to a fine point. Nieman picked it up and held it. He put it in his pocket. I might write with this, he decided. Or I might draw.

He got into his Jeep and drove over to Nora Jane and Freddy Harwood's house and parked in the driveway and walked up on the porch and rang the doorbell. The twins let him in. They pulled him into the room. "Momma's making étouffée and listening to the Nevilles," Tammili told him. "She's having a New Orleans day. Come on in. Stay and eat dinner with us. Daddy said you'd been in Willits. How is it there? Was it snowing?"

They dragged him into the house. From the back Freddy called out to him. Nora Jane emerged from the kitchen wearing an apron. It was already beginning to fade. Whatever had happened or almost happened or seemed to happen was fading like a photograph in acid.

"Come on in here," Freddy was calling out. "Come tell us what you were doing. We have things to tell you. Tammili made all-stars in basketball. Lydia got a role in the school play. Nora Jane got an A on her first English test. I think I'm going bald. We haven't seen you in days. Hurry up, Nieman. I want to talk to you."

"He's your best friend," Lydia giggled, half whispering. "It's so great. You just love each other."

THE BROWN CAPE

TAMMILI AND LYDIA were supposed to be cleaning up the loft. Their father was working on the well. Their mother was cooking breakfast and it was their job to make the beds and straighten up the loft and clean the windows with vinegar and water.

"Why can't we clean them with Windex like we do at home?" Lydia complained. "Just because we come to Willits for spring vacation they go environmental and we have to use vinegar for the windows. The windows are okay. I'm not cleaning them."

"You shouldn't have come then. You could have stayed with Grandmother. You didn't have to come if you're just going to complain."

"Why can't we have a ski lodge or something? Why do we have to have a solar house? We can't bring anybody. It's too little to even bring the dogs."

"It's a solar-powered house, not a solar house, and I don't want to take dogs everywhere I go. There're wolves and panthers in these woods. Those dogs wouldn't last a week up here. Dooley is so friendly he'd let a wolf carry him off in his teeth."

"You clean the windows and I'll get all this stuff out from under the bed. Everyone's always sticking stuff under here. I hate piles of junk like this." Lydia was pulling boxes and clothes out from underneath the bed where she and Tammili had been sleeping. It was the bed on which they had been born, in the middle of the night, ten and a half years before. Their father had delivered them and a helicopter had come and taken them to a hospital at Fort Bragg. Sometimes Lydia felt sentimental about that and sometimes she didn't like to think about it. It was embarrassing to have been delivered in a snowstorm by your father. Not to mention they had almost died. That was too terrible to think about.

"What are you thinking about?" Tammili asked, but she knew. She and Lydia always thought about things at the same time. It was the curse and blessing of being twins. You were never lonely, not even in your thoughts. On the other hand there was no place to hide.

"Who put this here?" Lydia dragged a long brown cloak out from underneath the bed. It had a cowl and a twisted cord for the waist and it was very thick, as thick as a blanket. It smelled heavenly, like some wonderful mixture of wildflowers and mist. She pulled it out and spread it on the bed. Then she wrapped it around her shoulders.

"I've never seen this before." Tammili drew near the cape and touched it. "It smells like violet. I bet it belongs to Nieman. No one but Nieman would leave a cape here. Let me wear it too, will you?" She moved into one half of the cape. They wrapped it around themselves like a cocoon and fell down on the bed and started laughing.

"Once upon a time," Lydia began, "there were two little girls and they were so poor they didn't have any firewood for the fireplace. All the trees had been cut down by ruthless land developers and there weren't any twigs left to gather to make a fire. They only had one thing left and that was their bed. We better cut up the bed and burn it, one of them said, or else we won't live until the morning. We will freeze to death in this weather. Okay, the other one said. Pull that bed over here and let's burn it up. Then they saw something under the bed. It was a long warm cape that their father had left for them when he went away to war. There was a note on it. 'This is for my darling daughters in case they run out of firewood. Love, your dad.'"

"Tammili." It was their mother calling. "You girls come on down. I want you to help me with the eggs." Tammili and Lydia put their faces very close together. They giggled again, smothering the sound.

"We're coming," Lydia called. "We'll be down in a minute." They folded the cape and laid it on the bed by Tammili's backpack. Then they climbed down the ladder to help their mother with the meal.

That was Wednesday morning. On Wednesday night their father decided they should go on an expedition. "To where?" their mother asked. "You know I have to study while I'm here. I can't go off for days down a river or in the mountains. One-day trips. That's all I'm good for this week."

"I thought we might overnight up in the pass by Red River," Freddy Harwood said. "Nieman and I used to camp there every spring. It might be cold but we'll take the bedrolls and I'll have the mobile phone. You can't go for one night?"

"I should stay here. Do you need me?"

"We don't need you," Tammili said. "We can take care of things. I want to go, Dad. We've been hearing about Red River for years but no one ever takes us. We're almost eleven. We can do anything."

"Get another adult," Nora Jane insisted. "Don't go off with both of them and no one to help."

"We are help," Lydia said. "Is it a steep climb, Daddy? Is it steep?"

"No. It's long but it's not that steep. Nieman and I used to do the trail to the top in three hours. Two and a half coming down. There's a bower up there under thousand-year-old pine trees. You don't need a sleeping bag. We'll take them but we could sleep on the ground. I haven't been up there to camp in years. Not since I met your mother. So, we'll go. It's decided."

"Tomorrow," they both screamed.

"Maybe tomorrow. Maybe Friday. Let me think about it." They jumped on top of him and started giving him one of their famous hug attacks. They grabbed pillows and hugged him with them until he screamed for mercy. "Tomorrow, tomorrow, tomorrow," they kept saying. "Don't make us wait."

"Then we have to get everything ready tonight because we have to leave at sunup. It takes an hour to drive to the trail. Then three hours to climb. I want to have camp set up by afternoon."

"What do we need?"

"Tent, food, clothes, extra socks. Vaseline for blisters, ankle packs for sprains, snakebite kit, Mag Lites, sleeping bags."

"We're going to carry all that?"

"Whatever we want we have to carry. We'll have extra water in the car. We'll take small canteens and the purifying kit. Go start pumping at the well, Tammili. Fill two water bags."

"Can't I fill them at the sink?"

"No, the idea is to know how to survive without a sink. That's what Willits is for, sweeties."

"We know." They gave each other a look. "So no matter what happens your DNA is safe." They started giggling and their mother put down the dish she was drying and started giggling too.

Freddy Harwood was an equipment freak. He had spent the summers of his youth in wilderness camps in Montana and western Canada. When he graduated to camping on his own, he took up equipment as a cause. If he was going camping he had every state-of-the-art device that could be ordered on winter nights from cat-

alogs. He had Mag Lites on headbands and Bull Frog sunblock.
He had wrist compasses and Ray-Ban sunglasses and Power Bars
and dehydrated food. He had two lightweight tents, a Stretch
Dome and a Lookout. The Lookout was the lightest. It weighed
five pounds, fifteen ounces with the poles. He had Patagonia synchilla blankets and official referee whistles and a Pur water purifier and drinking water tablets in case the purifier broke. He had
two-bladed knives for the girls and a six-bladed knife for himself.
He had stainless-steel pans and waterproofing spray and tent repair kits and first aid kits of every kind.

"Bring everything we think we need and put it on the table,"
Freddy said. "Then we'll decide what to take and what to leave.
Bring everything. Your boots and the clothes you're going to wear.
It's eight o'clock. We have to be packed and in bed by ten if we're
going in the morning."

The girls went upstairs and picked out clothes to wear. "I'm
taking this cape," Tammili said. "I've got a feeling about this cape.
I think it's supposed to go to Red River with us."

"Nieman saw baby panthers up there once," Lydia added. "The
mother didn't kill him for looking at them she was so weak with
hunger because there had been a drought and a forest fire. Nieman
left them all his food. He got to within twenty feet of their bur-
row and put the food where she could get it. Dad was there.
He knows it's true. Nieman's so cool. I wish he was going with
us."

"He has to study. He's going for a Nobel prize in biochemistry. That's what Dad told Grandmother. He said Nieman
wouldn't rest until he won a Nobel."

The girls brought their clothes and backpacks down from the loft
and spread the things out on the table. "What's this?" Freddy
asked, picking up the cloak.

"Something we found underneath the bed. We think it's

Nieman's. I was going to take it instead of a sleeping bag. Look how warm it is."

"I wouldn't carry it if I were you. You have to think of every ounce." Tammili went over and took the cape from him and folded it and laid it on the hearth. Later, when they had finished packing all three of the backpacks and set them by the kitchen door, she picked up the cape and pushed it into her pack. I'm taking it, she decided. I like it. It looks like the luckiest thing you could wear.

In a small, neat condominium in Berkeley, the girls' godfather, Nieman Gluuk, was finishing the last of twenty algebra problems he had set himself for the day. His phone was off the hook. His flower gardens were going wild. His cupboards were bare. His sink was full of dishes. His bed was unmade.

He put the last notation onto the last problem and stood up and began to rub his neck with his hand. He was lonely. His house felt like a tomb. "I'm going to Willits to see the kids," he said out loud. "I'm going crazy all alone in this house. Starting to talk to myself. They are my family and I need them and it's spring vacation and they won't be ten forever."

He went into his bedroom and began to throw clothes into a suitcase. It was three o'clock in the morning. He had been working on the algebra problems for fourteen hours. When Nieman Gluuk set out to conquer a body of knowledge, he did it right. When he had studied philosophy he had learned German and French and Greek. Now he was studying biochemistry and he was learning math. "If my eyes hold out I will learn this stuff," he muttered. "If my eyes give out, I'll learn it with my ears." He pushed the half-filled suitcase onto the floor and turned off the lights and pulled off his shirt and pants and fell into his bed in his underpants. It would be ten in the morning before he woke. Since he had quit his job at the newspaper he had been sleeping nine and ten hours a night. The day he canceled his subscription he slept twelve hours that night.

"The destination," Freddy was saying to his daughters, "is the high caves above Red River. They aren't on this map but you can see the cliff in these old photographs. Nieman and I took these when we were about twenty years old. We developed them in my old darkroom in Grandmother Ann's house. See all the smudges? We were experimenting with developers." He held the photograph up. "Anyway, we follow the riverbed for a few miles, then up and around the mountain to this pass. Four rivers rise on this mountain. All running west except this one. Red River runs east and north. It's an anomaly, probably left behind from some cataclysm when the earth cooled or else created by an earthquake eons ago. It's unique in every way. If there was enough snow last winter the falls will be spectacular this time of year. Some years they are spectacular and sometimes just a trickle. We won't know until we get there. Even in dry years the sound is great. Where we are camping we will be surrounded by water and the sound of water. It's the best sleeping spot in the world. I'll put it up against any place you can name. I wish your mother was going with us. She doesn't know what she's missing." He took the plate of pancakes Nora Jane handed him and began to eat, lifting each mouthful delicately and dramatically, meeting her violet-blue eyes and saying secrets to her about the night that had passed and the one she was going to be missing.

Tammili and Lydia played with their food. Neither of them could eat when they were excited and they were excited now.

"Is this enough?" Lydia asked her mother. "I really don't want any more."

"Whatever you like. It's a long way to go and the easy way to carry food is in your stomach."

"It weighs the same inside or out," Tammili said. "We're only taking dehydrated packs. In your stomach it's mixed with water so it really weighs less if you carry it in the pack."

Lydia giggled and got up and put her plate by the sink. Tammili followed her. "Let's go," they both said. "Come on, let's get going."

"I wish you had a weather report," Nora Jane put in. "If it turns colder you just come on back."

"Look at that sky. It's as clear as summer. There's nothing moving in today. I've been coming up here for twenty years. I can read this weather like the back of my hand. It's perfect for camping out."

"I know. The world is magic and there's nothing to fear but fear itself." Nora Jane went to her husband and held him in her arms. "Go on and sleep by a waterfall. I wish I could go but I have to finish this paper. That's it. I want to turn it in next week."

"Let's go," Tammili called out. "What's keeping you, Dad? Let's get going." Freddy kissed his wife and went out and got into the driver's seat of the Jeep Cherokee and the girls strapped themselves into the seats behind him and plugged their Walkmans into their ears.

Nora Jane went back into the house and stacked the rest of the dishes by the sink and sat down at the table and got her papers out. She was writing a paper on Dylan Thomas. " 'The force that through the green fuse drives the flower / Drives my green age;' " she read, " 'that blasts the roots of trees / Is my destroyer. . . .' "

Freddy took a right at the main road to Willits, then turned onto an old gold-mining trail that had been worn down by a hundred years of rain. "Hold on," he told the girls. "This is only for four miles, then we'll be on a better road. It will save us hours if we use this shortcut." The girls took the plugs out of their ears and held on to the seats in front of them. The mobile phone fell from its holder and rattled around on the floor. Tammili captured it and turned it on to see if it was working. "It's broken," she said. "You broke the phone, Dad. It wasn't put back in right."

"Good," he said. "One less hook to civilization. When we get rid of the Jeep we'll be really free. The wilderness doesn't want you to bring a bunch of junk along. It wants you to trust it to provide for you."

"Trusting the earth is trusting yourself. Trusting yourself is trusting the earth. This is our home. We were made for it and it for us." The girls chanted Freddy's credo in unison, then fell into a giggling fit. The Jeep bounced along over the ruts. The girls giggled until they were coughing.

"You have reached the apex of the silly phase," Freddy said, in between the bumps. "You have perfected being ten years old. I don't want this growing up to go a day further. If you get a day older, I'll be mad at you." He gripped the steering wheel, went around a boulder, and came down a steep incline onto a black-top road that curved around and up the mountain. "Okay," he said. "Now we're railroading. Now we're whistling Dixie."

"He hated that mobile phone," Tammili said to her sister. "He's been dying for it to break."

"It's Momma's phone so she can call us from her school," Lydia answered. "He's going to have to get her another one as soon as he gets back."

Nieman woke with a start. He had been dreaming about the equations from the day before. They lined up in front of the newspaper office. Gray uniformed and armed to the teeth, they barred his way to his typewriter. When he tried to reason with them, they held up their guns. They fixed their bayonets.

"I hate dreams," he said. He put his feet down on the floor and looked around at the mess his house was in. He lay back down on the bed. He dialed a number and spoke to the office manager at Merry Maids. Yes, they would send someone to clean the place while he was gone. Yes, they would tell Mr. Levine hello. Yes, they would be sure to come.

I'm out of here, Nieman decided. I'll eat breakfast on the way. They know I'm coming. They know I wouldn't stay away all week. I'll go by the deli and get bagels and smoked salmon. I'll take the math book and do five more problems before Monday. Only five. That's it. I don't have to be crazy if I don't want to be. An obsessive can pick and choose among obsessions.

He put the suitcase back onto the unmade bed. He added a pair of hiking shorts and a sun-resistant Patagonia shirt he always wore in Willits. He closed the suitcase and went into the bathroom and got into the shower and closed his eyes and tried to think about the composition of water. Hydrogen, he was thinking. So much is invisible to us. We think we're so hot with our five senses but we know nothing, really. Ninety-nine percent of what is going on escapes us. Ninety-nine percent to the tenth power or the thousandth power. The rest we know. We are so wonderful in our egos, dressed out in all our ignorance and bliss. Our self-importance, our blessed hope.

Freddy went up a last curve, cut off on a dirt road for half a mile, then stopped the Jeep at the foot of an abandoned gold mine. "Watch your step," he said to the girls. "There are loose stones everywhere. You have to keep an eye on the path. It's rough going all the way to where the trees begin."

"It's so nice here," Lydia said. "I feel like no one's been here in years. I bet we're the only people on this mountain. Do you think we are, Dad? Do you think anyone else is climbing it today?"

"I doubt it. Nieman and I never saw a soul when we were here. Of course, we have managed to keep our mouths shut about it, unlike some people who have to photograph and publish every good spot they find."

"Feel the air," Tammili added. "It tastes like spring. I'm glad we're here, Dad. This is a thousand times better than some old ski resort."

"Was a ski resort a possibility?" Freddy was trying not to grin.

"No. But some people went to them. Half the school went to Sun Valley. I don't care. I'd lots rather be in the wilderness with you."

"I'm glad you approve. Look up there. Not a cloud in the sky. What a lucky day."

"There's a cloud formation in the west," Tammili said. "I've been watching it for half an hour." They turned in the direction of the sea. Sure enough. On the very tip of the horizon a gray cloud was approaching. Nothing to worry about. Not a black system. Just a very small patch of gray on the horizon.

"Gather up the packs," Freddy said. "Let's start climbing. The sooner we make camp the sooner we don't have to worry about the weather. Those trees up there have withstood a thousand years of weather. We'd be safe there in a hurricane."

"What about a map check?" Tammili asked. She was pulling the straps of her pack onto her strong, skinny shoulders. Lydia was beside her, looking equally determined. This will never come again, Freddy thought. This time when they are children and women in the same skin. This innocence and power. My angels.

"Daddy. Come to." Lydia touched his sleeve, and he turned and kissed her on the head.

"Of course. Get a drink of water out of the thermos we're leaving. Then we'll climb up to that lookout and take our bearings." He handed paper cups to them and they poured water from a thermos and drank it, then folded the cups and left them in the Jeep. They hiked up half a mile to a lookout from where they could see the terrain between them and the place they were going. "Take a reading," Freddy said. "We'll write the readings down, but I want you to memorize them. Paper can get lost or wet. As long as the compass is on your wrist and you memorize the readings, you can find your way back to any base point."

"The best thing is to look where you're going," Tammili said. "Anyone can look at the sun and figure out where the ocean is."

"We won't always be hiking in Northern California," Freddy countered. "We'll do the Grand Canyon soon and then Nepal."

"Momma's friend Brittany got pregnant in Nepal," Lydia said. "She got pregnant with a monk. We saw pictures of the baby."

"Well, that isn't going to happen to either of you. I'm not going to let either of you get pregnant until you have an M.D. or a Ph.D., for starters. I may not let you get pregnant until you're forty. I was thinking thirty-five, now I'm thinking forty."

"We know. You're going to buy a freezer so we can freeze our eggs and save them until we can hire someone to have the babies." They started giggling again. When Lydia and Tammili decided something was funny, they thought it was funnier and funnier the more they laughed.

"Maps and compasses," Freddy said. "Find out where we are. Then find out where we're going, then chart a course."

"Where are we going?"

"Up there. To that cliff face. Around the corner is the waterfall that is the source of Red River." He watched as their faces bent toward their indescribably beautiful small wrists. The perfect bones and skin of ten-year-olds, burdened with the huge wrist compasses and watches. I could spend the day worshiping their arms, Freddy thought, or I could teach them something. "This is the Western Cordillera," he added. "Those are Douglas fir, as you know, and most of the others are pines, several varieties. Are the packs too heavy?"

"They're okay. We can stash things on the trail if we have to."

"In twenty minutes, we'll rest for five. All right?"

"I think I hear the waterfall," he said. "Can you hear it?"

"Not if you're talking," Tammili said. "You have to be quiet to get nature to give up its secrets."

"Stop it, Tammili. Stop teasing him."

"Yeah, Tammili. Stop teasing me." They walked in silence then, up almost a thousand feet before they stopped to rest. The path was loose and slippery and the landscape to the east was barren and rough. To the west it was more dramatic. The cloud formation they had noticed earlier was growing into a larger mass.

"A gathering storm," Freddy said. "We'll be glad I put the waterproofing on the tent last night."

"I am glad," Lydia said. "I don't like to get wet when I'm camping."

"Let's go on then," Tammili said. "That might get here sooner than we think it's going to."

They shouldered the packs and began to climb again. Freddy was drawing the terrain in his mind. He had planned on camping at a site that was surrounded by watercourses. It was so steep that even if there was a deluge it would run off. Still, there was a dry riverbed that had to be crossed to get to the site. We could make for the caves, he was thinking. There wouldn't be bears this high but there are always snakes. Well, hell, I should have gotten a weather report but I didn't. That was stupid but we'll be safe.

"He's worrying," Tammili said to her sister.

"I knew he would. He thinks we'll get wet."

"I don't know about all this." Freddy stopped on the path above them and shook his head. "That cloud's worrying me. Maybe we should go back and camp by the Jeep. We could climb all around down there. We can go to Red River another time."

"We're halfway there," Tammili said. "We can't turn back now. We've got the tent. We'll get it up and if it rains, it rains."

"Yeah," Lydia agreed. "We'll ride it out."

In the solar-powered house Nora Jane was watching the sky. She would study for a while, then go outside and watch the weather. Finally, she started the old truck they kept for emergencies and tried to get a station on the radio. A scratchy AM station in Fort Bragg came on but it was only playing country music. She was about to drive the truck to town when she saw dust on the road and Nieman came driving up in his Volvo. "Thank God you came," she said, pulling open the door as soon as he parked. "Freddy took the girls to Red River and now it's going to storm. I could kill him for doing that. Why does he do such stupid things, Nieman? He didn't get a weather report and he just goes driving off to take the girls to see a waterfall."

"We'll go and find them," Nieman said. "Then we'll kill him. How about that?"

The adventurers climbed until they came to a dry riverbed that had to be crossed to gain the top. It was thirty feet wide and abruptly steep at the place where it could be crossed. The bed was a jumble of boulders rounded off by centuries of water. Some were as tall as a man. Others were the size of a man's head or foot or hand. Among the dark rounded boulders were sharper ones of a lighter color. "The sharp-looking pieces are granite," Freddy was saying. "It's rare in the coastal ranges. God knows where it was formed or what journeys it took to get here. Hang on to the large boulders and take your time. We are lucky it's dry. Nieman and I have crossed it when it's running, but I wouldn't let you." He led the girls halfway across the bed, then let them go in front of him. Tammili, then Lydia. They were surefooted and careful and he watched them negotiate the boulders with more than his usual pride. When they were across he started after them. A broken piece of granite caught his eye. He leaned over to pick it up. He stepped on a piece of moss and his foot slipped and kept on slipping. He stepped out wildly with his other foot to stop it. He kept on falling. He twisted his right ankle between two boulders and landed on his left elbow and shattered the humerus at the epicondyle.

"Don't come back here," he called. "Stay where you are. I'll crawl to you."

"Don't listen to him," Tammili said. She dropped her pack on the ground and climbed back over the boulders to where he lay gasping with pain. "Cut the pack strap," he said. "Use the big blade on your knife. Cut it off my shoulder if you can."

"What time did they leave?" Nieman asked. He had called the weather station and gotten a report and put in a preliminary request for information on distress flares in the area.

"They left about six-thirty this morning. Maybe they're on their way back. Freddy can see this front as well as we can. He wouldn't go up the mountain with a storm coming. All they have is that damned little tent. It barely sleeps three."

"They could go to the caves. I'm going to try to call him on the mobile phone. If they're driving, he'll answer." Nieman tried raising Freddy on the mobile phone, then called the telephone company and had them try. "Nothing. They can't get a thing. We are probably crazy to worry. What could go wrong? The girls are better campers than I am. They're not children."

"Tammili only weighs eighty pounds. I want to call the park rangers."

"Then call them. We'll tell them to be on the alert for flares from that area. I know he has flares with him. He loves flares. He always has them. Then we'll get in the Volvo and go look for them. I guess it will go down that road. Maybe we better take the truck."

"We have to make a stretcher and carry him to the trees," Tammili was saying. Freddy was slowly moving his body but he wasn't making much progress. He couldn't stand on his left ankle and he couldn't use his right arm and he could barely breathe for the pain. There were pain pills in the kit but he wouldn't take them. "At least I can think," he kept saying. "I can stand it and I can think. We have to get a shelter set up before the rain hits. I want you to go on over there and wait for me. I can make it. I'll get there." Then he went blank and the girls were standing over him.

"Let's go over to that stand of trees and tie down the supplies and get the tent cover and drag him on it," Tammili said. "If you start crying I'll smack you. What do you think we went to all those camps for? This is the emergency they trained us for. Come on. Help me drag his pack to the trees. Then we'll come back and get him. Nothing's going to happen to him. We can leave him for a minute."

They pulled Freddy's pack to the stand of pine trees where they had left their own. They tied the straps around a sapling and then found the tent cover and went back for him. The sky was very dark now but they did not notice it because they were ten years old and could live in the present.

They laid the tent cover down beside their father and tried to wake him. "You have to wake up and help us," Tammili was saying. "You have to roll over on the cover so we can drag it up the trail. Come on, Dad. It's going to rain. You'll get washed down the river. Come on. Move over here if you can." Freddy came to consciousness. He rolled over onto the tent cover with his left shoulder and tried to find a comfortable position. "Clear the rocks off the path," Lydia said. "Come on, Tammili. Let's clear the path." They began to throw the rocks to the side. Working steadily they managed to clear a way from the riverbed to the trees. Freddy lay on the cover with the pain coming and going like waves on the sea. He rocked in the pain. He let the pain take him. There was no way to escape it. Nora Jane will call for help, he was thinking. I know her. This is where her worrying will come in handy. The truck runs. She will drive it into town and call for help. The rain was beginning. He felt it on his face. Then the pain won and he didn't feel anything.

Lydia and Tammili came back down the path to the unconscious body of their father. They folded the tent cover around his body and began to pull him along the path they had cleared. Every two or three feet they would stop and try to wake him. Then they would scour the next few feet for branches and rocks.

Then they would move him a few feet more. The rain was still falling softly, barely more than a mist. "It's good to get the ground wet," Tammili was saying. "It makes the tent slide."

"You aren't supposed to move wounded people. We could be making him worse."

"We aren't making him worse. His ankle's right there. We aren't moving it and his arm isn't moving. We're just going to that tree. We have to get away from the riverbed, Lydia. That thing could turn into a torrent. Keep pulling. Don't start crying. Nothing's going to happen. We're going to pull him to that tree and stay there until this storm is over."

"I don't believe this happened. How did it happen to us? We shouldn't have come up here."

"We only have a little more to go. Keep pulling. Don't talk so much." Tammili dug in her heels and pulled the weight of her father six more inches up and to the right of the path. Wind came around the side of the mountain and blew rain into their faces. She went to her father and pulled the tent cover more tightly around his body. She looked up at her sister. Their eyes met. Lydia was holding back her tears. "We only have one move," Tammili said. "We take the king to a place of safety. I'm a bishop and you're a rook. We're taking Dad to that tree, Lydia. We can do it if we will."

"I'm okay," Freddy said. "I can crawl up there. I'm okay, Lydia. Help me up, Tammili. This is just a rain. Just a rain that will end."

He half stood with Tammili supporting his side. He managed to hobble a few more feet in the direction of the tree. Lydia dragged the tent cover around in front of him and they laid him back down on it and pulled him the rest of the way.

Nora Jane and Nieman climbed into the Volvo and started across the property toward the old gold-mining road that Freddy and the girls had taken earlier that morning. "It's too low," Nieman said, after five minutes of driving. "It will never make it down that riverbed. Let's go back and get the truck."

"The truck barely runs."

"Well, we'll make it run."

"Let's call the ranger station again. I don't think we can overdo that. My God, Nieman, what's that noise?"

"I think it's a tire. It feels like something's wrong with a tire." He stopped the car and got out and stood looking at the left front tire. It was almost completely flat and getting flatter.

"You have a spare, don't you?" Nora Jane asked. She had gotten out and was standing beside him.

"No. I left it months ago to be repaired and never went back to pick it up. We'll have to walk back and get the truck."

"Call the ranger station first, then we'll get the truck." Nieman didn't argue. He got the ranger station on the phone. "No, we don't know they're lost. We just know they didn't know this weather was coming. You can put it in the computer, can't you? So if anyone sees a warning flare in that area they'll report it? He always has flares. . . . Because I know. Because I've been camping with him a hundred times. . . . Okay. Just so you're on the alert. We're going there now. It's the old gold-mining camp below Red River Falls. The waterfall that is the source of Red River. Surely you have it on a map. . . . All right. Thanks again. Thank you."

"Insanity. Bureaucrazy. Okay, my darling Nora Jane, let's get out and walk."

Halfway to the house it began to rain. By the time they reached the house they were soaking wet. They changed into dry clothes and got into the truck and started driving. This time they didn't talk. They didn't curse. They didn't plan. They just moved as fast as they could go in the direction of the people that they loved.

Tammili and Lydia had managed to drag Freddy almost to the tree. There was a reasonably flat patch of ground there and they surveyed it. "Let's put the tent up over him," Lydia suggested.

"We'd have to move him twice to do that. We haven't got time and besides we shouldn't move him any more than we have to."

"So what are we going to do?"

"We'll cover up with the tent and put all the packs and some rocks around to hold it down."

"Water's going to run in."

"Not if we fix it right. Get it out." Tammili was pulling things out of the packs. "We'll get him covered up, then I'll set off flares."

"You better set them off before it rains any more."

"Then hurry." They dragged the tent over to their father and draped it over his body. Lydia took the cape and wrapped it around his legs and feet. They pulled the tent cover up to make a rain sluice and set rocks against it to hold it in place.

"Finish up," Tammili said. "I'm going over there by the riverbed and set off flares." She had found a pack of them in the bottom of Freddy's pack. She pulled it out and read the directions. "Keep out of the hands of children. This is not a toy. Approved by the Federal Communications Commission and the Federal Bureau of Standards. Remove plastic cap carefully. Point in the direction of clear sky. Da. Pull down lever with a firm grasp. If three pulls does not release flare, discard and try another flare. Okay, here goes." She walked over to the cleared place. She pulled the lever down and a huge point of light rose to the sky and spread out and held.

"Do some more," Lydia called to her. Tammili set off four more flares. Then waited. Then set off two more. Rain was beginning to fall in earnest now. She went back to the pack and put the leftover flares where she had found them. Then she buckled up the pack and put the smaller packs on top of it. Then she dragged the synchilla blanket underneath the tent and she and Lydia lay down on each side of their father. The rain was falling harder. They arranged the synchilla blanket over Freddy's body and then covered that with the cape. They found each other's hands. The fingers of Lydia's right hand fit into the fingers of Tammili's left hand as they had always done.

A volunteer fire lookout worker was in a fire tower ten miles from were they lay covered with the cape and tent. He was a twenty-year-old student who had always been good at everything he did. He prided himself on being good at things. Every other Thursday when he spent his three hours in the tower he was on the lookout every second. He didn't go down and fill his coffee cup. He didn't read books. He kept his eyes on the sky and the land. That was what he had volunteered to do and that is what he did. Earlier, before he began his stint, he had pulled up all the local data on a computer and read it carefully. He had especially noted the memo about Red River because his mother was a geologist and had taken him there as a child. He saw the first flare out of the corner of his eye just as it was dying. He saw the second and the third and fourth flares, but lost the last two in the approaching storm. "I will be damned," he decreed. "I finally saw something. It finally paid off to stay alert." He called the ranger station and reported what he had seen.

Nora Jane and Nieman were driving the four miles of rocky trail between blacktop and blacktop. They were driving in a blinding rain. Nieman was at the wheel. Nora Jane was pushing back into the seat imagining her life without her husband and her daughters. I don't know why we built that crazy house to begin with, Nieman was thinking. I hate it there. Grass doesn't grow. You can't take a hot shower half the time. It's a dangerous place. We should have been down in the inner city building houses for people to live in. Not some goddamn, lonely, scary, dangerous trap on a barren hillside. He shouldn't have taken them up there, much less to Red River. As though they are expendable. As though we could ever breathe again if anything happened to them. But what could happen? Nothing will happen. They'll get wet, then we'll get them dry. He steered the old red truck down onto the blacktop and pushed the pedal to the floor. "I'm gunning it," he said to Nora Jane. "Hold on."

"Don't worry, Daddy," Tammili was crooning. "Momma will send someone to get us. Remember when Lydia broke her arm and it got all right. Her hand was hanging off her wrist like nothing and it grew back fine."

"It sure did," Lydia said. "It grew right back."

"Get behind the rocks," Freddy said. "Don't stay here. I'm okay. I'm doing fine." A sheet of lightning blazed a mile away. It seemed to be beside them. "It's okay," Freddy said. "Cuddle up. Rain always stops. It always stops. It always does."

"Sometimes it rains for two days," Lydia put in. She snuggled down into a ball beside her father. She patted her father's chest. She patted his ribs. She patted his heart. Another burst of lightning flashed even closer. Then the rain began to fall twice as hard as it had before. The earth seemed to sink beneath the force of the rain, but they were warm beneath the cape and the tent and they were together.

"These are Franciscan rocks," Tammili said. "The whole Coast Range is made up of the softest, weirdest rocks they know. Geologists don't know what they are. They used to be the ocean floor. Where we are, right now, as high as it seems, used to be stuff on the floor of the ocean."

"That's right," Lydia added. "Before that it was the molten center of the earth."

"The continents ride on the seas like patches of weeds in a marsh," Tammili went on. "Fortunately for us it all moves so slowly that we'll be dead before it changes enough to matter. Unless the big earthquake puts it all back in the sea."

"Who told you that?" Freddy tried to rise up on his good

arm. The pain in the other one had subsided for a moment. He was beginning to be able to move his foot. "When the storm subsides we'll put up the rest of the flares. They'll be looking for us. Somebody's looking for us now."

"We could drive the car," Lydia whispered. A third network of lightning had covered the mountain with clear blue light. Far away the thunder rumbled, but the lightning seemed to be only feet away. "One of us could stay with you and the other one could get in the Jeep and go for help."

"They'll find us," Freddy said. "Your mother will be right on top of this. If we don't come back, she'll send for help." The rain was harder now, beating on the flattened tent. Still, they seemed to be warm and dry. "This cape wicks faster than synchilla," Freddy added. "Just like Nieman to find this and leave it lying around." The pain returned full force then and Freddy felt himself going down. Don't think, he told himself. Turn it off. Don't let it in.

"Hold my hand," Lydia said and reached for her sister. "Tell more about the coast and the ocean. Tell the stuff Nieman tells us."

"It was a deep trench, the whole coast, the whole state of California. And the ocean and the hot middle of the earth keep churning and pushing and hot stuff comes up from the middle, like melted fire, only more like hot, hot honey, and it's very beautiful and red and gold and finally it turns into rocks and mud and gets pushed up to make mountains. Then the trench got filled with stuff and it rose up like islands and made California. Then the Great Plains got in the middle of the Coast Range and the Sierra Nevada and the Cascades. They are real thick mountains and all crystalized together with granite. But not the Coast Range. The Coast Range is made of strange rocks and there is jade left here by serpentine. And maganese and mercury and bluechist and gold and everything you could want."

"Serpentinite," Freddy said. "Manganese."

＊　　　＊　　　＊

Nieman was saying, "You stay in the truck and wait for the rangers. Work on the phone in Freddy's Jeep. You might get it working. I'm going up."

They were standing at the base of the path. It was still pouring rain. Nieman was wearing a foul-weather parka and was laden with signal devices, everything they had found in the house and cars.

"Go on then. Start climbing. I'll do what I can."

"Do whatever you decide to do." He looked at her then, this beautiful, whimsical creature whom his best friend adored, and he understood the adoration as never before. Her whole world was in danger and she was breathing normally and was not whining. Nieman gave her a kiss on the cheek and turned and began to climb. The rain was coming down so fast it was difficult to see, but he knew the path and he was careful. Maybe we should have gone for help instead of coming here. Maybe we should have done a dozen things. The rangers know. Surely to God they are on their way.

The ranger helicopter had turned back from the lightning and now a truck carrying a medic was headed in their direction but the road had been washed out in two places and they had had to ford it. "Plot the coordinates of the flares again," the driver said. "Are you sure twenty-four is the nearest road?"

"There's an old creek bed we might navigate, but not in this weather. An old mining road leads to within a mile. I'd rather take that. Here, you look at the map."

"Jesus, what a storm. A frog strangler, that's what we call them where I come from."

"Two little girls and their father. I'd like to kill some people. What the hell does a man want to go off for with kids this far from nowhere? It kills me. I used to teach wilderness safety at the hospital. What a waste of breath."

"Land of the free. Home of the foolhardy. Okay, I think I can make it across that water. Let's give it a try." He drove the vehicle across a creek and made it to the other side. As soon as they were across, the medic put on his seat belt and pulled it down tight across his waist and chest.

"Four hundred and three," Nieman was counting. "Four hundred and four. Four hundred and five."

Nora Jane sat in the passenger seat of the Jeep and worked on the phone. Once or twice she was able to hear static and she kept on trying. She took the batteries out and wiped them on her shirt and put them back in. She moved every movable part. She prayed to her old Roman Catholic God. She prayed to Mary. She made promises.

The storm was moving very slowly across the chaos of disordered rocks that is the Coast Range of Northern California. The birds pulled their wings over their heads. The panthers dreamed in their lairs. The scraggly vegetation drank the water as fast as it fell. When the sun came back out it would use the water to grow ten times as fast as vegetation in wetter climates. Tammili and Lydia held hands. Freddy slept. An infinitesimal part of the energy we call time became what we call history.

"Six thousand and one," Nieman counted. He wanted to stop and wipe his glasses but he could not bring himself to waste a second. Some terrible intuition led him on. Some danger or unease that had bothered him ever since the night before. He had come to where he was needed. It was not the first time that had happened to him. That's why I hated those movies, he told himself. When no one believed what they knew. When no one learned anything. The beginning of *Karate Kid* was okay. The beginning of it was grand.

He had come to a creek bed that was now a torrent of rushing water. I know this, he remembered. But how the hell will I cross it now? He stood up straight. He pushed the hood back from his parka and reached for his glasses to wipe them. A huge bolt of lightning shook the sky. It illuminated everything in sight. By its light Nieman saw the pile of tent and figures on the ground on the other side of the water. "Freddy," he screamed at the top of his lungs. "It's me. It's Nieman. Freddy, is that you?"

The rest was drowned by thunder. Then Nieman saw a small figure rise up from the pile. She came out from under the tent and began waving her hands in the air.

"I'll get there," he yelled. "Stay where you are." The rain was slacking somewhat. Nieman found a flat place a few yards down the creek and began to make his way across the rocks. Lydia met him on the other side. "Dad's broken his arm and foot," she told him. "We need to get him to a doctor."

The medic spotted the Jeep and the truck. "There they are," he yelled at the driver. "There're the fools. Let's go get them."

An hour later Freddy was on a stretcher being brought down the mountain by four men. The clearing was filled with vehicles. The brown cape was thrown into the back of an EMS van. It would end up at the city laundry. Then on the bed of a seven-year-old Mexican girl who had been taken from her mother. But that is another story.

Ten days later a party gathered at Chez Panisse to eat an early dinner and discuss the events of the past week. There were nine people gathered at Freddy Harwood's favorite table by the window in the back room. The young man who had seen the flares, the medic, the driver, Nieman, Freddy, Nora Jane, Tammili, Lydia, and a woman biochemist who was after Nieman to marry him. Her name was Stella Light and this was the first time Nieman had taken her out among his friends. It was the first time he had taken her to Chez Panisse and the first time he had introduced her to Nora Jane and Freddy and the twins. Stella Light was dressed in her best clothes, a five-year-old gray pantsuit and a white cotton blouse. She had almost added a yellow scarf but had taken it off minutes after she put it on.

"We had this magic cape we found under the bed," Lydia was telling her. "The minute we say something's magic, it is magic, that's what Uncle Nieman says. It's probably his cape but he can't remember it. He leaves his stuff everywhere. Did you know that? He's absentminded because he is a genius. Do you go to school with him? Is that how you met him?"

"Well, I teach in the department. Tell me about the cape."

"It kept us warm. Dad thinks it was synchilla. Anyway, it was raining so hard it felt like rocks were falling on us."

"It was lightning like crazy," Tammili added. "There was lightning so near it made halos around the trees."

"Tammili!" Freddy shook his head.

"You don't know. You were incoherent from pain."

"Incoherent?" Stella laughed.

"She always talks like that," Lydia said. "It's Uncle Nieman. He's been working on our vocabularies since we were born."

"I'm having goat cheese pie and salad," Nieman said. "I think he wants to take our orders. Menus up, ladies. Magic cape, my eye. Magic forest rangers and volunteer distress signal watchers." He stood up and raised his glass to the medic and the driver and the young man. "To your honor, gentlemen. We salute thee."

"To all of us," Freddy added, raising his glass with his good hand. "My saviors, my family, my friends."

Nieman caught Stella's eye as they drank. A long sweet look that was not lost on Tammili and Lydia. We could be the bridesmaids, Lydia decided. We never get to be in weddings. None of Mom and Dad's friends ever get married. Pretty soon we'll be too old to be bridesmaids. It will be too late.

"Stop it," Tammili whispered to her sister, pretending to be bending over to pick up a napkin so she wouldn't be scolded for telling secrets at the table. "Stop wanting that woman to marry Uncle Nieman. Uncle Nieman doesn't need a girlfriend. He's got everything he needs. He's got Mom and Dad and you and me." When she sat up she batted her eyes at her godfather. Then, for good measure, she got up and walked around the table and gave him a hug and stood by his side. Oh, my God, Stella was thinking. Well, that's an obstacle that can be overcome. Children are such little beasts nowadays. It makes you want to get your tubes tied.

"Go back to your chair," Nora Jane said to her daughter. "Let Uncle Nieman eat his goat cheese pie."

FORT SMITH

✤

THE SMALL BEAR woke in his nest of oak leaves and rolled over onto his back to attend the sky. The great ball of fire burned down between the leaves, warming his stomach and his snout. He sniffed the air, searching for food. He had not eaten anything of value in two days. Since the day when the large bear ran him off, cuffing him over and over with his paws until finally the small bear gave up crying to his mother for help and loped off into the strange woods. Which became stranger the longer he traveled. The place where he was now was a long wooded hill that ran down to a creek, then to a long white line that smelled gritty and strange, a smell that made the small bear grind his teeth and swallow. He kicked his feet up into the air, he closed his eyes and concentrated on finding food. A smell of something fine and new came to him, distant and alluring, and he rolled over onto his feet and followed it down the hill and across the creek and found the source of it beside the water. A crackly, ugly exterior he had trouble swallowing and then, a lovely salty taste. It was the small bear's first potato chip. An unopened sixty-nine-cent bag of chips a lady on a diet had flung from the window of a GMC Jimmy on her way home from a camping trip. That's it, she had decided. Out of sight, out of mind. A minute on the lips, forever on the hips.

The bear finished the bag and the chips and stood up to look around for more. On the white line huge animals went by at such a speed it seemed there was nothing to fear from them. Their smell was very bad, however, and he climbed back down into the creek to think it over. Mixed with the bad smell were other smells, good things to eat, fine new things to eat. He would wait until dark, then travel along the line to trace the smells. He crouched beside the water. He drank of it. He waited.

Minette had married Dell one May. The next May she had graduated high school. In between she had DuVal. Then she had two abortions. Then she got smart. Now she was a checkout girl in the Wal-Mart and her mother took care of DuVal and Dell was still good to her but he was depressed. He was working at the chicken-plucking plant and he hated the work. He had never intended to marry Minette and have DuVal and be stuck in a job, but here he was and the only relief he got was when he was drunk. He only got drunk on the weekends. He never touched a drop from Monday to Friday afternoon.

"There's a bear loose in town," he told Minette when they met by the garage after work. They had come driving up within a minute of each other. Minette hadn't even had time to take off her apron or go and get DuVal.

"One comes in every spring," Minette told him back. "Don't you remember that black bear we had last spring and they treed him by the bakery. It was on TV. You didn't see it?"

"Of course I saw it. Come here to me. What's that on the front of your dress." Dell moved in on her and she almost gave in and let him make her laugh. Then at the last minute she fought it off. "I got to go get DuVal. Momma said if I was late one

more time she'd stop taking him. She's been down in the back.
He's driving her crazy."

"He's a crazy little boy. Got a crazy momma." Dell pressed
her against the hood of the Chevrolet. He nuzzled her with his
chin.

"You need a shave, Dell. Go take a shower and get the chicken
feathers off of you. I'll be right back. I'll fry you a chicken if
you'll get it out of the freezer while I'm gone." She pushed him
away and walked out past the car to the Jeep and got into it and
drove off to get DuVal.

The small bear was getting very unhappy. There was food everywhere but he couldn't find it. When he found it the bark wouldn't
come off. He had broken a claw trying to break open one of the
shiny containers with the food inside that sat beside the clear-
ings. He had found some food but no more of the fine, salty
things he had found beside the creek. Deep in his brain a signal
kept going off calling for more of that ambrosia. He loped along
behind the line of trees he had found that morning. It seemed a
very long time since he had been playing with his mother and
his brothers. It seemed as if he were on a search that might never
end. Go on, his brain told him. You can find it if you look.

DuVal was packed and ready and standing on the porch. He had
his things in his little backpack and he was holding a package of
Lay's potato chips his grandmother had bought on sale at the
IGA. They had eaten part of them in the swing. The rest were
still in the sack, secured by a long green and red clip his grandmother had attached to it. "Don't eat any more of those chips
until after dinner," she had said. "I'm lying on this sofa resting
my neck. You wait on the porch if you like, but don't go down
them steps."

Minette drove up waving and DuVal ran down the steps and
got in. He was very coordinated for a three-year-old. One good

thing about Dell, Minette was always saying. He takes DuVal off to play ball. "Got you some chips," she said, leaning over to give him a hug. She fastened his seat belt. "Sit down then. Let's go home and cook some dinner for your daddy. Momma," she called out. "We're going."

She waited a minute, until her mother came to the door and waved. "She's all right," Minette said to DuVal. "She always thinks there's something wrong with her. It's just her way."

Minette did a U-turn on the street in front of her mother's house and drove fifty miles an hour down the side road and over to the housing development where their blue house stood on its acre and a half of ground. Dell had inherited it from his aunt. Someday that house and land would be worth some money, they were always saying to each other. If we just keep the taxes paid and hold on and wait, this house will put us on easy street. It was true. Fort Smith was growing so fast no one could keep up with it. Every year the outskirts of town grew nearer to the development, which had been way out in the country when Dell's aunt had spent her salary as a nurse to buy the blue house. Some people in the family said she never married because she had seen too much death. Others said it was because she was ugly. Dell's mother said she didn't like men. Anyway, out of all her nieces and nephews she had picked Dell to get to have the house. Of course he was the only one who was a father when the aunt died. Maybe it had been because of DuVal. Now they had the house and except for having to keep all that land cut in the summer it was a nice little nest. The taxes on it were three hundred dollars a year but they could pay it. DuVal loved the big yard with its trees. Practically the only thing he talked about when he learned to talk was about trees and birds and squirrels.

While Minette was frying chicken, DuVal walked out the back door and began to play around in the cleared place where they kept his toy trucks and his wagon and the tricycle he never rode because he was too small to ride it but Dell had bought it anyway one night when he was about half drunk. He couldn't wait to have a child who could ride a bike and he had gone on and bought this tricycle that only a four- or five-year-old could even reach the pedals.

The small bear lay in the curve of the cherry tree. There were small bitter berries on the tree and he had eaten several pawfuls of them, then chased the taste away with a pawful of grass. He lay back against the smooth bark. There were other fruit trees in the area and something about the place reminded him of better times. His stomach was small and flat again. Tonight he must try again to batter the bark of the shiny containers. Now he would rest in the heat of the late afternoon. Time had no meaning for the small bear. There was only heat and cold and smell, only pain where the big bear had scratched him on the shoulder and the smooth curve of the tree limb and the hot white ball in the sky. He lay back and closed his eyes, and slowly at first, and then more surely, he barely sensed and then smelled the potato chips. He sat up and reveled in it.

DuVal was taking the potato chips out of his pocket and putting them along the edge of the road he had built for his tractors. He lined them up. Every piece that was left in his pocket.

"Dell, bring the baby on in here and get him cleaned up," Minette called out. "Go on. I read in the paper that fathers never spend more than thirty minutes a day with their children. That's why so many of them go bad."

Dell got up from the television set and walked out the back door and scooped up DuVal and rode him on his back. "Your momma is frying a chicken, son. Proving once again that wonders never cease."

The bear sat for a long time smelling the fine, rare smell. It was mixed with other smells now, each one finer and rarer than the last. He shook his head and stood up on his hind paws and scratched at the tree. Then he began to move in the direction of the feast. The last rays of the sun moved down between the leaves. He squinted his eyes against the light and followed the smell.

A little brackish creek ran behind Minette and Dell Tucker's place. Dell had built a stile over the backyard fence so DuVal could climb it and think he was going somewhere. That had proved to be a mistake as Minette couldn't turn her back on DuVal without him starting climbing. In the end they had to put a little gate on the top and put a lock on the gate. "It makes the yard look like a prison," Minette said, when all the work and the additions were done. "I don't know why we started this in the first place."

"Because he needs to think he's going somewhere," Dell said. "When I was little we went anywhere we wanted to. We weren't all walled in all the time like he is. I was dreaming the other night about him trying to get out of the yard. That's why I built it."

"You are the craziest man I could have married," Minette said. "That's why I married you."

"Oh, yeah," Dell answered. "We'll see about that. I'll show you crazy." And he tackled her and laid her down on the sofa and started pretending to tickle her. "If I get knocked up I'm getting an abortion," she told him. "You just be prepared for that."

Now the small bear moved along the side of the brackish creek. The lovely smell was getting closer. He was lost in it. It smelled of ten good things all mixed together. He warmed in the smell. He moved happily along the ground, bringing his stomach with him.

On the back screened-in porch with the patched and ratty screens and the old painted table with its wobbly legs and the green chairs with the tall backs, Minette and Dell and DuVal feasted on the fried chicken. There was a platter of it on the table. Plus fresh boiled corn and butter and mashed potatoes and the blue and white dish of green peas and carrots. There was also a round loaf of Hawaiian bread, which was Dell's favorite and Minette's downfall. Tonight neither of them was paying much attention to the bread. The chicken was hot and crunchy and had been prepared by a combination recipe of the way both their mothers had fried chicken. It was dipped first in egg the way Dell's mother insisted it be done and then shook up in a brown paper bag with flour and salt the way Minette's mother did it. The deep hot fat boiling in the thick pan was agreed upon by everyone they knew who knew a thing about frying chicken. The fat was on the back of the stove where DuVal could never reach it. The table was set. The Tucker family was at dinner.

"I might make him a little baseball diamond," Dell was saying. "Back where we had that garden last year. It won't be long, Minette, he'll be playing T-ball."

"He won't play T-ball for three or four years. You got to quit rushing him into everything. He won't like it when he gets there."

"I wish we could have another one." Dell looked right at her when he said it.

"Another what?"

"Another one. A little boy or a girl. I think all the time what if something happened to him. Where would we be? It's too big a chance. Only having one."

"And how would we live then? On just our salaries? We can't do it, Dell. We wouldn't even be able to pay the taxes or fix the roof. What if I got sick? What would happen then? I don't think Momma would take care of two of them. She complains enough as it is."

"I only said I wished we could. I didn't say to do it." Dell reached for a third piece of chicken. He brandished it before he took a bite. He ate it with lovely manners. He was just a lovely man, Minette thought. But that didn't mean she was having any babies. A breeze stirred from the south. Beyond the fence the clouds were gathering. A front was coming up from Texas. It would be there by midnight. She helped herself to corn and ate it daintily. He wasn't the only one who could have manners.

DuVal was making a dam in his mashed potatoes. He had two sides built up but the melted butter kept dripping out of the other sides. He put his finger in it and sucked it off. "Get down," he said. "Getting down." He squirmed down out of the high chair and moved around the table to the door.

"Let him go," Dell said. "He's had enough. He was only playing with his food."

"Momma gave him potato chips," Minette said. "I told her not to, but she does it anyway."

DuVal had forgotten about the potato chips. Now he went into the kitchen and retrieved the bag where his mother had put it on the counter and carried it out the kitchen door to the backyard. They watched him going down the stairs carrying the bag. "Let him go," Dell said. "He looks so cute. What do you say, honey, is he the cutest child that ever lived?"

"He might be," she answered. They watched him moving out into the yard, the bag of chips dragging along in his hand.

The small bear arrived at the stile at precisely the moment that DuVal moved past the circle of toy trucks. The smell was now so overpowering that the bear ran up the steps of the stile and beat on the gate with his paws. When it wouldn't budge, he climbed around it and fell down the steps into the yard. DuVal froze. He had never seen a bear. He didn't know a bear from a hole in the ground but something in him knew to scream. The first scream was low-pitched. The second was bloodcurdling. The third was so terrible it stopped the bear in its tracks. By then Minette was out the door. "Oh, God," she screamed. "It's the bear. Get the gun." She ran toward her child. She ran twenty feet in a second. She grabbed him up and started toward the house. Dell was behind her with a 12-gauge shotgun in one hand and a pistol in the other. Minette reached the circle of toy trucks. Dell pulled her behind him. He drew a bead on the bear, which had moved toward them across half the yard.

"Don't shoot it," DuVal screamed. Minette had made it to the porch with him now.

"He hates that noise," Minette yelled. "Let me get him inside. Then shoot up in the air. It said on TV to shoot up in the air."

Dell wavered. The bear had stopped moving. Then, as they watched, he picked up the bag of potato chips and began to devour it. He bit into it, plastic bag and all, and chomped it down in five bites. Then he glanced their way, shook his head, bent over, and began to lick up all the crumbs.

"Throw him some chicken," Minette suggested. "Throw him the corn."

"Call the police, Minette," Dell answered. "Get the police on the phone." He moved back into the porch. He put down the pistol and picked up the plate of chicken and moved it to the end of the table near the door. He took a bite of a wing, then sailed it out over the bear's head toward the stile. Behind him Minette got the Fort Smith police on the phone.

Later, after the police had shot the bear with tranquilizer and the photographers had been there and the television cameras, and Minette's mother had shown up at just the wrong time, Minette and Dell wrestled DuVal to bed by promising to tape the photos of him on the ten o'clock news and after they did that they got into their four-poster bed and made love two and a half times before they finally fell asleep. It almost tied the record they had the time they went camping by Lee Creek. "Now everyone will know where we live and come and rob us blind," Minette said, cuddling down into her almost sleeping husband's arms. She was pretending to be helpless and dumb. "I'm going to be afraid to be alone a minute after this."

"No, you won't," Dell muttered, trying not to fall right asleep after the article she had made him read in *New Woman* magazine about women hating you to go to sleep after you made love to them. "You never are afraid of anything."

"Yes, I am," she said, but he was all the way asleep by then. She kept on saying the rest of what she had to say just the same. "I'm afraid of dying and I'm afraid I'll lose my job and I'm afraid of getting bit by spiders. I'm afraid something might happen to DuVal and I'm afraid you might start liking someone at the plant." Since he was definitely asleep and the moon was bright outside the open window and they had had such a narrow escape, she decided to let it all hang out. "I'm afraid of getting pregnant and I'm afraid if we wait too long I might never have a daughter. I'm afraid Fort Smith is getting too big or if it gets smaller we might both be out of work. I'm afraid we looked stupid on that television story and everyone will tease me to death tomorrow. I was afraid you'd shoot that little bear. As soon as you aimed at him I was about to cry thinking he'd be all blown up and bloody like people in Bosnia or somewhere. Well, to hell with it. We're the ones who caught him. If it wasn't for us he'd still be on the loose. What would you have done if you were me, that's what I'll say to them. We had DuVal to protect, for goodness' sake. To hell with it. What a day." Minette moved her body back over onto her own side of the bed and went dead to sleep. The moon moved across the sky. So did the earth we're riding on. Not that anyone notices it anymore what with all that stuff there is to keep up with on television.

A PROLOGUE

SIX MONTHS before he died he told his daughter that he had not wanted to remarry her mother. He was brushing his teeth while he told her. She liked to watch him brush his teeth. He was so efficient, so dedicated, so determined.

"I did it to save the children," he said. "I came back to save the children."

"You gave up the mistress to save what children?" the daughter asked.

"To save Juliet. She was running around with the wrong crowd. She was going out with a black."

"So you tore up the life Mother was making for herself and made her marry you again to save Juliet?"

"Had to do it. Had to stop that." He was flossing now. He had been the first person she knew who used dental floss. It had been given to him by the pathological dentist who had ruined all their teeth in the sixties.

The old man was eighty-eight when this conversation took place. The year after he lost all the money. The year before they took his car away and then his gun. He had had at one time almost twenty million dollars but he had lost it all. He had lost it by believing in his sons. Or else, he had lost it by being afraid to invest in the markets, by being afraid of the contemporary world, by being a racist and a misogynist and becoming an old man. His father had died a pauper and now he was about to die one too. Except for Social Security, a government program he would have ended if he could have. He had given at least one of his millions of dollars to the right wing of the Republican party. Now he was being taken care of by Social Security and Medicare. He saw the irony. What he could not see was how the weak destroy the strong within a family as well as in larger worlds. This happens in every family. It is as inevitable as the sun and rain. All the daughter wanted to know was how to keep it from happening to her.

A TREE
TO BE DESIRED

THE OLD MAN lay dying. His great-grandsons sat on either side of the bed. They had been there all night, barely moving or speaking. The only other person in the room was the black male nurse sent by Hospice. His name was Adam Harris. He was twenty-five years old. This was the fourteenth night he had sat by the bed feeding droppers of water to the dying man and wiping his mouth and tongue with the lemon-flavored glycerin swabs. He had sat by the bed on the two nights when the old man's sons had been there. He had sat by the bed when the youngest grandson had been there. He had sat by the bed when the old man's physician brother had come from Memphis and changed the medication. They had changed from Haldol to morphine. Now it would not be long. Now the long nights would soon be over.

The great-grandsons were the quietest men who had sat in the room all night. They were taller and sweeter and quieter than the redheaded sons and grandsons. Their sweet brown eyes met Adam's eyes with a deeper, stranger sadness than the sons and grandsons.

The old man had never screamed at them or hit them with his belt. They were not conflicted in their sadness. All the old man had ever done to them was laugh at them and give them candy and tell them about baseball games. He had never made them cut off their hair or work all day at meaningless chores or laughed at them for playing musical instruments. They did not live in Mobile where the old man lay dying. They lived forty miles away in Pascagoula, Mississippi, and worked in their father's dry cleaning establishment and played in a band that had gone to Jazz Fest in New Orleans the year before.

The great-grandsons were the children of the old man's oldest granddaughter. Once she had been the prettiest girl in Mobile. She was still pretty. Tall and agile and full of the sort of restless energy that the sons and grandsons had. She had been in the house every one of the fourteen nights Adam had sat in the room feeding drops of water to the old man and bathing his lips and the inside of his mouth with the glycerin swabs. The old man was starving to death and dying of dehydration. He could not swallow and he refused to be taken to the hospital and put on a feeding tube. On the night that his physician brother had sat by the bed many people had wept many times. The brother had wept continually and the youngest grandson had wept and Adam had wept. The daughter had been there that night. She had kept thinking they should send the old man to the hospital whether he wanted to go or not. "It is too late," the brother said. "It would do no good now."

That was the night they all gave up. They were crying because they knew they had to give up.

The old man did not give up. When it was too late he called the oldest granddaughter into the room and rasped out five words. Take me to the hospital, he told her, but it was too late to go now. That was the night they changed the medication from Haldol to morphine.

*   *   *

A TREE TO BE DESIRED

The granddaughter came into the room now. She went to Adam's chair and put her hand on his shoulder. "How is he?" she asked. She was wearing the long pink-and-white chenille bathrobe she had worn every night since she had come to stay in the house. It belonged to the old man's wife, who had almost stopped coming into the room. In the beginning, when the old man was crying out for her all the time, she came into the room many times. Now he had stopped asking for anything but water and she did not come in very often. She was in the kitchen, directing the maids to cook things for all the people who had come to stay in the house.

"I don't know. He seemed better a while ago," Adam answered.

"Come outside and talk to me," the granddaughter said. "Willie and Sam can watch him." Adam stood up. One of the great-grandsons got up from his chair and went to Adam's place and put his hand in the old man's. The old man couldn't talk anymore but he could squeeze their hands to mean yes and no.

The granddaughter's name was Juliet. She and Adam walked out of the room and down a hall to the den and went out onto a patio and lit cigarettes. It was beginning to be light in the sky. The moon was still visible, a clean new moon. Around it were six or seven bright stars. The planet Venus sat in the sky, right above the moon just like the fraternity pin of the old man who lay dying. There was a redwood picnic table on the patio and six or seven wrought-iron chairs. Juliet sat on one of the chairs and blew the smoke from her cigarette in a long thin line. A waft of air carried it toward a backyard swing. The robe had fallen open and her legs stuck out from the bottom of her short white night-gown. She was wearing pink sandals she had found in a closet and her toenails were painted a bright pale pink. She had not washed her hair in three days and it hung down her back and was tied with a faded red ribbon. She had been so beautiful when she was young that she had learned not to bother about her hair or clothes. She had become disenchanted with her beauty. Her husband had a girlfriend and that made her hate her beauty since it had betrayed and failed her. She looked up at Adam and smiled. He was more beautiful than she was because he was not sad. He had been sad when he had broken his ankle and ended his hopes of being a professional basketball player but he was not sad now because he had this job making twenty dollars an hour for staying up all night and he had a new Jeep Cherokee and an apartment of his own and the fourteen nights he had been in the Manning house had been pleasant compared to some of the places he had been sent by the Hospice people.

"What do you think is going to happen?" Juliet asked. "How long do you think it's going to be?"

"He's mighty strong. He's the strongest man I've ever seen as old as he is. How old is he again?"

"He will be eighty-nine in May. Next month, if he lives that long. He won't live that long, will he?"

"He was talking to your sons a while ago."

"Did you change the morphine patch?"

"No. I wanted to wait until the nurse got here at eight. His daughter told me not to give him the morphine unless the nurse was here."

"Don't pay any attention to her. She's going crazy. She can't take it. Neither can Grandmother. She's not doing very well."

Adam looked at the pink toenail polish. He was starting to desire her again. He had been suffering that on and off since the night the two of them had sat by the bed all night alone, or else since the night she had fixed a sandwich for him and brought it to him on a tray. He raised his eyes and met her eyes. She took a long drag on her cigarette and then put it out in a black wrought-iron ashtray made in the shape of a doll's skillet.

Adam walked across the patio to the basketball goal and picked up an old half-inflated ball and tossed it through the hoop. Juliet stood up and walked to where he was and picked up the fallen ball and shot a perfect hook shot. The robe was completely open now. She stopped and tied it tightly around her waist. Adam retrieved the ball and passed it to her. She shot again. This time the ball went through the hoop without even touching the rim. Swoosh. "You're good," Adam said. "Where'd you learn a shot like that?"

"Basketball camp," she said. "I ran the cafeteria so the boys could go to camp. At Auburn in the summers. We used to play in the afternoons. The staff would play. Did you ever play?"

"I played for Delta State, up in Cleveland, Mississippi. Then I broke my ankle. I still can't run." He stood back about fifteen feet from the goal and shot the ball, but it bounced off the rim. "Damn. It's not inflated."

"I know. Mine were lucky shots." She picked up the ball and held it against her waist. It was growing light behind them. There was a fence across the back of the property and behind the fence a stand of pine and oak trees. Light was spreading through the trees and illuminating the soft cirrus clouds that hung in the late April sky. It was still cool in the mornings in Mobile, especially when the wind was blowing from the east. Juliet shivered. Adam walked to her and took off his windbreaker and put it around her shoulders. They stood there then, not talking, watching the moon fade into the growing blueness of the sky.

Juliet's grandmother came out onto the patio. She was still wearing her gown and robe. "Come in and get some breakfast," she said. "Allison and your uncle Freddy are on their way. I need someone to go and get them at the airport."

"I'll go," Adam said. "As soon as the nurse gets here."

"I'll go with him," Juliet said. "I need to get out of the house for a while."

"Good," the grandmother said. "Then eat breakfast and get dressed. The plane gets in at nine-fifteen. How is he, Adam?"

"He had a good night. He woke up about three and talked to the boys. The morphine's better than the Haldol. He's a lot more comfortable now."

"Thank you for taking such good care of him." She moved to him and put her hand on his arm. Juliet was still holding the basketball. She put it on one of the wrought-iron chairs. She went to her grandmother and put her arm around her waist.

"The moon is very nice," Juliet said. "It has Venus in its arms. Remember when you used to show us that and tell us it was Granddaddy's fraternity pin?"

They went into the kitchen where the grandmother had bacon cooking and toast warm on a tray. Adam took a seat at the table. Juliet stood by the stove. She picked up a piece of toast and began to nibble the hard edges of it. Her grandmother made delicious toast. It was made of white bread with four pats of butter on each slice. There were little pools of butter with the hard edges all around it. She had eaten this toast all her life when she visited them. It reminded her of the pond on her grandfather's farm. Hard on the edge and soft in the center. After her grandfather got sick her grandmother had started making the toast with margarine instead of butter but this morning she had gone back to butter. "Sit down," her grandmother said. "Let me feed you."

"No, this is all I want." Her grandmother shook her head and served Adam a plate of scrambled eggs and bacon. Juliet stood by the stove watching him eat. He had elegant manners. He was an elegant man, elegant and still.

"At least have some orange juice," her grandmother said. "You aren't eating enough."

"This is good. This is fine. I'm going to get dressed."

Her grandmother poured a glass of orange juice and gave it to Adam. Then she poured another one and handed it to Juliet. Juliet drank part of it. "Thank you," she said. Then she left the kitchen and went into the spare bedroom and took off the robe and gown and put on a pair of slacks and a blouse. She went into her grandmother's bathroom and washed her face and hands. She put some of her grandmother's moisturizer on her face. She found a lipstick in her purse and put some on her lips. She started to leave the bedroom. Then she went back to the dresser and picked up a bottle of Guerlain's Blue Hour and sprayed it on her hair. She brushed her hair very hard and pulled it back behind her ears. She shook her head at her reflection and turned and left the room and went out to the side yard to wait for Adam. A tree her grandmother had planted the day she was born grew in the side yard. It was a sturdy oak tree, now at least two feet in circumference. She stood looking at it, imagining her grandmother directing the yard man to set it in the hole, imagining the roots searching and seeking for water far down into the ground.

"Are you ready?" Adam had come out and was standing by his car waiting for her.

"Let's go," she said. He held the door open for her and she got in and put on the seat belt. They drove almost all the way to the airport in silence. "Meet me somewhere this afternoon," she said finally. "Somewhere where we can be alone."

"You're married."

"He has a girlfriend and the question isn't marriage. The question is you're black and I'm white. And, yes, I mean it. If you want it too."

He looked away, then back to her. "Go to the Ramada Inn on the highway. Get a room. At four o'clock. I'll be there. I have to go home first and get some sleep."

"At four. I'll be waiting there."

They picked up Juliet's uncle and aunt and drove them to the house. Then Adam left and Juliet went inside and took off her clothes and got into the shower and washed her hair and shaved her legs.

Then it was afternoon and she went to the motel and got a

room and went up to it. Then he called and came up to the room and came inside and closed the door.

It was like silk. It was like water. It was without cruelty or ego. It confirmed everything she had believed all her life. It was a different thing, a completely different thing.

What was this difference? This vast unimaginable difference?

How flighty she seemed to him. How frightened. Like a bird imprisoned in a room, trying to find an open window or a door. "There should be music," he said.

"There is plenty of music," she answered. "I can hear it everywhere."

The old man died that night. Adam was in the room and one of the old man's sons and his oldest grandson. They sat with the body until the Hospice people came and took it away.

On the morning of the old man's funeral Adam woke up feeling lonely. His apartment was too quiet. There was no one there to talk to or eat breakfast with. It was a new apartment complex in a safe neighborhood and everyone had already gone to work. Adam's girlfriend had been there the night before but she had only stayed long enough to start an argument. She had gone there wanting to start an argument. She was sick of Adam. Sick of only seeing him in the afternoons. Sick of spending every night alone. She was twenty years old and ambitious. She had a job at a television studio and she got off work two hours before Adam had to go to work. Sometimes he even worked on the weekends. Sometimes he smelled like death. What he did reminded her of death and she was looking for life. She didn't care if he had a Jeep Cherokee and was the best-looking and most polite boyfriend she had ever had. She had young men waiting in the wings. She didn't have to sit around watching television all night by herself while he waited for someone to die. She went over to Adam's house to pick a fight and she picked one and then she left.

He woke up thinking he was glad she was gone. She was too bossy for him and too moody and unpredictable. Adam had gone to college for three years. He had a good job. He had a new Jeep Cherokee and an apartment with a new bed and a sofa and three good chairs. He had fifteen hundred dollars his father's insurance had sent him when his father died. He had a brother in law school and a mother who didn't bother him too often. He had a future in the health care provider world. He didn't have to sit around and wait for Janisa to decide to get in a good mood or have a dream come true of being a television anchorwoman. He had a life and he was going to live it. One thing about working for Hospice. You learned to appreciate your life.

I really liked that old man, Adam thought, as he eased his legs out of the bed and down onto the floor and walked naked into the bathroom and began to run the water in the shower. He was a strong old man and he held on. She's strong too, even if she is as scared as a bird. He stepped into the shower and felt the soft warm water caress his skin. Like her skin, so soft. She holds on like she is scared to death. There is danger in this. I won't even think about it.

He got out of the shower and thought about the old man's death instead. One of the old man's grandsons was a ship's captain on the Gulf of Mexico. He was the strongest of the men who had sat by the bed. He was as strong and quiet as the old man. The old man was quiet because his throat was paralyzed but the grandson was quiet because he had lived so long on the water and seen so much weather and such strange skies and many whales. The grandson took Adam's side of the bed and held the old man's hand. He did not ask questions and make the old man squeeze his hand to say yes or no. He just held his hand and was quiet and still.

About six in the afternoon the old man's second son came into the room and sat on the other side of the bed. He was the tallest of all the men. He was quiet too. He removed the bandages from the hand the old man had skinned the last time he stood up and tried to walk across the room. The son took the bandages off the hand and turned on the lights and examined the wound. "Goddamn it all to hell," he said. "This is getting infected. Get me some hydrogen peroxide, Jake. In there, in the bathroom." The grandson got up and brought the hydrogen peroxide. The old man's daughter came into the room and stood by the bed and watched. "What are you going to do?" she said.

"Treat this goddamn wound," the son said. He opened the hydrogen peroxide and poured it over the wound. The old man winced and shuddered. The daughter shook her head and moved back two paces. The grandson didn't move. The son opened a jar of aloe vera salve the oldest son had brought in from Texas the day before and began to spread it over the wound. "This will fix you up, Dad," the son said. "Goddammit, they're letting the goddamn thing fester."

Adam looked at the daughter. She returned his look and just kept shaking her head. Adam filled the syringe with water and put a few drops in the old man's mouth. Then he opened one of the glycerin swabs and began to gently swab the old man's lips. The son bandaged the hand with clean bandages. The grandson sat back down and took the old man's good hand. The daughter stood by the door.

"Turn the goddamn light off, Sister," the son said. "It's in his eyes."

She turned off the light. Adam pushed the button on the record player the oldest son had set up by the bed. They had been playing old Eddy Arnold albums and a three-record set of Christian hymns. "I come to the garden alone," Christy Lane started singing. "While the dew is still on the roses. And the voice I hear, falling on my ear, the son of God discloses. . . ."

When the old man could still talk a little and respond he had liked that song the most of anything Adam played for him.

The daughter came back into the room. She lay down on the bed beside her father and started saying something under her breath. It was the only thing she said when she was in the room the last three days. It was some sort of Tibetan chant. She had told Adam what it was but he had not understood what she was talking about.

Juliet had gone back to her house in Pascagoula to get ready for the funeral. She had washed her hair and rolled it up on heated rollers. She had put on makeup. Liquid foundation and powder and rouge and eyebrow pencil and eyelash thickener and blue eye shadow and lipstick liner and peach lipstick. She had put on her best dark blue suit and the pearls her grandmother had given her for her birthday. She put on black silk stockings and her highest black leather heels. She found a pair of black gloves to wear. She screwed small pearl earrings into her ears. Then she took them out and put in some amethyst earrings her husband had bought her once in New Orleans.

He came into the room. He wouldn't look at her. He hadn't looked at her since he started screwing his secretary. He had married Juliet when she was eighteen and he was nineteen. They had been allowed to get married because Juliet was pregnant with their oldest son. His father had been the mayor of Pascagoula. He was embarrassed by what his son had done. He had always been embarrassed by his children. He had died thinking they were failures because none of them had grown up to be governor of the state of Mississippi. Juliet's husband was not a failure. He had made a lot of money running dry cleaning establishments all up and down the Gulf Coast. He was fucking his secretary because he was a workaholic and she was the only person who would listen to him talk about his business. Juliet had lost interest in the business. She made her own money running a catering business. He wanted to look at her. He wanted to get rid of his secretary who wasn't even very pretty and make a fresh start with Juliet but he couldn't figure out where to start. "You ready to go?" he said. "The boys are in the car."

"Just let me turn off the lights," she answered. She didn't look at him. She walked around the room turning off the lights. He went out of the room and down the stairs. He was waiting by the car to open the door for her but she wouldn't let him open it. She moved around him and opened it herself and got in and put on her seat belt. The boys were in the back seat in their suits. She was proud of them. They were going to be pallbearers. There were going to be eight pallbearers. The old man's three sons, his three grandsons, and her two boys. The other great-grandsons were too young to carry a coffin.

Her husband got into the driver's seat. They pulled out of the driveway and began to drive to the old man's funeral.

The old man was being buried in a country cemetery five miles outside of Mobile. He had moved his headstone three times trying to make sure he was buried in an all-white cemetery. Now it sat beneath two live oak trees on a rise of land that had been a farm only four years before. It was a brand-new cemetery. There were scarcely twenty graves on the barren rise. The huge granite slab the old man had mined out of the Kentucky hills sat squarely in the center of a forty-plot area he had purchased for twelve thousand dollars.

To the right of the plot and down half a mile on the main road was the new funeral parlor where the old man had arranged to be pumped full of formaldehyde and laid out for viewing.

Juliet arrived after all the other cousins. Her husband had gotten lost trying to find the cemetery and funeral parlor. He was in a sweet mood, however, and did not seem irritated about having to miss a whole day's work in the middle of the week. He held her arm as they walked into the funeral parlor. He stood by her side as she embraced her cousins and her sisters and her brothers and her aunts and uncles. He was kind and sweet to her grandmother. He patted men on the back and embraced women. He was a part of the family. Secretary or no secretary there was not going to be a divorce in this family as long as he could help it. He loved his family. His family meant as much to him as his business. On this day, staring down into the coffin holding his powerful old grandfather-in-law, he thought that his family meant more to him than his business. He was proud of his sons as they took their places beside their great-uncles and cousins and closed the casket and picked it up to carry it to the waiting Cadillac. They were crying as they lifted it. He was proud of them for crying. He took Juliet's arm and led her to the car. This time she let him open the door for her. She let her skirt slide up her legs as she settled herself in the seat and she let him look and keep on looking. She opened her legs slightly instead of crossing them. She let him wonder.

The old man's brothers were there. One was a physician and the other was a general in the air force. The old man's first cousins were there. The one who had been a federal judge. The one who had been a naval commander. The one who was a newspaper editor. The cousin who had gone crazy and tried to kill his mother was dead. So was the one who had been the Speaker of the Mississippi House of Representatives. So was the girl cousin who had been a civil rights activist before there was a word for such a thing. All his first cousins who could walk were there and two who were in wheelchairs.

His second cousin who had given away his land and gone to a seminary when he was forty years old read the sparse, cold, Presbyterian burial service. The only music was a song played on a guitar by one of the old man's granddaughters' husbands.

Juliet stood behind her grandmother's chair. While the song

was being played she looked around and behind herself. There was a sea of suits with some women among them. The old man had been a man's man. The men he had led and organized and lectured and set an example for were gathered on the hill as if in regiments. Juliet had not known so many people would come to the service. She had not known that many men could find their way to the obscure funeral parlor the old man had chosen for his laying out and burial. As she looked she saw Adam move to the side of one group of men. He stood alone on a small rise, wearing a beautiful dark blue suit with a white shirt and a tie. He looked like a movie star in the midst of a field of bankers. He looked right at her and nodded his head but he did not smile.

When the service was over and the people began to leave, Juliet left her family and walked over to Adam and took his arm. They walked off together toward a rise of land where a yellow Caterpillar tractor stood waiting to shovel the pile of waiting dirt upon the old man's grave. A young black man sat on the tractor seat reading a newspaper folded into an inconspicuous size. He had taken off his cap and sat with his face and head bathed in sunlight. He was the only other black person at the funeral.

"I didn't know you'd come," Juliet said, still holding on to Adam's arm. It was very strange to be with him like this, in sunlight, dressed up, after all the nights they had sat beside the bed. After the strange afternoon, which already seemed like a dream, bathed in unreality.

"I loved Mr. Manning," Adam said. "I thought a lot of that old man. I've never been so sad when someone died. Someone I'd taken care of."

"How many have you taken care of?" she asked. She kept on holding on to his arm. She had not expected to see him again.

"Too many," he said. "I don't know how much longer I can keep this up."

"Come over to Pascagoula and work for us," she said. "We have three businesses down there. I could find a lot of things for you to do." She felt in her pocket for a packet of business cards she had for her catering business. She knew it was there because the last time she had worn the suit was when she catered a party where she had to get dressed up. She extracted a card and handed it to him. He moved away from her and opened his billfold and found one of his own cards and handed it to her. They stood like that, holding each other's cards. The boy on the tractor started up the motor. He began to drive very slowly and respectfully toward the open grave. Not many people were left by the grave. The old man's daughter and her sons and her grandchildren were there. The old man's sons were there and some of the grandsons. Juliet's sons had walked toward the car with their father. He stopped on the road and watched his wife and Adam walk to the grave and join the ones who were going to stay until the dirt was shoveled on the grave. He felt a stirring, as of some terrible unease or something he could not understand. He took a deep breath and began to walk back toward the grave.

Juliet and Adam each took a handful of dirt and dropped it carefully on the coffin. They took in deep breaths of the clean country air. They waited for the tractor to finish the job.

"*Oh, mani, padme hum, oh, mani, padme hum,*" the daughter was saying under her breath as the tractor pushed the dirt into the hole. Then she stopped saying it and followed her grandchild over to the huge granite stone. It said MANNING in large letters. On the lip of the slab were chiseled other names. They were the names of the old man's male ancestors in a line going back to 1750 when the first ancestors had left Scotland and come to the United States.

Juliet's husband came to her side and took her arm. "We better go," he said. "Someone's got to be at your uncle's to greet people when they come."

"There are plenty of people there," she answered. "Grand-mother's there. They're coming to see her."

"Your wife was the mainstay," Adam said. "She was a champ. I guess she needs some rest now."

"Adam's coming over to see about applying to my business," Juliet said. "You know I've been needing an overseer for the out-of-town trips."

"Good," her husband said. "I'm sure that will be fine."

The old man had had a saying in the fifties and sixties when the civil rights battles were going on. "Turn the niggers loose and the women will be right behind them," he had said. He would laugh uproariously when he said it. Many people who had heard him say that remembered it when it happened.

II

It was several weeks before Adam drove over to Pascagoula to talk to Juliet about the job. First he was sent by Hospice to watch a man who was dying of skin cancer. It had started with an un-treated patch over the man's ear, which his children had begged him to have treated. They kept saying that. "I told him to go to a doctor about it," the youngest daughter kept saying. "We told him a thousand times not to let that go."

Now it had spread everywhere. The man smelled terrible. It was all Adam could do to stay in the room with him. Everyone in the family hated to stay with him. They also seemed to hate each other.

After the third night Adam went to see his boss and told him he couldn't stay with the man another night. "It smells so bad," he said. "I think I'm going to faint."

"There's no one else to go," the boss said.

"I won't go back," Adam said. "I need some time off. I'm burned out. I can't do it anymore."

"Take a week." The boss had seen this before. There was no

good in arguing with it. "How long do you think it will be before he dies?"

"A long time. He's not near to death."

"Maybe we shouldn't have gone in. I'll reevaluate it."

"I'm sorry."

"Take a week. Call me when you're ready."

That afternoon Adam went to his bank and found a young man
his age and talked to him. He wore his suit and looked the man
in the eye and kept insisting. Finally he got a promise that he
liked. He stood up and shook the man's hand and went home
and called Juliet.

"I want to buy part of a business," he said. "I don't want to
work for anyone."

"Then come on over. We'll talk about it."

She told her husband about it that night. "The guy who nursed
Granddaddy's coming to see about my business," she told him. "I
might let him come in and help me run it. I need some help now
that the boys won't do it. He may want to buy into it. Maybe
I'll sell it to him."

"You don't need to go getting into any business with black
guys."

"The girls who work for me are black. They'd like a black
man for a boss. I might sell it to him if he wants it."

"You don't need to have a business, Juliet. We have plenty of
money. Come back and help me with the stores."

"I want my own money. I don't want to work for you." She
left the room and went out into the yard and lit a cigarette, thinking about having to work with his secretary-whore. Fuck you, she
was thinking. Fuck your business and your money and your dick.

✳   ✳   ✳

She was waiting on the porch of her house when Adam drove up in his Jeep Cherokee. She was sitting on the steps in a long flowered skirt. The azaleas were in full bloom all around the porch and the trees were green with splendor. So he came to her.

They went downtown to the building where she had her kitchen. Three young women prepared the food and a young man made the deliveries. Their main business was delivering lunches to businesses in the area. Also, they catered parties. When there was a party, Juliet went with them to the house and directed things and sometimes worked as a waiter.

"So that's it," she said, when she had shown him the operation. "It's pretty simple really. Let's take some sandwiches and go look at the water. Do you like turkey? That turkey looked good, didn't it?"

"Turkey's fine." He waited at her desk while she packed a lunch in a cardboard box. Then they got back into his car and drove to a deserted pier outside of town and walked out on it and sat down and began to eat the lunch.

"So what would you want me to do?" he asked.

"Help me expand the business. I need a salesman. Someone to go around and tell people what we're doing. Help out at the parties. Dress up and be a waiter. I don't know. Come in. Be my partner. Help me make some money. My boys used to help me but now they're busy with their music."

"If it works out would you sell part of it to me? I want a business of my own. I can borrow ten thousand dollars any time I want it. People want to do business with black men. It gets them in good with the government."

"You believe that?"

"I have to believe in something."

"Let's try it for a few months and see how it works out. I'll pay you by the hour, whatever you were making. I'll be fair to you. I'm always fair. Ask anyone who knows me." She sat back

on her arms. "Can you cook? Do you know anything about catering?"

"I can cook if I need to. I'll do whatever it takes to get a
start."

"Then come to work in the morning. I'll meet you there at
eight. At the kitchen."

"Whenever you want me." He was quiet then, looking out at
the water, waiting for her to speak about the other thing. It was
a long while coming.

"Do you ever think about that afternoon?" she asked.

"Yes."

"I don't really understand it. Why it was so different. Don't
look away. Turn around and look at me. It made me think we
are more different than I imagined. And you aren't even black.
You're half white. So why was it so different? I can't stop thinking about it."

"You don't care what you say, do you?"

"I want to know the truth. That's all right, isn't it? To want
to understand."

"Yes. I suppose it is."

"We have a house on the beach. In Pass Christian. We could
go there sometime."

"Not at his house. We'll go to my place if you like. Or to a
hotel. There are the casinos. Those hotels are nice."

"When?"

"What are you doing now?"

"Nothing. Then let's go." She stood up and he stood up beside her and took her hand. He decided she was right. It was different, the touch, the smell, the immediacy, the refusal of hesitation.
He packed up the lunch things and deposited them in a trash
can. Then he came back to her and took her hand again and they
walked together toward the car. She was sorry no one was around.
She wanted someone to see them. She wanted to be threatened

and afraid. It was spring and she lived in a free country. Land of the free, home of the brave. Besides, her grandfather was dead and her father had gone back to his whores in Texas. There was no one to fear anymore. No one who could make her do a thing she didn't want to do. No one to beat or shame her. No one to threaten to lock her up in a loony bin for loving or being brave.

"Come on." She turned and took Adam's hand and they walked on to the car. The sun was pouring down upon them. It was noon on the Mississippi Gulf Coast and they were going to take the afternoon and make it one to remember.

WITNESS TO THE CRUCIFIXION

❧ ❧

I WAS BRUSHING MY TEETH when she started in again. "I want you to be in Paradise with me," she said, leaning her long blond hair so close to the sink it was hard not to get toothpaste on it. "I was praying for it when I woke up."

"Jocelyn," I screamed, foaming Crest going everywhere. "You are a little eleven-year-old Methodist in a small town in the Ozarks. You are not a television evangelist. Now get the hell out of this bathroom before I kill you." I turned and glowered at her. She is almost as tall as I am now. She is growing extremely fast for eleven. She has reached back into the gene pool and brought up some of Dad's old Scandinavian genes from when his ancestors lived in Wisconsin and fought the snow. Now we are in Fayetteville, Arkansas, fighting madness, low IQs, and Christians. Dad and I are fighting them. Mom and Jocelyn have joined up. They go to church about five times a week. Jocelyn is a Christian Scout and wears a blue vest with a flowered cross embroidered on the pocket and another on the back that she added just to be different.

"Don't you respect me?" she says. "If you curse me that means you don't respect me." This is one of the things they teach the scouts to say.

"No, I don't respect you. I don't even like you and if you don't get out of this bathroom I'm going to have to kill you. I'm giving you three. One, two . . ."

She moved back three paces and stood in the doorway looking sad and sadder. They teach her things to say but they don't teach her what to say *next* if the person she is working on doesn't respond with guilt or fear.

I pushed her out the door and shut it. I finished my teeth and started putting on my makeup. I had a meeting at eight o'clock with the other editors of the literary magazine. We were trying to find a way to pay for a field trip to SEFOR, a breeder reactor in Strickler, Arkansas, which is only twenty miles from the town where we live. A breeder reactor so hot a Geiger counter goes off as soon as you get within two hundred yards of the silo. It was built in the 1960s by a consortium of German and American utility companies to see how much uranium 235 and plutonium 239 they could squeeze into a building and not have it go critical, melt down, or, in other words, turn northwest Arkansas into Chernobyl. We were lucky. One melted down in Detroit, Michigan, first, and after that the consortium cooled SEFOR down with liquid sodium, one of the most inflammable things in the world, talked the government into taking *most* of the uranium and plutonium up to Hanford, Washington, and then gave the reactor, the visitors' center for the reactor, and the six hundred acres of land around it to the University of Arkansas. The university took it. Can you believe that? And my dad teaches at the place.

"You didn't have to curse me," Jocelyn says when I sit down at the kitchen table to eat my scrambled eggs. For whose benefit, do you suppose?

"Aurora," my mother begins, getting her pitiful oh-how-can-this-happen-to-me-so-early-in-the-morning, why-is-my-life-this-way, where-did-I-go-wrong, why-am-I-here-in-this-terrible-family-when-I-meant-to-be-a-sculptor look on her face.

"I didn't curse her. I told her to get her goddamn hair out of the sink while I was brushing my teeth. It's okay with me if she wants to go to school with Crest on her ponytail but I bet old Jerry Hadler will want his friendship bracelet back if he sees it."

"Please don't turn this into an argument."

"Please tell her to stop pushing Jesus at me. She's out of control, Mother. You really ought to think of getting her some help."

"You're the one who killed your baby," Jocelyn said, so I got up and slapped her in the face with my napkin and went into my room and got my backpack and went out the side door and got into my car and drove off down Lighton Trail to school. I used to have a Camaro but it was wrecked when a truck ran into the side of it at the corner of Maple Street and University Avenue. Then my grandmother died and willed me her Toyota so I put the insurance money for the Camaro in my college fund and have been very happy driving Grandmother's baby blue car with leather seat covers. It's like having her around to get into her car every day. She adored me. She knew who I was. Sometimes I think she loved me more than anyone else ever will. The day before she died she got me in her bedroom and told me I was the only one in the family who had the genes. She didn't call it genes. She called it spunk. "I thought your daddy had it but then he married your mother and sank into stone," she said. "I love him. Don't get me wrong, but you're the one who has the strength to make something of yourself, Aurora. Thank God for you. I'm leaving you my car."

I never thought she'd die but she did. At eight o'clock the next morning, while putting on her makeup. She was living out in Cassandra Village where the rich people around here stash their parents while they wait to die. So, anyway, I don't want to talk about that. I want to talk about the goddamn abortion and get it off my mind.

I did not kill a baby. I aborted a six-week-old fetus that would have ruined my life. I'm not cut out to be a mother. Sixteen-year-old girls with high intelligence quotients have no business having babies they don't want. I guess I'm not as rabid about this as I used to be. All the goddamn anti-abortionists have planted doubts in my mind. They keep the balls in the air. They keep it on the table.

I stopped on my way to school to pick up my boyfriend (my new one, not the one who got me pregnant), Ingersol Manning the fourth, six feet five inches tall, completely sane in every way. What does he see in me? You aren't the first one to ask that question. He was walking to school because his Pathfinder is in the shop getting repaired. He worked all summer to make the money to have it fixed. Now it's taking two weeks and he's walking.

He climbed in the passenger side of the Toyota and wiggled around until there was room for his head. "What's going on?" he asked and handed me a strawberry toaster pastry.

"We have to do something about Jocelyn," I began. "She's gone crazy down at the Methodist church. They've captured her, Ingersol. She's completely lost it over Jesus."

"It's the music," he answered. "Bach. She's an artist. The music gets them every time. It happened to me when I was thirteen. It was several months before I stopped having talks with the air."

"You were wonderful when you were thirteen."

"I was fat. I was shaped like a pear."

"I don't remember you fat."

"You wouldn't even play with me that year. One Saturday I came over and you wouldn't let me come in."

"No, I didn't."

"Yes, you did." He reached over and put his hand on top of mine to let me know he forgave me. He was right. There had been a couple of years when he was in the sixth and seventh grades when his jokes were too childish and disgusting for me.

He had this friend, Charles Barton, who was on prednisone and would curse in strings of really gross, disgusting, bodily function words. Ingersol would egg him on to say them. Then he would die of laughter. I couldn't put up with that even if Charles Barton did have cancer. He lived, by the way. He is completely in remission and recovered so I don't have to feel guilty about thinking it was disgusting.

"We could get her to read Malthus or Darwin or Desmond Morris or Nietzsche. We could invite her over to my house and trick her into watching my new *Creation of the Universe* tape by Timothy Ferris." Ingersol was sticking to the subject, a great gift of his.

"Oh, yeah, as if she can read. This is all my mother's fault. She thinks the reason I'm not homecoming queen is because they quit going to church. She joined the church to get Jocelyn a social life. Now Jocelyn's bought the program and from the way she's acting Mother's bought it too. So what am I supposed to do? Move out or fight?"

"First we think," he said. "Then we act. If it's social, I see why she's drawn to it. She's a social creature. She loves the world. All we can do is hope to plant some doubts in her mind."

We weren't getting any help from chance or luck. That very night our old brown Labrador retriever began to gasp for breath and fall down every other step. Dad put him in the back of the Explorer and took him to the vet and left him there. Jocelyn disappeared into her room. When I found her she was on her knees by her cedar chest, crying and praying. "What are you doing?" I asked.

"I'm asking Jesus to save Bill Bailey," she said through her tears. "I'm asking that he let him live until it's spring and he can run after the squirrels and bark at them. It's the wrong time for him to die, when it's cold outside and we couldn't even find a pretty place to bury him." She cried on and I didn't try to say anything to make her feel better. She was having a ball, kneeling on the floor like the virgin of the spring or Joan of Arc or someone. As if it was up to her to save a dog.

About twenty minutes later I went back in her room and let her have it. "If Bill Bailey lives it will be because an army of atheist scientists and biochemists have been going into their labs every day of their lives and believing in science instead of superstition and religion. It will be the techniques and drugs they developed that save his life, if it gets saved."

"And who made the scientists and biochemists?" she answered. "Who gave them the brains to find the drugs? God did. It's God's world and He made it all."

"So you like a God that would kill a poor old dog right at the beginning of winter? That's your hero?"

"You're the devil's advocate, Aurora. You're as evil as a black star." She ran from the room and found Mother and told her some blown-up version of what I'd said and I ended up having to go to Arsaga's coffee shop to get any studying done.

The next day Dad picked up Bill Bailey and brought him home. He had been pumped full of anticoagulants and antibiotics and put on a strict diet of low-fat dog food. He was going to live. Jocelyn gave thanks to God and asked Mother to donate her allowance for two weeks to the United Way.

"It's hopeless," I reported to Ingersol. "She has been programmed past all repair. 'And who made the scientists and biochemists?' she told me. 'God did.'"

"Maybe you should just ignore her," Ingersol suggested. "Just try not to notice her for a few years."

"That's easy for an only child to say. She's in my face with it. She prays over every bite of food. Three-paragraph prayers for cereal at breakfast."

"We must record this time in her life. Why didn't I think of that sooner!" The year before, we had won a home video award

at the Walton Arts Center with a video we made of Jocelyn drawing one of her welcome signs on the street in front of the house.
It was a life-size colored chalk picture of a maple tree in full au-
tumn colors. Underneath the tree it said, WELCOME TO THE
FALL.

Ingersol had interviewed her while I held the camera. He had
gotten her to say some amazing things about why she painted the
street and if it bothered her when the rain washed it off and how
long it took her and things like that. She was so cute that year.
I have to admit she really is a pretty little girl. "Why do you
think you paint the street?" he asked her. It was the end of the
video.

"Because it looks so pretty when it's done and people like it
and it makes them feel better to see a painted tree." She stood
up with the brown chalk stick in her hand and beamed into the
camera, so sure of herself and of her world.

We had won second place but still it was a triumph. We had
been wondering if we'd enter the contest again. Now here it was,
right before our eyes, Jocelyn's conversion to the Methodist church.

"If we get it right," Ingersol said, "this could be the one we
send to the competition at the Museum of Modern Art. They
love stuff from the South. This will fit right in with their pre-
conceived notions about what goes on out here. If she will let us
interview her."

"If she will? She wants a podium more than she wants God.
Besides, she loves you. She'll do anything for you."

"I love her," he answered. "I think she's the cutest little girl
who ever lived. Oh, God, I hope she doesn't lose her faith before
we get it on film."

"Don't worry. Jesus spared Bill Bailey due to her intercessions.
This has months to run."

We waited until an afternoon when Mother was gone. Then
Ingersol brought over the video camera and Jocelyn put on her

Christian Scout uniform and sat on the piano bench and I filmed while Ingersol asked the questions. We got some good stuff but nothing noteworthy. I think she has become suspicious of our motives. Also, she kept making us run it back so she could see what she looked like on the monitor. We wanted her to wear the hat but she wouldn't because she said it squashed down her hair.

We wasted two hours and a lot of film. The next Saturday we tried again in Walker Park with her sitting in one of the swings. Still, nothing good enough for the Walton Arts Center contest, much less the Museum of Modern Art.

Then we had a stroke of luck. A girl in the scouts got the flu and the Monday-night meeting had to be moved to our house. It would have been Jocelyn's turn sooner or later anyway, but the way it turned out there was only a day's notice. All day Sunday she was in fury trying to get our house cleaned up enough for her new friends at the church to see. I called Ingersol as soon as it began and he came over and filmed the whole thing. He filmed her cleaning up the bathrooms with a towel tied around her head. He filmed her vacuuming the living room rug and behind the sofas.

He filmed her pushing poor old Bill Bailey out into the garage and yelling at him not to come in. He filmed her throwing her cats out the back door. He filmed her yelling at me to clean up my room. He filmed Mother coming in the door carrying sacks of groceries. He filmed the blueberry muffins being baked and Dad sweeping the sidewalks and the carport and trimming the hedges. *ALL IN THE NAME OF JESUS*, we called it. We got some great audio bits. We got the best one at five the next afternoon.

"Get out of the way," she yelled at me. "I've got to get this table set. Get your books out of here."

"Can't I do my homework first? It's only five o'clock."

"They're coming at seven. These are rich girls, Aurora. They live in rich houses. I have to get this place fixed up. And get rid of that dog. Every time I put him out he comes back in. I don't want that old sick dog lying around the living room."

"Could I help?" I volunteered, knowing Ingersol was getting every bit of it on tape and she was so stupid she had forgotten he was there.

"Put the bikes away. Go shut the garage so they won't have to look at Mother's old car. Then go get dressed. Put on some nice clothes for a change and some makeup. Please get dressed, Aurora. Don't embarrass me to death." She stood with her hands on her hips. Poor little Christian martyr, little social climber, little artist trying to make the world a more attractive place.

She was about to cry. Ingersol caught it all. Afterward both he and I helped her as much as we could and then we left while she got dressed and only came back and filmed the part of the meeting where they do the prayers and the pledge of allegiance. I have to admit they looked adorable all lined up in their uniforms and sashes with their hats on their heads.

Needless to say this video is going to make our reputations when it's edited and finished. I know I should feel guilty about taking advantage of Jocelyn and using her pitiful little life as material for our work, but I don't really have any choice in the matter. If she does these things in my presence, she had better watch out. I'm a creative person on my way to fulfill my destiny in the world. The Jocelyns of the world are here for me to plunder.

Besides, what do you think the chances are of her being at the Museum of Modern Art next year when they give out the prizes? Zero. My mother is a classicist. She doesn't even like modern art.

Let's say she was there, sitting in the audience watching herself on the big screen. Would she recognize her obsession and begin to doubt it? I doubt it. She'd be thinking about the opening scenes when she was sitting on the piano bench looking like a child movie star and reeling out the party line about love and service to the world. There is one thing I must admit, and Ingersol admits it too. Christianity is a force for good in the world in many ways. It is a civilizing force in the midst of chaos. Not everyone is able to look out over the chasm of space and time and say, that's it, that's how it is, maybe it's even beautiful. Some people have to have the Pope or the Methodist church. They can't all worship Freeman Dyson and Timothy Ferris like Ingersol and I do. We are studying like crazy. We can't wait to get to Princeton or Harvard or Stanford or wherever those guys are teaching. We are going to be happy just walking around a town where great minds live. Meanwhile, we are doing the best we can with Fayetteville. More later.

Aurora Harris

A LADY WITH PEARLS

WE WERE ON OUR WAY to the Vermeer exhibition when I realized I didn't love Duval anymore. We were on the plane, high up above the state of Mississippi, when I knew our love was through. All those years, children, friends, houses, all gone down the drain. He was a boring, depressed man and I was still young at heart and happy to be here, on the planet Earth, in the year of our Lord nineteen hundred and ninety-six.

"What do you have to be unhappy about?" I told him. "Here we are, on our way to see an exhibition that thousands of people worked for years to create. On our way to look into the heart of genius. We have a Carey limousine coming to meet us at the airport. The snow has melted. You are a rich man in reasonably good health. If you don't know what you are about to see, that's okay with me. When you see the paintings you will know. I wish I hadn't brought you with me. You are ruining my dream come true." I sat back in the seat. We were on our way to see twenty-six of the thirty-one extant paintings of one of my favorite painters. I had to appreciate that. Even if I did have this depressed sixty-two-year-old man by my side.

"I think we are going to lose Allen," he said. "He's lost, Callilly. We have to admit he's lost."

"He is not lost. He's living on a sailboat in the Virgin Islands. He has an adventure every day. He toils not. Neither does he spin. How can you feel sorry for him? He doesn't have children. Why should he care?"

"He's thirty-five years old. It's too late now. He'll never have a home. Never marry. It breaks my heart. I'm sorry I can't get excited about your paintings but I can't think of anything but Allen."

Our son, Allen, had showed up the day before. We live in Pass Christian, on the beach, in a house that was Duval's summer home when he was a child. At one time his family owned two newspapers and half the land in the Delta. Now the fortune has dwindled to a small pile of money in the bank. Duval's sister drank up a lot of it. His brother gambled away the rest. Then they died. There is nothing left of the family but us. Duval is a good and sober man. He is a lay reader in the Episcopal church and he talks to stockbrokers on the phone and does good deeds.

"Okay," I said. "Our kids didn't turn out well. It's not our fault. We are still on our way to see the Vermeer exhibition in Washington, D.C., even if Allen is staying in our house and will probably have a party and ruin the carpets while we're gone. I told you not to let him have the house but you did it anyway. Brighten up. Are you hungry? You didn't eat a bite this morning."

"Sally lives in an apartment with a cat. Allen lives on a boat. No one achieves a thing. I can't take it anymore, Callilly. What are we doing on this airplane?"

"Okay. That's it." I got up and went to the back of the airplane and sat alone near the bored stewardesses. I got out a book I was trying to read. *The Best Poems of 1994.* It was bleak. There were elegies, laments, sadness. I think I'll go to Mexico, I decided. I'll go feed the children on the streets.

I put down the book and took a magazine from a rack beside the stewardesses' station. It was *Mademoiselle*, the January issue. *Are You Having Orgasms?* the cover asked. No, I answered. I guess I forgot about that. I turned to the article. I read it. I got up and went back to my seat by Duval and sat down beside him and put my hand on his dick. "What are you doing, Callilly?" he asked. "What's this about?"

On the limousine ride into town I stroked his arm and leg. This is my life and I'm taking charge of it, I decided. As soon as we got to the Four Seasons Hotel, I took off my blouse and brassiere and followed Duval around until I got him into the bed. It was four in the afternoon. We made love like there was no tomorrow. We made love like we hadn't made love in months, maybe years. It was nasty and bad and fabulously fulfilling. Afterward, we fell asleep. We ordered dinner in our room. We drank wine and ate filet mignon and had dessert. Then we watched a movie on television and then we fooled around some more and then we went back to sleep.

"We are already under the spell of Jan Vermeer," I told him that night. "He had ten children and died young. Tomorrow we are going to view the record he left behind. I'm already starting to want to paint. As soon as we get home I'm going to paint."

The skies are very beautiful over the beaches of the Mississippi Sound, which runs into the Gulf of Mexico. Every moment they change. All day long the sky and sea make paintings of such intensity and wonder a mortal human cannot hope to capture a millionth of that beauty. That *should* free us to paint but it has always made me afraid and shy. After this, I won't be afraid, I decided. What do I have to lose, at age sixty-two?

When we woke in the morning Duval called Allen to see if he had destroyed our house yet. "Don't call him," I warned. "Don't spoil this happiness. Get back in bed. Let me make love to you again."

He called him anyway. It was eight in the morning in Pass Christian and Allen was up and dressed and on his way out to try to find a small house to buy. "I want a place to come to so I won't always have to stay with you," he told Duval. "I'll fix it up and rent it when I'm not here."

"How will you pay for it?" Allen asked.

"I have some money. I've been working in the islands. You never listen when I tell you that."

"Don't start thinking Allen is going to be all right," I told him at breakfast. "One sober morning does not a breakthrough make."

"I can hope," he answered. "Without hope, we're really lost."

The paintings were divine, that's all there is to that. *The Geographer* is the image that killed Duval. He couldn't stop looking at it. "These paintings prove how depressed women were in the past," I told him. "Of all the portraits, only the geographer looks really happy, really engaged. Of course the women look satisfied, with their satin dresses and their maids and their pearls. But only the geographer looks like he's in charge of what he's doing. Maybe we underestimate Allen. Maybe we just don't understand what he's doing. He's a geographer, Duval. He has sailed across the Atlantic Ocean. Why do we keep thinking he's a failure?"

"He doesn't have a home. He doesn't have a family. What will become of him when he's my age?"

"He has us. We'll probably never die. And he's buying a house. This very morning he's out looking for a house."

"He'll want me to co-sign the note."

"So what? The house we live in was given to us. Left to us in a will. Where would we be if we hadn't inherited money? Allen's okay. I've decided to believe he's okay."

"He's drinking. He'll never settle down as long as he drinks.

No one in our family can drink. He will die like my sister and my father."

"Duval." I pulled him over to a corner of the gallery and reached under his coat and put my hand on his dick.

"Oh, God," he said. "Not that again."

We returned to the exhibition the next day. It was still terribly crowded but this time we knew what to do to make our way into the center of the circles around the paintings. I was concentrating on looking at the musical instruments and Duval was caught up in the idea of camera obscura. I think we both forgot about Allen until after lunch.

"Let's go home and see him and help him out," Duval said. "I've had enough of Washington, D.C. I want to go home and talk to my son."

"Nothing will come of it. You'll just end up getting mad. He'll stomp out like he always does."

"Maybe not. Maybe I'll sit down with him and get him to show me on the map where he's sailed. Hell, maybe I'll go back to the islands with him for a week. We have to keep on trying, Callilly. Have to keep on believing something good will come of something that we did."

He hung his head. I could see the trip sliding away, all the good I had achieved going back to sadness.

"Okay," I said. "Let's go pack up. Let's go home and see about our child."

And so we did. It was, you might say, as T. S. Eliot did, referring to the journey of the Magi, satisfactory. Allen was getting better. He was growing up. He might live and thrive and flourish. We might get to have some pleasure from him and not end up going to his funeral. I guess that's hope. If it isn't, I guess I can always paint or take a walk.

THE SOUTHWEST EXPERIMENTAL FAST OXIDE REACTOR

THIS IS REALLY about how Kelly got a new boyfriend but it is also about why you should register to vote and vote in every election even if you don't know which one is the worst liar and scoundrel and thief. If you don't vote, somebody else will. If you don't have a say in what happens, you might wake up one day and find an experimental fast breeder reactor going up in your backyard and it's too late to stop it. I live in a town where thirty years ago when the whole town was dirt broke and scratching for a living the politicians who run things came in here and let a bunch of electric power companies and the West German government build a breeder reactor and use it to test whether it would blow up. This is exactly one mile from the Fall Creek cemetery where two of my father's uncles who were shot down in the Second World War are buried beside their parents and grandparents. I don't hate Germans or anybody else. Some of my ancestors are Germans. I'm just saying that in 1964, when the Second World War was hardly over, they let the West German government come into Strickler, Arkansas, and build a reactor to see if the Doppler effect would cool it down if it got too hot.

It contained plutonium oxide. One-thousandth of a gram of plutonium oxide will kill a human being within hours. One-millionth of a gram will cause cancer in a few years. This is not speculation. These are facts. The other thing about plutonium oxide is that it is a very active sort of powder. It moves around in a sprightly dance. It clings to things. Inside our reactor it was mixed with uranium. At one time at least half a ton of plutonium oxide was inside a building right here in Strickler, Arkansas.

The reason I'm so interested in this right now is that I ended up on the roof of the reactor for two and a half hours. And then I went inside. I was on the roof for two hours and ten minutes and inside for fifteen minutes. I keep thinking about that plutonium oxide and wondering if some of it might still have been there. I keep thinking of all the places it could have found to hide, the bark of trees, the tar on the roof, the dust on the walls, the shelves, the glove boxes in the wall.

This happened in December. My boyfriend, Euland Redfern, and my cousin Kelly Nobles and myself were sitting around one Saturday morning freezing to death because it was twenty degrees outside and Daddy still won't turn the heat pump up above sixty-five and Momma said she thought we ought to go out to Evane's Hardware Store and buy some insulation for the doors.

"Come on," Euland said. "We've been sitting around all morning. Let's go get something done." Kelly got up off the couch and giggled and started putting on her hiking boots. I was already on my feet. I don't watch TV. I hate it. I think it's ruined everybody's minds.

"I want to go up to Devil's Den and hike over to the old reactor," Kelly said. "You promised you'd go walking with me if I came over."

"We will," I answered. "As soon as we go to the store and get this stuff for Momma."

*   *   *

We all live in Strickler, which is near West Fork, which is just south of Fayetteville. All our families have lived there for ages. I guess my daddy would have moved to West Fork to be near the schools but then G.E. came in and built the reactor and that made work for all the contractors in town. Daddy paved the roads from town to the site. He made eighty thousand dollars that year, which is what built us the new house and dug the well and put money in the savings account. His brother sold the concrete for the silo. His older brother is the principal of the West Fork High School, which got the new gym paid for by the taxes G.E. paid. Now the university has to pay them.

Nobody in West Fork or Strickler is mad about SEFOR even if it is just sitting there, and Uncle Rafe says the concrete is okay but the metal is probably starting to deteriorate. Plus the liquid sodium they used to cool it will catch fire in water and they ought to get the government to come in and take it apart and get it out of here.

"It would make a really good tornado shelter if they just kept the outside," Momma always says. She hates to waste anything. That's the way she was raised.

So as soon as Euland and Kelly and I got the insulation we went straight to Devil's Den and decided to hike to the reactor and back. We are all babying Kelly because her boyfriend quit liking her. He's going out with a girl in Fayetteville who works at the university. I never did think he was good enough for her to begin with but I see why she liked him. He is a really good-looking man, and sexy. He looks a lot like Alan Jackson, who is Kelly's favorite singer. Sort of a cross between Alan Jackson and Don Johnson. There was no way he was going to stay with Kelly after she gained all that weight last year. I told her to go on a diet but she wouldn't do it. She is so stubborn it's unbelievable, just like all the Nobleses.

Now she has decided to walk six miles a day until some of

the weight comes off. I'm not going to be the one to tell her it won't do any good if she doesn't stop sitting in front of the television set eating snacks.

Devil's Den is our park. People come from all over northwest Arkansas to walk around it and be in nature. It has a waterfall and nature trails and is a good place to go if you're feeling sad or just want to remember you are on the earth. Euland and I have made love all over the place there, in tents, at night and in the daytime, and once in the car outside the visitors' center on a Christmas afternoon. It is never hard to get Euland and me to go to Devil's Den. We have such good memories of it.

"One thing about going to Devil's Den in the winter is you don't have to worry about chiggers," I said. We were in Euland's truck with the package of insulation on the floor.

"Are you sure we can get from the trails to the reactor site?" Euland said. "I think we'd have to cross Lee Creek to do that. I'm not in the mood to spend all day tramping around somebody's pasture."

"You just have to cross Fall Creek, and it's dry as a bone right now. Then we're on university land. They don't care if someone walks over there to look at SEFOR. It isn't even fenced in until you get to the building."

"Why are you so interested in SEFOR all of a sudden?" Euland asked. "It's been there all our lives."

"Because there was an article in the paper so I looked it up one day when I had some time on my hands." Kelly works at the Fayetteville Public Library. She's been there a year, the longest she has ever stayed at a job. "These guys that built it were using it to do experiments to see if it would blow up. They thought they could start it up and cool it down but they weren't sure. For three years, when all of us were babies, they were right over there mixing uranium and plutonium together and seeing if they could cool down the nuclear reaction fast enough to keep it from exploding." She leaned toward us and there was this look on her face I have never seen before, like maybe she had actually forgotten for a minute about her boyfriend and buying makeup at the Wal-Mart and watching television and charging things to her charge card. "They were releasing this plume of heat into the air above our pastures where our cattle feed and inside of it was God knows what. That's what that long pipe sticking up is for. That's where the steam came out. When they build a reactor now that pipe has to be six hundred feet above the ground. The one at SEFOR was a hundred feet. So why do you think they built this little experimental breeder reactor in the middle of nowhere in a pasture outside of Strickler, Arkansas? Because our politicians let them. Governor Faubus let them and Senator Fulbright let them, too, the senator who has everything in Fayetteville named for himself. I've been thinking about calling up *60 Minutes* or *20/20* and telling them to come down and do an investigative report on it."

"Just because you broke up with your boyfriend doesn't mean you have to call up *60 Minutes* and get them down here poking around in Strickler and causing a lot of trouble for everyone," I said.

"They shouldn't leave that thing sitting there that near to our houses," she said. "The companies that built it should come and take it down and take it away from here."

"Well, hell, let's go take a look at it and see how it's doing," Euland put in. "I would have gone to see it a lot of times but you can't climb the fence in front without messing with the Penningtons' dogs. I don't like those dogs. I got bit once by a dog and that's enough for me." He pulled me over close to him and put his hand around my waist right under my breasts. We were standing outside the visitors' center where we made love that Christmas day. I started getting really horny and I knew he was too. I wished Kelly wasn't there with us but she was. I guessed that meant it was just going to be that much better when we got home that night. Euland likes to be horny. He likes to go around all day thinking about screwing me that night. Not me. I like to do it the minute I think of it. I am spoiled from getting laid by him any time I wanted to since we were juniors in high school and he was All State in football and basketball and track. He was the best and I picked him out and I have kept him. Well, I know how to keep him, but that's another story.

Euland runs his daddy's heating and air-conditioning business and I teach at West Fork High School and, yes, we are going to get married but not until we can buy a house. We are happy just like we are and we don't need anybody telling us to have kids when we haven't even paid off our student loans. It's the nineties and we're living our own lives.

He got out of the truck and came around and opened the door for us. He has the loveliest manners of any man you could want to meet. Also, he's got those shoulders and those long straight legs and if I start thinking about it I'll never get this finished.

We started off down the path beside the waterfall. It was so cold and dry we had to really watch our step. It was the coldest day we had had all of December. "What a day for a walk," I began, but Kelly interrupted me. Part of her being stubborn is she never lets you finish what you are saying. No wonder she never keeps a boyfriend.

"I'm walking every day if it's over forty degrees," she declared. "I'm not going to stay fat. Fat is death and I'm going to walk it off."

"What did you bring to eat?" Euland asks. She was wearing her backpack. We knew she had food in it.

"Some graham crackers and low-fat cookies," she answered. "Well, are you guys ready?"

"Let's go to the reactor," Euland said. "You've got me interested now."

We hiked past the waterfall and down to the bottom of the trail and started back up toward the east. There wasn't a leaf left on a tree but there were bundles of bright orange pine needles on the path and beautiful hawthorn berries here and there. Hawthorn berries are the most beautiful color of red in the world. No Christmas decoration has ever been as nice as stark winter woods with hawthorn berries under a gray sky. There was also red holly and barberries and dark green mistletoe in the high branches of the oak trees. Everything you see is sexual if you start thinking about it. Everything is seed and reproduction and sperm and egg. Thank God for birth control pills. Well, it would have been too cold to make love even if Kelly wasn't with us so I stopped thinking about screwing Euland and concentrated on pulling my fingers back into the palms of my hands inside my gloves. I knew something was going to happen. I knew this was going to be a day that mattered and it wasn't just because I was cold and horny that I felt that way. There's Welsh blood in all the Nobleses. We know things we can't prove we know.

We hadn't been walking half an hour when we saw a man coming down the other way. He was wearing a black leather jacket and some sort of thick light brown pants and his hair was jet black and curly. He wasn't wearing a hat. I love a man who can stand the cold without a hat. If I see a man in a hat I think he's old, no matter what his age.

We stopped at a wide place in the path and let him walk down to us. He was smiling this lovely wide smile like we were just what he was hoping to find in the woods. When he got about three feet away he stopped. "Hello, there," he said. "I was wondering if I had this place to myself. It's so quiet you can hear a leaf drop." He smiled the gorgeous smile again and I could see Kelly changing gears. She pulled her old AMOCO hat with the earflaps off her head and shook out her long red hair. She has the best hair you've ever seen in your life. Brilliant golden red and so curly it is like a bouquet of flowers. She never cuts it. It hangs down halfway to her waist. Fat or thin, Kelly can get a lot of mileage out of that hair. So then she unbuttons the top button of her jacket.

"I walk any day it's above forty degrees," she said, throwing her hair down on her chest.

"Then you shouldn't be out today." He laughed and pulled back his sleeve and showed us a watch with a digital dial that gave you the temperature. The watch said thirty-two. We all laughed and he took out a package of cigarettes and offered them to us and Euland and I took one and we lit them and then we all stood there smoking.

"What are you doing out on a day like this?" Kelly answered.

"I'm the new professor in the botany department," he said. "I've only been in town a week. I'm lonely. Everybody's married so they sent me out to see the woods. It's very interesting. I'm from Massachusetts. This is all new to me." He waved his hand around at the flora and fauna and I thought, I may have given up on Jesus but that doesn't mean I don't believe in providence.

"You want to see something interesting you should go with us," I said. "There's an abandoned breeder reactor a mile from here. We live near it. We're walking over there because you can't get in the front. You want to come along?"

"A breeder reactor?"

"An experimental breeder reactor that was the only one of its kind in the world. We're going over to check it out." I loved the expression on his face. I love it when people think Strickler is the end of the earth and then find out it's not.

"I'm the one who thought up going," Kelly says. "No one pays any attention to it anymore but I'm interested in it. I just broke my engagement and I decided I'd better wake up and find out what's happening in the world." She had completely moved in. She isn't all that fat and even if she was you couldn't tell it underneath all the basic black ski clothes she was wearing.

"I'm Ed Douglas," he said. "I'd love to tag along."

So we set off back down the path with Kelly and Ed in the rear and Kelly telling him everything she'd been learning about SEFOR and Ed turning out to be a really good listener, something every Nobles finds seductive to the tenth power since we all talk too much.

"They built it right beside Fall Creek," Kelly is telling him. "Which runs into Lee Creek which is a category five white water river. Not to mention Fall Creek is where the people in my family teach their children to swim. All three of us learned to swim there, Chandler, Euland, and me. All our grandparents are from Strickler. And our parents too. Anyway, they built that nuclear reactor right beside our creek without asking anyone if they could do it. I think we can still sue them. I'm looking into it."

I didn't look behind me. I didn't want to turn into a pillar of salt and I didn't want to start giggling. I just held on to Euland's arm whenever there was a place where we could walk side by side. It was beginning to look like we might not be stuck with Kelly all weekend after all.

It wasn't as easy getting from the park to the pasture that leads up to SEFOR as we thought it was going to be. The path through the little woods was covered with honeysuckle vines. Euland and Ed had to get out pocketknives and cut vines every ten or twenty feet. I guess we would have given up if Ed hadn't come along but Ed was showing off for Kelly and Euland was showing off for Ed so they kept on hacking down the vines. It wasn't that far. I could see the pasture and the top of SEFOR through the trees. All this time Kelly is having the time of her life saying all the stuff she's been reading in the library and making copies of in her spare time. "The heat produced by the nuclear reactions was transferred to liquid sodium metal, then transferred to more sodium, then the steam came out of the pipe to float around on top of our pastures and houses and creek. Can you see why I got interested in this?"

"Well, of course," Ed answered. "It's one thing to think about nuclear power in the abstract. It's another thing to have it in your backyard."

"So one of these breeder reactors blew up in Detroit, Michigan. Well, they don't call it blowing up. They call it melting down."

"A disaster either way."

"You got it." She was letting him get a word in here and there, but not many. "Anyway," she goes on. "After that happened in Detroit they shut this one down and gave it to the university. Our uncle sold them the concrete. He says it's probably okay but that the metal might be starting to deteriorate."

"I can imagine it might."

"Anyway, I keep reading everything I can find but there's not much information. The university should sue the power companies that built it to make them take it down but they won't because SWEPCO, our local power company, was part of it and they contribute money to the university. There are other connections about that but I haven't finished finding them all out."

Kelly was casting herself in the role of some investigative reporter with secrets to keep. One thing about all the television she watches, she can find lots of outlets for her dramatic side.

We finished hacking through the vines and came to the rickety wire fence that separates the park from SEFOR. Euland climbed over it and held it while I climbed over and then Kelly and then Ed. Just as we got to the other side and were straightening up our clothes, the sun came out for the first time all day. It was so beautiful, this big patch of sunny sky in between the banks of clouds. It cast beautiful shadows all over the yellow pastures. It made the world look beautiful and interesting and gay. I moved over to Euland's side and started thinking maybe we ought to go on and get married in the spring. We could rent a house for a year or two before we buy one. Kelly was unbuttoning her jacket another button as if she isn't the most cold-blooded person in the world.

"It's just half a mile from here," Euland said. "Let's hike."

*   *   *

"This isn't the only time nuclear power came to Arkansas," Kelly was telling Ed. "I guess you know about the Titan II missiles in Damascus, don't you?"

"Damascus?"

"Damascus, Arkansas. It's a town down west of Little Rock. We had this representative named Wilbur Mills and he got so crazy from drinking and screwing whores that he let the government put eighteen Titan II missiles in the ground in Arkansas. He volunteered the state for all sixty of them but Kansas and Arizona wanted some so we only got eighteen."

"You are centrally located." Ed was laughing at everything she said, like she wasn't discussing the fate of the world. She still had her hat off. She gets terrible ear infections. I was hoping her hair would keep them warm.

"You got that," Euland put in. "We could guard the United States from east, west, south, and north."

"People aren't educated," Ed puts in. "If they were, they wouldn't let politicians get away with these things."

We stopped for a moment in a low protected place beside a man-made dam. We huddled together and Kelly finally put on her hat, turning it around so the AMOCO sign was in the back and her curly bangs fell down across her forehead. Before us was a long sloping pasture leading up to the reactor in the distance, the Southwest Experimental Fast Oxide Reactor, a concrete silo sixty feet below the ground and fifty feet above the ground with a smokestack rising another fifty feet. There was a power line running from the silo to the road and a chain-link fence with a gate. Above that the gray-blue skies of December in the Ozarks.

"So anyway," Kelly is saying. "They came down and dug these holes in the ground and put in the missiles, each one containing the most explosive devices ever aimed at an enemy in the history of the world. Right there, in Damascus, they put the one that melted down, blew up, whatever you want to call it. Two people were killed." She was losing her audience. We were freezing. Ed pulled out his watch and the temperature dial said thirty. "Let's walk while we talk," he suggested. "Let's get on up there."

We started hiking really fast in the direction of the silo, but the conversation was started now and no one could let it alone.

"I worked with this guy who was a soldier stationed in Little Rock when the Titans were down there," Euland said. "It was his job to drive one of the trucks that took the warheads back and forth to Fort Chaffee to be checked and cleaned up. There were two men driving each warhead. He said one night the brakes went out on the truck, that was before cellular phones, and they had to keep pouring water on the brakes every twenty miles to make it to the base. He runs Jackson's Air in Fayetteville now. He's a smart guy."

"Your tax dollars at work," Kelly puts in. Not that she pays anything compared to me. You ought to see what they take out of a single teacher's salary.

We were halfway up the pasture when we saw the dogs. I'm always worried in a pasture that I might meet a bull but it never occurs to me to worry about dogs. Everyone around here keeps their dogs tied up. If they didn't their dogs would be dead. So when I saw the dogs in the distance I didn't get worried at first. Euland was the one who stopped. Euland's been bitten.

"Are those dogs going to be okay?" Ed asked. He took hold of Kelly's arm. I guess it was the first time they touched each other.

"I don't like loose dogs," Euland answered. "I don't trust them. Hell, I wish I had a gun." We were within sight of the fence surrounding the reactor. There was a gate on it but it didn't look like it was padlocked. Euland picked up a dead branch from the ground. It broke in two in his hand. "Let's go," he said. "Run for the fence."

I guess it was a quarter mile. Too far to outrun dogs but we did what we were told. The dogs kept trotting in our direction.

They didn't bark. They just kept trotting with a big yellow dog in the lead.

"Stay in front of me," Euland yelled. He had the ends of the stick in his hands. I'll say one thing about boys from Strickler. They aren't afraid of the devil when the time comes. I'll say something for my cousin Kelly, too. She can sprint. We were on basketball teams together and you could count on her to get a basketball down the court. So Ed didn't have to wait on any girls from Strickler. We beat him to the gate. All three of us from Strickler were probably thinking about the dog pack last summer that killed a child near Hogeye. There are wolves and foxes in this part of the country and all sorts of wild creatures.

We got to the chain-link fence just as the dogs stopped trotting and started running. Euland threw himself against the gate and it opened. I don't know what we would have done if the caretaker hadn't left it open. He said later it was open because someone from the university was supposed to come by on Sunday and double-check the radiation badges in the containment vessel. Whether that was true or not, he had neglected to put the lock on and Euland pushed it and it opened. About the time we got inside these three dogs as big as mastiffs got to the fence and started throwing themselves against it.

"Do you have that cellular phone?" I asked Kelly.

"No, the battery was down. It's at home on the charger."

The dogs kept throwing themselves at the fence and at first I was sorry I'd made Euland stop carrying a gun in the truck but then I decided he wouldn't have had it out here anyway. "I'll be goddamned," he said. "Well, Ed, I guess you didn't plan on this much excitement. You think we could have scared them off if we hadn't gotten in the fence?"

"I'm glad we didn't have to try. I think they're feral. Will they go away, do you think?"

"I wouldn't trust it."

"Is there a caretaker to this place? Surely someone watches it."

"Just Mrs. Pennington. She lives in the old visitors' center. It's her dog that keeps you from getting in the front gate. I'll be damned. I don't know how we're going to get out. Well, I guess we can look around and find something to use for weapons. An iron rod would do."

"They check it every Saturday," Kelly put in. "That was in the newspaper article. A man from the university comes out every Saturday and sees about the radiation. Do you think he's been here yet?"

"Maybe that's why the gate was open." Ed turned and looked at the building behind us. The dome-shaped containment vessel and the flat-roofed building that adjoins it. It looked like a fallen rusting spaceship stuck in the ground, not really evil, just a pile of concrete and metal and bad ideas, abandoned and forlorn. The ladder going up the side of the dome was cut off twenty feet above the ground but there was still a ladder to the flat-roofed part. Ed buttoned his jacket up around his neck and walked over to the ladder. "I'm going up," he said. "Let's see if we can get inside. There might be an alarm we can set off or a phone." As soon as he was on the roof Euland started up after him. I looked at Kelly. "Let's go," I said. "I don't want to be left out."

I started up. As soon as I was almost to the top she got on and started climbing too. I was getting off the ladder when I heard it start to slip. "Jump," I screamed down at her. "It's loose. It's falling." She ignored me and kept on climbing, half her body on the ladder and half on the brick wall. Two years ago when she was going with a rock climber she put in a lot of hours on that fake rock wall in Fayetteville behind the brewery and I guess it wasn't all wasted time because she made it onto the roof. By the time she came over both Ed and Euland were holding on to her arms.

We stood in a circle. We looked at each other. It was cold as hell. It was Saturday afternoon. The ladder was on the ground.

No one on earth knew where we were. Not to mention that the University of Arkansas Razorback basketball team was playing Louisville in the Bud Walton Arena and anyone in northwest Arkansas who wasn't at the game was watching it on television.

"They'll find our cars," Ed said.

"There's a forecast for snow," Euland answered. "We better all just hope that doesn't happen."

"I hate dogs with all my heart." Kelly walked to the edge of the roof to look at them. They were still hanging around the gate. "I hate the whole idea of dogs and keeping them penned up and putting collars on them and if you let them go they get wild and try to kill you."

"Well, I wish I had my dog," Euland said. He has a Doberman. "I'd love to turn him loose to kill those hounds."

Ed had walked over to a black shed on the back of the roof and was inspecting the door. He took out his pocketknife and began to undo the screws on the side of the door. He didn't curse or act like he was mad or anything. He just stood there taking the screws out of the door with the flat blade of a Swiss army knife. I guessed that if we didn't catch pneumonia this was going to be the day Kelly finally found what she'd been looking for all her life. A ticket to a bigger world.

"I'll be goddamned. I'll just be goddamned," Euland said about six times. Kelly was just standing off to one side like she didn't have a care in the world. She had fixed the main thing wrong with her world by finding an unmarried professor out in the woods and getting herself marooned with him on top of a breeder reactor, so why should she care if we starved to death or caught pneumonia before someone missed us and came to help?

"Can you lend me a hand here?" Ed called out and Euland went to him and began to help with the screws.

"There might be an alarm we can set off." Ed took a different blade out of his knife and began to wiggle it around along the sides of the lock. I pulled a scarf out of my pocket and asked him if he wanted to put it on his head but he said no. It must have been about twenty-five degrees by then. The patch of sun we had seen earlier had entirely disappeared. There was nothing to be seen in four directions but the roof of Euland's mother's house on the hill near the cemetery and the old visitors' center looking deserted and the two-lane blacktop road no one could hear us from and snow clouds coming in from the west.

No alarm went off but the lock did begin to come loose around the door and Euland got really excited and started calling the hogs. "Sooieee, pig," he yelled out. "Go hogs." He was pulling on the lock while Ed cut around it.

All I could think about was my thin gloves and how it would be just my luck to get frostbite and lose a finger just when I had almost finished learning how to play Erik Satie's *Second Gymnopédie*. I was learning it to play for Euland's mother's sixtieth birthday party.

"It's coming," Euland yelled. "Sooie, pig, here it goes." There was this crashing, breaking sound and a big chunk of lock and wooden door was twisted and torn out of its place and then Ed and Euland kicked the rest down.

"A hollow-core door," Ed said. "This is the craziest thing I've ever seen in my life. Well, let's go in. There may be a phone that works."

"What do you think is down there?" Euland asked.

"Well, surely not the radioactive core." Ed stood with his hands on his hips. "If it's been decommissioned that's gone. In any case that would surely have been underground."

Only it wasn't underground. Later, when Kelly was poking around the files in the university library, one of the things she found was a letter from a nuclear engineer to the Atomic Energy Commission. It was dated 1972, the year SEFOR was decommissioned. It said one of the problems with SEFOR was that they had no idea whether they would be able to cool down the nuclear reactions they were starting and they should have built it underground just in case. The nuclear engineer is named Richard E. Webb. We wanted to write him a letter but Kelly can't find an address for him anywhere although she has used up about six hours of Fayetteville Public Library computer time in the search. When last heard of he was in West Germany working for some organization called the Greens. The part of the letter I liked most was the very end. He told them, "As officers of the federal government, who are bound to support the Constitution, the AEC and the Joint Committee on Atomic Energy should recommend that Congress submit an amendment proposition to the states so that the people can make a value judgment of whether a civilian nuclear program is both necessary and safe, *as is their right.*"

Also, he says twice they should only build something like SEFOR *deeply underground* in case something to do with safety had been overlooked.

The something that was overlooked was me sleeping a mile down the creek. The something that was overlooked was Euland's parents' house up on the hill and Kelly and her brothers right down the road.

"I would think this was the lab area," Ed was saying. "I don't know much about nuclear reactors but I've seen plans. There had to be a lab and they wouldn't want it near the core. I visited Los Alamos once when I was a graduate student."

"Let me go in first," Euland said. "I know about equipment. I'll be able to tell if there's anything that might be contaminated. Let me find the lights."

"Imagine this being out here in the middle of nowhere." Ed buttoned the top of his leather jacket and turned to look at Kelly and me where we were huddled together watching them.

"Strickler isn't nowhere," Kelly told him. "It's where we live. I learned to swim in that creek. That one right over there. The one you can see from here."

"I'm going in," Euland said. Ed held open the broken door and Euland disappeared into the hole. "It's a ladder," he called back. "There's a ladder going down."

"I'm right behind you," Ed called back. "You stay here, girls. Don't come in until we find some lights."

We've found out something else since that afternoon. The half ton of plutonium oxide that was in the core doesn't take up much room. Stacked all together it wasn't much bigger than, say, eight six-packs in a pile. For some reason I find that comforting when I start worrying about the dust that was everywhere when Kelly and I finally went down the ladder and were inside.

"Come on down," Ed called up. "We found a light but it's not much. Watch your step. There's a steel ladder with fourteen rungs. Count them."

Kelly went down first and I followed her. The light was only one bulb in a ceiling fixture. And it wasn't a laboratory or a nuclear core. It was an abandoned office with desks and three chairs and a stack of wire baskets pushed against a wall. A set of stairs led down to the space below.

The lower level was a laboratory with beakers and stacks of equipment and sealed containers marked GENERAL ELECTRIC. There was a steel door locked and padlocked. DECONTAMINATION CHAMBER, it said. DO NOT ENTER.

In the laboratory Ed had found two lights that worked. It was much brighter than the upstairs part. We stood in a group looking around. There were glove boxes in the corner. That gave us a chill. If there's a glove box in a laboratory it means something was inside it that no one should touch.

We stood there for a minute not saying a word. Then Euland

walked over to a table and picked up a telephone and held it to his ear. "It works," he said. "I've got a signal."

"Call the West Fork police," I suggested. "It's 555-8777. Jo Lynn works there on the weekends."

Euland dialed the phone and our cousin Jo Lynn Nobles answered and then she put him through to Dakota Jackson, who used to go out with Kelly in high school. "Get out of that building," Dakota said to Euland. "Get back up on the roof. I've been there when they tested those badges. Don't stay in there any longer than you have to."

"Dakota said get out of the building," Euland said. "Go on. You girls go first. They're coming as fast as they can. They've got to get the fire truck for the ladder."

Kelly was already running up the stairs with Ed behind her, but I refused to run. I just walked back up the stairs and across the office and up the ladder.

It was snowing a soft light snow when we reached the roof. A darling misty snow that filled the air with mystery and a hundred shades of white. The soft yellow hills and evergreen trees were disappearing into white. Above us the sky was turning every color of pink and gray and violet. Then the black leafless trees. The dogs had disappeared. "Well, at least you got to see the prettiest part of the country," I said to Ed. "This is our home. I guess we can't help it if we think it's gorgeous."

"It's beautiful country," he answered. "This is the first time I've felt at home since I got off the plane a week ago. That's a joke, isn't it? Feeling at home on top of a decommissioned nuclear reactor. Not many people would understand that, I guess."

"We understand," Kelly said. "Why do you think we all still live out here? Why do you think I haven't moved to town? I'm a librarian at the Fayetteville Public Library. I have to drive fourteen miles every morning to get to work."

*   *   *

It gets dark at five o'clock in December in the Ozarks. It was pitch-black dark by the time we saw the four-wheel-drive vehicles coming down 265 in our direction. It was another twenty minutes before they got the jammed front gate open and drove in and put up the ladder from the fire truck and took us down one by one.

"I'm going to kill those goddamn loose dogs," Euland kept saying to anyone who would listen. "I'm coming back tomorrow and hunt those bastards down."

"We'll trap them," Dakota agreed. "It's part of that pack that attacked that kid last month. I'm glad you flushed them. You aren't the only one with those dogs on a list."

Kelly and I rode as far as Devil's Den in the deputy's truck. The men rode in the police car and made out the reports. "I'm going to ask him to stay and have dinner with us," Kelly said. "You think we can take him to that sushi place we went to last month? Or should we just stay home and cook something for him?"

"Let's just go to El Chico's like we always do," I answered. "Don't go changing your personality just because he's a professor. Besides, Euland hates Japanese food. He's had all he needs today."

They took us to our cars at Devil's Den and Kelly rode with Ed to show him how to get to Momma's house and we all went in and saw Momma and Daddy and told the story and then Kelly and I put on some fresh makeup and the four of us went in Ed's car to get some supper. We'd decided to just stay in West Fork and go to the White Tiger Haven and get a hamburger and a beer. We played the jukebox and talked about nuclear energy and the global warming meeting in Japan and told Ed all about Fayetteville and what there is to do there. We tried to teach him to call the hogs, but he wasn't ready for that yet. They had beaten Louisville 87 to 65, by the way, after our embarrassing loss to them the year before.

Then Ed took Euland and me home and he and Kelly went off and spent the night at his apartment although I had begged her in the ladies' room not to do it.

I had had an epiphany up on the roof of SEFOR. As soon as we were alone I told Euland I wanted to get married in April for my birthday.

"I don't know," he said. "I don't know if we should rush it, Chandler. Everything's all right like it is, isn't it?"

"No, it's not. We've been going together since the dawn of time. It's time to get married. We're a laughingstock for not getting married. I'm sick of it."

"I can't believe you'd start this tonight. After all that happened to us today."

"I'm starting it. So just get used to that."

The next day I threw away my birth control pills. I knew he'd never leave me or let me go but I wanted some insurance.

Postscript: Euland and I got married on April 28, 1998, out in my mother's backyard by the wisteria arbor, which is where McArthur Wilson and I used to play doctor together. He was at the wedding with his wife, Cynthia, and their two little girls. He runs a television station in Fayetteville. He's gone pretty far in the world.

No, I wasn't pregnant or pretending to be but I'm still off the pill. Nothing's happened yet but we're not worried. No one in the Nobles or Cathaway or Redfern or Tuttle families has ever had any trouble having babies if they wanted them. I kind of want it to happen and then again I don't.

I wore Momma's wedding dress with new lace all around the sleeves and hem. It's been in a box for thirty-six years. It had not turned yellow thanks to Mrs. Agnew's having sealed it up so well when she ran the cleaners down on Main Street.

*　　*　　*

What else? Nothing has happened about SEFOR. Not a single thing has been done and Kelly is still thinking about calling 20/20 but she hasn't done it yet because she doesn't want to make trouble for the university while she's dating a professor. She thinks Ed's going to marry her but Euland and I think the odds are about fifty-fifty. Of course, Kelly *will* get pregnant if she needs to. She is the most ruthless of my cousins, plus the most stubborn. She has lost eleven pounds. She doesn't look like some starving model yet but she is definitely back in the game and holding cards.

Well, that's all from Strickler for the moment. It's October again. Time to start getting ready for the winter. Euland's so busy this time of year I hardly see him. Everybody wants to get their heat pump checked before it snows. We like to keep things working around here.

Also by Ellen Gilchrist

Flights of Angels
Stories

"Readers will find the penetrating intellect, deep compassion, and dark sense of humor that mark Gilchrist's best work and place it among the best writing coming out of the South — or anywhere else, for that matter — today."   — Ron Carter, *Richmond Times-Dispatch*

The Courts of Love
Stories

"Some of the most indelibly etched characters in contemporary fiction. . . . This is the first book I've read in years that I found myself consciously *not* wanting to finish, wanting it to last forever."
     — Hart Williams, *Washington Post Book World*

Rhoda
A Life in Stories

"Rhoda's feisty, sexy, and devastatingly acute sensibilities make her one of the most engaging and surprisingly lovable characters in modern fiction."   — Robert Olen Butler

 Available in paperback wherever books are sold